CW00802780

Sixty Seconds of Silence

SIXTY
SECONDS
of SILENCE

by
David
Porter

XULON PRESS

Xulon Press
2301 Lucien Way #415
Maitland, FL 32751
407.339.4217
www.xulonpress.com

Paperback ISBN-13: 978-1-6628-5778-2
Ebook ISBN-13: 978-1-6628-5780-5

Dedicated in loving memory of:
Doc & Betty
Alan, Bob-O, Bruce, Frank, James, Mike, and Wendell

FOREWORD

I am an avid reader and writer, but honestly, I never read fiction because I usually read things that are specifically related to my studies. As I write this, I have a stack of books sitting next to my desk that are waiting to be read. When my friend, David Porter, sent me a copy of *Sixty Seconds of Silence*, I was wondering how I would fit it into my busy schedule of teaching and traveling; however, as I began to read it, I found myself engulfed in the story. I was reading it on the airplane, in the airports, traveling in the car and in my hotel...I wanted to find out what was going to happen with Matt Davenport!

David has been one of my best friends for over twenty years. We went to Bible school together, played on the basketball team together, we were in each other's weddings...needless to say, I know a lot about David – but I didn't know that he is a phenomenal storyteller!

Sixty Seconds of Silence is a masterful novel of the adventures of Matt Davenport filled with adventure, mystery, Jewish history, Muslim culture, and the Bible. What starts with the back stories of several different people is seamlessly woven together as all of their lives collide into a powerful ending.

One of the things I loved about David's writing is that from the beginning to the end, not only did I find myself wondering what was going to happen next with Matt Davenport, I was also learning factual information about Jewish and Muslim cultures that I did not know. From important landmarks in Jerusalem to spiritual beliefs of Islam, it was obvious that a tremendous amount of research went into this novel.

Ultimately, I loved the supernatural element that was woven like a thread throughout the story. By the time I was finished reading, I was not only entertained but also reminded of some tremendous spiritual truths that you would be hard-pressed to even hear about in church today.

It is my utmost pleasure to recommend to you *Sixty Seconds of Silence*. It is a tremendous story with lots of twists and turns and an ending that is absolutely amazing. I guarantee with every chapter, you will want to read another just to find out what's going to happen next!

— Dr. Chad Gonzales, DMin.
Host of *The Way of Life* Television Broadcast and *The Supernatural Life* Podcast, Bestselling Author of *Possessors of Life* and *The Supernatural Prayer of Jesus*, and founder of *The Healing Academy*.

PREFACE

When I was in elementary school, I heard stories about a Christian adventurer and archaeologist who had discovered the most amazing Biblical finds — peoples, locations, and artifacts that proved the stories in the Bible were fact. By the time I reached my early teenage years, in my mind the adventurer rode horses across deserts, fought against hostile government leaders who were determined to hide the truth, and had adventures with his sons who often came along for his discoveries in all parts of the ancient world — on land and under the sea. He probably even carried a whip! And, he was a Christian! These were the days before the internet and my imagination was able to run wild at the thought of what this man had found. I imagined myself along for the journeys to Saudi Arabia, Israel, Turkey, Egypt, and many other places, fighting and running from men in long tunics and turbans who were chasing us on horseback and brandishing the long, curved swords I had seen in movies. It turns out, my imagination may have been just as active as his! Since his death, many of his "discoveries" have been criticized by recognized archaeologists, scientists, historians and even some Biblical scholars. There are very passionate people on both sides of the argument. Either way, when I was a kid, I wanted to do those things and go to those places with him.

At the same time, as I was growing up, I also had a fantastic Children's Pastor at my church. He is a brilliant man and a wonderful storyteller. He had a way of capturing my attention that made me feel involved in the stories he was teaching. When he taught us about David and Goliath, I felt like I was *there*. I felt like I was actually helping David pick out which of the rocks would be his five smooth stones. I was *with* Noah as we were building the ark and loading the animals. I could almost feel the first drops of rain on my face. I was *with* Elijah when we were outrunning Ahab's chariot. We didn't even break a sweat! From an early age, he helped me realize these characters from the Bible were *actual* people, and these were *actual* events. And, they were *amazing!* In my mind, the Bible was *awesome!*

As an adult, I stumbled upon the online video of an interview that an archaeologist gave to a radio station. Very quickly, I could tell he was a brilliant Israeli man who was doing the real-life work that I had imagined the Christian adventurer doing when I was a teenager. The archaeologist was actually finding things in the ground of Jerusalem that proved what the Bible said happened, actually did! I watched hours and hours of videos and when I reached out to this man, he responded to my email. I was beside myself. Then we spoke on the phone. He helped me, answered my questions, and directed me to people in Israel who could help with my research, all while I was unable to travel due to a pandemic.

The stories of the Christian adventurer, along with the storytelling style that my Children's Pastor employed, and the real-world knowledge of Jerusalem from an archaeologist's perspective, worked in conjunction with my imagination and became part of the foundation for my love of the Bible, its history, and telling stories that would capture people's imagination while pointing them to Jesus and His story. I bring this to light because the influences of these three men — one I never met, one I have spent many hours with, and one on the other side of the world — shaped the style and story of *Sixty Seconds of Silence.* I pray the content of this book blesses you, encourages you, entertains you, and most importantly, points you to Jesus.

— *David*

There is a natural realm and a spiritual realm.
Open their eyes that they may see...

Prologue

JERUSALEM. 3:37 PM.

Darkness. Total and complete. Nothingness in its purest form. Matt couldn't tell if his eyes were opened or shut. He tried moving his hand up to his eyes, to check if he could see it, but that's about the time he realized his arm was pinned under something. Was he lying on it? Was his wife, Jessica? His body felt completely unfamiliar. His bed felt completely unfamiliar. And so did his apartment. Their apartment, in the middle of the city, had never been this dark or this silent since he and Jessica had moved in. "Jessica, is the power out?" he whispered to his wife. Matt tried to roll over to face the side of the bed she normally slept on and that's when the slicing pain hit him. Everything hurt, but his head *hurt*. This wasn't just a 'headache' kind of pain, this was gold medal pain. Numero uno pain. Worst-hangover-in-the-world kind of pain. Matt laid his head back down on his pillow, but realized it wasn't his pillow. It was hard, jagged. He noticed his ears squelched a high-pitched noise. "What is going on?" he finally said out loud, but the sound was foreign to him. Different, just like everything else about this moment.

Matt again tried to move his arm and realized that not only could he not move it, but he also couldn't really feel it either. He slowly used his left arm, his free arm, to try and determine what was going on. It turns out, his arm was pinned under a very large piece of concrete, or something, right above his elbow. That's when things came back to him. This wasn't concrete, this was the cave itself trapping his arm. Matt had a vision of Aron Ralston, the mountain climber that had his arm pinned under a boulder while climbing in Utah. The way he escaped? He cut off his own arm![1] And he did it with a pocketknife! Fear started to dig its claws into Matt's emotions.

How do I keep getting myself into these situations?

"Hello? Can anyone hear me?" he shouted. The sound made his head throb even more.

Nothing. Silence. Total and complete. Nothingness in its purest form. It was like his surroundings swallowed the sounds he was making.

"Well, that's not good," Matt whispered to himself. "I'm *not* cutting off my arm..." his words trailed off.

Again, the fear tried to set in. Matt's brain was running a thousand miles an hour. He remembered seeing the news reports from a few years ago when a youth soccer team had been exploring a cave in Thailand.[2] What was supposed to be an hour inside a cave dramatically changed when a sudden rainstorm had pinned them in the belly of the cave. Completely cut off from the outside world, trapped, without food or way of escape, they stayed there for over two weeks before the Thai Navy Seals rescued them.

Can I survive that long? If it rains right now, I'm pinned. I'll drown!

The fear was gaining a stranglehold on him.

Matt made a decision. Matt resolved within himself that no matter what the circumstances looked like, how dire the situation turned, that

---

[1] Katie Serena, "Aron Ralston And The Harrowing True Story Of '127 Hours,'" All That's Interesting, September 4, 2021, https://allthatsinteresting.com/aron-ralston-127-hours-true-story.

[2] History.com Editors, "Thai Soccer Team Becomes Trapped In Cave," History.com, June 18, 2019, https://www.history.com/this-day-in-history/thai-soccer-team-becomes-trapped-in-cave.

God was *for him* and not against him.[3] Matt resolved that he would *live* and not die and so he began the process of continuing his life.

Matt was lying on his back, completely surrounded by fallen rocks. It was like he was in a small cocoon, completely protected from the falling mess. If he had been six inches taller or had fallen six inches to the left or right, it might have been a completely different story. He didn't have room to sit up. In fact, if he were to sneeze, he would hit his head on the slab of rock directly in front of his face. It couldn't be any more than eight inches away from the tip of his nose.

If I move any of these rocks, the whole place may cave in on me. I could be completely crushed. On the other hand, just on the other side of this rock might be daylight. No, I don't think that's right. Anyone could have heard me scream, and I would be able to hear them. I can't hear anyone. Do they know I'm missing? Is anyone even looking for me?

Don't panic.

Breathe.

"Lord, you're going to have to get me out of here." *How long was I unconscious, two minutes? Two hours? Two days?!? Focus Matt. Focus. Don't get overwhelmed. Attack one problem at a time.*

Matt again began fighting the crippling panic that was trying to set in. The ceiling slab gave a loud **crack** as dust and debris fell into Matt's open mouth.

---

[3] Romans 8:31

CONTENTS

PROVENANCE:

*/'prävənəns/ 1. the place of origin or earliest known history of
something.*

2. the beginning of something's existence; something's origin. [4]

"Thus saith the Lord of hosts, the God of Israel...
'And now have I given all these lands into the hand of
Nebuchadnezzar the king of Babylon, my servant; and
the beasts of the field have I given him also to serve him.
And all nations shall serve him, and his son, and his son's
son, until the very time of his land come...'"
— Jeremiah 27:4, 6-7

---

[4] Oxford Dictionary

JERUSALEM, KINGDOM OF JUDAH. 586 BC.

The young father placed his hand on his thirteen-year-old son's shoulder, pulling him close and, bending down on one knee, whispered to him in Hebrew, his native tongue. "Now watch closely, Leshem.[5] The Kohen Gadol, the High Priest, will take the blood of the bull into the temple, through the Holy Place and into the Holy of Holies."

Asher ben Osip had been preparing his adolescent son for his first Yom Kippur, the Day of Atonement, since before he entered manhood on his twelfth birthday.[6,7] Asher knew that Leshem had a tender heart, and it would be hard for him to understand all of the different nuances of the day, particularly the blood sacrifices.

"Our God, the one true God, is a holy God," Asher continued. "He wanted to have an intimate relationship with His people, that's us, the chosen ones, the children of our father Abraham, the Kingdom of Judah. God wants us in His presence. That has been his desire since time began, since Adam, but because He is so holy, anything unclean cannot survive in His presence."

"What does 'unclean' mean, Abba?" Leshem asked.

---

[5] Leshem – Hebrew name meaning "Precious stone"

[6] Asher – Hebrew name meaning "Fortunate"

[7] Osip – Hebrew name meaning "God will multiply; God will add"

Asher patiently answered his excited son's question. "How to describe unclean? Well, do you remember when you took your sister's bread at the evening meal? That wasn't right, was it?"

Leshem's face turned red, embarrassed. "No. I told her I was sorry. You made me give it back and I had to give her what was left of mine."

"Right," Asher said. "When you took her bread, when you stole it from her, that was wrong, it was sin. Sin makes you unclean or a better way to think of it is that sin made you impure."

The color from Leshem's face drained as he connected the dots. Beginning to panic he asked, "Am I unclean? Does that mean I cannot survive in God's presence? Am I going to die?"

Lovingly smiling, Asher answered, "In this instance, you are unclean. You have been touched by sin. You made things right with your sister, but you still need to make things right with God. You need to wash that sin away and get clean. *Everyone* here today has sinned in the last year, and we are *all* unclean. That is what today is all about, making things right with God. But do not worry, son. The only way you would die is if you went into the Holy of Holies while you were unclean."

"The Holy of Holies, Abba?" Leshem asked.

"The Holy of Holies is the sacred room in the Temple where the Ark of the Covenant rests on a large stone in the middle of the room. The Ark is the most important treasure in the Temple. As long as we have the Ark, we have access to God. God *lives* in the Ark and the Ark rests in the Holy of Holies. Only the Kohen Gadol can enter the Holy of Holies and he can only enter one time a year. That day is today. You are safe, son. You are not going to die." Leshem exhaled in relief as his father stood and looked toward the city gate. That is when the boy noticed the troubled look on his father's face, a look he had been seeing more and more recently. Leshem still did not know what was bothering his father.

"So, only the Kohen Gadol can hear what God says? God doesn't speak to me or to you?" Leshem asked.

Asher answered, "No, Son. God only speaks to a small number of people, certain ones that He chooses, like the Kohen Gadol, but he must do several things in order to make himself clean before he can enter into the room where God lives. That is what the whole morning has been about. Remember a little while ago when he killed that bull?" Asher asked.

"Yes, Abba, it was really bloody," Leshem answered.

"Yes, I know it was. That was the High Priest's sin-sacrifice, to make him clean, so that he would be able to enter the Holy of Holies for us. He will be standing in our place, so we do not have to go in there. Only once a year, the Kohen Gadol stands in our place. But he must be clean himself before he can represent us, and the blood sacrifice ensures that he is clean."

"How does blood make us clean?" Leshem asked.

"The price of sin," Asher paused. "Son, whenever there is sin, a price has to be paid for it to be taken away. The price of taking your sister's bread was giving yours to her. The price of sin is death and for us to be clean, these animals must pay that price; their blood has to be spilled. Somehow, their blood absorbs the unclean and impure nature of our sin."

Leshem was quiet for a moment, taking everything in. He was a quiet young boy, eager to learn and even more eager to please his father. Finally, he asked "And, the Kohen Gadol has to do this every year?"

"Yes, Leshem. The Kohen Gadol does this every year, once a year, on the Day of Atonement, Yom Kippur. The Priests have been doing this for one thousand years," Asher answered.

"So, if I sin tomorrow, I have to live with it for a whole year?"

"That is one reason God gave Moses the law, to give us a way to remain clean. But if you break one of these laws, you remain unclean until you can find a way to get clean in God's eyes."

"Wouldn't it be better, Abba, if there was a way to get clean and stay clean once and for all time?" Leshem asked.

Asher chuckled quietly as the ceremony continued. "Yes, my son. I think it would."

Leshem nodded as he turned his attention back to the continuing ceremony. "So, the Kohen Gadol killed the bull to get clean from sin and then what happened? He walked into the temple and disappeared. What did he do in there?"

"Killing the bull did not make him clean. When he walked into the temple, he also took some of the blood from that bull. He walked all the way through the Holy Place and into the Holy of Holies, behind the huge veil separating the two rooms. Then the Kohen Gadol took the blood of that bull and sprinkled it on the lid to the Ark of the Covenant. That lid is where God's glory shines. That is God's throne. When he sprinkled the blood on the lid, on God's seat, that is when he made atonement for his own sin." As Asher was speaking, the Kohen Gadol emerged from the Temple and began the next part of the ceremony. "Now, he is ready to undertake the duty of making atonement for the sin of the people. That is what he is working on now. See? He is selecting the goats."

"Abba, this does not make any sense to me. The part with the goats? I do not understand that at all."

Asher nodded. "Up until now, everything the Kohen Gadol has done has been to get clean himself. The part with goats starts the process of getting the nation clean. Two goats are selected as a sin-sacrifice, but only one of those two goats will be killed, the other will be let go."

"Why is one let go, Abba? And how does the Kohen Gadol decide which one is which?" Leshem asked his father.

While Asher is teaching his young son, Leshem, about it, the ceremony continues. It is a bloody ordeal. The sea of people in attendance holds their breath as the High Priest lays his hands on one of the innocent goats, symbolically transmitting the sins of the people to the animal. Then, the people gasp as they watch the High Priest, taking out a knife, ritually kill the selected goat on the large, horned altar; the young goat's life snuffed out in a moment with a pained yelp. The High Priest collects some of the blood and disappears inside the large stone temple.

"Once the Kohen Gadol selects the two goats, he casts lots to decide which one will die and which one will get to live. After the selection is made, the High Priest lays his hands on the goat, transmitting our sins onto him, places the chosen goat on the altar and then kills it. The sin of our people, the children of Israel, which is you and me, Leshem, our sin is symbolically transmitted to the goat. He is dying in your place and in my place. He is our sin substitute."

Over the past few weeks, Leshem had noticed the despondent look on his father's face but could not find a cause. Was it because of the sick people in the city? Was it because there wasn't much food? For his part, Leshem tried to eat less so his younger brothers and sisters could have food. He had heard his father talk and argue with the other men, the elders of the city, but did not understand what was happening. What he did know was that none of the local families had been able to leave the gates to gather grain from the fields because of an enemy, the Babylonians.

At night before he went to sleep, Asher told Leshem about the victories of past kings, David, Jehoshaphat, and others. These stories seemed to comfort Asher while exciting Leshem's imagination. "Since the days of Uzziah, the nation has made shields, spears, helmets, bows and slings, and given those weapons to the men." Asher had told him while showing Leshem his sword. "And today is no different. The army has the ability to raise the catapults to sit on the city walls.[8] The past kings had victories, but so can current kings!"

After the family was asleep, Leshem would lie awake and worry about his father, trying to understand why he was concerned. The gates were closed and locked. The people were safe inside. They even had fresh water from the tunnels that King Hezekiah had built. God is on our side. So, what had been bothering his father?

As the atonement ceremony continued, Leshem noticed his father's clenched fists, and that he seemed even more worried now than he had been lately. "What is wrong, Abba?" he asked.

"Nothing is wrong, son," Asher answered. "This is the most crucial part of the ceremony. I always get nervous at this moment. I wish that I

---

[8] Reference II Chronicles 26:14-15

could go with the High Priest into the Holy of Holies. I wish that I could make sure he was actually atoning for my sins. I cannot. Just like you, I cannot enter into the Holy of Holies because I am unclean. I must stay here, with the rest of the nation, and trust by faith that the blood of a goat is going to atone for my sins and the sins of my family."

"What is happening in there right now, Abba?"

"The Kohen Gadol makes his way into the Holy of Holies. He stands before the Ark and before God. Underneath the lid of the Ark, remember, that lid is God's Seat?" Leshem nodded but said nothing. "Under God's Seat, inside the Ark, are the laws that God gave to Moses. God wrote those laws in stone with His very own finger.[9] Every day of the year, God sees those laws and it shows Him how unclean we are. We have broken his commandments. It reminds Him of our stony hearts, of the rebellion in our hearts against Him and His decrees.[10] The penalty for breaking those laws is death. It should mean our death, mine and yours, because it seems no man born on this Earth can keep all of the laws because we have been born with a sin-nature. But God knew this and set up a way for the price of that sin to be paid for us. To keep *us* from having to pay the penalty for sin, an animal must pay the price when we break His laws, for when we become unclean, for having sin in our lives. God declared that an innocent sacrifice would take our place and cover our sins.

"So, right now, the Kohen Gadol is in the Holy of Holies, and he will sprinkle the blood of the innocent sacrifice as our substitute over God's Seat. And, in that moment, God will look down and He will no longer see our sin, our uncleanness. All He sees is the blood. That blood tells Him that a life has been given to pay the penalty for sin. When God sees that blood, the throne changes from a place of *judgment* to a place of *mercy*. His throne becomes a Mercy Seat.[11] That is what we call God's throne — the Mercy Seat." Asher concluded.

---

[9] Reference Exodus 31:18

[10] Reference Zechariah 7:12

[11] Reference Exodus 26:34

A deafening roar snapped Asher and Leshem away from the lesson that Asher was teaching and drew their attention towards the gate of the Temple. The blood-soaked Kohen Gadol had reappeared signifying that God had accepted the atoning sacrifice of the innocent goat. The joy of the people could not be contained. It would seem that God had not abandoned them. Perhaps their pending doom could be avoided. Perhaps the voice of the prophets Ezekiel and Jeremiah were, in fact, wrong.[12] God had accepted their sacrifice.

Leshem could not believe the joy his father exhibited. Asher, along with all the people cheered, screamed, danced, jumped, sang, praised, and played all sorts of different instruments. Most of the people laughed, but some cried with joy. Whatever had been bothering his father and the men of the nation, seemed to be gone, replaced by relief, by joy, by exhilaration.

Asher picked Leshem up and twirled him around and around. "God is with us! God is with us!" He sang. "He has not abandoned us! He is for us!" He shouted.

Leshem reveled in his father's joy. It had been many days since he had seen his father smile, let alone dance and be merry. When the dizzy father put the boy back on the ground, the whole world seemed like it was spinning. As he started to regain his composure, Leshem noticed that the Kohen Gadol was still performing part of the ceremony. Tugging at his father's sleeve to get his attention, he asked "Abba, what is he doing now? What is he doing with the other goat?"

Breathlessly answering, Asher said, shouting above the noise, "He is finishing the ceremony. See, the Kohen Gadol needs a way to *show* the people, to demonstrate to the people, that the sin has been dealt with and it no longer is counted against us. So, he is setting the other goat free! We are clean! We are saved!"

Asher eventually noticed the confused look on Leshem's face and realized he needed to give the boy a more thorough explanation. Again,

---

[12] Reference Ezekiel 4, 5, 21

he knelt down beside him and said in a more fatherly way, "The blood of the first goat represented us. The blood of the first goat was evidence **to God** that the penalty for all of our sin had been paid. But we were standing out here. We couldn't go inside, so we didn't get to see that our sin had been atoned for. So, the Kohen Gadol comes out, places his hands on the goat, see? In exactly the same way that he did with the first goat, the Kohen Gadol symbolically transmits the sins of the people on to the other goat. The second goat is evidence **to us**! That goat will be taken outside the city gates and set free. It shows that our sin has been separated from us. God has accepted our sacrifice!" Asher began dancing, singing, twirling, again.

It seemed the whole nation of Judah, all of the people, were rejoicing. A loud cheer, erupting like a volcano, swept inside the city walls, engulfing men, women, children as they all danced, cheered and praised God. Their worst fears, it seemed, would not be realized. The enemy would face God after all. The people of Judah would not have to fight on their own.

Leshem danced with his father, enjoying a side of him that the boy had not seen in a long time.

King Nebuchadnezzar's men heard an unusual sound, a sound they never thought they would hear coming from inside the city walls. It sounded like joy. It sounded like victory. It sounded like relief.

For almost two years, the army had been encamped outside of the walled city of Jerusalem. Nothing went into the city and anything that happened to come out of the city was killed. No messengers survived. No food was returned. Their army surrounded the entire city, far enough away from the reach of arrows and catapults that there was no danger. It was only a matter of time before the people locked inside the city gates would starve or surrender. Why were they celebrating now?

They should have learned their lesson years earlier. Nebuchadnezzar had shown mercy. This time would be different.

Hearing a new and unusual sound, the King stepped out of his tent. His patience had worn thin. Tomorrow Nebuchadnezzar would begin his campaign to cement his victory.

That night after the celebration had finished, as Leshem was preparing to sleep, his father came to him ready to tell of another ancient king's victory. Leshem interrupted his father's thought, "Abba, tell me, please, what is going to happen to the enemy outside our walls."

Asher was surprised that his son, whom he had tried to protect from the knowledge of the enemy, was aware of the danger. "Son, how do you know…. Yes, I will tell you. You are a man and deserve to know.

"When you were just a baby, our evil king, Jehoiakim, set his heart against Babylon. The prophet Jeremiah, God's mouthpiece on Earth, warned us that God had given all the lands to Nebuchadnezzar, the Babylonian king and that we should not set our hearts against him.[13] Our king did not listen and withheld the yearly tribute. Since we were in rebellion against God, our nation was alone to face the Babylonian king. Jehoiakim died and left his son, King Jehoiachin, who was not much older than you are now, to face the consequences of his poor decision."

Interrupting, Leshem asked "How old was he, Abba?"

"The young king was eighteen, unlearned in the ways of war and was outmatched. He surrendered within three months. It could have been very bad, but Nebuchadnezzar had mercy on us and our young king and offered a treaty." Asher answered.

"What is a treaty, Abba?"

"A treaty is an agreement between two parties, son. Each side agrees to certain terms. In this case, the Babylonian king took our king captive,

---

[13] Reference Jeremiah 27:5-6

along with all the noble men, the educated, the rich, the trained. Anyone who could be of value, ten thousand people in total, Nebuchadnezzar took them back to his kingdom. That is where they are now. He took all of the treasures of the king's palace and even some of the treasures of the Lord's Temple — the ones that were not hidden — like the Ark."[14] Asher smiled broadly and winked at his son. "Nebuchadnezzar also let the rest of us live, he didn't destroy our city or houses. Then the Babylonian king set up a new king to rule over us, King Zedekiah. Those were his terms."

"And what were our terms? What did we have to do?" Leshem asked.

"We were to accept our new king and we were to pay even more taxes for our yearly tribute. For almost ten years we paid the tribute, but we lived in fear of what might happen if Nebuchadnezzar returned. We have lived without our people. We have lived without our kin. We have lived without our rightful ruler. We have lived without peace. We have felt abandoned by God. But we paid the yearly tribute to keep the Babylonian king away."

"Then why is he back and why is his Army here?"

"To earn the love of the people, the new king, King Zedekiah, decided to withhold the payment to the Babylonian king. Nebuchadnezzar is here, *he thinks*, to destroy us."

"Oh no!" Leshem said, a little too loudly, causing his younger brother to stir in his sleep.

"It will be ok, son. Yes. Almost two years ago, Nebuchadnezzar returned. Until today, we lived in fear that we would be destroyed, that God had forsaken us, that our families would be killed, and our city destroyed. Today, God accepted our sacrifice. We believe we are saved." Asher replied.

Leshem sat up, serious, concerned. "Did the Kohen Gadol hide the Ark and the temple treasures again, Abba?" Leshem asked.

The question surprised Asher. Instead of sensing relief from his son, Asher was noting fear, anxiety, and dismay. "Yes. I am sure they

---

[14] Reference II Kings 24:13

took them through the hidden tunnels, outside the city walls and hid it there in the caves, where the Babylonian king will not find it. No one can find it without help from one of the priests. Even the men who built the tunnels and caves do not know where the Ark is hidden in them. What's wrong, son?"

Leshem asked his tired father, "Abba, can God forgive us, make us clean and the city still fall?"

ARCHAEOLOGY STAGE ONE: IDENTIFICATION

Determine the absence or presence of an archaeological site in the area.[15]

"The flurry of archaeological work in Jerusalem over the years has not been without conflict. For instance, in 1996, when the Israeli government opened the entrance to the underground historical site called the Hasmonean Tunnel, which is located in the heart of the Muslim Quarter, it ignited Muslim fears that the excavations might undermine the Islamic structures on the Temple Mount and rioting ensued. Palestinian Arab Muslims even fought running battles with the Israeli army over the opening of the archaeological tunnel. The Jews are not innocent of this either. There is no trust on either side." — Dr. Cooper Kenyon

"The observant Jew believes Israel is their 'Promised Land' and they await their coming Messiah. The Christian mistakenly believes that the land of Israel was given to all peoples through Jesus, that he was the promised Messiah and is somehow, the Son of God. The Muslim believes that this region belongs to them, that Jesus was a prophet of Allah, and good man, but nothing more. These beliefs are the bedrock to all conflict in the region." — Rabbi Eliyahu Kaduri

---

[15] "Phases of Archaeology," Job Monkey, 2022, https://www.jobmonkey.com/archaeology/phases/

OLD CITY OF JERUSALEM

Approximate location
of Dr. Kenyon's discovery

Herod's Gate

Damascus Gate

Lions' Gate

CHRISTIAN
QUARTER

New Gate

Tzahal Square

TEMPLE MOUNT

Golden Gate
(sealed)

MUSLIM
QUARTER

CHURCH OF THE
HOLY SEPULCHRE

DOME OF
THE ROCK

Jaffa Gate

Mount of Olives

JEWISH
QUARTER

ARMENIAN
QUARTER

Dung Gate

CITY OF DAVID
Location

Zion Gate

N
W — E
S

Chapter 1

PRESENT DAY. SOMEWHERE OUTSIDE JERUSALEM.

The instructions came to the three-fingered man in the usual way. A mark on a wall, a symbol, informed him it was time to go to a pre-arranged place located within the Muslim Quarter of the Old City of Jerusalem. Once there, someone would approach him with coded words or in extreme cases, a prepaid cell phone. Usually, it was a young boy or woman, who was told to look for the middle-aged man, clean shaven with three fingers on his right hand. The missing digits was the only trait that distinguished him from the thousands of other Palestinians living outside of Jerusalem. He was neither fat nor skinny, short nor tall. He was neither balding nor overly hairy. He was not unusually good-looking nor hideously grotesque. In fact, there were absolutely no distinguishing features about him other than the smallest two fingers missing from his right hand — which could be easily concealed in a pocket. Most of the time, he took pleasure in his anonymity. He could disappear in a crowd, and no one would even notice him. He could move in and out of locations, in and out of groups, in and out of situations without detection, a trait that had served him well over the years.

The bomb making was not a profession. It was a duty, a rite that had been handed down from father to son, father to son, father to son, for almost five hundred years. He would have the honor of seeing

1

the 500th anniversary in his lifetime. When it became necessary to protect the hidden place, *his* portion involved bombs. Sometimes that meant bombing a market. Sometimes that meant bombing a bus or an embassy, but it was always done to protect the hidden place. No other reason. There was no other reason for murder. That was clear from the holy Koran. Islam, in his opinion, was a religion of peace. But sometimes Islam needed to be protected and protecting the hidden place meant protecting Islam. Many times, his bombs had been detonated around the city. Each time, the authorities concluded the attack was random, a suicide bomber, intent on ill will. They never understood the surgical precision with which he operated. They never understood he was the author of each episode. They were all his creations. He was what the other members of his small group called, *The Bringer of Death*. According to Muslim scholars, it is not forbidden to give someone a nickname as long as the name does not contradict Islamic principles. Since he is protecting Islam by bringing death to infidels, the name is accepted, but rarely used, and certainly never to his face. There is a reverence to the myth of the man.

The three-fingered man was on his way home from the market, where he had spent the morning drinking coffee and smoking cigarettes with other men from his village, when he saw the symbol instructing him back to the Muslim Quarter of the Old City. He did not want to go. He worked close to the Muslim Quarter six days a week and he wanted to spend the day at home. Today was his day off and he had planned on concentrating his time with his sons. Specifically, today was to be the beginning of instruction for his oldest son. Yusef would soon learn what it meant to protect the hidden place and how he was to do it. But not today. The three-fingered man would need to tell his wife where he was going and that he didn't know when he would return. Sometimes making contact was a lengthy process. He couldn't just wave his hand around and scream, "I am The Bringer of Death! Point me to my target!"

There was a specific intersection in the Muslim Quarter where he was to wait for contact. Sometimes he found himself leaning against a wall with his hand in his pocket, subconsciously hiding the disfigured hand. It made the waiting that much longer, but he was not in a habit of flaunting the bite of a bomb. That is what had happened to his fingers. A moment of carelessness. A fleeting moment of a wandering mind, a lack of attention and in an instant, a flash of light, blinding heat and two fingers detached from his hand. Black powder is a cruel mistress if not given all of one's attention. It was a lesson he had learned and learned well. He realized how quickly something can happen and how much worse it could have been. His sons would learn from his mistake. But not today. Today, he was being summoned and that only happened when it was necessary to protect the hidden place.

"Laila, I must go to work," the three-fingered man said as he entered the house.[16] Even though he and his family spoke English, inside the house they only spoke Arabic. He knew his wife would be upset, but there was nothing that could be done. Laila was in the kitchen and the three-fingered man intentionally stayed in the next room.

"But it is your day off! You said you were going to spend time with the boys. They will be so upset. They won't be boys forever," she replied from the kitchen, annoyed more than angry. She knew it was now falling to her to occupy the boys' time, to keep them out of trouble. Not an easy task. "Why do you have to work? Can't it wait until tomorrow?"

Stepping into the kitchen, the three-fingered man replied, "I saw the sign. I have to go make contact." He sighed and Laila saw the disappointment all over her husband. It was evident that he was looking forward to the time with the boys as much as the boys were looking forward to the time with their father.

"Perhaps contact will be quick. Keep your hand out of your pocket where it can be seen. Make contact and get home quickly. Off you go," she said as she took a dishrag and waved it at him, affectionately chasing him out of the kitchen.

---

[16] Laila – Arabic name meaning "Sweetheart, ecstasy"

3

"I will speak to the boys before I leave," he said as he was making his way out of the kitchen.

"You will do no such thing! Grab your keys and get going. I will explain it to them when they wake up. Maybe you can make contact and return before they are done with their breakfast."

"I think I will take Yusef with me.[17] He would like that, wouldn't he? This might be the beginning of his lessons, a chance to teach him some of his destiny."

The boy's mother nodded. Tears began to fill her eyes. She knew this day would come but had hoped to keep her son's childhood intact as long as possible. The beginning of his lessons would mean the ending of his childhood.

"We will take it slow and take our time. I was about his age when my father started my lessons. Don't worry, wife. I will teach him to be careful. I learned my lesson, so he won't have to learn the same one," the man said while subconsciously looking down at his right hand. The woman turned her back to the three-fingered man, raised the dish towel to her eyes and while wiping them, nodded her approval.

The three-fingered man gently woke his sleeping son. "Yusef," he whispered. "Get dressed. You and I are going into the Muslim Quarter. Don't wake your brothers and don't forget your watch," he said with a smile. Yusef realized this meant a unique opportunity to spend time with his father while his brothers stayed home.

The three-fingered man grabbed his keys and walked to his 1976 Land Rover, which his sons had affectionately nicknamed *The Rock*, after the famous American wrestler who was now starring in movies. Sitting down in the driver's seat, the engine turned over on the first try, the result of a loving hand caring for the nearly half-century old

---

[17] Yusef – Arabic name meaning "God increases"

truck. The rugged vehicle coughed a few puffs of putrid scented black smoke — the neighborhood could 'smell what *The Rock* was cooking' and roared to life. He always liked to give the truck a few minutes to warm up, before putting it into gear. Like his bomb making duty, this vehicle was special and had been passed from father to son. When his son was ready, the three-fingered man would pass the vehicle to him. The truck was a dinosaur compared to modern day SUVs, but there was something about driving it that he enjoyed. There was no glass in the side windows, no air conditioning, it didn't even have power steering, but if there was ever a need to get off of the road, nothing could match *The Rock's* rugged power. And sometimes, in his line of work, there was that need.

The drive west to the Old City of Jerusalem was, for the most part, uneventful and took less than 45 minutes, only slightly delayed due to the large number of tourists and the tour buses that always increased as the holy days neared. At least, the three-fingered man always thought, the Sun wasn't in his eyes as he made his way towards Old Jerusalem. And today was different. He had Yusef along for the trip.

"Where are we going, Abee?" Yusef asked excitedly in English. It was a rare treat to be with his father when his brothers were not around.

"Arabic, Yusef. Today we speak only Arabic," the three-fingered man replied in his native tongue. "Today begins your training. You have a divine destiny, just as I do, and I must teach you how to perform it. Allah has chosen us. Today, you begin to learn."

"Does Allah speak directly to you, Abee? Will he talk directly to me?" Yusef asked in excited Arabic.

The three-fingered man smiled at his son. "No, Yusef. Allah, in his great wisdom, only speaks to his prophets, a small chosen few. We cannot hear directly from him. And before you ask, I do not know why." Yusef knew that meant it was time to be quiet… *children are meant to be seen, not heard.*

The Old City of Jerusalem is divided into four quarters, the Muslim Quarter, the Christian Quarter, the Armenian Quarter and the Jewish

Quarter and there are eight different gates into the city.[18] Each quarter and each gate has a different story to tell. Walking into the Old City with someone who had never, or rarely ever entered the city, like young Yusef, always brought joy to the three-fingered man. The three-fingered man parked *The Rock* in a familiar neighborhood where he knew it would be safe and walked with Yusef towards the beautiful Damascus Gate. A student of history, he loved seeing the ancient city through the eyes of a stranger-to-the-city. Among the three entry ways into the Muslim Quarter — the Damascus Gate, Herod's Gate, and the Lions' Gate — the Damascus Gate was, by far, his favorite entrance, even though the Lions' Gate was closer to where he needed to be.

Named for having been the traditional starting point for travelers headed to the ancient Muslim capital of Syria, the Damascus Gate is the most direct entry into the large Muslim Quarter of the city and the gate is always busy. "Suleiman must have had important visitors on his mind as he constructed this magnificent gate" he said to his young son as they stopped to look. "The gate has two towers on either side, and they are covered with those decorative battlements. See them, up at the top?" asked the three-fingered man as he pointed to the top of the tower to the right. Starting to walk again he added, "And look here, at this ancient inscription on the gate, *There is no god but Allah, and Muhammad is his prophet.* May peace be on him. Look how well preserved the inscription is! This inscription reminds us each time we enter or leave the city of why we live the life we have chosen."

Yusef looked at his father quizzically. "We get to choose this life? I thought Allah chose my life."

The father patiently answered his son, "Allah sets the path. It is up to us to walk it."

The three-fingered man loved everything about the Muslim Quarter and could feel himself pulled into the history of the place each time he

---

[18] "Jerusalem Within The Walls," Israel Ministry of Foreign Affairs Website, Accessed March 9, 2021, https://mfa.gov.il/MFA/AboutIsrael/State/Pages/Jerusalem%20within%20the%20Walls.aspx

entered through the gate. The opening was large but narrowed quickly, making a ninety-degree left-hand turn and then quickly another ninety-degree right-hand turn. The gate area was filled with shops, and locals selling souvenirs to passing tourists. These were the prime spots for people selling goods as the entrances and exits were limited by the walls surrounding the city. The three fingered man knew his son would be wide eyed entering the gate. "You know, Yusef, Muslims came to Jerusalem in about 638 AD, which is almost fourteen hundred years ago and have been a driving force behind the character of the Old City."

"That is *forever* ago, Abee," Yusef said in English.

"Arabic, Yusef!" demanded the three-fingered man. Then with more patience, added, "This is *our* city! Muslims have ruled the city for over one thousand years! The only time that rule was interrupted was for only a brief blink in history when Jerusalem was captured by Christian crusaders. We do not speak their language in this city unless it is absolutely necessary. Understand?"

Yusef nodded and smiled at his father.

As the three-fingered man stepped through the gate area, he understood and wanted to show his son that they were stepping into the world of Islam. The first step to emphasize that fact was speaking Arabic. "Tell me Yusef, what is the first connection that the Prophet had with Jerusalem? Do you remember?" The well-aged narrow, brown, cobblestone streets were filled with life, people buying and selling, colorful burqas worn by the women in the market, and Arabic being spoken all around.

Still looking, eyes wide with fascination, the question forced the young boy's attention back to his father. "I think so," Yusef said. "The angel Gabriel woke up the prophet Muhammad, may peace be upon him, woke him up from a dream he was having in the holy city of Mecca. Gabriel somehow... removed and washed his heart and... took him on a trip that night, here, to Jerusalem."

Smiling broadly, the three-fingered man asked, "And what did he do here?"

"He visited all the holy places... and then... he met the other prophets like Moses... and Abraham... and David... and Jesus... way up there, under the Golden Dome, on the Foundation Stone," Yusef said, pleased with his memory.

"Yes, but the Dome was not there. It had not yet been built. What happened while he was there on the Foundation Stone?"

"The Prophet climbed a ladder of light through... seven heavens and appeared before Allah, himself. Allah then taught Muhammad about prayer and... other things."

"You have answered well, Yusef. Here is your first lesson. Allah instructed the Prophet in prayer and in 'other things.' Those other things are part of *our* destiny. They are special to *us*, me and you. Allah chose us by way of our ancestors, through Suleiman the Lawgiver," the three-fingered man said, smiling. "Do you know who Suleiman the Lawgiver was?"

"No, Abee, who was he?"

"He built the beautiful gate we came through a moment ago. Suleiman the Lawgiver, sometimes he is referred to as Suleiman the Magnificent, ruled the Muslim Ottoman Empire for 46 years and the Ottoman empire ruled Jerusalem, too. He ruled over 25 million people during his reign. He is the one that selected our ancestors and set our destiny."

"What *is* our destiny, Abee?" he asked.

"We are the protectors of the hidden place. Suleiman chose your ancestors to be protectors of the hidden place because of their loyalty, their bravery, and their discretion. The duty has been passed for generations. You are the next in that line."

Yusef's eyes opened wide. He knew that made him special to the Prophet.

"Do you know what the word discretion means, Yusef?" the three-fingered man asked.

"No sir."

"Discretion means we keep this a secret. We tell no one. You do not tell your brothers or your friends. If you tell, it could mean your life. We do not want to disappoint the Prophet. Do you understand?"

Yusef nodded and he did understand. He took his father's words seriously. The three-fingered man knew his son was young, but he also knew Yusef was smart and eager to please. He would do everything in his power to keep their secret.

As they continued their walk through the streets of the Muslim Quarter, the three fingered man continued teaching his son about the history of the Old City. "The Dome of the Rock, what we call 'The Most Holy Sanctuary' was built in 691 by Abd al-Malik. He covered the exterior with tile mosaics and on the interior, on the walls, words from the Koran are written in elaborate calligraphy. The building is in an octagon shape. Do you know how many sides an octagon has, Yusef?"

The boy, distracted by a shop with antique silver goods for sale, did not hear the question and had stopped walking with his father. By the time he noticed it, the three-fingered man had to backtrack several steps. "Yusef!" he said. Startled, the boy jumped to attention and caught up with his father.

"The Most Holy Sanctuary has an octagonal shape. How many sides does an octagon have?" he asked again.

"Six, Abee?"

"No, son. Try again."

"Oh, I remember, eight. Octagons have eight sides."

"That is correct. Do you know..."

Yusef interrupted his father, "Abee, my friend at school, Amit, said that where the Dome is, that it really belongs to them, the Jews. He says that... that is the place where the Jews set up their temple a million years ago or something. He said it was called something... something like their most Holy Place or something. And, he said that the Foundation Stone was where their God's gold box sat. *And* he said..."

The three-fingered man had heard enough and knew his son would keep talking if he didn't interrupt him. "You are not to listen to the lies of the Jews. *There is no god but Allah, and Muhammad is his prophet.* That Jew has no idea of what he is speaking, and I will not have him putting wrong ideas into your head. You can no longer be friends with him."

Yusef knew better than to argue with his father but wished he had not told his Abee which of his friends had told him those things. Amit had just been given the latest PlayStation video gaming system for his birthday and Yusef *really* wanted to go to his house and try it out. He simply nodded and said, "Yes, Abee."

"Did you remember your watch, Yusef?" the three-fingered man asked.

The boy was happy that the subject had so easily been changed and looking down at his wrist, again said "Yes! Abee," but this time it was with curiosity, not disappointment.

The three-fingered man said, "We walked in the Damascus Gate and stayed on that street until we came to the Convent of the Sisters of Zion where we turned left. That is down there on this street. We have walked in this city for about fifteen minutes. Do you see where we are standing now? Be back here, at this exact spot, in one hour. Not one minute before, not one minute late. It is 9:03 right now. Be back here at 10:03. You are free to explore the city but stay inside the city walls. For one hour, Yusef. Do you understand me? One hour. I do not want to have to come looking for you or it will be judgment day for young boys," he said with a wink.

Yusef was beside himself. He could not believe he got to be alone with his father and that his father was giving him the freedom to explore the city without him. Yusef had one hour and wanted to go back to that store that sold silver things. He wished that he had known to bring the money he had been saving.

"Remember, Yusef. Only Arabic. No English," the three-fingered man said. And then, as if on cue, the three-fingered man pulled his left hand out of his pocket and handed his son some coins, Shekels, the currency used in Israel. "Don't buy any junk. That is for some breakfast when you get hungry. Do you understand? Off you go. I will see you in 57 minutes," he said with a smile. Yusef was a good boy and trustworthy. The three-fingered man knew his son would return in 50 minutes and then try to hide until the exact moment he was supposed to show up. The real reason for the time limit was to keep the boy close, in the Muslim Quarter at least, where he knew the people of the city would take care of an Arabic speaking boy.

The three-fingered man was only a few steps away from his rendezvous destination, the real reason for his trip into the Old City and made his way there. He pulled out his cigarettes and, taking one in his right hand, lit it with a lighter pulled from his jacket pocket. Keeping the cigarette in his right hand would force him to keep it out of his pocket, out in the open where his contact could see it. Surprisingly, his contact approached him quickly, before the first cigarette was finished. A woman, wearing a traditional hijab, a scarf covering the head and chest to show modesty, approached him and without speaking, handed him a cell phone, turned and walked away. As he was watching the woman walk away, the phone rang in his hand, startling the three-fingered man. He had never been approached that quickly and contact had definitely never happened the same day.

The three-fingered man pressed the green button on the cheap phone. The voice was processed through a distortion device and amplified through the speaker portion of the phone. "Alhimaya, the attempts to protect the hidden place, by traditional means, have been ineffective.[19] It falls to you, Alhimaya. Kill the leader and block the path. Make it look accidental. Do it Monday. Do you have questions?" The three-fingered man dropped his head in sadness and disappointment but before he could speak, the distorted voice said "Good. Keep this phone. We will be in touch again." The line disconnected. The three-fingered man hated being referred to as Alhimaya. Alhimaya was not his name, it was not even a name. It was a word that meant protection, like a nurse cares

---

[19] Alhimaya (or Al Himaya) – Arabic word meaning "Protection"

for and protects their patient. He understood his role in protecting the hidden place, but The Bringer of Death was no nurse.

"Monday?" the three-fingered man said to himself. That was not much time. He needed to gather the supplies necessary to construct the bomb. He also needed time to inspect the site so he would know the size of the charge that would close the path — a task he could do before heading back home. Finally, he would need the time to construct the bomb. It would be a difficult task to accomplish, but he knew he could do it, but the short timeframe would ensure a rough final product.

The three-fingered man made his way back to his prearranged meeting spot with Yusef, found a place with some shade and sat down to wait. On cue, at 10:03, Yusef magically appeared, proud of himself for finding his way back to his father and for not being one minute late.

"Let's make our way back out of the Gate, son. I have to make a stop on the way home. Did you have a good time? Did you get some breakfast? Would you like to see a cave?"

This was turning out to be the best day of his young life. Yusef answered, "Yes, yes and *yes!*"

The three-fingered man smiled at his son but wished he had come alone into the city. He resolved himself for what he knew he must do. He must begin, in earnest, his son's lessons. Today he would show him, for the first time, the place he must protect.

"Son, remember when I told you about your destiny?"

Yusef nodded emphatically.

"Son, we are protectors of a place most people on this Earth do not know even exists. Today, by chance, we are forced to visit it. We are going to look at the entrance to the hidden place, the cave of wonder. Come with me. It is a short walk from here."

Chapter 2

———•◆•———

MONDAY. 6:33 AM.

T he harmonic notes produced by the electric guitar screamed in unison over the driving beats of the bass, drums, and electric rhythm guitar. The thumping of the song pulsed like a hard rock heartbeat through the small apartment. It was easily the third time in a row the song had played, and it showed no signs of changing.

"Really? Again? How can you listen to that kind of music? I thought you said you were studying…" Jessica said a little louder than the music was playing. To his credit, Matt didn't play his music so loud that it disturbed the neighbors, but when he played Stryper, particularly the 1988 album, *In God We Trust*, it got on Jessica's nerves. She called it classic rock and that got on *his* nerves.

"I *was* studying, and now I'm finished! I was reading the Bible, in the book of Daniel, chapter 5, and it reminded me of this song. When the music starts in my head, I gots to gets it in my ears!" Matt replied.

"Why don't you gets yo' earbuds in yo' ears and save the rest of us from that noise pollution!?" Jessica teased playfully.

"You don't know it, but you owe a debt of gratitude to this band and specifically to this song. This song is the reason we are married."

"What?!?" Jessica asked incredulously.

"Yeah. Here's the story. I was just a kid the first time my friend's older sister played this cassette for us. Yes. I am 'cassette' years old." Jessica rolled her eyes, but Matt laughed at his own joke. "This song, called *The Writing's On The Wall,* is really what sparked my interest in Old Testament history and that specific story showed me that Bible history can be cool, funny even. If I had never listened to this cassette, if I had never heard this song, I probably wouldn't be here in Israel with you right now, babe."

"How in the world did this song get you interested in Old Testament history? And nobody has ever called Bible history 'funny,'" Jessica said as she was continuing to put on her makeup. She turned away from her makeup mirror and saw Matt staring at her. "You're doing it again," she said to him.

To say that Matt Davenport was living his dream life would be a massive understatement, but it was a completely different story in the not-too-distant past. A little over a year ago, he had found himself right in the middle of a situation involving a terrorist network, intent on destruction, and Mossad, the elite Israeli anti-terrorist organization. In a matter of two days, Matthew Davenport, just a normal, nervous dude from the suburbs had changed. At the start of the ordeal, he had been a timid, little, wimpy Christian, afraid to tell strangers about his belief in God and the supernatural, afraid to tell the love of his life his true feelings about her, afraid to simply be a man. *"Man up and grow a pair,"* the handsome terrorist had once said to him. Now, after he had been involved in multiple car chases, gunfights, helicopter and airplane flights on different sides of the globe, he was different, not just because he had found himself in the middle of an international terrorist plot, but because he found what the Bible declared was *actually* true. In the midst of the torrential rain of bullets, in the middle of explosions, in the uncertainty of the moment between jumping out of an airborne helicopter or staying inside with the terrorist, Matt found that God, through the Holy Spirit, would talk to him and help him if Matt was willing to listen and do what was said. Even when it seemed crazy, Matt obeyed that still, small voice and it saved his life, on more than one occasion.[20] God protected Matt in the most supernatural of ways and provided a way of escape.

Some people think that hearing from God is a myth, that it sounds crazy, that it just can't be true, but Matt knows God wants to talk to His followers and is a very present help in time of trouble.[21] Matt relied on God to save him, to help him figure out the mystery of what the terrorist was planning, and he relied on God to help him save the life of the woman he loved, Dr. Jessica Adams. That was then. This is now.

"I said, *you're doing it again*," Jessica said, laughing. And he was. Matt was staring at his beautiful wife, Jessica. He sometimes had trouble believing how wonderful his life had become and often Jessica found Matt staring lovingly at his wife.

"It's just because you're so beautiful, Jessica. I can't help it!" Matt said laughing. Then, changing back to the original subject, he continued, "Yeah, this song is what turned me on to Old Testament history. Today I was reading the Bible, in the book of Daniel, and came across the story. Do you know the story of the 'writing on the wall'?" he asked.

"I know... the phrase... 'the writings on the wall,' but I don't know what you're referencing in Daniel chapter 5," Jessica replied.

"Well, then Dr. Davenport, let me enlighten you." Matt teased. Jessica had been Dr. Adams until recently when the two of them were married. It had been a nightmare trying to get her last name changed on everything. From simple things like access passes at worksites to more involved things like passports and work visas, it had taken almost a year for everything to actually have her new last name, Davenport, on it. "Someone ring the bell; class is in session."

"Matt, just tell me, already. I don't have time for an in-depth lecture today. Remember, I'm meeting Professor Kenyon this morning?"

"Ok. Ok. Settle down class. I'll make this quick, but it's a really cool story, so you'll want to go back and read it for yourself. Here's

---

[20] Reference I Kings 19:12 (King James Version)

[21] Psalm 46:1

the background: the Babylonian king, Nebuchadnezzar had demanded payment, a yearly tribute, from the kingdom of Judah and they refused. So, he marched his army into town and forced them to pay and then, he took all the nobility, the upper class people, the military leaders, anybody that he could gain knowledge from or had any skills to help his kingdom, he took them back to Babylon and told the new, puppet king, Zedekiah, to keep up the yearly tributes, the yearly payments. You know what I mean by puppet king? He was just a power broker, a client king. He had some regional power, but he was still under the authority of Nebuchadnezzar. Anyway, that doesn't really matter to this story. What *does* matter is that one of the guys that old King Nebbie took back to Babylon with him was a dude named Daniel — of 'Daniel and the Lion's Den' fame.[22] You've heard that story, right?" Matt asked.

Laughing Jessica said, "Yes, I have heard the story of Daniel in the lion's den. Old King Nebbie, now *that's* funny. Did King Nebbie have a daughter named Little Debbie?" Matt groaned at the bad joke.

Continuing, Matt said, "Well, King Nebbie also took the treasures out of the Temple in Jerusalem as part of his payment, think gold and silver chalices and stuff like that. These were God's golden vessels. So, fast forward a few years. King Nebbie has died and the new king, Belshazzar, throws a great feast and all of his friends, family, nobility, wives and even his concubines are there. There were a thousand people in attendance.[23] They were gettin' their party on, getting drunk and all that… and King Belshazzar has the brilliant idea to go and get the Temple treasures and fill them with wine and use them to get drunk. But see, these were God's vessels and God didn't like that too much.[24] Well, the next thing you know, they were drinking out of God's vessels, and they started praising these false gods, gods of gold and brass and wood

---

[22] Daniel 6

[23] Daniel 5:1

[24] Daniel 1:3

and silver and stuff.[25] Then all of a sudden, this huge hand appears and starts writing words on the plaster of the wall. That's where the title of the Stryper song comes from *The Writing's On The Wall,* from this giant hand, writing on the wall, out in the open for everybody to see. Now, the Bible puts what happened next, delicately. It says, let me find the verse, oh, here, verse 6 'Then the king's countenance was changed, and his thoughts troubled him, so that the joints of his loins were loosed, and his knees smote one against another.'[26] Basically, what happened when the king saw the hand writing on the wall, it scared him so bad that his knees were literally knocking together and he dropped a deuce in his fancy pants." Matt said, laughing as he went along.

The comment caught Jessica off guard and when she quit laughing, she said "Eww! Gross! Ha ha! What happened next?" Jessica asked, fully into the story now.

"Well, King Belshazzar wanted to know what the writing said, right? So, he starts asking everybody at the party if they can read and interpret the words and nobody can. So, he sends word out, 'Call all the smarty-pants, nerdy types, in the kingdom and see if any of them can read or interpret the writing,' he even offered them a reward but none of them could interpret the writing.[27] Then, the queen was like 'I remember a dude, named Daniel, from when Nebbie was king, I bet he can interpret the words.'[28] So they called for Daniel.

"Daniel shows up and the king tells him, 'Nobody has been able to tell me what these writings are about. You're my last hope. If you can interpret these words, I'll give you all kinds of gifts and make you the third highest ruler in my kingdom.'

Daniel politely declines. He basically tells the king, 'I don't want any of your stuff, keep your rewards and keep your leadership positions to

---

[25] Daniel 5:4

[26] Daniel 5:6

[27] Daniel 5:7

[28] Daniel 5:10-12

yourself. I'm not interested.'[29] But Daniel says he *can* interpret the writings. So, Daniel says, 'Here are the words that are written, *Mene, Mene, Tekel, Upharsin.* That literally means *numbered, numbered, weighed, divisions.*' and then Daniel tells him what those four words mean. *Mene* or *Numbered* means that God has numbered your kingdom and it is finished. *Tekel* or *Weighed* means you, Belshazzar, have been weighed in the balances and found wanting. *Peres* or *Divisions* means that your kingdom and your kingship will be divided between the Medes and the Persians."[30]

"So, what happened to the king? How do you say his name? Beltshezzer?" Jessica asked.

"Belshazzar. *Bell* not *belt.*" Laughing, Matt continued the story, "Well, the king wanted to give Daniel all the stuff he had promised him. Daniel was like, 'Bro. Did you even hear what I said? I'm out of here.' And *that night*, the kingdom was attacked and overtaken by the Medes, just like Daniel had said and King Belshazzar was killed. The new king was named Darius. He's the guy that threw Daniel in the lion's den, but that is a story for another time.

"So, class, let's recap. Over twenty-five hundred years ago, God used a miracle to let Belshazzar know he was doomed, writing words on a wall in an unknown tongue that Daniel interpreted. Over thirty years ago, a Christian rock band, Stryper, wrote a song, using a phrase coined by the event and in my curiosity to understand where the phrase came from got me interested in Old Testament history. See? It *can* be funny. If I wasn't interested in Old Testament history, we might not have connected the way we did, I might not have been in your life, and you might not have fallen in love with me. Hence this song is the reason we're married and I'm currently living in Israel! Turn it up!!"

Jessica turned and looked at Matt directly, face to face, gave him one giant eye roll and went back to her makeup. "Cool story, bro," she said laughing.

---

[29] Daniel 5:17

[30] Daniel 5:25-28

Turning the music off in the bedroom, Matt said, "I am going to make some breakfast before I head into the Old City to meet Rabbi Kaduri. Do you want me to cook you some pancakes, too?"

"No, I'm going to meet Professor Kenyon for breakfast before work," Jessica answered.

"I thought you were going out to his dig site, and he was going to show you around the place. When did your plans change?" Matt asked as he was moving towards the kitchen.

Jessica, finishing up her makeup, put down her eyeliner and made her way out of the small bathroom and moved towards the kitchen area as well. She said, "Yeah, I was going to go out to the site, and I really want to see it, but I just had one of those negative nudges about it. So... I decided I would just meet him for breakfast, let him tell me about what he is working on and what he has found and then try and visit it at some other point. I didn't have any kind of negative feeling about meeting him for breakfast, so that's what we're doing. Sounds crazy, doesn't it?"

Matt, through the ordeal with the terrorists, had learned to trust those nudges, both positive and negative, knowing that the Holy Spirit often used them to direct their paths, to keep them safe or to reveal His goodness in their lives. "Nope. Doesn't sound crazy at all. Maybe God has something awesome in store for you guys wherever you are getting breakfast! Maybe there's a contact to be made there or something. Do you know where his dig is? Know anything about it?"

"Yeah, he's been working on this particular site for a few years. It's located on the north side of the Old City, outside the walls of the Temple Mount, but I'm not exactly sure where. You know, Dr. Kenyon told me that in Israel there are something like 37,000 historical and archaeological sites and less than seven percent of them have been excavated. It has taken him this long to excavate down to the level where they are now, finding artifacts from different time periods all along the way. Dr. Kenyon was excited about a recent discovery and, I think, I'm kind of hopeful anyway, the reason he invited me out was because he wants some of my expertise in dating some of the finds. I *hope*... but I could be completely off base. Maybe he needs some of my contacts to help with testing or permits or something."

"That would be cool, something a little different than what you have been working on these past few years. Would it be a paying gig?" Matt asked.

"Matt, we make good money. Even if he offered, I would probably refuse a salary for this. It would be an honor to help one of my old college professors and a delight to help my friend."

"Nerd!" Matt said jokingly.

"You just told me all about King Nebbie and you're calling *me* a nerd!?" Jessica laughed as she was gathering her purse, jacket, and briefcase. She gave Matt a kiss and started towards the door. "I love you, husband. I'll see you tonight. We're still going to try to cook that new recipe your mom sent us, aren't we?"

"Yes, we are, and I can't wait! I love you, wife. See you tonight!"

And with that, Jessica was out the door and, on her way, to meet her old professor, Dr. Kenyon. Matt turned his Stryper back on and looking down at his watch, immediately turned it off again, realizing he didn't have time to listen to the song again or cook the pancakes before he was supposed to leave to meet Rabbi Kaduri in the Old City. "Why does he always want to give these private tours at breakfast time on Monday mornings?" Matt said aloud, but he knew the answer — early Monday mornings were a great time to move easily about the Old City of Jerusalem before the tourists showed up and clogged the cobbled city streets with their slow-moving pace. Matt also knew that today was going to be a little bit different, and he was glad that he and the Rabbi had become friends. Today, some politicians from the United States were making their first trip to the Holy Land and wanted a local guide, one with an in-depth knowledge of the Old Testament, to show and explain where some of the great Biblical stories took place. Somehow, these politicians had been referred to the Rabbi and the Rabbi invited Matt along for the VIP tour.

Matt jumped at every chance to learn something new about Israel and her history. After having seen Israel, the Bible came alive to him. He had once told Jessica that before he saw Israel, before he saw Jerusalem, when he read his Bible, it was like watching an old movie, in black and white, without any sound. He read the words on the page, but there wasn't a lot of depth to it for him. After having been to the Holy Land, after having been to the exact places, walking where the Biblical patriarchs walked, having seen the land where they lived, it made the Bible come alive. Instead of being like a silent, black and white movie, it was now a 3D, 8K, super high-definition movie with 7.1 surround sound.

Matt grabbed his keys and put on his leather jacket because it looked cool, not because he thought he would need it all day. In fact, the March morning might be chilly, but he knew he would end up carrying the jacket in the afternoon. It didn't matter. He didn't get the opportunity to wear a leather jacket many times in Israel, and he was going to do it now. He also grabbed his crossbody, sling bag. Ever since 'the incident' with the terrorists and the bombs, Matt had become a little paranoid, though the feeling was dissipating more and more daily. He carried the bag with him every time he left the apartment, because, like he told Jessica repeatedly, "I never want to be unprepared again."

Jessica teased Matt saying things like "Don't forget your purse!" and "Your purse really matches that outfit, handsome." When he would wear his leather jacket along with the bag, Jessica called him 'Indiana Davenport' though she admitted it didn't have the same ring to it that Indiana *Jones* did.

Matt didn't care what Jessica thought of it. Just like Batman and his utility belt, Matt was determined to be prepared. In his bag, he kept an extra phone and charger, a Swiss Army pocketknife, some simple medicines like headache and diarrhea pills, some extra money, both American and Israeli, a small flashlight, and he always had several large bags of his new favorite candy, *Wild Berry Skittles,* the ones in the light purple bag. Family size? Sharing size? Nope. Matt Davenport size!

Matt left the apartment, excited about the new things he would see and might learn on today's tour with Rabbi Kaduri. The place was an oxymoron, to him there was always something *new* about the *Old* City and there was always something he could learn from his intelligent Jewish friend. He had a couple of questions he had been saving up and he planned to ask the Old Testament scholar today, if he had a few minutes in private with him.

Chapter 3

MONDAY. 7:09 AM.

The Sun was warming the cool, crisp morning as Jessica made her way to the prearranged meeting place with Dr. Kenyon, a small coffee shop called *Cofizz*, located in the Downtown Triangle area of the more modern Jerusalem, about a ten-minute drive to the Damascus Gate. Since Dr. Kenyon had not arrived, Jessica ordered some coffee and found an unoccupied table outside, where she sat to wait for him. Dr. Kenyon had the well-earned reputation for always being a few minutes late. Jessica had kept an extra block of time available this morning for just this thing.

Jessica had met Dr. Kenyon while attending his archaeology class at Penn State University while she was completing her undergraduate work. She was under the impression that this "Kenyon: Archaeology of the Holy Land" course was being taught by Kathleen Kenyon the British archaeologist who excavated Jericho in the 1950's. When she signed up for the class, Jessica was unaware that Kathleen Kenyon died in 1978 and Cooper Kenyon was the wrong age, nationality, gender and even had the wrong life status — he was alive. Jessica had only signed up for the class because of his last name. Through the semester, Jessica had shown so much promise that he later invited her to become one of his teaching assistants. They shared a common bond, the love of archaeology, history, geology and Jesus Christ, but not necessarily in that order. Being a Christian in the academic world was a rarity. When he retired from full time teaching and found his way to Israel, Dr. Kenyon and Jessica reconnected and occasionally met to catch up, like this morning.

About fifteen minutes after seven in the morning, Dr. Kenyon showed up, his wild gray hair trying to escape from under the fedora that he had always worn. He was wearing a blue, wool cardigan over a plaid shirt and it looked like he hadn't shaved in a week. On him, it wasn't the 'cool' kind of stubble, it was 'why hasn't the old guy shaved?' kind of stubble. He waved to Jessica, motioned like he was drinking out of a cup and mouthed that he was going to order and would be right back with her. Jessica nodded and smiled.

After a few minutes, Dr. Kenyon emerged from *Cofizz* with a cafe' Americano in his hand and as he joined Jessica at the table said, "Hey there, you! How is the married life treating you? Still in the honeymoon phase? You know, after forty-three years, Sheila and I still are. Best decision I ever made!"

Jessica had never met Sheila but felt like she had known her forever because of all of the stories that Dr. Kenyon had told her about his wife. "Absolutely," Jessica answered. "I'm never planning on leaving the honeymoon phase! I didn't know life could be this wonderful, this fulfilling. I'm so blessed to be *Mrs. Davenport!*"

"Oh, that's wonderful, Dear. We're so incredibly thrilled for you." Dr. Kenyon had a way of including his wife in his excitement for people that he cared about, even if they had never met her. "Have you been waiting long?"

Jessica answered "No, no. No big deal. Tell me about your dig site. I want all the details! What's new since we last spoke?" Jessica knew that once she got Dr. Kenyon started on his work, it could be a while before she had the opportunity to speak again. To be so slow everywhere else, the elderly man's mind was sharp and moved at a lightning pace. He spoke so quickly and gave facts at such a rapid pace that his students had nicknamed him 'Machine Gun' Kenyon because of his staccato delivery style. Jessica eased back into her seat and used her cup of coffee to warm her hands from the cool spring air.

"As you know, we have been excavating on the north side of the Old City for several years. With all of the different controlling factions here, the Israeli Antiquities Authority, the Muslim religious leaders, the Jordanians who control the administration of the Temple Mount, to the poor people who think we're trying to displace them, it is really hard to get any work done. It feels like we take three steps forward and then two steps back every single day.

"You really should come out to the site. It will make so much more sense when I tell you about this if you could visualize it."

"Next time, I promise," Jessica said.

"Deal! Ok. Where to start? You know, Jerusalem has been conquered over forty times throughout history. Each time it was conquered, a newer iteration of the city was built on the ruins of the previous one. Each new city is still there and can be found, right beneath our feet. At our site, we have dug down through several layers and we were excited when we found coins from the first century, silver minted coins from the city of Tyre. I think I told you about that? These are the types of coins that Jesus used. These could have been in His pocket!

"But we kept digging, layer by layer, moving backwards in time, city by city, empire by empire. And we have come across something truly amazing! Truly! Truly amazing! But before I can tell you about it, I need to set the context.

"Jessica, you moved into a related field, history and geology, but let me remind you a little bit about archaeology, *true* archaeology. In the field of archaeology in Israel, we use three sources of information. First, is the Bible, particularly the Old Testament. It is a history book of the land and the peoples in the land. If we remove the theology portion, we have a fantastic, *accurate* recording of the place we are currently located, the country of Israel. But as you know, not everyone wants to believe the Bible...

"So second, we have outside sources, documents, parchments, clay tablets and stelae and the like from outside the Bible. These are contemporary accounts that sometimes happen simultaneously as Bible events but are recorded from a different viewpoint. Many, many times, they confirm what the Bible says.

"And finally, we have the ground. The ground is pure. We know that those coins we found have been there for 2000 years. We know this by the minting, the image, the style. They laid there undisturbed for 2000 years until we came along and dug them up. It is *pure* history. People might try to refute the Bible. People might try to refute a lesser-known ruler's decree on a parchment from history, but there is no refuting the *pure* history of what is found in the ground. But the best is when those three things, the Bible, outside documents or sources, *and* what is found in the ground converge, then we have an unbreakable, airtight case. Then we know, with a certainty, what happened at a certain location at a certain time in history."

As 'Machine Gun' Kenyon stopped to take a sip of his coffee, Jessica was able to interject, "I wish my husband could be here to listen to you. He *loves* Bible history. He was telling me a funny story this morning about an ancient Babylonian King."

Kenyon barely let Jessica finish her thought before he started back up again. "That is incredibly coincidental, as you will soon see. I wish you had brought him along as well. He might enjoy this," Dr. Kenyon said with a huge smile as he put his coffee down. "So, where the three things align – the Bible, the outside documentation, and the ground, we have an unbreakable case. That is what we have found at my site!

"We dug down several layers and we started to find a layer of ash. In that layer of rubble, we found fragments with people's names on them, specific people that are mentioned in the Bible. We found arrowheads. Oh... I'm getting ahead of myself. Let me back up. Have you ever heard of the Babylonian Chronicles?"[31]

---

[31] Joel Shurkin, "Archaeologists Find Evidence Of The Iron Age Siege Of Jerusalem," Inside Science, September 20, 2019; *https://www.insidescience.org/news/archaeologists-find-evidence-iron-age-siege-jerusalem*

With a mouth full of coffee, all Jessica had time to do was shake her head before Dr. Kenyon started back up.

"The Babylonian Chronicles are a series of ancient clay tablets found in Iraq, written in cuneiform and then hardened in ovens. They document the major events in Babylonian history. And in one of the Chronicles, often abbreviated ABC 5 and known as the Jerusalem Chronicles, we find the story of a siege.[32] A very specific siege, the siege of Jerusalem.

"In 586, the Babylonian army was the strongest in the land. Their king, a ruler named Nebuchadnezzar, a nasty fellow, was intent on ruling the whole of the Earth and setting himself up as a god. You can read about him in the Bible, in the books of 2 Kings, Ezra, 1 & 2 Chronicles, Jeremiah and some in Daniel, too. Anyway, Nebuchadnezzar had besieged the land of Judah. So, the king of Judah, a man named Zedekiah, calls in Jeremiah, the prophet, and asks him to intercede on his behalf to God. Jeremiah answered the king," Dr. Kenyon pulled out a Bible and said, "It is better to read it out of the book than for me to tell it! Here, in Jeremiah 38 starting in verse 17, *'Then Jeremiah said to Zedekiah, "This is what the Lord God of Heaven's Armies, the God of Israel, says: 'If you surrender to the Babylonian officers, you and your family will live, and the city will not be burned down. But if you refuse to surrender, you will not escape! This city will be handed over to the Babylonians, and they will burn it to the ground.'"*

"But I am afraid to surrender," the king said, "for the Babylonians may hand me over to the Judeans who have defected to them. And who knows what they will do to me!"

Jeremiah replied, "You won't be handed over to them if you choose to obey the Lord. Your life will be spared, and all will go well for you. But if you refuse to surrender..."[33] Dr. Kenyon stopped reading, but continued the thought, "And refuse to surrender he did! So, just as the

---

[32] Titus Kennedy, *Unearthing The Bible,* (Harvest House Publishers, 2020), 152.

[33] Jeremiah 38:17-21 (New Living Translation)

prophet had foretold, Zedekiah was captured, and in a terribly cruel act, Nebuchadnezzar forced him to watch as his family was killed in front of him and then they put his eyes out. The last thing he saw in his life was his family being murdered.

"The final act and the whole point of that story was to tell you this, Nebuchadnezzar burned the whole city to the ground. There was nothing left. He destroyed it all." Dr. Kenyon turned a couple of pages in his Bible and read, *"Meanwhile, the Babylonians burned Jerusalem, including the royal palace and the houses of the people, and they tore down the walls of the city."*[34]

"So, we have the Bible talking about the destruction of the city of Jerusalem by the Babylonians, burning it down. We have the Babylonian Chronicles, the clay tablets, which tell of the destruction of Jerusalem by the Babylonians and now the ground confirms what the Bible and the Chronicles state. That's what we found! We found a layer of ash where the city had been destroyed. And as we continued sorting through the debris, we found arrowheads that were *specific* to the Babylonian army. They are made of bronze and have a very unique, distinctive shape. We find them all over ruins in Iraq, where ancient Babylon was, but there they were, right outside of the city walls, in a layer of ash about a meter thick, where the city had been burned. We found these bullas, umm these little impressions, like small seals, like you would seal an envelope with. Are you familiar with bullas?" Dr. Kenyon asked but didn't give Jessica a chance to answer before continuing.

"Well, these carved stones were probably part of a man's ring that he would wear on his finger. The stones had engravings in them, etchings with names and titles. Now, when he needed to seal a document, a contract for instance, he would put a piece of clay on the document, warm the clay and then put the seal into it. That way, you couldn't read the document unless you were to break the seal. It would also inform whoever was receiving the document, the name and title of whoever

---

[34] Jeremiah 39:8 (New Living Translation)

sent the document to them because it would be etched in the clay. It's like in the United States, when you get something notarized, when you have to get that seal, that stamp from the notary, to make it official. The clay seals are called bullas.

"We found several of these seals, but we actually found ones with some of Zedekiah's government officials' names on them! We found one that says *Gedalyahu son of Pashur*, and he is specifically mentioned by name in Jeremiah 38:1.[35] We found another that says *Gemaryahu son of Shaphan*.[36] He is specifically mentioned by name in Jeremiah 36:12! It's amazing! The Bible, outside documentation and the ground, all proving that Nebuchadnezzar had burned the city, and that Zedekiah and his government leaders had actually been there. It is an airtight case. A slam dunk. A home run. It's like these men are waving to us from 2600 years ago, through history!

"As amazing and life changing and history affirming as all of that was, that was just the beginning! We continued excavating and we found something truly special. We have found something truly wonderful. We have found the entrance, a cave, to a system of tunnels. At least that's what we think it is, a network of tunnels that crisscrosses under the city Old and Modern. We are still in the very beginning of the excavations, but it seems to be an incredible find! We cleared the opening, and the tunnels were clear! The caves look like they have been untouched since before the city was destroyed in 586 BCE! It is a *pristine* find. This is like 'Howard Carter finding King Tut' level of potential! It looks like the entrance to the tunnel system was purposefully hidden, which would explain the undisturbed nature of the site and we found it purely by accident. It is really a funny story..."

---

[35] Artifact was found in 2005. Rich Deem, "Seal of Gedaliah, Son of Pashur, Confirms the Existence of One of Jeremiah's Persecutors," Evidence For God, August 21, 2008, https://www.godandscience.org/apologetics/seal_of_gedaliah.html

[36] Artifact was found in 2008. Tsvi Schneider, "Six Biblical Signatures," Center for Online Judaic Studies, http://cojs.org/six-biblical-signatures/

Jessica saw an opportunity to jump in the conversation before the old professor could get started on the new story. "Who dug the tunnels and when?" was all that she got out before 'Machine Gun' Kenyon started up, rapid fire style, again.

Chapter 4

Monday. 7:30 AM.

The three-fingered man parked *The Rock* in his usual place, but it was much earlier than he was accustomed to being there. He needed to stop the current excavations and was following instructions to kill the archaeologist, but he wanted to do that without injuring anyone else, if possible. He knew the old man's routine, and this would be the best way. Early. When no one else was on the site. He stepped out of the rigid vehicle and made his way to the passenger side door, opening it carefully. Sitting in the passenger seat was a sleek, professional camera, a Nikon D5600 that looked like it could be perfectly at home recording finds of historical significance at an archaeological site or slung around the neck of a wandering tourist that had stumbled onto an archaeological site. Beside the camera was sitting a new, professional camera bag. The three-fingered man carefully picked up the bag and wrapped the strap around his neck and arm so that it hung safely around his neck and shoulder. Inside of the camera bag was the hastily assembled bomb. With very little regard for the expensive camera, he picked it up by the lens and moved away from *The Rock*.

The three-fingered man was a man of precision. He was like a surgeon when it came to his craft, but only if he had the proper length of time to scout, survey, note, and plan every single detail needed for the execution of his duties. That was not the case today. So, he gingerly carried the bag across his chest, camouflaging the deadly contents, as he made his way to the entrance of the cave.

The site was exactly the same as it had been a few days earlier as he and Yusef had scouted the location. It seemed as if no one had visited the place since their reconnaissance mission. It had been easy then, as it was today to get into the site. What had not been easy was answering all of Yusef's questions. That boy had asked more questions in one day than the three-fingered man had asked in his entire training period. Most of the questions were easy enough to answer, but there was one question asked multiple times and in multiple ways, that the three-fingered man had not been able to give a sufficient answer; *"Why are we protecting this cave? What are we protecting in the cave? What about this cave is special so that we need to keep it hidden? Why did Suleiman want to keep this place a secret?"* The truth was the three-fingered man didn't know. Neither did his father. And most likely, neither did his father's father. Somewhere along the line, the truth as to *why* the cave needed protecting was lost. He just knew it was his duty to keep it hidden. Something in this cave was so important or so dangerous that Suleiman had blocked off the entrance to *every cave* in the area, just to keep this one and its contents, whatever they were, hidden. It was his job, along with others, to make sure it remained so.

The three-fingered man found the path to the small cave entrance in the light of the early morning. Shadows from the Old City's walls were receding, and the light of the day made the trek down the steeply sloping incline easier than walking it in the dark, especially with a bomb strapped to his chest. He didn't want to accidentally fall and be obliterated by his own bomb. It was a curious fact that suicide bombers bodies were almost always completely destroyed, leaving little evidence of who they were. The major exception to this rule was that their heads were almost always found completely intact, minus the body, having been blown free at the first instances of the explosion. In studying his craft, he had once found an article online that said: *"The vest's tight constraints and the positioning of the explosive pouches would channel the energy of the blast outward, toward whoever stood directly in front of him. Some of that energy wave would inevitably roll upward, ripping the bomber's body apart at its weakest point, between the neck bones and lower jaw. It accounts for the curious phenomenon in which suicide bombers' heads are severed clean at the moment of detonation and are later found in a state of perfect preservation several yards away from the torso's shredded remains.*"[37] He had tasted enough of his own bombs to know he didn't want to visit Allah today. Giving two of his fingers was enough, he wanted to keep his head exactly where it was. So, he walked with a delicate step, placing one foot carefully in front of the other.

When he reached the entrance, the mouth of the cave, he moved the camera bag to the side and squeezed into the opening. Once inside, he opened the camera bag and removed the flashlight he had placed there. He clicked the button on the side and the light immediately illuminated the small path hewn out of the side of the towering hill. It had not been so easy with Yusef. The three-fingered man had not known he would be entering the cave on that day and had not brought a flashlight with him. He was forced to use the small flashlight setting of his cell phone to try and illuminate the path for himself and his young son. It was a lesson he remembered for today.

The three-fingered man arrived at the place he had prepared two days earlier and laid the flashlight on the ground, propped in between the wall and his Nikon camera so that the flashlight illuminated what he needed to see. He had found a carved indentation in the upper ceiling structure of the cave, in between the carved roof and the wooden support beam that was working to hold the ceiling structure in place. A well placed, carefully crafted charge would cause a minor cave-in, and it would seem like a horrible accident. He carefully removed the bomb from the camera bag, set the timer for 40 minutes, turned it on and then placed it in the ceiling crevice. The three-fingered man had studied the archaeologist and knew his patterns. He knew that he would arrive early,

---

[37] Joby Warrick, *The Triple Agent: The Al-Qaeda Mole Who Infiltrated the CIA.* (Vintage Books, 2012), 151.

before any of the other workers, to assess how much had been excavated on the last day of the dig. He would mark where he wanted to proceed and make plans for when the rest of the crew arrived. The three-fingered man knew that the archaeologist would be there within the hour because the crew started arriving at 9 AM and the archaeologist needed to be done with his initial surveys before then so he could be working on the day's plan. That would be his chance to kill him, when he was alone in the cave. The three-fingered man could block the tunnel, hide the truth — whatever that was — and potentially make it look like the cave just collapsed on the man. Finishing it, he gathered his camera, placed it in the camera bag and slowly, carefully stepped away from the bomb, inspecting his work. Where it had been placed, the device was utterly invisible and unless someone was explicitly looking for it, it would not be found. The timing of it all would take precision which excited him, but the thought of killing the archaeologist saddened the three-fingered man.

Chapter 5

MONDAY. 7:42 AM.

M att stepped off of the city transit bus, crossed the street when traffic was clear and made his way to the Jaffa Gate of the Old City of Jerusalem. The metro station, the closest point where Matt could get off the bus, was actually closer to the Damascus Gate, but it only took Matt about ten minutes to walk to the meeting place, near the Jaffa Gate, where he would connect with Rabbi Kaduri and the VIP tour group. Matt put a handful of *Skittles* in his mouth and sighed a moment of relief as he realized that he had arrived before Rabbi Kaduri or the VIP group. Matt never liked to make the Rabbi and his groups wait for him, as he was just a tagalong to the tours. Matt was around ten minutes early but knew Rabbi Kaduri would be there at any moment and chances were extremely high that the tour group would actually be late, as usual.

Standing there in the shadow of the city walls, Matt was glad he had decided to wear his leather jacket. Not only did he look cool, but it was keeping the chill of the morning off him. The Jaffa Gate is where most non-Muslim foot traffic enters the Old City. It is certainly the most convenient entrance to the newer pedestrian friendly area of Jerusalem, but at this time of the morning, the foot traffic was still very slight. Other than the vendors and shop owners getting ready for the day, there wasn't much going on at this hour, certainly in regards to tourists.

Seemingly out of thin air, Rabbi Kaduri showed up wearing the same style of clothing that Matt had always seen him wear, a black suit and a white shirt, a small hat sitting on the crown of his head called a yarmulke and comfortable dress shoes, built for walking. The Rabbi was, Matt guessed, somewhere in his late fifties to mid-sixties. He had a long graying beard and short cropped graying hair, styled neatly to match his neatly dressed appearance. Matt had never seen the Rabbi in any other style dress than the black suit. Once, Matt asked him about it, "Why do you always wear the same outfit?"

Rabbi Kaduri had replied, "There are several reasons, but the main one and one that you will find is important to all Jews, everywhere around the world. *Tradition.* When you see someone wearing a black suit, a white shirt, has a long beard and a small hat on his head, do you think to yourself, 'Is this guy is Jewish?' No! You know! We all know! *Tradition.* Men wearing black jackets and pants is both simple and formal and say that the person wearing them is both dignified and humble. *Tradition.*" Rabbi Kaduri had the same accented English that all Israelis did if Hebrew was their first language. Matt often tried to imitate the accent, but Jessica said he only sounded like a weird vampire when he tried.

Matt greeted his friend, "Ma shlomkha?" which was the way to ask, "How are you?" or a more literal translation would be "How's your peace?" in Hebrew.

"Tov toda! Ve at, Matthew?" Rabbi Kaduri replied, Hebrew for "Very well, and you, Matthew?" He seemed surprised with how well Matt's Hebrew was coming along.

"Tov, tov. Good, good, Rabbi. I have some new questions for you, but I can't do it in Hebrew. Mind if we stick to English today?" Matt answered.

"Of course. You know I enjoy practicing my English with you. We probably have a few minutes before the group arrives. What do you have for me today? What are your questions?"

Matt and Rabbi Kaduri had been enjoying getting to know each other over the course of the last few months. Matt had an inquisitive mind and the Rabbi lived to teach. It was a perfect combination. Matt usually asked questions trying to get a better understanding of the Old Testament from someone who knew and studied the Words and could read it in its original written language, something Matt thought was an advantage. Matt had trouble learning to speak Hebrew, let alone how to read the oddly shaped letters. Even a simple *Google* search on how to say an easy phrase returned answers written in the weird looking style. It had also been difficult to learn the spoken language when everyone wanted to practice their English with him.

"Ok. Can you explain to me something that I have been wondering about for a long time? In Genesis, the account of the Garden of Eden. The woman, Eve, took the fruit…"

"A fig," the Rabbi interjected. "Westerners always think the fruit was an apple. It was a fig. I apologize for the interruption, please continue."

"Yeah, so Eve ate the *fig* and then gave some to Adam and he ate the *fig*, too. Then the Bible says this, I memorized it so I could ask you about it: *'And the eyes of them both were **opened**, and they knew that they were naked'*[38] So, my question is, weren't their eyes already opened? I mean, before that, they weren't running around blind, right? So, what does that mean? How were their eyes then opened when they ate the fruit, uh, fig?"

"What an excellent question, Matthew. Let me posit this answer to you in this way — what if, when Adam and Eve ate the figs, their eyes were then opened to the world we currently live in? What if their eyes were opened to their humanity? What if, until that moment in time, mankind's eyes were opened into the Spirit realm, the place where God lives? Their eyes were opened to their place alongside the Divine. Once they ate the figs, the thing God forbade them from eating, perhaps their eyes opened to the humanity of this world. From that point on, with very, very few exceptions, humans have been dealing with their sin nature and floundering in their flawed, natural, Earthly, non-spiritual

---

[38] Genesis 3: 7 (King James Version)

vision. In effect, their eyes were blinded to the 'spiritual realm' and only opened to the earthly realm," The Rabbi could tell Matt was struggling with this explanation and went down a different track of thought.

"Have you ever known anyone that only saw the best in people? A person that only saw the good traits of someone, even if that person was a complete *shmendrik*, eh, a complete jerk?"

Matt nodded. "Yeah, sure. Jessica, my wife, is like that. She only sees the good in people."

"Wonderful. A beautiful trait. Well, imagine that's what Adam and Eve were like. They only saw the best in *everything*, in all of God's creation, they only saw the good in it. They never saw evil. Never saw lack. Never saw anything other than *good, the perfect, the God-realm*. Then, when they ate of the fig, their eyes were opened and for the first time in history, they began to see things, other than just the good. Does that begin to make sense? When they ate the fig, they became blinded to the divine side and had their eyes opened to the natural, physical realm. Again, we could go very deep down this trail if we have more time at some point."

"I think it makes sense Rabbi," Matt answered, "and I appreciate our limited time right now, but let me see if I have a handle on this. Before Adam and Eve ate the fig, they could see only the good, which is the spirit realm? Then after they ate the fig, they could only see the bad, which is this natural realm we live in? I think I'm starting to confuse myself."

"Hmmm. Maybe it could be better understood like this, Matthew," the Rabbi said. "When mankind was created, he had a filter, like sunglasses, over his eyes. Like sunglasses block out the harmful rays of the Sun, these 'God-glasses' blocked out anything that had a natural, sinful nature to it. When they ate the figs off of the tree and tasted sin for the first time, their 'God-glasses' were removed — their eyes were opened to the sinful nature and desires of mankind. They saw that they were naked. The 'God-glasses' that had been blocking out the desire and need to commit sin were gone. They became aware of it. Their eyes were opened to it. And we have been dealing with the consequences ever since."

"Wow! I think I'm understanding. But you said there were some exceptions to this, some exceptions to being blind to the God realm? That there were some times that humans had their eyes opened to the spirit realm, the spirit world, the place where God exists? People were able to wear their 'God-glasses' again?"

"Oh yes. For short periods of time. I will do my best to confine my answers to examples you will be familiar with, answers from, what you call the Old Testament. One example is from the book of Numbers, the twenty-second chapter. You are probably familiar with a prophet named Balaam. You know the story of the talking donkey, yes?"

Matt nodded and Rabbi Kaduri continued, "The text actually says *'Then the Lord **opened the eyes of Balaam**, and he saw the angel of the Lord standing in the way, and his sword drawn in his hand: and he bowed down his head, and fell flat on his face.'*[39] The Lord opened Balaam's eyes and he saw into the spirit realm, an angel that was prepared to kill him and he would have if Balaam had not repented of his evil ways. The Lord let Balaam look through some 'God-glasses,' and it saved his life.

"Let's see, oh, another place where someone had their eyes opened was Abraham's servant girl from Egypt, Hagar. You are familiar with Hagar? Abraham and Hagar had a son, but Sarah, Abraham's wife, was angry about it. She had Abraham send Hagar and her son, Ishmael, away. They were in a desert place and Hagar was crying out to God for water so that her son wouldn't die. Again, the book of Genesis says, *'And God **opened her eyes**, and she saw a well of water; and she went, and filled the bottle with water, and gave the lad a drink.'*[40] Hagar and her son would have died in the desert except that God opened her eyes to the spirit realm. Through the spirit realm, she was able to see a hidden source of water and she and the boy were saved.

---

[39] Number 22:31(King James Version)

[40] Genesis 21:19 (King James Version)

"But the most famous of Bible stories I can tell you, the one you are probably most familiar with, and hopefully we have time to finish it before the tour arrives, comes from the Prophet Elisha. This comes from the second book of the Kings."

Matt, a student of the Bible, was always amazed at Rabbi Kaduri's seeming memorization of the Old Testament and his instant recall of the exact words of the text. It was, Matt was positive, a result of a lifetime of dedicated study.

Rabbi Kaduri continued, "The king of Syria was making a war against Israel. His war council would meet in private and make their plans. The Syrian king would tell his war ministers to make their camp in a certain place that would be a perfect place to ambush the army of Israel. God would then tell the prophet Elisha about this, and Elisha would warn the king of Israel not to go to that place. It happened a second time. The king of Syria found the best place for an attack on the Israeli army, but Elisha warned the Israeli king not to go to that place. It happened a third time and a fourth time. Finally, the Syrian king got angry with his war ministers and asked who was telling their innermost secrets. 'Who among you is the traitor?' he asked. But a servant said, none of us are traitors. He said *Elisha, the prophet that is in Israel, he tells the king of Israel the words that you speak in your bedchamber.*[41] As you can imagine, this made the king furious!

"So, the king sent out spies and found where Elisha was located, in a city called Dothan. This is near the modern-day village of Bir al-Basha, in the West Bank. So, the furious king sent his army, all of them, to surround the city, by the cover of darkness. Elisha's servant rose early in the morning to draw water, feed the animals and get ready for the day. Looking out, he saw the massive Syrian army encircling them. He was scared out of his wits! So, he ran back to his master, screaming that they were doomed.

---

[41] 2 Kings 6:12 (King James Version)

"Now the text reads like this, '*And his servant said unto him, Alas, my master! How shall we do? And Elisha answered, 'Fear not: for they that be with us are more than they that be with them.' And Elisha prayed, and said, 'Lord, I pray thee, open his eyes, that he may see.' And the Lord opened the eyes of the young man; and he saw: and, behold, the mountain was full of horses and chariots of fire round about Elisha.*[42] The servant was able to peer into the spirit realm and see the angel hosts of the Lord Almighty. Elisha prayed that the servant could wear "God-glasses" and see what was *really* happening.

"So, there are three examples, three exceptions to that natural course, in your Bible, of times when God, through his miraculous ways, somehow closed the eyes of men and women to the natural realm and opened their eyes to the spiritual realm," Rabbi Kaduri concluded.

Matt thought about it for a moment and said, "I love that scripture, '*for they that be with us are more than they that be with them,*' It reminds me of another scripture, this time in my New Testament, written by Paul to the Romans. It says, '*If God be for us, who can be against us?*'[43] And, most of all, I think, I love that Elisha was able to pray, '*Lord, open his eyes, that he may see.*' and God did it! God did it! Can you even imagine that? These are some things that I need to meditate on and think about. Thank you for shedding some light on their eyes being opened. I mean, Adam and Eve and all of the rest of them."

About that time, Matt and Rabbi Kaduri's attention was drawn to a black van that could seat around fifteen people that had pulled up close to the Jaffa Gate a little distance from where Matt and Rabbi Kaduri were standing. A group of well-dressed elderly men and women began slowly exiting the van. The whole thing was so ungainly and took so long that Matt and the Rabbi both knew this had to be his tour group. The procession was blocking traffic, people were starting to stare as more and more horns started honking. The Rabbi shuffled over, gave

---

[42] 2 Kings 6:15-17 (King James Version)

[43] Romans 8:31 (King James Version)

some instructions to the elderly driver, obviously a member of the group himself, showed him a better place to let his passengers out and where to park his oversized van. Matt looked at his watch and noted that the group was only about ten minutes late.

By the time the passengers had all disembarked from the over-sized van, the driver had found a place to park that was big enough for the large vehicle, the group had gathered and made their slow trek to the new assembly point, close to Tzahal Square, a midway point between the Jaffa Gate and the Damascus Gate, Matt noticed that it was almost 8:25 in the morning. The group was already over twenty minutes behind schedule as Rabbi Kaduri was trying to get the group together so he could go over some instructions with them. Then something strange happened.

A tremor.

Matt felt the vibration in his feet and knees before he heard anything. It was just a slight tickle in his soles before he actually heard and could identify the sound. In reality, they were almost instantaneous, but it was that first vibration that alerted Matt to the fact that something was out of the ordinary. The noise, like a concussive wave, washed over him and the group. A detonation nearby made their chests pump and their ears ring. The explosion startled the group and Matt saw panic in Rabbi Kaduri's eyes. Then he watched fear set in with the group. Who could blame them? Jerusalem is a powder keg of religious and political tension just waiting to explode.

As the Rabbi was about to lose control of the situation, Matt spoke up with a loud voice and said, "It's ok! It's ok. Don't be afraid!"

Matt was different than he used to be...

A scared little old lady with blue hair screamed, "Was that a suicide bomber?"

Matt screamed even louder to calm the brewing panic from the tour group and others that were in the vicinity, "No! That was not a suicide bomber! Stop that kind of talk! Everyone gather around so you can hear me." Matt looked to the Rabbi, they made eye contact and Matt could see that by taking control of the situation, it was helping his friend relax and gather himself.

As the elderly group gathered around Matt, the little old lady with the blue hair said to him, "How do you know that wasn't a suicide bomber? They are all over the place around here! They want to kill us all!"

Matt answered, "Ma'am the Israeli army does a very good job of keeping people safe here. Besides, a suicide bomber wouldn't detonate a bomb this early in the morning. No one is in the city yet. A terrorist of any kind would wait until they could maximize the extent of human damage. They don't bomb empty places and trust me; this place is empty right now."

That answer seemed to calm the group for a moment and then the little old lady with the blue hair asked another question, the question that was on everyone's mind. "Well then, what was it?"

"Yes, ma'am," Matt said. "That's a great question. Without going over there to investigate, I can't be one hundred percent sure. My best guess, do you see all the scaffolding all around the outside of the city?" The group turned to look where Matt was pointing, across the street from where they were standing. "See those? Those are archaeological excavations going on. They are everywhere. Literally, everywhere. You can't walk 200 yards in any direction from where you're standing and not run into an archaeological site. Sometimes, they use small explosive charges to clear debris from an area. I'm sure that's what we heard. We don't hear any sirens, no police or military vehicles. I'm sure there's nothing to worry about."

The VIP group seemed satisfied with that answer and by that time, everyone else in the vicinity had moved along going about their business. Life had gone back to normal in the Israeli neighborhood. The little old lady with the blue hair had one final question for Matt. "Who are you and where is our tour guide? I thought we had a Jewish man that was leading the group today. You don't look Jewish."

"You're right, I'm not. But he is. This is Rabbi Kaduri, your guide."

Matt nodded to Rabbi Kaduri, and he took over. Rabbi Kaduri said to the group, "See where that dust plume is, see it rising over there, in the general vicinity where the explosion took place? That is approximately where the traditional site of the Garden Tomb is located. That is one of the places we will see on our excursion today, but we will wait… *until the dust settles.*" Rabbi Kaduri chuckled at his joke, but no one else seemed to get it. He continued speaking to the group, "We will go over there later in the morning. Our first stop is a short walk from where we are now. We will be headed just inside the city walls to the Church of the Holy Sepulchre, which is built over another site which *may* be the place of the crucifixion *and* tomb of Jesus. But, before we get started, I would like to introduce this young man to my right. This is Matthew Davenport. He is my *mishpokhe*, my good friend, like family, and he will be helping us on our tour today." Turning to Matt, the Rabbi said, "Thank you, my friend." Turning back to the group, the Rabbi continued, "I will be leading the tour today and Matt will be bringing up the rear for us. I need all of you to stay between the two of us." Then Rabbi Kaduri started with the formal beginning commentary of his tour for the VIP group.

"Jerusalem's Old City is smaller than a square mile, yet it contains some of the holiest sites in the world, for Jews, like me, for Christians like Matthew, and for Muslims, like the suicide bombers." At this, the group of politicians laughed at the politically incorrect joke. Matt laughed a little too loud, caught off guard by the perfectly timed zinger. "For centuries, people thought that Jerusalem was the center of the world because it was the meeting place of three continents, Europe, Asia, and Africa. Another reason Jerusalem has been so important and such a hotly contested place throughout history is because it lies on the edge of the Judean Desert, but it has water! The water comes from natural springs bubbling up inside of the numerous caves all around and below us. Think about it, all of the great empires throughout history sprang up around Jerusalem: Egypt to the southwest, Sumer to the southeast, Babylon, Assyria and Persia all to the north and east. Then you have Greece and then Rome to the north and west. All of these great civilizations left their marks on *this* land and *this* city. Today we will be looking at some of those places. Now, how many will be walking with us today? Let's get a headcount... Matthew, will you handle that while I start with the recent history of the city?"

Matt nodded and began his count.

Rabbi Kaduri began his tour lecture, "A brief *modern* history of Jerusalem, so you can better understand the tension and hopefully, when you get back to the United States, can continue to help us. I say 'continue' because it has been an incredible lift to my people and this nation having the United States of America recognize Jerusalem as our capital. Let's walk back around to the Jaffa Gate as that will be our entry point to the Old City today.

"A brief history; we will start with the Ottoman Empire. They first ruled Jerusalem beginning in 1517."

The little old lady with blue hair said "You call that *recent*? That's over five hundred years ago!"

"Oh yes, around here, five hundred years is considered *modern*." Rabbi Kaduri answered.

"Five hundred years is twice as old as the United States! Oh my. This is something to take in," the little old lady said.

Rabbi Kaduri smiled and continued, "The walls you see here and what we refer to as the Old City, is not what you think of from biblical times. The city from Biblical times is what we call the City of David, which is currently being excavated to the south of the Temple Mount and the Jewish Quarter. Keep in mind that everything that we will see today was outside of the city walls during the time of the prophets and most of it was outside of the city walls when Jesus walked here."

The little old lady with the blue hair stood there silently, mouth hanging open.

"Now, where was I? Oh yes. Suleiman the Magnificent began ruling the Ottoman Empire in 1520 and was Sultan for over forty years. He expanded and fortified the walls that you see here now. The Ottoman

Empire ruled Jerusalem all the way until 1917, when the British, under General Edmund Allenby took control of the city.

"The British began to relinquish control of the city in 1947 with a United Nations approved partition plan which would create a Jewish *and* Arab state. The Arabs rejected the plan and attacked the new state of Israel the day after they declared their independence. This was 1948."

The group finally made its way back to the original meeting place and Rabbi Kaduri continued his lecture, "This is the Jaffa Gate you see here in front of us. As you can see from all of the indentations, pockmarks, and holes, this gate has seen some serious action. All of those holes are actually bullet holes, grenade shrapnel, and the scars of the 1948 war. There was fierce fighting here and at one point, we thought we would never breach the walls.

"But something miraculous happened and the new Israeli nation won the war! This meant that we would be allowed to exist! But Jerusalem became a divided city. The western half became part of Israel, while the eastern half, including the Old City, was controlled by the Jordanians. For the displaced Palestinian people, the Old City became a rallying point, a place they could call their own.

"Modern Jerusalem was really created the way we know it now, during the Six Day War in 1967. Five Arab nations invaded us, Egypt, Syria, Jordan, Iraq and Lebanon. But again, a miracle! The Israeli nation won the war in only six days! We would be allowed to exist! This is the point where Israel gained control of the West Bank and East Jerusalem from the Jordanians and the Gaza Strip and Sinai Peninsula from Egypt. You may have seen the photographs of the Israeli soldiers praying at the Western Wall... It is a quite moving image because it was the first time in thousands of years that Israelis were actually able to pray there.[44]

---

[44] Mona Boshnaq, Sewell Chan, Irit Pazner, Garshowitz and Gaia Tripoli, "The Conflict In Jerusalem Is Distinctly Modern. Here's The History," The New York Times, December 5, 2017, https://www.nytimes.com/2017/12/05/world/middleeast/jerusalem-history-peace-deal.html

"The Old City is still divided but now it is sorted by people groups, not by countries. We have four quarters: the Jewish Quarter, the Christian Quarter, the Armenian Quarter and the Muslim Quarter. The Temple Mount is still controlled by Israel, but we handed administration of the site back to the Jordanian government to try and help ensure that peace is maintained.[45] As you can imagine, things here, relationships, are delicate and temperamental. There is tension all around, building from the inside, the love of the land and our holy places within each group, Jew, Christian and Muslim.

"Now, let's all make our way inside the beautiful Jaffa Gate."

---

[45] Dov Lieber, "Amid Temple Mount Tumult, The Who, What And Why Of Its Waqf Rulers," Times of Israel, July 20, 2017, https://www.timesofisrael.com/amid-temple-mount-tumult-the-who-what-and-why-of-its-waqf-rulers/.

CHAPTER 6

J essica had only been home from her long day of work for just a few
minutes when Matt swung the door to the apartment wide open
and shouted, "Hey Lucy, I'm home from the club!" in his best Cuban
accent. Matt and Jessica had started watching reruns of the old black
and white comedy *I Love Lucy* in the evenings as they were getting
ready for bed. The show always put them in a good mood — nothing
like some good, clean fun. As Jessica liked to say, "A merry heart does
good like a medicine."[46]

Jessica couldn't help herself and laughed at Matt's goofy antics. He
always seemed to know just the right thing to do or say to make her
smile. Even if her day had been extra stressful at work, like today, as
her latest project was drawing to a conclusion, he had a way of making
her smile. Jessica had plopped down on the couch, turned on the small
television and had just flipped her shoes off as Matt came barreling
through the door.

"Uh-oh, Ricky!" Jessica said mimicking the red-headed comedienne,
Lucille Ball.

"Lucy, you got some 'splainin' to do!" Matt answered. The two of
them laughed at each other's jokes. Matt plopped down beside his wife,
gave her a kiss on the cheek and asked, "How was your day?"

"Nope. You go first. I've got to give my brain a break. I just want
to listen. How was your day? Did you learn anything new today from

---

[46] Proverbs 17:22 (King James Version)

Rabbi Kaduri on your *hundredth* tour of the Old City?" Jessica asked with a smile.

"Well, now that you mention it, I did learn something really cool from the Rabbi. You know that question I've been wondering about with Adam and Eve? About their eyes being opened? I asked him about it, and he gave the most insightful answer… like always."

"Well," Jessica said, "What did he say?"

"First, he explained that when Adam and Eve ate of the forbidden fruit, which, he is positive, was a *fig*, their eyes became blinded to the spiritual realm where God lives and abides. At that moment, their eyes became open to the natural world we live in, which by that point was a sinful world. That's why they noticed, for the first time, that they were naked. Their eyes were opened to the natural realm in a way that they had never been before. That's also why they were ashamed to speak with God. They were blinded to Him and that realm for the first time and it made Him seem unfamiliar to them."

"Oh, man. That's deep," Jessica said.

"Understatement of the decade," Matt sarcastically replied.

"Heeeeey. It's been a long day. Cut me some slack! What else did he say?"

"It was really, really enlightening," Matt said, turning to face Jessica at a more direct angle. Jessica was still sitting facing the television but had turned her head in Matt's direction. Matt continued, "Would you mind muting the TV? I'll tell you all about it."

As she was looking in the cushions of the couch for the remote Jessica said, "Oh. Yeah. I, uh, I didn't even realize it was on." She found the remote, pressed the mute button and the room went silent.

Matt said, "Thanks, I was having trouble concentrating while the sound was on. Anyway, Rabbi Kaduri explained that since Adam and Eve ate of the forbidden fruit, the fig, man has been blinded to the spirit realm. *But,* and this is the part that I think is so fascinating, he said that there are times when that blindness is *suspended*, somehow."

49

Jessica's eyes opened wide in amazement, "When? How? I want to see in the spirit realm! Is that really possible? Do you think it is?" Jessica was starting to become her old self again; the weariness of the long workday was wearing off and she was starting to have more energy.

"I'm not sure. He gave me three Old Testament examples. You know he is Jewish and doesn't really understand the New Testament…"

"Yet!" Jessica interrupted. "He doesn't understand *yet*! I believe your friend will come to understand the beauty of the New Testament and its message and I think you will have a part to play in it."

"Maybe we both will," Matt said with a smile. "Anyway, he doesn't understand the New Testament *yet*, so he gave me three examples from the Old Testament where people had their eyes opened, the blinders to the spirit realm were removed."

"Well, give me one of them and then we probably need to get started working on dinner."

"Dinner can wait. Or we'll go out. I'll give you this example, but then I want to hear about your day, too. Deal?"

Jessica nodded and Matt continued, "So, are you familiar with Balaam and the talking donkey?"

Jessica laughed. "What are you talking about, a talking donkey? You mean, like in *Shrek*? Donkey!" Jessica did her best Michael Myers imitation of the cartoon ogre saying the name of Eddie Murphy's character 'Donkey'.

"You mean to tell me with all those years of church attendance you've never heard about Balaam and his donkey?" Matt asked incredulously.

"I have no idea what you are talking about. Are you even speaking English right now?" Jessica answered.

Matt laughed, "Yes, I'm speaking English! Hang on, I'll be right back." Matt stood up and went into their bedroom. A moment later, he returned and sat in a chair that was placed perpendicular to the couch and television, so that he was at a right angle to Jessica and the television. Continuing he said "Let's just read it from the Bible, shall we? Numbers 22. So, here's the set up to the story. The Israelites are conquering the land of Israel, as God had commanded them. They defeated an army of Amorites, and it scared the other people in the region, in particular the people of Moab, the Moabites, and their king, Balak. Look here, in verse two and three *'Balak son of Zippor, the Moabite king, had seen everything the Israelites did to the Amorites. And when the people of Moab saw how many Israelites there were, they were terrified.'*[47]

"Balak realized there were too many Israelites to fight, and he freaked out. So Balak sent some of his royal court to Balaam, God's prophet, to try and convince him to curse the Israelites. Balaam said, 'I tell you what, I need to pray about this, and I'll let you know what God says about it.' Well, as you can imagine, God told Balaam to stay home and to tell the royal court people to 'kick rocks.' Get that? God told Balaam to stay home and not go with the royal ambassadors. He said in verse twelve, *"Do not go with them. You are not to curse these people, for they have been blessed!"*

"Well, the royal court people went back to Balak and told him that Balaam wasn't coming. So Balak sent different royal court people to Balaam with an offer of great riches if he would go and curse the Israelites. Now, remember, God told Balaam to stay home.

"So, the new royal emissaries showed up, offered Balaam some extravagant riches and initially, Balaam said no. Then he said, 'Well, hang on. Let me see if God has changed his mind.' Can you imagine that? God changing his mind about cursing his chosen, blessed people? Well, God basically said, 'I told you to stay home, but if you want to go, go! See what happens... but don't you dare curse my chosen people.'"

Jessica said, "Oh, this sounds like a bad move. Did Balaam go with the royal ambassadors?"

Matt nodded. "Yep. His greed got the better of him. Let's read the next part straight from the Bible: *'So the next morning Balaam got up, saddled his donkey, and started off with the Moabite officials. But God was angry that Balaam was going, so he sent the angel of the Lord to*

---

[47] Numbers 22:3 (New Living Translation)

stand in the road to block his way. As Balaam and two servants were riding along, Balaam's donkey saw the angel of the Lord standing in the road with a drawn sword in his hand. The donkey bolted off the road into a field, but Balaam beat it and turned it back onto the road. Then the angel of the Lord stood at a place where the road narrowed between two vineyard walls. When the donkey saw the angel of the Lord, it tried to squeeze by and crushed Balaam's foot against the wall. So, Balaam beat the donkey again. Then the angel of the Lord moved farther down the road and stood in a place too narrow for the donkey to get by at all. This time when the donkey saw the angel, it lay down under Balaam. In a fit of rage Balaam beat the animal again with his staff.[48] Remember this morning when I was telling you that there is cool, even funny stuff in the Bible? You just have to know where to look. Well, here's another one of those funny stories.*

"Let's continue reading in verse twenty-eight, *'Then the Lord gave the donkey the ability to speak. "What have I done to you that deserves your beating me three times?" it asked Balaam. "You have made me look like a fool!" Balaam shouted. "If I had a sword with me, I would kill you!"*[49]

"So, let's stop right there for a minute," Matt said. "Do you understand what just happened in the story? The donkey started **talking** to Balaam. **Talking!** And Balaam in his fit of rage, in his anger, wasn't shocked or freaked out by the fact the donkey was **talking** to him. Balaam *answered* the donkey! Then they started having a conversation!! Here, look!"

Jessica was laughing as Matt went back to reading the story straight from the Bible, "Here comes the donkey's reply: *"But I am the same donkey you have ridden all your life," the donkey answered. "Have I ever done anything like this before?" "No," Balaam admitted. Then **the Lord opened Balaam's eyes,** and he saw the angel of the Lord standing in the*

---

[48] Numbers 22:21-27 (New Living Translation)
[49] Numbers 22:28-29 (New Living Translation)

roadway with a drawn sword in his hand. Balaam bowed his head and fell face down on the ground before him.[50]

"So, God opened Balaam's eyes and he was able to see into the spirit realm. The talking donkey, while maybe was the star of the story, the important thing to recognize and the thing Rabbi Kaduri was showing me was that for a brief moment, God recovered Balaam's spiritual sight and for a brief moment he could see into the spirit realm. That's what was lost, one thing anyway, that was lost when Adam and Eve ate the fruit."

"Oh, wow. Oh my gosh." Jessica said. "That's incredible. And he gave you three different examples?"

"Yes! That's one thing I really like about Rabbi Kaduri. If you ask him a Bible question, I mean, an Old Testament question, he will give an answer with multiple explanations and examples. He just knows *so much* and can explain it *so well*. It's like he has the whole book memorized. Have you ever met someone like that?"

Jessica answered, "Not so much with the Old Testament, maybe some preachers I've known, but in the professional world, I've known people that could spout off scientific numbers or research or... like Dr. Kenyon, my old professor that I had breakfast with this morning, he can recite history, dates, times, peoples, groups, etc. And he *loves* it. It just *flows* out of him."

"Oh yeah. How was breakfast with Dr. K?" Matt asked.

"Matt, you would have *loved* it! In fact, I hope this is ok, but I set up for the both of us to go to breakfast with him tomorrow and then he is going to take us to his archaeological site."

"Ummm. Ok. Yeah, I can make that work. Tomorrow? Why the rush?" Matt asked.

"Well, Dr. Kenyon has asked me to be a part of his documentation and verification team. Basically, he wants an outside, credible source

---

[50] Numbers 22:30-31 (New Living Translation)

to maintain and document the integrity of this new site. He told me all about it and I'm so excited. You're going to love it!!"

"Why do you think I'll love it?" Going to look at dirt and rocks with some old professor didn't seem like the most interesting thing to Matt, even if Jessica thought it would be.

"You know you told me about King Nebbie this morning? Dr. Kenyon is excavating a site where he has found all sorts of artifacts from when Nebuchadnezzar destroyed Jerusalem. He has found bullas and arrowheads and, I mean, King Nebbie was *really* here! Dr. Kenyon said he would let you hold some of the artifacts, these things are 2600 years old! But that's not even the coolest part of his site!" Jessica's excitement level was rising to match Matt's; he had that effect on people.

Matt's eyes lit up. It was one thing to be in the city and to learn about the history, which Matt *loved*, but it was another thing to actually *see* and *feel* and *touch* the history. Matt loved museums but this was an even better opportunity! This was more than dirt and rocks. He was actually going to see some of the things as they were being pulled out of the ground, not behind glass in a museum.

"Count me in!" Matt said. "What could be even cooler than the Nebuchadnezzar stuff?"

Jessica gave Matt a two-word answer, "Suleiman's caves," and then enjoyed the puzzled look on Matt's face as he tried to figure out why that was more interesting than King Nebuchadnezzar's artifacts.

"Do... what?" was all that Matt was able to ask, with a dumbfounded look on his face.

"Yeah. Are you familiar with Suleiman the Magnificent?"

"I'll admit, I'm not as familiar with Suleiman the Magnificent as I am with King Nebuchadnezzar."

"You mean to tell me in all of those tours you've taken of the Old City, you haven't learned anything about Suleiman the Magnificent?" Jessica asked.

"Wait, didn't Suleiman build one of the gates to the Old City?"

"That's right!" Jessica exclaimed. "He built the Damascus Gate in the 1500's and much of the existing wall structure we see today. Dr. Kenyon gave me a history lesson on him this morning."

"So, this Suleiman guy is from five hundred years ago and King Nebbie is from 2600 years ago. Remind me why we're talking about Suleiman and why I should be more interested in his artifacts than King Nebbie's?" Matt asked.

"His caves, babe! His caves!" Jessica answered, brimming with excitement. "See, Suleiman built the Damascus gate and refortified the Old City's walls. They weren't using poured concrete and rebar in wall construction five hundred years ago, right? They were using cut stones. They got those stones from limestone quarries. Those quarries are underground! Those quarries form a network of caves and tunnels located partly under the Muslim Quarter and partly in the adjacent area just outside of the city walls. Suleiman used some preexisting quarries to get these stones, right? So, he had these teams that were tasked to locate the old quarries and once they did, they were instructed to find the best stones to use to build the walls. To find the best stones, they had to find the best quarries, and the best quarries in Israel are underground. They're caves. So, Suleiman had teams of cave hunters. You following me so far?

"Yes, but I don't know where you're going with all of this," Matt replied.

"Ok. Here's what we know from history: in 1540, Suleiman abruptly and without explanation, halts all exploration in the caves, stops hunting for caves and *seals up* all of the existing caves around the city.[51] Boom. One day things are normal and the next day, everything is closed, sealed off. Stopped. Complete radio silence. Why did he do that?"

"Are you asking me? I don't know. You tell me! Why?" Matt asked.

---

[51] Thomas L. Friedman, "Quarrying History In Jerusalem," The New York Times, December 1, 1985. https://www.nytimes.com/1985/12/01/travel/quarrying-history-in-jerusalem.html

"Well, that's the thing. That's the mystery. That's one of the things Dr. Kenyon wanted to talk with me about. He found a cave that had been sealed by Suleiman."

"Ok. But you just told me that *all* the caves were sealed by Suleiman. What's unusual about this one?"

"This one was never *used* by Suleiman, never quarried by Suleiman, actually, it was never quarried by *anyone*, it was never even *touched* by Suleiman. But Dr. Kenyon thinks this one, this cave, this network of tunnels is the reason that Suleiman sealed all the caves. There is something special about this one that freaked Suleiman out enough to seal *everything.*"

"Why does Dr. Kenyon think *this* cave is the reason?" Matt asked.

"Because not only was this cave's entrance sealed off like all the rest of the caves, this cave entrance was also *hidden.* None of the rest of them were. Not only that, the cave and tunnels were *untouched, pristine.* Why? And, of all the caves in the area, all of them are stone quarries. This one isn't. It's just a series of tunnels. Why do that?"

"How does he know it was never quarried if he just uncovered the cave entrance?"

"Because the tunnels aren't wide enough to get quarried stones out of the mouth of the cave *and* unlike the rest of the 'quarry caves' in the area, this one is more like a traditional mine, an earthen cave with wooden, cross-braced supports holding up the walls and ceiling of the tunnels," Jessica answered.

"Where exactly is this cave or where is his dig site or whatever?" Matt asked.

"Somewhere just outside of the Muslim Quarter, probably somewhere close by where you were today. He said it was just a few minutes from the Damascus Gate."

"Hmmm. Archaeology *and* a mystery? I'm officially interested. When do I start?"

CHAPTER 7

The three-fingered man looked down at his watch as he walked in the front door of his modest home. It had been a long, hard day. And it was only Monday. It had been a long, hard Monday. The time was only 6:33 and he knew his day was really only half over. He loved his children, but he was tired, and he knew he needed to spend time with them. He walked into the main living room of the house where his children were inside playing a game together. When they saw him, the game stopped. He became the game. Hugging, climbing, swinging. He was a human jungle-gym. Right until he heard the unfamiliar, yet piercing, unique sound of a cheap cell phone ringing in his jacket pocket. He knew this was a call he could not miss. The three-fingered man had long thought that he was under surveillance. The calls came at the most 'opportune' or depending on perspective, 'inopportune' time. Two days ago, while with Yusef in the Old City, the call had come almost as soon as he received the phone. Now, almost the moment he walked in his house the phone had rung. The three-fingered man was sure someone was watching him. He hated the thought.

"Children! Children! A moment! I need to answer the phone! Stop, stop!"

When the children didn't immediately stop playing, the three-fingered man's tone became much more urgent, "I said *stop!*" The children, scared of what *that* tone meant, immediately shied away from their angry father. "I am not mad. I have to answer..." the three-fingered man abandoned trying to explain to the small children and pressed the green button on the cheap cell phone just as his wife, Laila, was entering the room to console the children. Looking at his wife, he mouthed an apology.

The three-fingered man didn't even have a chance to say anything into the phone's receiver before the distorted voice on the other side of the line said, "Alhimaya. Perhaps we were not clear. The leader has been killed, but the hidden place is still exposed. It was meant to look accidental. It is only a matter of time before excavation resumes. Keep this phone with you at all times as it is now the only way we communicate. We will be in touch, Alhimaya." And then the line went dead. The three-fingered man knew the charge had been too large once he saw the carnage, but on such short notice, with limited scouting and placement investigation, and with the limited supplies he was able to gather, it was the best he could do. Next time would be different. The three-fingered man's heart sank at the thought of it all. He did not enjoy this life. He felt like he was on a leash, destined to be at the beck and call of some unknown puppet master for the rest of his life… and he was about to commit his beautiful son, Yusef, to a lifetime of the same slavery.

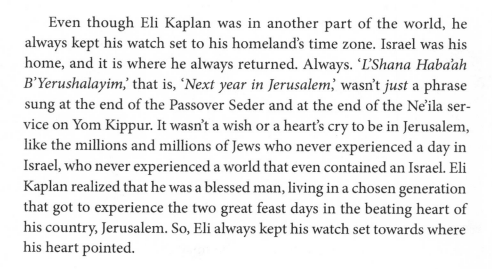

Even though Eli Kaplan was in another part of the world, he always kept his watch set to his homeland's time zone. Israel was his home, and it is where he always returned. Always. *'L'Shana Haba'ah B'Yerushalayim,'* that is, *'Next year in Jerusalem,'* wasn't *just* a phrase sung at the end of the Passover Seder and at the end of the Ne'ila service on Yom Kippur. It wasn't a wish or a heart's cry to be in Jerusalem, like the millions and millions of Jews who never experienced a day in Israel, who never experienced a world that even contained an Israel. Eli Kaplan realized that he was a blessed man, living in a chosen generation that got to experience the two great feast days in the beating heart of his country, Jerusalem. So, Eli always kept his watch set towards where his heart pointed.

"6:33 pm. I imagine she will be having dinner about now. Should I make contact and interrupt her evening or wait and spare her the news until tomorrow morning?" Eli asked himself. "Matthew will be with her. He will console her. Better to do it now than cost her a day at work tomorrow."

Dr. Eli Kaplan owned the research company, Laboratory Nedaviah where Jessica Davenport had worked for the last several years.[52] He had recruited her while she was in college because of her specialized degree. Little did he know what kind of treasure he had found when he began grooming her for her role at the company. Shortly after they had met, Jessica's father died and Eli, familiar with gut-wrenching, unexpected loss after the death of his wife and daughter years prior, was able to comfort and help Jessica make her way through the painful ordeal. And Jessica was helping Eli, too. It became obvious that the elderly scientist was still, to this day, dealing with the heartache associated with the death of his daughter and wife. He had become a father figure to her, and they shared a connection that most bosses don't have with their subordinates. When Eli retired, or passed from this life to the next, whichever came first, Jessica was the first in line to take over the company, not only because she was very, very good at her job, and not only because she was the closest thing Eli had to family, but also because she knew Eli's secret; that he was as much a Mossad agent as he was a scientist and his company was as much a front for Mossad and their research as it was a genuine research company. Jessica was smart, dedicated, loyal and like a daughter.

She deserved to know.

Eli picked up his phone, opened the text messaging app and found the running thread he had going with Jessica. He typed out his message, reviewed it, erased it and typed it again. After a few minutes of typing, erasing, typing and erasing, he decided he had worded the message in a

---

[52] Nedaviah – Hebrew name meaning "Generosity"

way that would convey the news and his sympathy. Just before he hit the send button, he had the idea of including Matthew on the text as well.

Matt and Eli Kaplan had met through their mutual acquaintance, Jessica, but Matt and Eli's connection went much, much deeper than that. A year earlier, when Matt finally realized what the terrorists were planning, he risked everything, even his life to save Jessica and her work. In doing so, it had saved Kaplan's company and the nation of Israel. Eli was able to see the quality of man that Matt was. Eli respected Matt from that moment forward, but as he got to know Matt, to see him and understand Matt's character, Eli treasured him and trusted him. If Jessica was like his daughter, Matthew was the man he would have chosen to marry her.

Eli scrolled in his phone to the *M*'s, found Matthew Davenport in his list of contacts and added him to the text message. Eli hated that he couldn't call, but where he was and what he was doing at the moment wouldn't allow it. A text would have to do... and he knew Jessica and Matthew would understand. He reviewed the message one last time and hit the *Send* button on his phone.

Maybe he would be able to find a way back to Israel earlier than he had planned.

CHAPTER 8

J essica and Matt had made a fantastic mess while trying out the new 'easy' recipe that Matt's mother had emailed them. Matt had a favorite dish growing up, a specialty that his mom had 'discovered' purely by accident. The meal was actually a deconstructed 'Chicken Pot Pie' without crust and served over white rice. His family had named the meal 'Chicken and Rice' to simply differentiate the meal from other dinners with similar ingredients and because 'Deconstructed Chicken Pot Pie served over rice' was a mouthful for a name.

The problem that Jessica and Matt ran into while trying to prepare the meal was the lack of American ingredients. When Matt's mother put '3 cans *Veg-All*' as one of the steps, she had no idea that Veg-all wasn't widely available in Israel. They couldn't just run to the grocery store to pick it up. To get the necessary vegetables into their dish didn't mean just opening a few cans, it meant cutting, chopping, shredding and peeling various fresh greens and neither Jessica nor Matt could do it efficiently or neatly. After what seemed like a long time of chopping carrots, and looking at the mess, looking at his wife who he could tell was tired, looking at the rest of the recipe which also included the cook time, Matt came up with a wonderful idea. He looked down at his watch and thought, *yeah, let's do it.*

"Hey Gorgeous," Matt said to his wife, "Let's put all these freshly cut veggies in the fridge. It's almost 7 pm and this still has to cook and everything. Let's go out and get dinner tonight and now that everything is prepared, when we come home from work tomorrow, we can actually cook the meal tomorrow night. How's that sound? Go get on some comfy clothes and I will clean all of this up and put it away."

Jessica let out an immense sigh which Matt at first thought was a sigh of frustration. Actually, it was a sigh of relief. "Yes! That sounds perfect. I'll be ready in a minute." Jessica left everything sitting right where it was, including her phone that she had been using to read the recipe. Free from the thought of cooking dinner, she made her way from the tiny kitchen and into the bedroom. A moment after she left, the phone, sitting on the counter beside the refrigerator, chimed. Jessica had a new text message.

Almost instantly, Matt's phone, still in his pocket, vibrated. He had a text message. Matt's hands were full of carrots, so he dropped them in a zip-top bag and placed them in the refrigerator. He walked to the sink, washed his hands and dried them on a towel Jessica had been using as a placemat for the potatoes. When his hands were dry, Matt pulled the phone out of his pocket, opened his text app and read the message. He was glad that Jessica had left her phone in the kitchen.

About that time, Jessica walked out of the bedroom wearing jeans and a sweatshirt from her Alma Mater, Penn State, and started towards the kitchen. Matt intercepted her and kept her away from her phone. He said "Hey. Sit down with me for a second," and guided her towards the couch. She sat on the couch and Matt again sat in the chair at a ninety-degree angle to Jessica.

Before Matt could say anything, Jessica's phone chimed again and in the quiet of the apartment, this time she heard it. She started to get up and Matt put his hand on her knee. In a soft, sympathetic voice, he said "Hang on a second, sweetheart. There's something I need to tell you." Jessica recognized there was something going on, by the tone Matt was using. She rocked back into a sitting position and when she did, she saw the television, still on, still muted and she immediately knew why Matt had asked her to sit down.

"Oh no!" Jessica exclaimed as she looked at the television. There, being broadcast, was the evening news. The lead story of the night was about an explosion at an archaeological dig site. "Where is the remote? ***Where is the remote?!?***" Jessica shouted as she dug through the cushions looking for the television remote so she could turn up the volume. "How did you know? Or were you about to tell me something else?"

Matt just shook his head and watched the television.

"More on that story in just a moment, and also new emerging details of kidnapped Indian nuclear scientist, Laksh Aditya, which point to Israel as his last known destination, but first a look at tomorrow's weather," the nightly news personality was saying as Jessica found the remote and turned the volume up. [53] [54] [55] It was just the teaser introduction to the broadcast and the rest of the story would be coming up in a few moments.

Jessica turned to Matt and said, "How did you know?"

"I got a text message from Eli, we both did. That was the message you heard *ding* on your phone." Matt pulled out his phone, unlocked it, found the text, and handed it to Jessica as a weather forecast was being explained on the television by a young woman in a pink and blue dress. The text read:

Kids, I have some horrible news. Jessica's friend, Dr. Cooper Kenyon, Z"L, was killed today in an explosion at his dig site. We are not certain of the details, but I know about this and that should tell you something. Jessica I am sorry I am not there to give you a hug, but I am glad you were able to see him today. Matthew, take care of your sweet wife. She is stronger than she knows but will need your gentle, loving hands around her.

How Dr. Eli Kaplan, a million miles away, in a different country, in a different time zone, in a different world altogether, knew that Jessica had spent time, today, with Dr. Kenyon was anyone's guess, but it didn't surprise either Matt or Jessica. That was just par for the course with

---

[53] Pitamber Kaushik "India's Vanishing Nuclear Scientists," Asia Times, July 22, 2019, https://asiatimes.com/2019/07/indias-vanishing-nuclear-scientists/

[54] Laksh – Indian name meaning "Aim, Target, Goal"

[55] Aditya – Indian name meaning "The Sun"

him. Matt was familiar with Z"L, the abbreviation Eli had put in his text. Z"L is a Hebrew abbreviation placed after someone's name to indicate that they have passed away and are fondly remembered. It stands for *zichrono livracha.*[56] This translates as, '*May his memory be a blessing.*' But it was the other part of the text, the thing that Eli *didn't* say that caught Matt's attention. Dr. Eli Kaplan, secret spy with the Israeli Mossad, in a different world altogether, knew about Dr. Kenyon's death. That fact alone was enough to put Matt on high alert. His paranoia level immediately vaulted from mild jitters to just short of 'terrorists are out to get us!'

Jessica looked at Matt with tears in her eyes. Matt, moved with compassion for his wife, relocated from the chair to the couch and sitting with her, held Jessica in his arms. She buried her head in his chest as the tears flowed. "Oh, sweet wife. I'm so sorry, so, so sorry," he said. "It never makes it any better to hear it, but we know that he is in Heaven. We know he is with his Lord and Savior. We know that he is dancing and singing and having a wonderful time. It's only us here, still on Earth that are sad. He is at peace."

"You're right," Jessica said. "It doesn't make it any better to hear it." But Jessica knew he was right. She knew Dr. Kenyon was a Christian and at his death he passed over and was enjoying Heaven. Then her mind turned to Sheila, Dr. Kenyon's wife of forty-three years. What would she do now?

The television news anchor was back from commercial and starting up with the lead story of the night. On a large, flatscreen television beside the standing news anchor, was a black and white photograph of Dr. Kenyon with his date of birth and today's date. It turns out the news story was not about the archaeologist's death, but the details of the pending investigation and problems it would soon face.

"Dr. Cooper Kenyon, acclaimed archaeologist from the United States of America and professor of Archaeology at Pennsylvania State

---

[56] Benor, Sarah Bunin. 2012-present. "Zichrono Livracha, entry in Jewish English Lexicon." Los Angeles: Jewish Language Project. https://jel.jewish-languages.org/words/636

SIXTY SECONDS OF SILENCE

University, was killed this morning when an explosion went off at his archaeological dig site on the north side of the Old City of Jerusalem, just a few blocks from the Damascus Gate. No one else was injured during the blast which occurred at approximately 8:25 am. Israeli police arrived on the scene, hours later, after workers at the site found part of their dig unrecognizable and feared the place had caved in. The workers found it unusual that Dr. Kenyon, an early riser and always punctual, was not at the worksite. He was known to arrive before the rest of the team to inspect the site and set the day's schedule, but when he did not show, the workers called and spoke with his wife who thought he was at work. At that point they feared he had been killed in a rockslide. Israeli police report that several neighboring communities heard a blast that shook the foundation of homes and businesses at approximately 8:25 in the morning. Authorities are unclear if it was some sort of professional sabotage gone awry, with a miscalculation of the strength of an explosive charge, or perhaps the archaeologist was planning to clear debris, and it was an accidental detonation as the experienced scientist placed the charge or if there were potentially other forces at work."

Other forces at work, Matt knew, was code for suspected terrorist activity, and in his paranoid state, could be the only explanation for why Eli knew about the archaeologist's death.

The news anchor continued, "The problem now facing the investigation is who actually has jurisdiction over the archaeological dig site. Being so close to the Temple Mount, it is uncertain who should perform the investigation — the Israeli Police, the Israeli Defense Force, that is, the Israeli Army, the Muslim Waqf who oversees and manages the current Islamic edifices on and around the Temple Mount in the Old City of Jerusalem, including the Al-Aqsa Mosque and the Dome of the Rock, the Palestinian Authority because the neighborhood in which the explosion took place is predominately Palestinian or if the Americans will get involved because of the unnatural death of one of their citizens. It could take weeks to sort out jurisdiction and months to determine…"

65

"Turn it off, please, Matt," Jessica said. "I've heard enough. At least now I know why I had the negative nudge about going out to his site. If only I had paid more attention to it, I might have saved his life…"

"No, you can't think that way," Matt interrupted Jessica's thought. "I know you want to take the blame, but Dr. Kenyon serves the same loving, caring God that we do. Dr. Kenyon had the same opportunity to hear God's voice, just like you did. Either he didn't recognize it, or he didn't pay attention to it. You're not responsible for him. Don't let the enemy try to give you the care of it. That's not your cross to bear." Matt said as he hugged his wife.

Matt and Jessica sat in silence for several long minutes. Then it seemed to dawn on Matt, and he said, "I was right there this morning, I was two blocks from the dig site. I heard the blast. I felt it. It scared the tour group, bad, and I was the one that calmed them down. I was trying to help Rabbi Kaduri. I told them it was probably some archaeologist using explosives to clear debris. That happens, right? I guess, since the site was empty, that explains why there weren't any police, any sirens, any emergency personnel. I'm so sorry… I wish that I had gone and checked it, investigated, instead of just talking."

"You wouldn't have been able to do anything. It's sweet of you to think of others the way you do, but even if you had gone to investigate you wouldn't even think anything was out of the ordinary. There was no way to know and nothing you could have done."

Matt and Jessica were quiet for a few minutes, holding each other as Jess continued to cry in her husband's chest. Finally, Jessica got up, went to the kitchen and picked up her phone, unlocked it and sent a text to Eli Kaplan. She made her way back to the couch and sat close to her husband. A few short moments later, her phone dinged as Kaplan replied.

"What's that?" Matt asked.

"I asked Eli to find… Dr. Kenyon was married for forty-three years. I asked for his wife Sheila's telephone number. It didn't take him very long to find it and reply. I think, no, I feel impressed that I *need* to call her… I… I… don't know what to say…"

Jessica stood up, walked toward the bedroom looking for a small bit of privacy, and started dialing the number that Eli had sent her. Matt, understanding what his wife was about to do, started putting his shoes back on and said, "I'll go grab us some food. I'll be back in a few minutes." Jessica nodded and pressed the call button on the phone. Matt stepped out of the apartment and as he closed the door behind him, he said "Lord, please help my wife. The Bible says that you are 'always ready to help in times of trouble.'[57] Well, these are troubling times for Dr. Kenyon's wife. So please help my wife give Sheila the comfort of Your 'peace that passes all understanding and keep her heart and her mind stayed on you.'[58] The Bible says that 'the Lord is our helper,' so I'm asking for your help.[59] We know that you have sent the Comforter and I am asking for your supernatural comfort for both of these ladies.[60] I thank you for it, Lord, in Jesus' Name.[61] Amen."

---

[57] Psalm 46:1 (New Living Translation)

[58] Reference Philippians 4:7

[59] Reference Hebrews 3:6

[60] Reference John 16:7

[61] Reference John 15:16

CHAPTER 9

"Hello?"

"May I speak to Mrs. Kenyon, please?"

There were a few sniffs and a clearing of a throat before the woman's voice, finally able to compose itself, was able to reply, "This is she. Who's speaking, please?"

"Mrs. Kenyon, we have never met, but I knew your husband and through all the stories he told me about your lives together, I feel like I know you. After I saw the news, I felt compelled to call you. I don't mean to upset you in any way, but I did want to reach out to you and let you know how much your husband meant to me and let you know if there's anything I can do for you, I will." Jessica could feel herself getting emotional and did her best not to cry. She was only partially successful. "I was one of your husband's students and then teaching assistants at Penn State, but he was more than just one of my professors. He was my friend. I *know* he's in Heaven right now, but I am so sad he's gone." The tears were flowing now, and Jessica could hear Sheila crying on the other end of the line. "I'm sorry, Mrs. Kenyon. I didn't mean to make you cry."

Through tears, Sheila said "You... still haven't... told me your... name."

"I'm so sorry," Jessica answered. "My name is Jessica Davenport and..."

With a seemingly renewed strength, Sheila interrupted Jessica and said "Oh, thank the Lord. Sweet girl. Coopy has told me all about you over the years — he even told me about your breakfast this morning while he was driving to work. How ever did you find me?"

Jessica was slightly taken aback with Sheila's recognition of her name and was definitely thrown for a loop with *Coopy*, a name she had never heard anyone call her old professor. She tried to phrase her response delicately so as to not give away Eli's involvement. "I have a friend that has an 'in' with the phone companies. He was able to get me your phone number so I could get in touch with you."

"Please, thank your friend for me. I'm so thankful he connected us. There are some things I need to ask you and some things that I need you to do."

Now Jessica was really shocked. What could Sheila Kenyon, a woman that Jessica had never met, possibly need her to do? Jess' mind furiously began trying to figure it out. Funeral arrangements? Letting Professor Kenyon's peers know what had happened? What could Sheila need Jessica to do?

She said, "Yes, ma'am, I will thank him, for the both of us. What can I help you with? I'll do anything I can."

"Jessica, let me tell you about my last conversation with my husband. You know that man was like no other man alive. Most men aren't like this but once you got Coopy talking, he would talk and talk and talk. And in that regard, this morning was no different. What was different was the *way* he was talking. He was excited as he told me all about your breakfast and the things you talked about, but then something seemed to change. It was almost like he knew something was going to happen. It was almost like he knew God was warning him, but he was trying to shake it off, saying things like 'I'm just being paranoid....' I guess we know now it wasn't just paranoia... God really was trying to warn him." Sheila paused and took a moment to compose herself. "Anyway, once he started talking, you know, it's hard to get a word in. And then he started down this path of talking, he said 'if anything should ever happen to me, Jessica is the one to take over the site. She's the one that will know what to do and how to finish it up. Make her understand. Her field is a little different than straight archaeology, and she will probably give you some pushback, but she's the one to continue my work. She *has* to be the one. I don't know why, but she *has* to be the one.' When he finally stopped to take a breath, I tried to change his thinking, telling him it would be years before it came to that." Sheila stopped talking and Jessica could hear her crying over the phone. "I'm so thankful he called me this morning. I'm so thankful the two of you had breakfast and he was in a good mood while we talked. Thank you for that, sweet girl. I'm so thankful that he was able to give me some instructions about what to do. But you know what I am most thankful for?" Sheila said through the tears, "I'm so thankful that I got to tell my husband one last time that I love him."

The two women sat in silence together, in different parts of the city, and wept for the loss of Cooper Kenyon, a man they both loved and respected, in very different ways.

ARCHAEOLOGY STAGE TWO: EVALUATION

Determine historical and cultural significance of
archaeological materials located during Phase One survey.⁶²

"The tunnels below the Old City are vast and unexplored and potentially filled with a wealth of knowledge and information, but until the Jews, the Muslims, the Christians, the Israelis, the Palestinians, the Jordanians, the Israeli Antiquities Authority, the IDF, all of the extremists on every side, and all the rest that are jockeying for power and territory can come to an agreement, the tunnels will remain unexplored and the knowledge will be lost for yet another generation." — Eli Kaplan

---

⁶² "Phases of Archaeology," Job Monkey, 2022, https://www.jobmonkey.com/archaeology/phases/

CHAPTER 10

It had been a few weeks since Dr. Kenyon's funeral and during that time, Jessica and Sheila had bonded over their mutual love, admiration, and loss of Dr. Kenyon. It was during those moments of being with Sheila and learning about some of the details of Dr. Kenyon and his work, that Jessica began to doubt her place as site leader and was still unsure of what Dr. Kenyon had expected of her and what she could bring to the excavation. But she had agreed to take over the dig site, at least temporarily, until she could figure out why he wanted her for the position. Because of some prior work engagements, today, Monday, would be her first day on the job and her first opportunity to see the site, meet the workers, read the journals that Dr. Kenyon kept, and begin trying to understand, firsthand, why he wanted her to be the one to take over the dig. Jessica had been able to work out a deal with her boss, Eli Kaplan, for her to be loaned to the archaeological team on a temporary basis. They would start with a six-month timeframe and then reevaluate where things stood and what she wanted to do.

For her first day on the job, Jessica wanted to show the excavation team that she was a serious worker, that she would be a fair leader, just like Dr. Kenyon, but also that discipline would be maintained on her dig site. She knew that some of the crew might have a hard time respecting her authority because she was a woman and certain cultures did not believe women should do anything but stay home and raise the children, cook, clean, and wait on their husbands. So, Jessica was up early on that Monday morning, along with Matt who had decided to join his wife on her first day at the job. Jessica dressed for business. She wore her jeans and work boots, a sturdy, long-sleeved shirt that buttoned down the front, a light jacket, a work hat with a floppy brim and sunglasses. It was still cool in the spring morning, but the Sun would be beating on her and her team by mid-day and she wanted to make sure she didn't get sunburned on her first day. Matt, on the other hand, was dressed for total comfort, jeans, tennis shoes, a short-sleeved t-shirt with a picture of Bigfoot and the decorative script that read "Hide and Seek World Champion," a crimson-colored baseball cap representing his favorite college football team, the *Alabama Crimson Tide*, his leather jacket and his over-the-shoulder sling bag. When Jessica saw him, she just laughed and said, "You'll fit right in at the site with the exception of the Alabama hat. You realize no one will know what that is."

"It doesn't matter," Matt said with a chuckle. "I'll know what it is. I'll know I'm representing the greatest football team to ever play the game! And maybe somebody, somewhere will recognize the hat! I mean, even Steely Dan said, '*They got a name for the winners in the world…*'"[63] Matt was always amazed at how many people actually recognized the script 'A' logo of the school and how many times he would hear "Roll Tide!" while out in the city of a foreign country. *Some teams travel better than others,* he thought to himself.

Jessica and Matt arrived at the dig site early, very early. Jessica wanted to prove a point. Jessica wanted her team to know that as long as she was in charge, she would be the first one working in the morning and the last to finish in the evening.

As Jessica and Matt stepped away from their car and made their way up the slight incline to the entrance of the archaeological site, they did a quick survey of the area. At the top of the hill where they had entered the site was a large tent, with several tables and what looked like power cords snaking away to an unknown source. From where they were standing, they could see that the site sloped away from them,

---

[63] Steely Dan. Lyrics to "Deacon Blues." *Aja.* ABC Records, 1977.

down a hill into a small valley and then up another hill that was facing them. In between where they were standing, and the top of the next hill, were several smaller, individual research areas. The large tent where they were standing looked like the headquarters of the dig site.

Jessica could see the look on Matt's face. He was ready to explore. "Let's get the stuff out of the car and set up in here before the team starts to arrive," Jessica said before he could wander off.

But the Davenports were both in for a surprise as they were not the first people at the excavation site. As they were unloading their car, hauling it to the site and setting up their gear, notebooks, computer, cooler with water and their lunches, in what appeared to be the command center tent, the couple happened to notice a man, in the shadows of the early morning light, wearing a bright yellow hard hat, making his way out of the opening to a tunnel at the bottom of the opposite hill that was sloping away from their tent. As Jessica and Matt had not had a chance to really survey the site yet, neither had noticed the entrance to the tunnel until then, so it was odd to see a lone man walking around the place. Before Jessica had a chance to call out to him, the man noticed the couple, smiled, waved, and started walking toward them.

When the man finally made his way up the hill and to the tent where Matt and Jessica were setting up, he looked to Matt and asked, "Dr. Davenport?" Matt chuckled and without saying anything, awkwardly pointed to his wife who was standing on the other side of the tent, across a worktable from where Matt and the visitor were standing.

"Oh. I'm so sorry, Dr. Davenport. I speak English good enough, but I don't read it too good. When I read the report stating that Dr. Jess Davenport was going to be in charge now, I immediately thought it said Jesse, a man's name. I am so sorry, Boss. Please excuse my ignorance. This is not the way I wanted to start our first day together. I came early to meet you, to start on the best foots."

Jessica was torn. She wanted to laugh and tell the man that it was a simple mistake, to think nothing more of it, but she also knew she needed to set a precedent, to let this man, whoever he was, know that *she* was in charge and that she expected excellence. In the end, she said "It's fine," in a very serious tone. Then she asked, "Who are you and what is your role here?"

To his credit the man understood Jessica, smiled politely and answered in accented English, "My name is Faysal Mohy al-Din abu Yusef. [64,65] I know that is a mouthful, so please, just call me Faysal. I am your foreman and here to help in any way that I can. Again, I apologize for my earlier mistake."

Jessica returned the man's smile and was about to say something when Matt blurted, "Hey Faysal! I'm Matt, Matt Davenport. No, not Matt-Matt. Just Matt. Uhhh…I've got to quit doing that. I'm Dr. Davenport's tongue-tied husband," and laughing stuck out his right hand to shake hands with the foreman. The foreman, understanding Matt and his own poorly worded predicament, laughed and shook Matt's hand.

Something seemed odd to Matt, but the moment quickly passed as Faysal said in reply, "Roll Tide. Is that how you say it?"

Matt laughed a hearty laugh. "Do you hear *that* Dr. Davenport? He said Roll. Tide. Faysal, you and I are going to get along really well! Yes, that is *exactly* how you say it. Roll Tide Roll." Jessica did not respond in any way, only turned back to her work.

Faysal sensed even more tension in the tent now and remarked, "I can see you are a serious woman and I respect the job you are being asked to do. If you do not want to be bother, I will go start my duties. When you are ready, I can teach you about our site and what we has been doing and what is going on."

Jessica let up with the tough exterior. She had made her point. "Faysal, please, I would appreciate your filling me in on what has transpired here over the time since the explosion. I would also appreciate it

---

[64] Faysal – Arabic name meaning "Decisive, Judge"

[65] Mohy al-Din – Arabic name meaning "Reviver of Religion"

very much if you would stay here with me as the other workers show up. As they arrive, maybe we can have an informal get-to-know-you time where I can start trying to learn names and job functions. I would also like to have a meeting with everyone, as a group, when they get here before work begins for the day. I am guessing not everyone speaks English, and since my Hebrew is only barely understandable and my Arabic is even worse, I will need an interpreter. Can you do that for me?"

Faysal smiled broadly, nodded and proceeded to tell the Davenports what had happened at the site since the explosion a few weeks earlier. As he spoke, Matt began to notice not only the foreman's accent, but also the odd syntax he used putting sentences together, something that Matt was becoming familiar with in the land where English was a second language. Matt let the thought pass and listened as Faysal began speaking.

"We found Dr. Kenyon's body the night of the first day, as it turned out he was not too deep inside the tunnel at the time of the explosion. That is why he had timely funeral. He was a sweet man, thorough, diligent, a good worker and a good friend. He will be missed greatly. Did you know Dr. Kenyon?"

Jessica somberly responded, "Yes. Cooper was a friend that I have known for many years. His wife Sheila and I have become friends as well. You're right, he was a sweet man and I know we all will miss him."

When Jessica finished speaking, Faysal said, "In the time since Dr. Kenyon's death, work has continue, to an extent, on the site. By order of the authorities (who are still arguing about who should investigate the Professor's death), the workers have continue clearing the debris from the entrance of the cave so that it could be more explore and documented. We have not started that exploring yet. We want an archaeologist to be here, first. You.

"It is almost a miracle, the tunnel and cave system seem mostly intact, having avoided a total collapse during the explosion. Only the entranceway was demolish during the blast, the tunnel acting like the barrel of a cannon, sending the force of the explosion and debris towards and out of the opening. No one has yet checked to see if the cave system is safe structure to begin exploring. I go inside the cave a couple of times, like this morning, but I never want to go far enough inside that I need a flashlight. I do not want to be crushed in a cave-in. I just go in to make sure people are not sleeping in the cave, where it is warm. I also make sure our team stay out until it is safe. No one has been in the tunnel since the accident. The next step will be to get people here to check the safety of the cave. If you want my opinion, I think we should abandon this site. There is nothing more to find."

Jessica let that last statement go and pulling out her notebook, began a list of things to do. There were already a handful of things on the list but finding someone to check the structural integrity of the cave would be one of the first things she needed to work on. Excavation work inside the cave and tunnel couldn't begin in earnest until the safety of the site could be assured and because the cave was now the primary reason for the excavation, until the site was deemed 'safe' there wouldn't be much work that could be done there. Every day that had unproductive people at the site was wasted grant money and Jessica knew that archaeological sites needed to prove their worth, by showing meaningful progress to keep funding flowing. She also knew that meaningful progress meant finding significant artifacts and discoveries, things that would make a splash in the media and museums and keep the donors' dollars flowing. When she eventually turned over the site to someone else, Jessica felt she owed it to Dr. Kenyon to leave this site in an even better place than where it was when she inherited it. So, along with doing a job she didn't feel qualified to do, with people she couldn't always understand, who possibly wouldn't respect her right to be the site leader because she was new, an outsider and a woman, there was also the added pressure of making sure Dr. Kenyon's work would continue. She needed to get the site opened and producing results quickly and she also needed everyone on board, pulling their weight, moving in the right direction. Quickly. That would be her message in the meeting this morning.

Over the course of the next few minutes, people started showing up to the work site. Jessica had been correct when she said that Matt would fit right in. Everyone from Faysal to the college interns was in jeans, tennis shoes and some sort of t-shirt. The only visual difference between Matt and the regular workers was that Matt's clothes seemed relatively clean and unstained and Matt had practically the only clean-shaven male face at the site. From the look and sounds of them, the people were a hodgepodge of ethnic backgrounds, American, Palestinian, African, Jewish and even some people that must have been transplants from some Eastern Bloc countries.

As each new person arrived at the site, Faysal and Jessica greeted them. The first to arrive had been a studious looking young woman carrying a laptop computer, notebooks and wearing a backpack, too. Immediately, Matt thought she looked familiar, and his suspicions were confirmed as she entered the site and he heard what Jessica said. Faysal introduced the young, thin, college intern with an incredibly pale complexion to Jessica. "Dr. Davenport, this is Nava, a student at local university. [66] She was Dr. Kenyon's, how do I say, note taker? She will be of great benefit to you."

Jessica, visibly shaken, said "Oh my word. You look so much like a friend I used to have; a co-worker named Nuria Melamed. You could be sisters!"

Nava blushed. "I'm sorry to say it, but I'm an only child, but it's really nice to meet you...?"

"Oh. I'm sorry. I'm Dr. Davenport, but you can call me Jessica. I am the new leader of the site."

A large smile crossed Nava's face as it dawned on her that the new person she would be working closely with was a woman! "Cooper and I spent most of our time together along with Faysal when he was not actively working in the site. I have a pretty good idea of what is going on, what our next step was going to be before the accident, and I'll be happy to get you caught up." Nava was obviously not American, but her English was very, very good.

---

[66] Nava – Hebrew word meaning "Beautiful." The word appears in the Bible, in Song of Songs 2:14.

"That's wonderful," Jessica answered. "Thank you very much."

About that time other workers began arriving at the site. Nava realized that Jessica needed to meet them all and moved on towards the tent that Matt and Jessica had used as their headquarters. Faysal did his part, speaking to each one in either his accented English, his native Arabic or what Jessica figured was heavily accented Hebrew. The workers poured into the site and just before the day was set to begin there was a mad dash of people trying not to be late. Faysal stood there and noted each person as they arrived, keeping tabs on who was there and whether they were late or not. Jessica realized Monday mornings, just like bosses or the foreman of a job, are the same everywhere in the world.

Jessica looked around and noticed Matt trying to slip out to go exploring. "Stay close, babe. You'll have plenty of time to see everything after our meeting. Don't wander off too far," she semi-yelled to him as he was starting to walk towards the site. Matt nodded back in her direction with a huge smile on his face. Jessica decided to give all of the workers a few minutes to get their day started and then asked Faysal to round everyone up so she could properly introduce herself and have their initial meeting.

Faysal seemed to be a no-nonsense kind of guy when work needed to be done. He called the group together and had them all roughly assembled in a matter of moments. There was still a lot of chatter going on with the group as Jessica moved toward where Nava and Faysal were standing and asked, "Is this everybody and has anyone seen my husband?"

Before either of them could answer, Matt entered the tent with an enormous smile on his face and his hand held in front of him, palm side up. "Hey Gorgeous! Look what I found!" In his hand was something small, circular and was once recently covered in dirt. "I think it's a coin!" Jessica, Faysal and Nava rushed to him. Sure enough, in his hand was a small, dirty, silver coin that Matt was using his thumb and his saliva to clean. It looked like it was very, very old.

"Stop Matt!! Stop! **Stop! Stop!!**" Jessica shouted.

Matt froze, not daring to move a muscle. He didn't know what he had done wrong, but didn't want to make it any worse, especially with people around. "What's wrong?" he asked.

There were several small zip-top bags lying around the tent and Faysal picked up a few. He took the coin and placed it in one and handed the rest to Matt. "If you're going to be an archaeologist or even a worker at the site, you'll need these."

Jessica, still fuming, followed it up with, "We have to protect the integrity of the finds. You know this Matt. Where did you find it? Exactly where? Were you digging or was it lying in the open? Why did you pick it up? Why didn't you tell someone?"

Matt didn't know what to say. He thought he was helping. He didn't know he was hurting anything. "I'm so sorry. I just saw something shiny and picked it up. I can show you exactly where I was, because I only went to one place. I thought I was helping." Matt lowered his head, dejected.

Faysal thought the point had been made and said, "My friend. We find a lot of coins here. We average a coin finding about every fifteen minutes. This is not unusual. But your wife is correct. Any time you find something, you *must* document it and put it in a bag."

Nodding, Matt unzipped his cross-body sling bag and put the zip-top bags inside. "Sorry, guys. I didn't know. I'll do better next time, if there is a next time."

Faysal and Nava smiled, but Jessica was ready to get back to business. "Is this everybody?" She asked again, looking towards the group standing outside of the tent.

Faysal did a rough count, trying to match faces with his clipboard and looking around said, "Almost. There is at least one person missing that I notice. Wally." Looking over the site, Faysal and Jessica saw a man standing at the lower portion of the worksite, in front of the cave entrance, holding his phone in front of him, taking what looked to be selfies. It was one of the most unusual sites to behold. "That's Wally," Faysal said. "He is a total muscle-head. You know what I mean by that?

All muscle and no brains. But if you point him in the right direction, keep him on task, he is the best worker we have on the site. Strong as a bull. Allah put him on Earth to move heavy rocks." Wally was a mountain of a man. It looked like he had been born in a weightlifting family and they had started his training at birth. Even from where they were standing, Jessica could see that Wally's arms were as big around as her waist. Faysal continued, "Wally is very interesting man. He never talks about it, but what I have pieced together is that his name is actually Wallace, which, I think, was his mother's maiden name. She was from England or has an English background or something. Anyway, Wally's father was the strictest of Muslims and would not allow his wife to speak English or teach any to Wally. He has an English name but doesn't speak a word of it. I'm sure there is more to the story, but I have never been able to get him to speak of it."

"Weird," Matt said.

"Could you ask him to join us?" Jessica asked Faysal.

"Certainly," Faysal replied and started moving down the hill towards where Wally was still taking selfies.

"Care if I join you?" Matt asked. He was looking for an opportunity to get away from Jessica and was itching to see everything the place had to offer.

"Certainly!" Faysal again replied.

As the two men neared Wally, they noticed he was not taking pictures, but was shooting a video. When he noticed Faysal and Matt, Wally finished the video and turned to them with a smile on his face. He said something to Faysal in Arabic and Matt understood one of the words: *Instagram*. It seemed Wally was shooting an Instagram video. Matt was not big on social media. He understood Facebook enough and a little bit of Twitter, but he never downloaded the apps for anything else, like Instagram or TikTok.

To say Wally was huge, would be an understatement. If he had been a boxer, the *tale of the tape* would have read something like this: 6'3" tall, 247 pounds, long, thick arms. Every inch of him was muscle. His muscles had muscles. Those muscles had muscles. He looked like he was in his mid-thirties, but his jet-black hair looked like it was just starting to thin. He had a long, bushy beard that had one streak of gray down the right side. Even though Matt had never seen Wally before, there was something oddly familiar about him, so much so that Matt studied the man's face intently. Faysal and Wally were having a brief conversation in Arabic and then Matt noticed that both men turned toward him. Matt awkwardly smiled and waved to Wally. Wally laughed and grabbed Matt in a bear-hug, pinning his arms to his sides and picking him up off the ground. Matt felt like a child in the massive man's grip. He was powerless to escape. This must be what it feels like to be held in the grasp of a professional wrestler.

Faysal, laughing, said "I told him you saved me when I embarrassed myself with the new leader of the site. Wally said that since you protected me, he will protect you!" Wally sat Matt down and slapped him on the back, laughing. Faysal said, "I told you he was a muscle head!" Matt shot Wally a look, but then remembered he couldn't understand English. The last thing he wanted to do was get on the big man's bad side.

The three men were laughing, but for obviously different reasons. Wally because of his display of strength and Faysal and Matt because of the joke at Wally's expense. Then Faysal, looking down at his watch, said something to Wally in Arabic and his mood changed. Wally looked up towards the top of the hill where the group had gathered and immediately started making his way up the slope. Faysal walked with him, but Matt, sensing an opportunity to check out the dig site alone, stayed where he was. The other two men didn't immediately notice.

At the same time Matt and Faysal were heading down to talk with Wally, Nava saw that Jessica was finally alone and went to talk with her. Not knowing exactly where to start a conversation, Nava decided to ask about the woman that Jessica had mentioned. "Dr. Davenport, you said I reminded you of an old friend. I think you said her name is Nuria. Who is she?"

Jessica smiled a sad smile. She was happy to talk about her good friend, but sad that she had been killed during the terrorist incident a year earlier. Jessica replied, "Nuria was a very close friend of mine who worked with me for a few years after she graduated college. She was so smart and funny, pretty, talented, intuitive, well-spoken, and a good friend. She could keep a secret and she gave great advice. I know that it must seem weird, but you look *so much* like her it is astonishing." Jessica smiled again.

"Wow, I hope I can live up to that!" Nava said. "You keep talking about her in the past tense. Has she moved out of the country or something?"

Jessica's shoulders dropped, "Do you remember the terrorist attack on the building in Tel Aviv last year?" she asked.

"Oh, no! Was she killed in the explosion?"

"Not in the explosion. There were other elements to that terrorist attack that the news media didn't know about. She was killed because of some information that the terrorists thought she had. The media never put the two pieces together — they reported that she was killed in her home by an unknown assailant. To them, it is an unsolved murder."

Nava was unsure how to react. So, she just stood there mouth open, with an amazed look on her face. Did her new boss have some information that the media didn't have, that the authorities didn't know, or was she some conspiracy theory nut who was grasping at straws trying to connect two unconnected threads? Before she could really respond, Jessica noticed Faysal and the large man almost to the top of the hill, walking towards the tent.

Her attention focused on the two men, Jessica asked Nava, "Now that we have just about everyone here together, I'd like to have a quick meeting. Would you mind being my interpreter for the Hebrew speakers? I am going to get Faysal to interpret to the Arabic speakers and I'll talk directly to the English speakers."

"Oh sure! In fact, I'll get the groups separated so it will make it easier for everyone to hear. The Arabic speakers will comprise the largest group. Faysal can handle it though." With that, Nava turned and in a loud voice started separating the groups by language, Hebrew speakers to Jessica's left, English speakers right in front of her and the Arabic speakers to the right so that Faysal could address them directly.

"Just like Nuria would have done," Jessica said under her breath. "I miss you, girl."

CHAPTER 11

In the days leading up to her first meeting with the crew, Jessica gave serious thought to what she wanted to say to those at the dig site. It would be the first time any of the workers would really see and hear her and Jessica knew she needed to make the right impression. She also knew she wanted to start her meeting by honoring the man they surely all missed, Dr. Kenyon. Now, as she looked out over the group, she didn't know if she could do it without getting emotional. She began by saying, "I know I have not had the chance to meet all of you, so I guess I should start by telling you that I am Dr. Jessica Davenport and to let you know that we *all* have suffered a great loss. As you all know, Dr. Kenyon was a fantastic leader, a wonderful mentor, a dedicated husband, a masterful communicator and a genuinely good friend. It is a loss that we *all* feel." Jessica paused every few sentences as Nava and Faysal interpreted her words. "You may not have known, but I knew Dr. Kenyon for over a decade… and I am still feeling his loss… as I know you all are. I am not here to try and replace the man. I would never be able to. I'm here to try to finish what he started, to continue his work, to make his wife and all of *you*, proud of what we can accomplish, together, in his memory. We will do it with excellence. We will do it with pride."

About that time, there was a loud *pop*, a cracking noise and then a rumbling. Jessica was the first to see it as she was facing the direction of the sound, followed closely by Nava and Faysal. They were addressing their respective groups and facing the same direction as Jessica. Across the worksite from them, a dust cloud began sweeping out of the mouth of the cave as the hillside entrance began to collapse. This time, it wasn't just the entrance to the cave, but the collapsing structure began sweeping a growing track up the hillside opposite of where the group was standing. It started at the cave entrance and then grew into a depression that resembled a snake weaving back and forth along the opposite hillside. The rumbling grew louder and louder as the sound wave reached the crew in force. It began to look like the whole hillside was crumbling in on itself.

The people assembled to listen to Jessica all turned in horror toward the sound. When they realized what was happening, there were a mix of reactions. Several of the women shrieked, and several of the men shouted. Even Wally showed his disgust by taking off his hard hat and throwing it to the ground. All the work, all the progress that the team had made of clearing the cave entrance over the last several weeks had been wiped out in an instant. What had taken weeks to accomplish took less than thirty seconds to destroy. Jessica was immediately grateful that she had called this meeting. Everyone was with her and away from the danger.

As she tried to regain everyone's attention, Jessica said with a loud voice, "Everyone it's ok." Then to Nava and Faysal she said, "Continue to interpret, please." Then, back toward the group she said in her best, most inspiring coach-talk way, "We are going to clear this. This is just a small setback, but it will not stop us. We will accomplish what we set out to do. There is nothing that can stop us if we all work together. And I know that we all want to accomplish the same thing. We want to honor the life of Dr. Kenyon through this site." Turning to the foreman, Jessica continued, "Faysal, please do a roll call. I want to make sure each and every person on this site is accounted for."

Faysal, sensing the calming effect the new leader's presence was having on the crowd, immediately sprang into action. He ran the few feet from where he was to the table inside the tent headquarters, grabbed his clipboard and returned. Jessica raised her hands in a calming motion and said, "Everyone please keep calm and stay quiet. We need to do a check. Please bear with us." Nava moved toward Faysal and between the two of them had called roll, and made sure everyone was accounted for, within a matter of minutes.

It was during that moment of quiet, that Jessica realized that she had not seen Matt for a few minutes. Immediately she thought that he had run to investigate the cave-in.

Didn't he know it wasn't safe, yet?

As Faysal and Nava finished up their check, they reported to Jessica that all team members were accounted for and safe. Jessica said, "Faysal, would you please, from a very safe distance, survey the site. See if you understand what happened, what was the cause, the extent of the damage, any and all of that. *Safely.* Do it safely. And tell my husband to stay away. Since everyone else is already present and accounted for, I'm sure he will be the only other person foolish enough to get close to the damaged site. Take someone with you and the both of you be safe!"

Faysal nodded and turning, said something in Arabic to Wally. Wally nodded, picked up his hard hat and the two men made their way off, cautiously walking down the hill through the smaller work sites and towards the place where the opening of the tunnel had once been. With their eyes, they followed the damage for what looked to be several hundred meters, but an exact measurement would, in coming days, reveal how much damage there really was.

Jessica turned to Nava and more to herself than to her subordinate said, "That's so unfortunate. We are at a crossroads. That might have been the entire cave system that just collapsed. We can sort through the ruins, but what do we expect to find? Anything of value? Or we could shut the site down, call it unsafe, cut our losses. Does it make any sense to spend more money to try and clear this debris to only find that was all of it? Or, what if there is more to this cave system? What could we find?" Then realizing what she was saying, finished with "Oh, I'm sorry. I'm just talking out loud."

Nava nodded and said, "You'll figure it out. That's what you were brought here for. I've only known you for a minute, but I can already tell that you're a good leader and you'll find the right thing, make a plan and put it into action. These people are good people, and they'll follow you. Just lead them."

Jessica smiled, nodded, and stepped away, taking a moment to herself. Under her breath she began praying a quick prayer. "Lord, please help me. I'm feeling overwhelmed, but I know that you are my refuge and strength and my very present help in time of trouble.[67] I am asking for the helper, You Lord, You are my helper.[68] Please help me as I navigate this situation. I thank you for it in Jesus' Name, amen." Immediately, deep on the inside, Jessica knew she was supposed to continue the work Dr. Kenyon had started. A knowing. She *knew* it. Even though she couldn't explain why, she just *knew* that she was supposed to continue the work, that this was a setback but not a defeat.

A few moments later, Faysal and Wally returned with their rough initial report. Without actually moving onto the hillside, from what they were able to see, the entire cave structure looked like it had collapsed. In the prior episode, the one that killed Dr. Kenyon, it looked like the cave had disintegrated from just inside the mouth of the cave and worked its way toward the opening. This time, it looked like, at least initially, that the damage had started at the mouth of the cave and caused a chain reaction along the interior of the tunnel. Each piece falling caused the next piece deeper within the cave to fall, much like lined up dominoes fell, each knocking the next one in line over. Jessica, nodding and taking it all in, knew she had, on her very first day, her hands full. Once the information had been relayed and Jessica had taken a few moments to process it, she asked "Do we have a survey team? Can we get them geared up to report the damage? Or are we going to have to hire one to come in? Oh, and did you keep Matt away? Where is he?"

Faysal said something to Wally in Arabic and the muscled man shook his head. Faysal turned back to Jessica and said, "Neither of us

---

[67] Reference Psalm 46:1

[68] Reference Hebrews 13:6

has seen your husband since the three of us made our way up here to the meeting. Are you sure he is not up here somewhere?"

Nava could see the immediate panic in Jessica's eyes and put the pieces together quickly. She turned to the still assembled group and in a loud voice said, first in English and then in Hebrew, "Dr. Davenport's husband. Has anyone seen Dr. Davenport's husband since the cave in? His name is Matt. Anyone?" Faysal did the same for the Arabic speakers. There was a mostly silent murmur among the group with several people shaking their heads. "Carefully, everyone spread out and start trying to find him. His name is Matt. And those of you who want to be on the emergency response team, gear up!!" Turning back to Jessica, Nava finished with "Call his cellphone and see if he answers. Maybe he went to get coffee or something."

The large, assembled group started moving out across the dig site, frantically calling Matt's name in a host of different accents. But the group knew that it had been over thirty minutes since the cave-in had occurred and if Matt was buried underneath it, there was very little chance of his survival. A human can only remain buried in soil for just a few minutes.

"Good idea," Jessica said. She ran over to her bag and pulled out her cell phone, found Matt's contact information and hit the green 'call' button. The phone rang four times and then Jessica heard the familiar voicemail greeting of her husband. "No answer," she said to Nava, and immediately dialed it again. "But that's not unusual. If he is already on the phone, he lets my call go to voicemail and then calls me back. Maybe if I call him several times, he will get the idea that this is important and take my call." Again, the call went to Matt's voicemail. "C'mon Matt. Answer me. You know how much it frustrates me when you don't answer," Jessica said as she was calling his number again. For the third consecutive time it went to Matt's voicemail. This time, Jessica left him a message. "Matt, there's been an accident at the site and the tunnel has caved in. I need to know you are alright. *Please*, call me back," and hit the *End Call* button. "I'll send him a text as well. Maybe he can't answer the call for some reason…" Jessica began typing her text. As soon as Jessica finished the text and hit send, she immediately dialed his cell phone again. For the fourth consecutive call, Jessica heard the beginning of Matt's voicemail greeting. She was having a hard time keeping her cool and could feel her heart beating heavily in her chest.

Nava moved toward her new boss and took her hand. "He will turn up. I know he will." She paused for a moment and then continued, "I don't know your personal beliefs, but I am a Christian and I would love to pray with you about this. Would that be ok?" Jessica looked at the young intern and hugged her.

"Yes. Yes. I would absolutely love that. Let me try his phone one more time, first." Jessica hit the call button on her phone and saw Matt's name light up on the screen. Once again, the call went to his voicemail.

CHAPTER 12

As Faysal and Wally turned away from Matt to head back up the hill for Jessica's very first meeting as head of the dig site, Matt sensed an opportunity. He knew this might be his only chance to explore that tunnel by himself. Matt took a couple steps with Wally and Faysal so they would think he was walking with them, then slinked away and headed for the tunnel. He pulled his cellphone out, walked inside the mouth of the cave, and turned on the flashlight app. He bumped his head as he stepped inside the small and narrow opening. Matt thought to himself, *maybe I should grab a hardhat. Nah. I'm only going to be in here for just a minute and I won't go very far inside. I'll be fine.* Matt had a little negative nudge, just an uneasy feeling, but he dismissed it as quickly as it had shown up. He wrote it off as that spark of excitement at the thought of doing something just a little devious, something he knew he shouldn't be doing. He was more upset at the possibility of getting his *Alabama* hat dirty.

Stepping inside the cave, Matt took a moment to try and get his bearings, to understand the layout of the space. The small entrance he had walked through had four, roughly carved steps that went downward and connected to a small interior space. That small interior space was a tunnel, a hallway of sorts that was only two or three feet long, a very, very small space. Matt rubbed his hand along the wall as he walked and felt the rough dirt and rock that had been carved by hand. That tunnel, hewn out of the earth, made a hard right hand turn at about the five-foot mark. It turned out to be a ninety-degree angle. If someone had just looked in the cave, they would think it was a dead end because the perpendicular cave and its opening were almost completely out of sight. Looking in from the mouth of the tunnel, this cave would look like a short, tiny little space. The opening into the next space was small, barely even there. It looked like someone had gone to great lengths to keep it hidden.

As Matt turned the corner into tunnel number two, he was immediately bathed in darkness. The only light in the space was one faint glow from the entrance and his cell phone flashlight app. "This was dug by someone over two thousand years ago," he whispered to himself while trying to understand the place. After about three steps, it was complete darkness outside of the halo of light being emitted from the phone. The darkness of the cave was stark and engulfing. His phone's little light struggled to fight the darkness away. This right-hand hallway, tunnel number two, went on for approximately thirty yards, up a slight incline, and made a left-hand turn. As Matt turned the corner into the third tunnel, he wanted to see exactly how dark it was in the cave, so he turned off the flashlight app. It was dark. Very. Very. Dark. He stopped and reversed course, looking back at where he had entered. He could see the little sliver of light from the entrance, but other than that, he could not see anything. As his eyes started to focus, he noticed what seemed to be little blinking red and green lights. He turned his flashlight app back on. Until that moment, he had not noticed the wooden support beams that stretched across the top of the tunnel, and he probably wouldn't have noticed them then if not for the tiny, faint, blinking lights. The support beams crossed the ceiling of the hallway, every seven to ten feet. "This looks just like the iron ore mines back home," he said. "Why would the ancient people of this land dig a mine? Are there gold or precious jewels in the ground here?"

Matt turned back around and pressed onward, turning the corner and walking along hallway number three. This hallway seemed to continue the inclined pathway, but it was steeper. Matt felt like he was walking uphill for another thirty to forty yards. When he came to the end of tunnel number three, the tunnel looked like a dead end, but gave two options; turn right or turn left, again at ninety-degree angles heading off in opposite directions. He had a choice to make. At this point, Matt started to get a little bit uneasy. He did not want to get lost in this cave system. Until now, there hadn't been any choices to make, it was pretty straightforward. Until now.

Matt stopped, turned, and looked at where he had just come from. Again, he turned off his flashlight app and this time, it was complete, total, stark, darkness. It was black. Pitch black. Matt didn't know if he had ever been somewhere that was as dark as this cave. As his eyes adjusted, as much as possible to the complete darkness, Matt again noticed the little blinking lights, but this time, instead of sitting on each crossbeam along the length of the hallway, they only ran about halfway up to where he was standing, stopping about fifteen yards from where he currently stood. It was *so* dark, and the lights were several yards from him. He really had to stare to even see them. And then something came back to Matt, something Faysal had said less than a half an hour ago. Faysal had said he never went so far into the cave that he needed a flashlight. He said that he only went a short way in to make sure that there weren't any people sleeping in the cave. There wasn't enough room for people to sleep in that entrance area and Faysal would need a flashlight after about 6 feet in this cave system. He also said that he didn't allow anyone else in the cave. They were waiting on an archaeologist, on Jessica, to get here before they started their exploration. Who then, who was the person that lined these two tunnels with these blinking lights? What were they used for? Some sort of stability maintenance? Was this archaeology's version of a Richter Scale or something?

Where did the blinking lights come from?

Matt was thinking about that when he heard a distant *pop*, a *crack* and a rumbling noise. A split second later, it repeated, *pop, crack, rumble.* A split second later, it repeated again, *pop, crack, rumble.* Over and over and over, it repeated. Each time, it was slightly louder. *Pop, crack, rumble. Pop, crack, rumble.* It was moving towards Matt. Quicker and quicker. *Pop, crack, rumble. Pop, crack, rumble. Pop, crack, rumble.* Louder and louder. *Pop, crack, rumble.* Then, Matt understood what was happening. Looking down the tunnel from where he had just walked, he saw the crossbeam at the far end of the tunnel spark in a brilliant light. That was the *pop.* The crossbeam immediately shattered into pieces. That was the *crack.* And then the ceiling structure came crashing down. That was the *rumble.* Almost immediately, the process repeated on the next crossbeam. The noise was deafening. The tunnel was forcing all of the sound, the noise, the shockwaves, and the debris up the tunnel and toward Matt. It hit him full on, in the face, in his chest, in his thighs, knees and shins.

Immediately, Matt turned away from the mini explosions and tried to escape down the left-hand tunnel. Was it the correct choice? He didn't know. Would it lead him to safety? He wasn't sure. Would he live? Only God knew at this point. Matt's flashlight app was still off. It was completely dark in the tunnel. He ran full speed in the darkness, as hard and as fast as he could. Each step he took was a step away from the danger. The path was uneven and loosely packed, making it slippery and unnerving as he tried to run. Matt couldn't tell it, but behind him, the *pops* stopped. Had he been paying attention instead of running full speed, he would have noticed that the cracking and the rumbling continued, following him as he raced away. It was almost like being trapped inside an awful set of dominos, each crossbeam crashing and bringing the next one down with it which then brought the next crossbeam from the ceiling to the floor. It was an avalanche in the cave, chasing him as he went. Matt sprinted hard down the declining hallway which added to the speed with which he ran. Ten yards. Twenty yards. The rumbling was getting closer. Thirty yards. The carnage was catching him. Forty yards of complete darkness. Could he escape it? With the tunnel caving in around him, behind him, below him, Matt ran as hard as he could toward the end of the tunnel he was in. He was running as hard and as fast as his feet and lungs would take him. Then… nothing.

CHAPTER 13

J essica called Matt's phone one more time. No answer. Voicemail. "Come. On. Matt. Answer your phone!!" Jessica was exasperated. Frustrated. She turned back to Nava who could see the fear and tension in her new boss' actions, words, even her gestures.

Nava said "Dr. Davenport, I…"

"Call me Jessica. I can't deal with the formality of being called Dr. Davenport right now." Her voice started rising. Angry. Not at Nava, at Matt.

Nava calmly started again, "Jessica, I can't tell you how I know this, but he is going to be ok. I just know it. "

Jessica didn't know what to think. Was this God speaking through this young, college intern? Or was this some kid who was just trying to cheer her up? Through all of her time walking a Christian life, she sometimes still had a hard time getting her brain and emotions under control, especially in emergency situations, like this. Jessica could clearly hear the voice of the Lord when she was in her special place of prayer, with her perfect music at the perfect volume. In times like this, in high stress moments, highly charged emotional moments, hearing from God was still a challenge for Jessica.

Nava took Jessica's hand and calmly continued, "I'd still like to pray with you."

Jessica took a deep breath in and slowly let it out. She took a second breath in and slowly let it out. Calmer now, Jessica said, "Yes. I would like that very much. I'm sorry I'm being short with you," and gave a slight, reassuring squeeze to the younger woman's hand.

"I completely understand. Don't worry about it."

Just then Jessica's phone, still in her free hand, began vibrating and playing the familiar klaxon ringtone she had set. Startled, she fumbled and ultimately dropped the phone and then had to scramble to pick it up before the call went to her voicemail. Without even looking at the caller ID, Jessica answered the phone and frantically said, "Matt, is that you? Are you ok? Where are you? Talk to me!"

There was a brief moment of silence and then the calming voice of Eli Kaplan, Jessica's friend and boss, said "This is Eli. Tell me what's going on and what I can do to help."

Jessica was frazzled and it showed as she responded to the gentle words of her friend, "Oh. I ummm… I'm sorry. I thought you were Matt. Ah. This… This morning is my first day at the site and we *just* had a cave-in. Matt is missing. I… uhhh… I don't know."

Eli, in his usual calm manner, asked, "Have the authorities been called?"

"I… uh… I don't think so."

"I'll take care of that. I'm on my way back in country. I'll have excavation teams there within the hour, sooner than that probably. My people. People we can trust. Sit tight. If Matt calls you, let me know. Otherwise, I'll have people there shortly."

Jessica had renewed strength at the calming sound of Eli's voice. He had done for her what she had done for the archaeological team. "Thank you, Eli. I'll talk to you soon," but Eli was off the line before Jessica had finished her thought. She lowered the phone and reexamined her surroundings. Nava was still standing there, looking at her expectantly.

"Jessica, let's finish that prayer," Nava said as she took Jessica's hand. At the same time, Faysal stepped back into the tent and saw the two women holding hands. He didn't know what to say or what was going on. Nava said to him "We're about to pray for Jessica's husband's safe return. Please join us," and extended her free hand toward the man.

"But I am not a Christian, am I allowed?" Faysal asked.

Nava answered, "Yes. We *all* want Matt's safe return. Please, join us."

Faysal stepped toward the ladies and with his left hand took Nava's hand and with his right hand, took Jessica's. The three of them formed a small circle. Jessica noted the unusual way Faysal's hand felt in hers — it felt smaller, somehow, than normal. The thought drifted away as Nava began her prayer. "Lord above, maker of Heaven and Earth, be with us as we wrestle with what to do about this situation. Be with us as we decide how to move forward. Be with Matt wherever he is. In your Son's holy Name, Amen."

The three of them opened their eyes and looked at each other, but Jessica didn't let their hands go. She said, "Thank you, Nava. I want to add my prayer to yours. Please indulge me as I pray as well." Nava nodded and the three of them again bowed their heads as Jessica continued speaking, this time with authority. "Lord, I come to you in the Name of Jesus.[69] You said in Your Word that 'A thousand shall fall at our side, and ten thousand at our right hand; but it shall not come nigh us. For You have given Your angels charge over us and they keep us in all our ways. They shall bear us up in their hands, lest we dash our foot against a stone.'[70] I pray for Matt now! Keep him alive! Angels, protect him! Keep him from being crushed by those stones and bring him back to me. Thank you, Lord, that you hear us when we pray.[71] In Jesus' Name, Amen." When Jessica opened her eyes, the other two were just staring at her, mouths open, stunned. "What?" she asked, still holding hands with them.

Nava looked at Faysal and back to Jessica. Faysal looked at Nava and back at Jessica. Finally, Nava said, "I've never heard anyone pray like that before. You almost commanded God…"

---

[69] Reference John 15:16

[70] Reference Psalm 91:7,11,12

[71] Reference 1 John 5:14-15

Jessica sweetly replied, "Yes, the Bible tells us to 'come boldly unto the throne of grace, that we may obtain mercy, and find grace to help in time of need' and that's what I was doing.[72] This is a time of need... we need mercy and grace right now! We have a 'new and better covenant' with God and because of that new covenant we can ask boldly for what we need. [73] 'God *shall* supply all our need,' is what the Bible tells us." [74]

Faysal asked "How did you send the electricity through my hands?"

"What are you talking about?" Jessica asked.

"I felt it, too. It was like an intense heat coming from your hands," Nava added.

Jessica took a quick moment to compose herself. "That's what that was. I felt the power leave my body... I'll be happy to explain all of this in *much* more detail when we have more time, but... well, sometimes the Lord gives us a physical demonstration, like heat in the hands, or a supernatural joy that causes laughter even in the midst of horrible circumstances, just to confirm that He is working on the thing we prayed about." [75] Turning to Faysal, Jessica continued, "It wasn't me that sent electricity through your hands. It was God's Holy Spirit."

Faysal had a reaction that Jessica wasn't expecting. Looking him in the eyes as she was speaking, Jessica saw... fear. Faysal dropped her hands, afraid, almost flinging them away. Then, acting like Jessica was diseased or something, quickly started moving backwards across the tent, bumping into tables and knocking over chairs as he made his way out.

"Well, I wasn't expecting *that*," Jessica said to herself.

Nava replied, "Don't worry about Faysal. He will be fine in a few minutes. He is *so* superstitious. If it has anything to do with anything unusual, supernatural, even scary movies it really, *really* freaks him out.

---

[72] Hebrews 4:16

[73] Hebrews 12:24

[74] Philippians 4:19

[75] Reference Mark 5:30, Luke 8:46

Give him a minute and he will act like nothing ever happened. As long as you don't bring it up, he definitely won't."

"It doesn't even matter to me. I've got bigger things on my mind. What did you mean when you said, 'those of you who want to be on the emergency response team, gear up?' Does that mean you don't have a plan in place for things like this?"

Nava paused a minute and then answered, "We started talking about putting one together after Dr. Kenyon's accident, but because we didn't have someone here as a leader, to make the decisions and take the action *and* be responsible for it, it sort of fell off our radar after a few days. We have some people who volunteered to be on the emergency response team, the ERT, but they haven't had any kind of training and don't have any kind of true emergency equipment."

"That's not good," Jessica said as she started making her way out of the command tent. But what she saw amazed her. To her complete shock and surprise, the group who had been looking for Matt was now mounting a rescue attempt in the debris of the cave-in. They formed a long assembly line. At the head of it, was the beast of a man, Wally. He was pulling rubble up and handing it to the next person or multiple people if that's what it took to carry the load. They passed it on down the line to clear the area and turned back to Wally to take the next piece of debris from his massive grip. Over and over the process went. Making small progress, but progress just the same.

Wally was a machine. He never got tired. He never stopped. With each piece of debris he moved, he shouted, "Matt!?!" He met the silence of non-reply with brute force of clearing more debris. Over and over and over. The people in the assembly line behind him quickly tired and were replaced by fresher backs. Then after moments, those people were replaced. Wally kept working. Kept digging. He was made for this. He was unstoppable. He looked like he would move earth all night if that's what it required.

Jessica stood there watching, helpless, prayerfully looking to God for His help, secretly willing the muscled man, Wally, to continue and find her husband, uninjured.

Faysal made his way back over to Jessica and acting as if the prayer-electricity event never happened said, "Like I said, Wally is best digger we have. A total muscle head but when you get him pointed in the right direction, he is the best. When he meet Matt this morning, Wally told him that he would be Matt's protector while he was on site. Wally said it in jest, but it has given him extra motivation to try and get your husband back."

Jessica stood there slightly in shock. Matt had a way with people. People gravitated towards him, somehow. Matt had only been on site for a short time, and he already had people attached to him emotionally... and some of those people, like Wally, *didn't even speak English!* It was that way everywhere he went. He was genuine and compassionate, outgoing and a little naive. He had a childlike quality to him, and people were drawn to him. They just *liked* him. Jessica *loved* him and with each piece of rubble that Wally moved, she nervously waited for Matt to be found.

CHAPTER 14

Darkness. Total and complete. Nothingness in its purest form. Matt couldn't tell if his eyes were opened or shut. He tried moving his hand up to his eyes, to check if he could see it, but that's about the time he realized his arm was pinned under something. Was he lying on it? His body felt completely unfamiliar. His bed felt completely unfamiliar. And so did his apartment. Their apartment, in the middle of the city, had never been this dark or this silent since he and Jessica had moved in. "Jessica, is the power out?" he whispered. Matt tried to roll over to face the side of the bed she normally slept on and that's when the slicing pain hit him. Everything hurt, but his head *hurt*. This wasn't just a 'headache' kind of pain, this was gold medal pain. Numero uno pain. Worst-hangover-in-the-world kind of pain. Matt laid his head back down on his pillow, but realized it wasn't his pillow. It was hard, jagged. He noticed his ears squelched a high-pitched noise. "What is going on?" he finally said out loud, but the sound was foreign to him. Different, just like everything else about this moment.

Matt again tried to move his arm and realized that not only could he not move it, but he also couldn't really feel it either. He slowly used his left arm, his free arm, to try to determine what was going on. It turns out, his arm was pinned under a very large piece of concrete or something, right above his elbow. That's when things came back to him. He had been in the tunnel when the support beams started failing. This wasn't concrete, this was the cave itself trapping his arm. Matt had a vision of Aron Ralston, the mountain climber who had his arm pinned under a boulder while climbing in Utah. The way he escaped? He cut off his own arm![76] And he did it with a pocketknife! Fear started to dig its claws into Matt's emotions.

"Hello? Can anyone hear me?" he shouted. The sound made his head throb even more.

Nothing. Silence. Total and complete. Nothingness in its purest form. It was like his surroundings swallowed the sounds he was making.

"Well, that's not good," Matt said to himself. "I guess this is how Jonah felt. I'll tell you what, I'm not spending three days and nights in the belly of this whale![77] I know you hear me, Lord. Save me from this mess![78] And, just so you know, I'm *not* cutting off my arm!"

Again, the fear tried to set in. Matt's brain was running a thousand miles an hour. He knew he shouldn't have ever entered the cave, shouldn't have been here without a hardhat, shouldn't have ignored Jessica. He started beating himself up over it. Then the problems started clouding his thoughts. He remembered seeing the news reports from a few years ago when a youth soccer team had been exploring a cave in Thailand. [79] What was supposed to be an hour inside a cave dramatically changed when a sudden rainstorm had pinned them in the belly of the cave. Completely cut off from the outside world, trapped, without food or way of escape, they stayed there for over two weeks before the Thai Navy Seals rescued them.

Can I survive that long? If it rains right now, I'm pinned. I'll drown! The fear was gaining a stranglehold on him.

---

[76] Katie Serena, "Aron Ralston and The Harrowing True Story Of '127 Hours,'" All That's Interesting, September 4, 2021, https://allthatsinteresting.com/aron-ralston-127-hours-true-story.

[77] Reference Jonah 1:17

[78] Reference Jonah 2:2

[79] History.com Editors, "Thai Soccer Team Becomes Trapped In Cave," History.com, June 18, 2019, https://www.history.com/this-day-in-history/thai-soccer-team-becomes-trapped-in-cave.

Matt made a decision. "God, you haven't given me a fearful spirit. You have given me life; you've given me power and you've given me a steady mind.[80] I *will not* be afraid. I shall not die, but live, and declare the works of the Lord.[81] You said you came that I could have life and have it abundantly.[82] *That's* what I'll have! I know you have a plan for me and that's why I love Jeremiah 29:11! It says 'For I know the plans I have for you, says the Lord. They are plans for good and not for evil, to give you a future and a hope.'[83] I've got hope for a beautiful future. Let's get on with it! Now, the first thing I need to do is get up and get moving. Here we go."

Matt resolved within himself that no matter what the circumstances looked like, how dire the situation turned, that God was *for him* and not against him.[84] Matt resolved that he would *live* and not die and so he began the process of continuing his life.

Suddenly, Matt remembered the discussion that Rabbi Kaduri had with the little old lady with the blue hair. During the VIP tour, Rabbi Kaduri talked to the group about why Jerusalem has been such a sought-after location for thousands of years, about why men had fought over this plot of land long before the world's three largest religions had claimed it, and why the city had been conquered over forty times. The city of Jerusalem is located in the mountains, on the edge of the Judean Desert. But Jerusalem has *water*. It has its own natural springs that well up from deep within the Earth. Jerusalem doesn't depend on rain for its water because it doesn't rain much. Jerusalem has its own water that bubbles up from the Earth and that's why the city has been sought after and controlled by so many different people groups. Water. Jerusalem could lock the gates and have a constant source of water inside the city walls. A desert city with little rain.

---

[80] Reference 2 Timothy 1:7

[81] Reference Psalm 118:17

[82] Reference John 10:10

[83] Jeremiah 29:11 (The Living Bible)

[84] Reference Romans 8:31

Something on the inside was talking to Matt. He knew he wasn't going to drown. It doesn't rain here. Matt's brain started calming down. *Relax, Matt. Relax.*

Just then, Matt remembered that he was wearing his over the shoulder, cross-body sling bag for exact situations like this. With his free hand, Matt clumsily unzipped the bag and started rummaging through the things he was carrying: an extra phone and charger, a large, Swiss Army pocketknife — *I'm not using that to cut off my arm* — some simple medicines like headache and diarrhea pills, some extra money, both American and Israeli, the several large bags of his new favorite candy, *Wild Berry Skittles*. He dug until his hand landed on what he was looking for, the flashlight. Matt clicked the button and immediately the light chased the darkness from around him. He squinted and blinked at the immediate change as his eyes adjusted. Fighting fear the whole time, Matt turned to look at his trapped right arm. To his surprise and amazement, he could see almost his entire arm, it was only partially pinned. A large, flat, angled rock, like the point of a triangle, was lying across his arm just above the elbow, but he could see his hand on the other side of it. It was actually turning blue from the lack of blood flowing to the extremity. Matt held the flashlight in his mouth and used his free hand, his left hand to push on the stone. As he did, the stone teetered. It reminded Matt of when he was eating at a fast-food restaurant back home — sometimes the table would rock back and forth either because the floor was uneven or because the table leg was bent. Matt usually used a couple of packs of sugar to even up the table legs. The stone that had pinned Matt's arm down was acting the same way. Matt pushed it towards the opposite corner and when he did, there was just enough wiggle room that he was able to free his arm. With his arm freed, Matt dropped the stone and it crashed, sending dust flying into the area where he was. Immediately the blood started flowing back to his arm, hand and into his fingers. Matt shouted "Pins and needles, pins and needles! Oh Lord, that hurts!" As he did, the flashlight dropped from his mouth, hit him in the chest and rolled on the ground, light blinking in the fall. The sounds from the crashing stone, his shouts, and the banging of the flashlight intensified the pounding of his head.

Matt rubbed his arm, wrist, and fingers trying to get the blood flowing again. His biceps were scratched and bleeding. It looked like road rash or a raspberry. When he finally moved his attention back to the flashlight, he finally understood the true nature of his predicament.

Matt was lying on his back, completely surrounded by fallen rocks. It was like he was in a small cocoon, completely protected from the falling debris. If he had been six inches taller or had fallen six inches to the left or right, it might have been a completely different story. He didn't have room to sit up. In fact, if he were to sneeze, he would hit his head on the slab of rock directly in front of his face. It couldn't be any more than eight inches away from the tip of his nose.

"Thank you, Lord, for keeping me safe… Now, how am I going to get out of here?" Matt took stock of the situation.

If I move any of these rocks, the whole place may cave in on me. I could be completely crushed. On the other hand, just on the other side of this rock might be daylight. No, I don't think that's right. Anyone could have heard me scream, and I would be able to hear them. I can't hear anyone. Are they even looking for me? Don't panic. Breathe. "Lord, you're going to have to get me out of here." *How long was I unconscious, two minutes? Two hours? Two days?!? Focus Matt. Focus. Don't get over-whelmed. Attack one problem at a time.*

As he was thinking about what to do first, Matt's flashlight blinked again and went dim. "Well, that's not good either." Matt took a few moments to work his way so that he could pick the small flashlight up. He banged it a couple of times against the side of his leg. The light blinked and shone a little brighter. "I wonder how long these batteries are going to last. Why don't you have any spare batteries in your man-purse?" Matt paused, regained his composure and said, "Focus. One problem at a time."

Matt laid there another moment, unsure of how to proceed. He took the flashlight and tried examining his surroundings. The light hurt his eyes and his head was still pounding. Matt wiggled his arms enough to squeeze his right hand up to feel his head. His hat was gone and there was crusty stuff just above his forehead. Matt assumed it was blood. There was crusty stuff on the back of his head as well, matting his hair to his head and causing it to slightly stick to the ground. Matt assumed that was blood as well, but nothing seemed to be bleeding currently. *So, I've been here long enough for the bleeding to stop.* While he was sore, bruised and hurting, nothing seemed to be broken, and if he could find a place to move, he was physically able.

Turning his attention back to his surroundings, it seemed every inch above his head and to the sides of his shoulders was completely packed with debris. Still lying on his back, Matt tried looking behind him, but the only way to do that was to roll his head back and act like he was trying to look at his hair. He could see that it was completely blocked. There was a large rock that came to rest just above his head and traversed the length of his body at a slight angle. The part by his head looked to be resting on the same thing Matt was, and it moved the length of his body at a very slight upward angle so that it was a few inches higher above his feet than it was above his head. Matt followed the large slab until it was blocked from sight by other debris protruding from the left and right. Looking down the length of his body, Matt could see his feet. Matt pointed his toes and when he did, they hit something solid, but Matt noticed something. To his astonishment, to the left and to the right of his feet, seemed to be completely free. Matt wiggled his legs and realized that from about the waist down, he had much more freedom than from the waist up. Matt sensed that freedom from this hole, might just lie at his feet. His problem became how to get his body to where his feet were. He had no room to use his arms to push his body. He had no way to get any leverage to slide his body in that direction. His feet didn't have any grip to 'pull' him in that direction, but Matt knew, he just *knew* on the inside, that he was supposed to move *forward* in the direction of his feet. Again, in an instant, a Bible story came to his remembrance: Moses leading the Israelites out of Egypt, what is known as the Exodus story — but Matt was reminded of a very specific, often overlooked part.

Matt was reminded of the part of the story where the Israelites have been on the move for three days. They are tired, complaining, and afraid. And that's when things go from 'pretty-ok' to 'oh-no-we're-all-going-to-die' territory. The Egyptian Pharaoh sent his army to either bring the Israelites back or kill them and leave their bodies where they landed. That army had just arrived when the Israelites made it to the Red Sea, a massive, impassable barrier. Water in front of them. Enemy army behind them. A mutiny against Moses was brewing.

The Israelite people 'said to Moses, "Why did you bring us out here to die in the wilderness? Weren't there enough graves for us in Egypt? What have you done to us? Why did you make us leave Egypt? Didn't we tell you this would happen while we were still in Egypt? We said, 'Leave us alone! Let us be slaves to the Egyptians. It's better to be a slave in Egypt than a corpse in the wilderness!'"

But Moses told the people, "Don't be afraid. Just stand still and watch the Lord rescue you today. The Egyptians you see today will never be seen again. The Lord himself will fight for you. Just stay calm."[85]

Matt knew that's where people usually stopped and found comfort in the story — knowing that God would fight the battle for the people. Matt also knew that's not what *God* said. God never said, "Stand still and I will fight the battle for you." *Moses* said that about the Lord. What God actually said comes next in the story and was the reason Matt knew what he needed to do, right now.

"And the Lord said unto Moses, Wherefore criest thou unto me? speak unto the children of Israel, that they go *forward*."[86] God didn't tell the Israelites to stand still. Moses did. God told them to *go forward*.

So, Matt decided to move *forward*, towards the freedom of his feet. Then, he began trying to solve the first problem: *How do I move that way*

---

[85] Exodus 14:11-14 (New Living Translation)

[86] Exodus 14:15 (King James Version)

without using my hands to push off on something? And that's when the second problem hit him, literally in the face: the ceiling structure made a loud 'crack' and started dropping dust, pebbles, and other small debris on him. Matt realized he didn't have long before the weight on top of the large slab would cause it to crack and crush Matt in the process. Frantically, Matt started the worming process of using his feet to pull him, inch by inch toward the potential freedom. That's when problem three hit him; because of how low the ceiling structure was, he could only raise his knees a slight amount which meant each 'worming' action only moved Matt less than an inch, a horribly painful, scratching inch. He used his fingers to try and claw his way out. It would only be a matter of minutes before his fingertips were bloody and his fingernails were gone. To get all the way out, to get to a place where there might only be a few more inches of freedom, to get away from the falling ceiling would take minutes, possibly hours and would be physically exhausting, let alone would rub his back and fingernails raw. Matt again began fighting the crippling panic that was trying to set in. The ceiling slab gave another loud **crack** as dust and debris fell into Matt's open mouth.

CHAPTER 15

Off in the distance, Jessica could faintly hear the sounds of sirens blaring. Wally was still moving debris, buckets of dirt, and huge boulders and slabs of stone, and the other men on the site had all taken their turn following him. The next replacement was just getting ready to take his first slab from Wally's hands. It was huge, but the replacement was able to handle it. Barely. The sirens were getting louder.

"Finally," Jessica said to herself, "I think that's the authorities coming to help us." She turned from her spot where she was watching the debris removal and started making her way up the hill to the command center tent. Nava was by her side and the two ladies reached the tent as the first of the rescue workers showed up. He was an unimpressive man, short and round, but he moved well along the uneven footing at the site. Perhaps he had been an athlete at a prior point in life. He was bald on top with a crown of hair around his ears and had a thin, dark mustache.

"My name is Doron Raz, and I am looking for Jessica Davenport."[87, 88]

"That's me," Jessica answered and extended her hand.

Shaking her hand, Doron said in very good English, "Eli Kaplan sent me. Tell me everything you know as quickly and as thoroughly as possible. My team will be here momentarily, and I need to be able to place them correctly."

---

[87] Doron – Hebrew name meaning "Gift"

[88] Raz – Hebrew name meaning "Secret"

Jessica answered, "We have one person missing, my husband. He is untrained and only here as a visitor to support me on my first day as project leader. The rest of the group had assembled here, in this area, for a meeting when the cave, there, across the slope, started crumbling under its own weight. It started at the entrance and crumbled into the mess you see before you. At first, we were relieved that we were all gathered here, and it wasn't until 20 or 30 minutes later that we realized my husband was gone. The team started frantically digging shortly after that. You can see the assembly line, with Wally, the big man leading things, but we are making very slow progress. It has been more than an hour since we started digging."

"Thank you, Dr. Davenport. You are sure that he was in the cave?"

"Well, yes, I think. Our car is still here, and he hasn't answered any of my phone calls or texts. It is the only logical explanation. He would *not* pull this sort of prank, if that's what you mean."

"That thought never crossed my mind. But before my people get set up, I wanted to make sure that was the most likely scenario — that he was indeed in the cave." Jessica just nodded.

About that time, people, rescue workers began pouring into the site. There were scores of them, all dressed similarly and carrying heavy equipment. "Would you mind assembling your people together and introducing me? We are going to take over and oftentimes this news comes better from the project leader."

Jessica turned to Nava but before she could say anything Nava said, "I'm on it boss. I'll get Faysal and we'll get everyone assembled like before," and turned to walk away.

Jessica replied, "Give us just a few minutes. And thank you. Please save my husband."

"We will do our absolute best. You have my word. Eli emphasized how important this job is. If it is that important to *him,* it is that important to me. Don't worry. We're on it. I'll be back with you in a few moments."

About that time, Faysal walked to Jessica and said, "Hey Boss, can I speak with you for moment?"

"Is it good news?" Jessica asked.

"I am sorry, not so much good news. Not bad news either. What I mean is can I talk to you about the site for moment?" Jessica nodded and Faysal continued. "I know you want to honor your friend and continue his work, but I fear it is waste of time, people, and resources. Dr. Kenyon's death was horrible, and we do not know why he was using explosive. Now, this site is just too dangerous. It just caves in on its own now. I know you do not have too much experience at excavating, but I have been doing this work all my life. This place is too dangerous. Not only that, the caves are empty. I have been walking in them many times. There is nothing in them. Empty passageways that lead nowhere. I do not want see anyone else get hurt for no reason."

A group of hot, tired, sweaty people had made its way to where Faysal and Jessica were talking, and several members of the group were nodding in agreement with what Faysal was saying to her. As people were being taken off the assembly line, more and more were making their way to the area outside of the command center tent.

Another man in the group, barely older than a teenager remarked, "We ones take risks. For what? So, rocks can crush? No thanks you. It no safe. I go home."

Jessica started to say something just as a third, older man started speaking. Jessica continued to talk as the man continued to talk so that no one could understand either. The man became visibly angry at Jessica, raised his voice, and stepped towards her. Faysal stepped in between them and, patting the air, tried to calm the man. That's when Jessica noticed that Faysal only had three fingers on his right hand.

Jessica turned to Faysal and asked him to assemble the entire group, turned and walked to the spot she had used earlier as her point of communication. Nava, making her way up the hill, saw what was going on and following Faysal's lead, started assembling the Hebrew and English speakers as well.

Jessica addressed the group. "Team, what we have here is a momentary setback to our work. But right now, my highest priority is finding my husband. I am *so thankful* for your rescue efforts. We assume he has been trapped in the cave-in." Jessica paused long enough for Nava and Faysal to interpret. She continued, "The emergency response team is here now, and this is Doron. He is the team leader. Please give him your complete cooperation. They will be taking over the rescue of my husband. If it is not absolutely necessary, don't get into the damaged area and please give the rescue team room to work." Again, she paused and let the others interpret. "We will make a more informed decision about the future of this site when we have more information and after my husband has been found. Anyone who wants to leave for the day has my permission. Please check out with Faysal as you go."

Jessica made her way back into the command center tent and sat down in a chair. She put her elbows on the table, held her head in her hands and contemplated calling Eli again. Besides hearing Matt's voice, Eli's was the only other one she wanted to hear. "Lord, I am relying on you. I can't do this alone and I know I don't have to. I am relying on you. You said you would never leave nor forsake me."[89]

She picked up the phone and dialed Matt's number again. Four rings and his voicemail, just like before. She started preparing herself for a long day ahead.

Before she had a chance to put the phone away, it rang again, the familiar klaxon tone she had set so that she would be able to hear it over the digging sounds at an excavation site. Hurriedly looking at the caller ID, Jessica realized it was her friend Eli calling her back. "Hey Eli," she said. "Thank you for calling me again. I needed to hear a familiar voice."

"Matthew hasn't turned up?"

"Not yet, but your team has. Thank you." she replied

"You're welcome sweet girl. I'm sorry to do it, but I need to ask you another serious question. Do you think, do you have any reason to

---

[89] Reference Hebrews 13:5

suspect foul play? Dr. Kenyon was killed in an explosion, was this the same thing? Was there an explosion? Give me some details. Start at the beginning."

Jessica responded, "No… it was nothing like what I imagine Dr. Kenyon's explosion was like. Matt told me he heard that explosion from blocks away — he was outside the Jaffa Gate, close by when it happened. Today, there was no explosion at all that I could tell. We had all met at the entrance to the site, so we were a good distance away. I was making my formal introductions, telling them we would continue the work of our friend when I heard a rumbling noise. I was already facing the cave and saw it just… crumbling. It started at the cave entrance and made its way along the length of the cave system, just crumbling under the weight of the hillside above it. There was no explosion that I could see or hear. Everyone just thinks the place isn't safe. My foreman wants me to abandon any more work on the place. It looked just like I imagine a cave-in would look like. It wasn't until much later that I even realized Matt wasn't around."

"Sweet girl. I'm sorry this has happened. I will be there as soon as possible. Sit tight. My people know what they are doing." And with that, Eli was gone again.

Faysal and Wally stepped into the tent and said, "Most everyone has gone home. We stay with you all night if needed." Faysal paused and then almost apologetically said, "I hope you will at least *consider* abandoning this project. Please tell your superiors. There is nothing to find here. Just more death." Faysal realized what he said and tried to back up from it. "No, no, no — not your husband. This place is the death of dreams. There is nothing here to find. I don't want anyone else to get hurt."

CHAPTER 16

There weren't many places he could look, but Matt couldn't find his cell phone. It was gone. It had been in his hand when he was running in the dark and now it had disappeared. Fighting panic, he dug around in his cross-body sling bag and found the cheap spare, the pay-as-you-go phone that he had been carrying for times just like this. He pressed the green button to turn it on and watched the screen, waiting for the phone to connect to the cellular network.

He waited.

And waited.

And waited.

The battery icon dropped down from 63% to 62%. Matt pressed the red button to turn the phone off.

"I must be so far underground that I don't have cell service. How long has it been since I charged this thing? Lord, I wish I could let Jessica know that I'm ok." Matt said. Then something unusual happened. From deep inside him words bubbled up.

For God so loved the world… For God so loved the world… For God so loved the world…

The phrase came to Matt and repeated and repeated. It lodged itself in his brain. Matt was trying not to panic but took a moment to rehearse the scripture from the book of John. "For God so loved the world that he gave his only Son, that whosoever believed in Him would not perish but have everlasting life."[90] But it was the opening phrase that stuck with Matt, *For God so loved the world... For God so loved the world...* and then a second phrase came to Matt, one that he had not thought about since childhood.

His banner over me is love... His banner over me is love... His banner over me is love...

Matt recognized the second phrase as another verse from the Bible, this time in the book Song of Solomon.[91] He realized that God was trying to tell him something. *God loves me so much that He sent Jesus, and His banner, His protection over me is His love!* Matt knew that he was going to have enough time to get out of the predicament he was currently in.

Something changed inside of Matt.

He had an awareness of God's love for him. It was like he was clothed in the love of God, like a warm winter coat had been placed on his shoulders, wrapping him, surrounding him, enveloping him.

"I am called to be an ambassador of God's love," Matt said aloud, surprising himself. "Where did that come from?"

All of a sudden and out of nowhere, Matt began to laugh. He laughed a hearty, belly laugh. His head throbbed at the sound and the effort, but it just continued. It welled up from deep within his heart. He laughed and laughed and laughed. It was a Supernatural laugh, a physical expression of an inward witness that he was going to make it out of this situation, alive.

"Well, ok then. Let's get out of here." Matt said to himself as he was wiping a laughter tear off his cheek. Again, his flashlight blinked and went dim. Matt decided to preserve the batteries and turned the flashlight off and was again engulfed in darkness. "I don't need any light to see that I need to slide down towards my feet." He put the cheap, spare phone and the flashlight in his bag and zipped it closed.

---

[90] John 3:16

[91] Reference Song of Solomon 2:4

Matt continued the process of inching his way towards the opening where his feet were. The soles of his tennis shoes had a slight lip to them, and he was able to use his heels to pull his body in that direction. Because the large rock above him was so close to his body, he couldn't raise his knees very high, but slowly, inch by inch, minute by minute, Matt made his way towards the exit of his cocoon. Matt had no sense of time. He had no idea how long he had been in the cave and no idea how long it would take him to make his way out of this spot.

The large slab above him shuttered again with a loud crack and dust and debris rained down on him, but he also heard it hitting the floor where his head had once been. He was making progress, but the cracking noise spurred him on and gave him another boost of adrenaline. Inch by inch by inch by inch, Matt scraped his way towards the freedom of his feet.

After what seemed like hours, but might have been only minutes, Matt sensed that he was past where his waist had been. The air seemed different, a degree cooler, maybe. He sensed that he had a little more freedom to move. He put his hand up and felt the slab above his head, further away than it had been previously. He moved his hands to his side, spreading them out like they were wings and found that he had much more room. His feet were still touching something solid, but he was able to move his arms and shoulders and pull himself more toward his feet until he was curled up in a ball. Finally, he reached in his bag and pulled out his flashlight to try and understand his surroundings better.

He clicked the light on, and it illuminated the situation. The large slab that Matt had been staring at in front of his face had been part of the ceiling of the hallway before the collapse. It had fallen and the part that had been by his head rested on the floor of the cave. The opposite end of the slab had come to rest on the wall at the 'end' of the hallway that Matt was in. It basically formed a right triangle with the ceiling slab that Matt had been lying under acting as the hypotenuse. Matt must have run full speed into the end of the hallway, which would explain his blood-crusted forehead, and fallen, hitting the back of his head on the floor, which would explain the blood-crusted crown of his head.

Much like hallway number three had come to an end with a choice to make — turn left or turn right — this hallway did the same. Both exits looked like they were at ninety-degree angles to the place where Matt was lying. He had another choice to make, turn left or turn right? He had no way of knowing which way to go. The slab above him gave another loud crack and Matt rolled to his right just as the hallway imploded in on itself. The large slab surrendered to the weight of the hillside above it. Matt scrambled away from the carnage, coughing in the dust cloud that engulfed him.

"Thank you, Lord, for your protection! Now what?" Matt asked more to himself than to the Lord, but the Lord answered him in the form of a song. It was a song that Matt had heard before, one that his father would play on their home stereo when he was a kid. The song was titled, *Whom Have I?* and the name of the band was *Lamb*. But it was the verse they sang about that returned to Matt now. It was found in Psalm 73. "Nevertheless I am continually with You; You have taken hold of my right hand."[92] Matt knew that as long as he was depending on God and His help, that God would lead him, like He was holding Matt's right hand. It was a comfort to Matt; his fear and panic being replaced with God's peace, and he could almost *feel* God's love radiating towards him.

The new hallway that Matt found himself in seemed almost completely intact, but the structure of this hallway was different. Matt was able to stand up. Again, his flashlight blinked and went dim. Matt slapped it in his free hand to try and get the light to shine brighter. When it did, Matt saw something different than he had experienced in the other hallways up to this point. First, while the other hallways had been dug out of the ground, out of the Earth like an abandoned mine, this hallway seemed like it was carved out of rock. There were no cross beams holding the ceiling up. It was like someone had taken a jackhammer to the limestone bedrock of the city and cut a path through it. It was narrow and

---

[92] Psalm 73:23 (King James Version)

cold and contained rough chisel marks all along walls, ceiling, and floor the length of the hallway. But there was something else. The hallway was roughly one hundred yards long and as Matt took a few steps forward, he saw that there were openings all along this hallway, matching entrance ways across from each other. Moving towards the first set of openings that stood opposite each other, Matt flashed his light in the first opening and then again in the second. He saw long hallways in each direction, both had multiple openings in them. Staying in his original hallway, Matt moved forward a few feet to the second set of openings. This set of openings was different. The one on the left-hand side was a simple room and across the hallway was another long passageway. Matt again moved forward to the third set of openings. He looked to the one on the right-hand side and saw there was another set of rooms and then across the hallway was another long passageway that had openings the length of it. The hallway where he currently stood contained eight or nine openings on either side. As he investigated the different hallways, rooms and openings, he saw many were wide open, but many were blocked by rubble, either just partially or almost completely.

Matt realized he was in a labyrinth, but for some reason, he was at peace. It was a supernatural peace, something outside of the ordinary hope he would normally carry as an optimist. The more Matt looked to God, the more at peace he was. This was something that welled up from deep within him... somehow. A scripture came back to his memory, a scripture from the book of Isaiah. "You keep him in perfect peace whose mind is stayed on You, because he trusts in You."[93]

"Where do I start? Which path do I take?" Matt said aloud. "Too bad I don't have a spool of thread in my man-purse. I could tie one end off and then follow it all the way back here if I came to a dead end."

The amount of time and manpower put into carving this cave was unimaginable. And for what reason? Why would these people go through the process of carving out these passageways that seemingly

---

[93] Isaiah 26:3 (King James Version)

lead to nowhere? And who were they? Who did this? Matt was beginning to understand why people were drawn to archaeology as a profession. They might get to answer some or all of those types of questions. They might get to solve the mystery of it.

Matt looked down at his feet while he was trying to figure out his next step and noticed something on the floor. It looked like a coffee cup handle that had broken off the cup, but it was old. Really, really old. It was brown in color and looked like it had broken off of a jug or something. This was the *first* find in this cave system. He knew that this would be important to the team, and he remembered the tongue-lashing that Jessica had given him. He knew he needed to do two things: collect the sample and be able to tell the team where he found it. Matt pulled out one of the zip-top bags that Faysal had given him, picked up the handle, and carefully placed it in the bag. But how would he mark the spot where he found it? Matt was thinking about this as he put the zip-top bag in his cross-body sling bag. Matt saw something in his sling bag that led him to an idea. The idea was to mark the spot where he found the jug handle with a few pieces of his new favorite candy, *Wildberry Skittles*, the ones in the light purple bag. He opened one of the new bags he was carrying, pulled out a handful of the candy bites, separated all the bright green ones out to mark the spot of the find and then put the remaining candies in his mouth. A large smile crossed his face when a second idea formed in his mind.

"Who needs a spool of thread when you are carrying *Wildberry Skittles?* I'll just *Skittle* myself out of here, *Hansel and Gretel* style!"

Matt moved forward, intending to start at the far end of the tunnel, the opposite end of the tunnel from where he entered… but there was… something… He couldn't explain it, but he just knew, he shouldn't start at that end of the tunnel. It was a strong *stop*. Perhaps this was the Lord steering him towards an exit. Matt backtracked and started his exploration at the first doorway from where he entered the tunnel. "Seems as good as any place to start," Matt whispered. "Let's do it!"

CHAPTER 17

J essica realized that she was an unwilling participant in a waiting game. Not much had changed in the hours since the cave-in had occurred, outside of her dig team being replaced by the professional rescue squad. She couldn't do anything to make a difference; she wasn't strong enough physically to move dirt and rocks, wasn't trained enough to use some of the machinery that the emergency response team was using, wasn't at peace enough to go home. She was just... there.

Wally and Faysal had stayed with Jessica, trying to keep her spirits high. As a way to pass the time, Faysal had suggested that the group of three remaining team members still on site, try to sift through the earth that was being removed to see if there were any artifacts to be found. Sifting dirt is one of the activities that occurs on almost every archaeological site, everywhere, whether it is a cave or a traditional excavation site. It can be found on every site, in every country, directed by any nationality team leader. The process involves putting all dirt recovered from the excavation through a mesh wire screen. The mesh wire screen, usually contained in some sort of frame, is held between two of the dig team members. A third team member takes a bucket of dirt and slowly pours it onto the screen. As the two team members hold the frame and shake the screen, the dirt and fine particles pass through the mesh and any larger rocks, coins, pottery, bones or other larger items remain on the screen. It is labor intensive and mindless, but it was something to occupy their time.

Over and over, Wally scooped buckets of dirt and dumped them on the sifting frame. Over and over, the dirt was sifted through the mesh. Over and over, the frame was empty of anything important or useful. For hours the process was repeated. Dump, sift, nothing. Dump, sift, nothing. They swapped places and repeated the process. Faysal or Jessica dumped dirt, the other two team members sifted and came up with nothing. Over and over and over and over. Nothing and nothing and nothing and nothing.

It is a very important job, but it is not unusual to go hours without finding anything while sifting dirt, which is why team leaders usually assign interns or volunteers to do the job. However, at this excavation site, outside of the cave, they found coins very often. They found pottery pieces very often. It was completely unusual to go this long without sifting some sort of find. To his credit, Faysal realized that what was meant to occupy their time and give them a *win*, had now turned into bucket load after bucket load of defeat, laughing in their faces. It had become a reflection of what was happening with the emergency response team — sorting through debris and finding nothing — but the response team was not emotionally invested, and it did not affect them the way it seemed to be affecting his new boss. So, Faysal suggested a break for some food. It was late afternoon, and no one had eaten all day.

Jessica realized that everyone needed a break, needed to get away for a few minutes, needed a moment to refocus. She hated to leave but realized it might be a long night. "Let me go tell Doron that we are going to get some food and give him my cell number in case they need me for anything. After that we can go, but let's go someplace close, if that's ok," Jessica said. Faysal nodded and said something to Wally in Arabic. Wally smiled and replied to Faysal.

"He said he knows a great place that is close enough to walk to and if you haven't had Shakshuka for an evening meal your mouth is about to be in paradise! How does that sound?"[94] Faysal asked.

---

[94] Lisa Bryan, "Shakshuka," DOWNSHIFTOLOGY, December 19, 2018, https://downshiftology.com/recipes/shakshuka/

Jessica replied, "I don't know what shakshuka is, but I'm not a particularly picky eater. That's Matt. I swear, he has the tastebuds of a three-year-old."

Faysal chuckled and said, "Shakshuka is a combination of tomatoes, onions, garlic, spices and gently poached eggs. It will fill you up and stay with you for while so you not hungry soon after."

"That's fine," Jessica said as she turned to walk towards where Doron was standing. "I'll be with you in just a minute."

True to her word, Jessica returned quickly and the three of them walked to a nearby place to get some food. The chain had a storefront that was only large enough to take orders, but it had a few tables outside on the sidewalk where they could eat their meal. The three of them ordered their meals and found a place to sit. Jessica felt bad that Wally couldn't join in the conversation held mostly in English, but he was cheerful, kept a smile on his face most of the day and particularly during the meal. Faysal did a decent job of interpreting and trying to keep him informed of the highlights of the conversation. Eventually, Wally said something to Faysal in Arabic, Faysal interpreted and everyone at the table realized the can of worms had been opened.

"Wally thinks it is strange and also telling that we have not found anything in our sifting today. Strange because we find so much normally and telling because he believes, like I do, the caves were empty," Faysal interpreted and then added "I think we should call off any further excavation. I think that the cave system has been completely destroyed and there is nothing to find."

"I understand *you* feel that way, but Dr. Kenyon thought there was something truly special to find in this cave system. We met for breakfast the morning he was killed, and he was so excited about it. He specifically asked me to join the team that day. Then, after his death, his wife told me his final wish was for me to take over the site. Why would he do that if everything was empty and there was nothing to be found?"

Faysal sat for a moment thinking and finally said, "How often did you see your friend in the days and weeks prior to his death?"

"Not very often, I'm afraid."

"In the months before his death, Dr. Kenyon had been acting different, unlike himself. There were signs of how do you say, 'olds-timers'? You know where people cannot remember things?"

"Alzheimer's disease," Jessica answered.

"Yes, yes. That. He was just different. Perhaps he was thinking of another place and time. Maybe he was just being hopeful that there might be something of value to close this chapter of his life. I do not know. All I know is that the caves are empty, we have proven it today with our sifting."

Jessica could feel her anger rising. The events of the day coupled with Faysal's determination to get her to call off the dig was almost more than she could bear in the weight of Matt's disappearance. Her voice rising to match her anger level, Jessica said forcefully, "I will not call this dig off, today. I will not make any decisions until my husband is found! Why is that so hard for you to understand?"

Even though he did not speak English, Wally could understand that Jessica was upset. He interrupted, said something in Arabic to Faysal, stood up and walked off. Jessica looked back to Faysal questioningly. Faysal said, "Wally is going to relieve himself. He will return in a few moments."

Faysal used his fork to move the scraps of food on his plate around a little when he heard the klaxon sound of Jessica's phone ringing. "Is it your husband?" Faysal asked expectantly.

"No, it's my friend who put together the rescue team. I need to take this." Jessica answered. "Hello, Eli. Are you in the country?"

About the same time that Eli started answering Jessica's question, Faysal's cell phone rang in his pocket. Not his normal cell phone. It was a cheap phone he had been instructed to carry at all times. He pulled it out of his pocket, pointed to it and stepped away from the table so that he could carry on a conversation without anyone overhearing it.

"Alhimaya, you have done well. You have protected the hidden place and it will remain hidden. It must remain hidden forever," the heavily

123

distorted voice said over the cheap speaker at his ear. "If the new leader will not give up the dig, if the new leader reopens the site, the new leader must die. We will be back in touch within the week. Start making your plans now." Faysal started to argue, but the person on the other end of the call ended it before he could speak. He stopped walking and dropped his head. He hated this.

By the time Faysal turned and walked back to their table, Wally was sitting, waiting for him to return and waiting for Jessica to finish her call, unaware of whom either of them had been talking with. Faysal sat down and said to Wally in Arabic "Jessica was talking to the man who had coordinated the rescue team. She is not crying, so he is either alive or unfound. I do not know which. I will let you know what she says."

"Thank you for letting me know, Eli. We will be back on site in a few minutes," Jessica said as she was wrapping up her call. "I'll talk to Doron when I get there. See you in a little while." Pulling the phone away from her ear, Jessica pushed the red *End Call* button on her cell phone and looked up to an expectant Faysal and Wally.

Jessica said, "While Doron and his team were working to clear the site, there was another cave in, deep in the slope of the mountain. It was in the same area as our site, so they think it was connected, but it was distant from where they are currently working. They do not know if they created it or if it was just a byproduct of what has already happened. So far, there is no sign of my husband."

Faysal nodded and interpreted for Wally. Wally responded in Arabic and Faysal interpreted for Jessica. He says, "Your husband is strong and will survive. We should get back to the site so you can see him when he shows up." Wally smiled at Jessica as Jessica did her best to hold back the tears and return his smile.

The three of them stood up and started back towards the excavation site.

CHAPTER 18

Matt had been walking, crawling, scraping in and out of rooms and hallways for so long, his body hurt. Not just the scrapes on his arms, legs, stomach and back, but he was sore. His head still pounded. This had taken effort. And he was thirsty. And hungry. It was a high stress environment. The labyrinth was like a tree, each opening in a hallway was like a new branch. Each branch had branches and those branches had branches. And most resulted in a dead end. It was a maze. Whoever had designed and constructed this cave system had done it to keep any uninvited visitors completely confused.

Matt's flashlight was all but dead, barely giving any light when he clicked it on. What felt like hours earlier, he had swapped to his cheap cell phone's flashlight app, but because the battery wasn't fully charged, the battery on it was soon completely depleted as well. So, he was back to using his flashlight, as sparingly as possible. Every ten feet or so, he dropped a *Skittle* on the left-hand side of the hallway he was in.

As Matt was trying to *Skittle* his way out, *Hansel and Gretel* style, he realized early on that he would sometimes need to backtrack in order to move forward. He would come up on the small candies but didn't know the direction he had been walking. Had he just moved in a circle? Was he backtracking? Was the candy following a trail towards him or away from him? That's when he started putting the candies along the left-hand side of the wall. That way, he would always know which direction he had been walking. The candies had a shiny coating that reflected the light from his flashlight pretty well, so he could shine his light down a hallway and quickly determine if he had already tried to find a way of escape through that path.

Matt stepped into a new hallway, one that looked just like the hundreds he had already stepped into. He clicked on the flashlight and in the dim light it provided, he saw that it wasn't exactly a hallway. It was a room and inside there was a stack of rocks that blocked something. Matt went over to the blockage and realized that these rocks were intentionally stacked in this location. These were cut stones, chiseled rocks. These weren't scraps and hadn't just fallen here. They had been placed, stacked one on top of another, intentionally blocking something. Everywhere else that there had been rocks, they were haphazard, they were obviously debris from construction or minor cave-ins. This was different.

Matt's hopes soared. Maybe this was another exit. Perhaps whoever had carved this cave had blocked this entrance, this exit, and relied solely on the entrance of the cave where Matt had entered. Perhaps this was his way out. Matt clicked his flashlight off and started removing rocks in the dark. It wasn't hard to do in the dark and he was used to it by now. The room was empty except for the stack of rocks, so Matt pulled one from the top and threw it in the opposite corner, away from the entryway he had used to come into the room. Over and over, Matt repeated the process. Slowly, the blockage moved from above his head, down to chest height. He clicked his flashlight on and realized the other side had been closed up from that side as well.

"This has to be the way out!" Matt said to himself. "Nobody stacks rocks on both sides of a doorway, unless it is an entry or exit point!" The adrenaline rush was just what Matt needed. He clicked the flashlight off again and started pushing rocks that were stacked on the other side of the doorway, so that they fell away from him. Matt's arms burned with fatigue, but he was so close to freedom, he pressed onward. After a short while of intense labor, Matt clicked on his flashlight again. The light didn't come on. Matt beat it against his leg, clicked it on and off and on and off and on and off and on again. The light never turned back on. The batteries were dead. Matt felt the stacked rocks on his side of the entryway that were just below chest level. He felt the stones that were still stacked on the opposite side of the doorway, they were just above his chest level, but he could stick his arms through the opening and there was no blockage. Matt decided to squeeze through the opening, and hopefully, to his freedom.

Matt squeezed into and through the entryway and slid painfully down the stacks of rocks until he came to rest somewhere at the bottom, lying on his stomach. When he opened his eyes there was an intense light burning into them, the brightest light he had ever seen. Matt couldn't explain it, but he *heard* a scripture inside of himself. It was a scripture he had read many times, but now, it was like someone was *saying* it, *speaking* it to him, inside of his own head, *"Then spake Jesus again unto them, saying, I am the light of the world: he that followeth me shall not walk in darkness, but shall have the light of life."*[95]

The light was blinding to Matt, having been in complete darkness just moments earlier. He rolled over, trying to get into a sitting position so that he could stand, and that's when he realized that his flashlight had fallen out of his hand, and now, somehow was shining full strength, directly into his eyes. "How in the world…?" Matt mumbled. He grabbed the flashlight and began looking around the small, small room.

It was not an exit.

Matt's hopes were crushed. He stood up, picked up the flashlight and when he turned it so that it wasn't shining directly in his eyes, that's when he saw the man standing there facing him, holding a sword. It startled Matt so badly that he screamed and dropped the flashlight. It banged down the stacked rocks and came to rest on the floor again and Matt better understood what he was looking at. It was a corpse. The man must have sealed himself in the room as someone or something sealed him in from the other side. "Who would do that?" Matt asked aloud.

---

[95] John 8:12 (King James Version)

The corpse was obviously old, Matt couldn't tell how old or from what time period, but the guy was wearing a long tunic which could have been white at one point, a belt made of leather and sandals. His body was incredibly well preserved. Again, Matt remembered that Jerusalem is on the outer edges of the desert, and it does not get much rain and inside the cave it is almost a perfectly controlled climate. This was a mummy. When the man died, there wasn't enough room for him to lie down, and must have died leaning against the stones, sword in hand. Matt took a moment to look at the mummy and then shone his light around the room. It was small, but it was also full. There was an aura to it, almost like the room had a presence. There were several stacks of cut stones that looked like they intentionally buried different things, like someone was trying to hide or protect something. It gave the already small room a claustrophobic feel. On a small ledge in the back of the room there was a stone box, maybe four feet wide, three feet tall and three feet deep. The lid was at Matt's eye level and broken in two. From what he could tell, it looked like someone had given it a giant Karate chop, breaking the stone in the middle and leaving two pieces. But that wasn't what grabbed Matt's attention. What grabbed Matt's attention was the black substance that was on the box and the wall behind the box. The dried substance had something to it that reflected the light of Matt's flashlight. It was strange. It reminded him of the reflective material that was made to help joggers who ran in the evening be more visible, but this was very, very old and dried and cracked. It wasn't material either. It was something... else. Dried liquid? Algae? Ancient paint? And the dark material itself didn't seem to be reflecting the light. It was some-thing *within it,* inside the substance that was reflecting the light, like it had glitter in it or metal flakes or something. How could something black, have anything that reflected light? It was very, *very* unusual.

Matt looked closer and saw that the dark stain was very specific and only in certain places. It looked like it started at the ceiling, made its way down the back wall and came to rest on the now broken lid of the box. Possibly, more of the black substance had dripped directly onto the lid, but at least some of it had trickled down the back wall. All of it contained elements that reflected the light. It was surreal. Because of the height of the ledge, and how full the room was, Matt decided it would take too much effort to see what was in the box right now. He had other things to think about and he could investigate that with Jessica, later. But Matt knew this room and its contents were special and made a mental note to be sure to tell Jessica about it.

As Matt turned to leave the room, he had a thought. He had watched enough science type shows that he knew he wanted to collect a sample of the black substance to have it tested at the 'nearest laboratory.' At least that's what they would do on one of those crime-scene investigation cop shows. Matt pulled out a zip-top bag and his new, Swiss Army pocketknife from his cross-body bag. To avoid cross-contamination, Matt used the knife to scrape some of the black substance into the zip-top bag. He wasn't sure how much he needed, so he collected what he would call, scientifically speaking, a *bunch* of it. He put the zip-top bag and his knife back into his sling bag and zipped it up. Then he decided to get out of the one room in the whole place that contained a dead man.

Matt pushed the stones out into the larger room, creating a much more manageable opening to move through. When he was back out into the open room, that's when it struck him — Matt realized that his flashlight was shining very bright, like the batteries had been recharged, somehow. Again, the same scripture came back to him. *"Then spake Jesus again unto them, saying, I am the light of the world:* **he that followeth me shall not walk in darkness, but shall have the light of life."**[96] And as the verse welled up from within him, a cool breeze started blowing.

"There's something going on here..." Matt whispered. "Thank you, Lord, for your help." Matt's attention began to focus on the breeze. Where was it coming from? Matt hadn't felt fresh air in hours. The air had been stale and unmoving. Until now.

---

[96] John 8:12 (King James Version)

Another scripture welled up inside of Matt. *"It is his voice that echoes in the thunder of the storm clouds. He causes mist to rise upon the earth; he sends the lightning and brings the rain, and **from his treasuries he brings the wind."*[97]**

It dawned on Matt that the breeze was blowing from the room he had just left. Matt also realized that was an impossibility. It was a closed room. Sealed. One way in. One way out. How could there be a breeze flowing *out of* that room? He put his hand in the opening he had cleared, and he could feel the breeze flowing out of the room. Then Matt knew. These are miracles that God was performing in Matt's life — the flashlight working, the light of life — the breeze, flowing from His treasuries. It was God fulfilling His Word.

Matt decided to follow the breeze. It was steady and it was leading. He just knew, instinctively, that he should follow it. Matt decided he would trust this as God's intervention. He didn't know if the breeze would lead him anywhere, but he stepped out in faith to follow it. Trusting God to guide his footsteps. As Matt made this decision, another scripture came to mind, *The steps of a good man are ordered by the Lord: and he delighteth in his way.*[98] Matt smiled as he began walking because he knew God was showing him the steps, the path to walk. Again, he had an overwhelming sense of God's love.

Matt stepped out of the slightly larger room and stood still a moment until he could find which way the wind was blowing. The breeze was flowing from his left to his right and so he turned to his right and started following it. He came to an intersection, a T-junction, where he had to again turn ninety degrees left or ninety degrees right.

He could feel the breeze blowing from behind him, gently urging him forward. He stepped into the right hallway and noticed it was dry, stale, stagnant air. He stepped back and into the left chamber and felt the still, small breeze nudging him forward. Over and over this process

---

[97] Jeremiah 10:13 (The Living Bible)

[98] Psalm 37:23 (King James Version)

repeated; Matt doing his best to follow the breeze, taking a step, making sure it was the correct path and continuing if it was. If Matt ever got out of the flow, as soon as he realized it, he patiently made his way back to where the breeze could lead him. His flashlight never dimmed.

Matt understood something. God was not only helping him, leading him in this time of trouble, but God was teaching him something. This was the perfect *natural* example of something that was truly **supernatural**. Hearing the voice of the Lord, and following His leading was very much what Matt was experiencing now. God used simple nudges, a small voice, a velvety feeling or as one preacher Matt listened to would put it, a green light or a red light, but on the inside. God rarely shouts, instead He uses simple nudges to guide, just like the breeze that was leading Matt now. Spiritually, if Matt ever got out of the flow of where God was leading him, he just took a moment to reset, find the flow and follow where God was leading him.

Just like now.

CHAPTER 19

As Jessica, Faysal, and Wally made their way back to the excavation site, Jessica was struck by the changes that had been made since she had slipped away for dinner. The rescue team had split in two. One group of workers were in the same general area they had been in when Jessica and her team had left, just further along the path they were working. The other team had moved forward and were just beginning to start work at the far end, where the additional cave-in had occurred. It looked as if the two groups would be working at opposite ends, but moving towards each other, hoping to meet somewhere in the middle. To Jessica's profound relief, it looked like they were being extremely cautious and extremely thorough.

While Faysal and Wally waited in the headquarters tent, Jessica made her way to where the team was working, trying to find and hopefully rescue Matt. Doron saw Jessica coming and made his way down the slope of the hill to meet her.

"Can you fill me in on what has happened?" Jessica asked.

"Yes. As you can see, we have split the team into two parts. Just beyond where the second team is now working, there was a slight rumble and then a stretch of about 10 feet of what I guess was more tunnel, caved in. We were nowhere near it, so everyone is safe, but we decided to investigate it and work our way back together. The thinking is we can clear more areas in this fashion. The second team is just now starting to work. So far, we have found nothing out of the ordinary and no sign of your husband, yet, which I consider a very good thing!"

"I hope you're right, Doron. I hope he's only trapped in a safe place and hasn't been crushed. Maybe it is good news that we haven't found any signs of him." Jessica knew she was grasping at straws, but she was willing to grasp at anything at this point.

Doron said, "Why don't you just go on home? It has been a long day and there is still a lot of ground for us to cover. I will call the moment we find anything. I promise."

Jessica started to protest but realized that what Doron was telling her was probably the smart thing to do. "I'm going to wait for Eli to get here and after I see him, I will go home. I appreciate your thoughtfulness as you are speaking with me," Jessica said. She recognized that Doron was trying to help, trying to be thoughtful, but also trying not to give her false hope. It was a delicate balance that Doron was walking well, most likely from years of experience.

Jessica made her way back to the command center tent and to her complete surprise, discovered Eli in deep conversation with Faysal. The two men were nodding and obviously in agreement about whatever they were talking about. Wally was sitting at a table playing on his phone. When Jessica saw Eli, all of her emotions rushed to the surface, and she was unable to contain them. She started crying as Eli hugged her and he held her like a father would hold his daughter. That was the type of relationship they had.

"I'm so glad you're finally here," Jessica said as she buried her head in the older man's chest.

"Me too, Jessica," Eli replied.

After a few moments, Jessica composed herself and stepped back. Trying to move the attention away from her, Jessica asked "What were you guys talking about?" to both Faysal and Eli.

Eli nodded to Faysal and said, "I suggested to your foreman that all further excavation at this site be discontinued. It is much too dangerous and not worth the potential for injury or loss of life. Your foreman agreed."

Jessica was ready to explode. She turned toward Faysal, pointed her finger right in his chest, and shouted "How dare you!?"

But before Faysal could reply, Eli gently took Jessica's hand and said "No, no. This was my decision. He only confirmed what I was thinking. I brought it up to him. Trust me, sweet girl. Let's get you home. It's been a long day."

Jessica had been the head of the excavation for exactly one workday and now she was being removed from office. Impeached. Through no fault of her own it was over. Her shoulders slumped slightly, Jessica replied, "I trust you, Eli. Let me gather my things and then we'll go back to my apartment." She turned to grab her belongings, but almost as if she remembered something turned back to Faysal and said, "I apologize for shouting at you and I sincerely thank you for helping me today, for staying with me, for keeping my mind occupied, even when I was acting like a jerk to you. Please tell Wally 'Thank you' for me as well. I'll be in touch."

Walking past where Wally was sitting, Jessica put her hand on his arm and even though she knew he couldn't understand her, said "Thank you."

CHAPTER 20

Matt followed the still, small breeze for what seemed to be hours. His flashlight still burned bright, but inside the cave, time stood still. Matt had no way to gauge how slowly or quickly time was passing. Following the breeze was easy, but at the same time it was difficult. As long as Matt was moving in a straight line, it was easy, but when he needed to change direction, when he came to a place where a decision needed to be made, it wasn't always easy to follow the breeze. Several times Matt had taken a path, realized it was not the right way and had to get back to where he could feel the moving of the wind. But he was always able to find the breeze again. God loved him so much, he never held Matt's mistakes against him, never gave up on Matt, never punished him for missing the right path.

Matt was still amazed at how similar all of this was to his relationship with God and hearing God's voice. Matt knew God wants to give direction to those who call on Him, but the way He does it is usually through small nudges, like the breeze, not through shouts or hurricane strength winds. And God loves people so much that He is willing to wait on them if they make mistakes, make wrong turns, or get distracted along the way. He is there waiting on them when they decide to come back to Him.

Matt was thinking about these things as he came to another T-junction, a place to turn ninety degrees left or right. Matt took a step, felt that cool breeze and continued in the next hallway. That's when he saw it, the pile of green *Wild Berry Skittles*. The same pile of green *Wild*

Berry Skittles that he had left when he found the first artifact inside the cave. He had walked for hours and hours or maybe even days, Matt wasn't sure, but all of his walking had led him right back to where he started. Matt felt dejected, but then the wind blew, his hair ruffled, and Matt was reminded that regardless of the place or his situation, he was on the right path. It didn't matter what his circumstances looked like as long as he was following God's path. He decided to do what an ancient leader in Israel's history once did, a man named David — the same David from the story about the giant named Goliath.

In this particular instance, David was leading his army home from battle. They made their way back to the town where they lived only to find that it had been ransacked by an enemy and all of the women and children, David's wife and kids included, had been kidnapped. If anyone ever had a reason to feel dejected, if there was anyone who felt like he had missed God's direction, it was David. He was in the throes of depression. Even his army was ready to stone him. But then the Bible says that "David encouraged himself in the Lord his God."[99] And God answered David and told him to chase the enemy and everything that had been stolen and all of the people that had been kidnapped would be recovered without any loss.[100] And, that's what happened. David and his army pursued the enemy and recovered everything that had been taken.

Because David looked to the Lord, encouraged himself in the Lord, and sought-after God's direction throughout his life, God was able to bless him and lead him to victory in every area of his life. And in time, David became one of Israel's greatest warriors and strongest kings.

Matt began whispering, quoting a Psalm of David, "Lord, You're as real to me as *bedrock* beneath my feet, like a castle on a cliff, my forever firm fortress, my *mountain of hiding*, my *pathway of escape*, my *tower of rescue where none can reach me*. My secret strength and shield around me, you are salvation's ray of brightness shining on the hillside, always

---

[99] 1 Samuel 30:6 (King James Version)

[100] 1 Samuel 30:8 (King James Version)

the champion of my cause. All I need to do is to call to you, singing to you, the praiseworthy God. When I do, I'm safe and sound in you."[101] Matt felt his spirits lifting. "The joy of the Lord is my strength![102] You give me the strength to continue, because I am walking in your path." The cool breeze again blew, ruffling Matt's hair and flapping the sleeves of his t-shirt.

Matt took a moment to think about David. David became a mighty king and shining example of God to the world he lived in, but David wasn't perfect. David messed up several times, he committed adultery and then had someone killed, but when he turned back to God, God was always there waiting for him. There were real world consequences for David's actions, but God was faithful to him through it all.

Eventually, David became the first Israelite king who was able to conquer the walled city of Jerusalem, the city above where Matt was currently trapped. Rabbi Kaduri had told Matt about how David's heavily armed men took the defenders by surprise. Matt stood there in the cave trying to imagine the story recorded in the Old Testament.

The Jebusite city was much smaller than Jerusalem is today and was confined to the low ridge to the south of what is now the Temple Mount. Again, the Rabbi's words came back to Matt: *Jerusalem is on the edge of the Judean Desert and the city historically got its water supply from natural springs bubbling up from inside of caves.* When the Jebusites built their defenses, their walls around the city, they didn't include the Gihon Spring and left it outside the city walls. David's men learned that the Jebusites used a sloping tunnel to haul water up from the spring, into their fortified city on top of the ridge. David's men used that to their advantage. They climbed the tunnel to gain access to the city and once they were inside the city walls, it didn't take David's men long to gain control of the city. In time, the old Jebusite city became known as the City of David and the ridge on which it stood was renamed from Mount

---

[101] Psalm 18:2-3 (The Passion Translation)

[102] Nehemiah 8:10 (King James Version)

Moriah to Mount Zion. This was the same Mount Zion that Matt was currently trapped under… somewhere. Matt stood there in awe as a thought dawned on him: possibly, close to 3000 years ago, the legendary King David could have been somewhere in *these* very caves…

Matt took a step in the direction that he thought the breeze was leading him, but when he did, everything became stale. He took another step and another. There was no breeze and Matt was beginning to get a sickening feeling in his stomach. He realized he was walking a path that he had earlier felt the Lord was preventing him from following. He had received a *hard stop* and Matt had listened to it. Matt realized now that he was off the correct path, the one God had intended him to take. He took a moment to reset and whispered, "Lord, I didn't mean to stray from Your direction, show me where to go and I will follow You." Immediately, the breeze was gently blowing in his face, beckoning him to turn around and leading him to a different tunnel. "God, you are so cool. The minute I turn back to you, you are there waiting for me. I love it! It's always amazing to me to know that you're not mad at me, not trying to teach me a lesson. Thank you for being so awesome to me!"

Matt backtracked a few steps and then waited to find out which direction the Lord wanted him to go. He understood that he was back at the beginning, the place where he had originally entered this tunnel portion. He had originally taken the opening that was now on his right, but the breeze was blowing the opposite direction now, leading him to his left. As Matt started in this tunnel, he noticed that it began gently sloping downhill. Matt shined his flashlight down the hallway and noticed that it looked almost identical to every other hallway he had been in since he had become trapped. It was long, narrow, and chiseled out of the bedrock. There were openings along each side of the pathway, but this tunnel seemed much longer than any other he had been in. It was straight for several hundred yards, but then seemed to bend and curve rather than come to a perfect right angle like the other places he had been during this ordeal.

Matt followed the breeze as it followed this path. On each side of the hallway there were rooms and additional hallways, but the breeze never turned, never leading him into any of those rooms. Matt took his time, making sure he was following the correct path. He looked into each opening he passed. The further he walked, he realized that the rooms and hallways looked different — they started containing artifacts. Matt could see pottery, could see bones, could see things that glinted in the glow of his flashlight. The more he walked the more inhabited the place looked. It encouraged and excited Matt. He wanted to stop and explore, but his greatest desire was to let Jessica know he was alive and so he pressed onward. He walked for what seemed to be miles and miles.

The hallway Matt had been following came to an end in another T-junction, and that's when the unexpected happened. Matt's flashlight went dark. He turned it off and on, over and over, but nothing happened. He rapped it first on his leg and then on the wall, but the flashlight remained off. The breeze was still urging him forward, but he was forced to move in darkness. Matt stepped to the right, arms outstretched. The breeze was there nudging him forward. He took two steps and the hallway ended. He turned left and walked two more steps and that hallway ended. He turned left again, and that hallway ended in two steps, but looking to his right, Matt saw something he wouldn't have seen if his flashlight had been working. Matt saw a pinhole of light shining into the cave. Matt wanted to run to it, but there wasn't enough light in the cave to see if there were obstacles, so he took his time. When he finally made his way the few feet to the place where the light was shining, he realized that this was truly an exit. He could feel the heat from outside the cave opening. He pushed on whatever it was that was blocking the exit and after a few minutes of effort, it crumbled, and Matt came pouring out into a bright light. Shielding his eyes from the extreme difference in lighting, Matt saw that there were a group of men standing close by, staring at him. Until his eyes adjusted, Matt couldn't really make out anything about the men, except the way they were dressed — black suits and white shirts, small hats sitting on the crown of their heads, hats called yarmulkes and comfortable dress shoes, built for walking. *Tradition!*

"Matthew, is that you? Matthew, what are you doing here? Are you injured?" a concerned voice asked out of the darkness.

Matt took a step to his right and out of the blinding light. When he did, he saw the group of Jewish men and a familiar face in Rabbi Kaduri. Matt saw that where he had exited the cave was just beside a rock-built sign that had "City of David" written in Hebrew and English and the lights that had been shining in his eyes were the lights illuminating the sign. Somehow, Matt had made his way across the entire Old City of Jerusalem. The dig site where his misadventure had begun was located just north of the Old City and now, he was south of the Temple Mount, outside the Jewish Quarter.

Out of the direct light, seeing his friend and noting the concern in his voice, Matt answered "Yes, Rabbi. It's me. I will be fine. Do any of you have a phone I can borrow? I need to call my wife. She needs to know I am alive."

Chapter 21

It was well past midnight as Jessica and Eli sat in the small apartment. Eli, sitting in the chair beside the couch, was trying to stay awake for Jessica's sake and Jessica, lying on the couch, was trying to doze off for Eli's. Neither were having much success. The television was on in the background barely giving enough noise to keep the silence of the room from being deafening.

Suddenly, there was a man's deep voice, booming in the quiet of the room, "Captain, there's an incoming message!" Jessica and Eli both jumped, startled out of their semi-non-sleeping state.

Eli said, "I'm sorry, sweet girl. That is my text message notification. I turned it off of vibrate so I wouldn't miss anything tonight. This is a message from Doron, asking me to call him. Give me a minute."

"I need to use the restroom anyway. Take your time." Jessica had a bathroom just off of her bedroom and so she made her way there. She closed the door to the bedroom and finally changed out of her dirty excavation clothes and into her comfy Penn State sweatshirt and jeans and then made her way to the bathroom. She used the facilities, washed her hands and her face and did her best not to cry while looking at her reflection in the mirror. "Come on Matt," she whispered. "You've got to be alive. Come back to me." When she finally made her way out of the bedroom, Eli was finishing up his brief call with the leader of the rescue operation.

"How bad is it?" Jessica asked.

"What do you mean?"

"Well, if it had been good news, Doron would have called me. Either it is bad news, or they are shutting down for the evening, which is bad news, too. How bad is it?" Jessica asked again.

Bzzzz. Bzzzz. Bzzzz.

Eli said, "They are not shutting down, they will be working around the clock for the next number of days. They have actually had several teams working shifts today and this evening, but Doron is going home for the night. His replacement has arrived and been briefed on the situation." Eli paused.

"What are you not telling me, Eli?"

"They found something, but it doesn't mean *anything* so don't read anything into it."

Bzzzz. Bzzzz. Bzzzz.

Jessica's phone vibrated on the coffee table, but she didn't notice.

"What did they find, Eli?" Jessica was sitting on the edge of her seat and had an edge in her voice.

Eli responded in his soft manner, defusing the situation as much as possible. "They found a crimson red hat with a white script "A" on it. Jessica's shoulders slumped and tears formed in her eyes and rolled down her cheeks. Eli continued, "Doron wanted to know if Matt was wearing a hat when he disappeared. I told him about Matt's infatuation with the silly college sporting team."

Bzzzz. Bzzzz. Bzzzz.

Jessica's whole world was spinning. She simultaneously felt like she was going to throw up and pass out. The tears flowed down her cheeks. Eli did his best to comfort her, but there was little consolation that he could give. Jessica had lost all hope.

Jessica's phone had stopped vibrating, but then chimed as a new text message arrived. Jessica was in no shape to process new information, so Eli picked up her phone and without unlocking it, said, "Does this make any sense to you? The text says, *'You're not alone! I'm ok. Call this number back.'*"

"Give me the phone! Give me the phone! That's Matt, he's alive!!" Jessica screamed. She unlocked the phone and dialed the number. Matt answered on the first ring.

"Hello gorgeous. I hope you've had a better day than I have," Matt said.

"Oh my gosh!! Where are you? What happened to you? Are you ok?" Jessica screamed into the phone.

"I'm fine. Tired and hungry. I'll explain everything to you when I get home. I'm in the City of David, but I'll be home in a few minutes."

"I'll come and get you."

"No, just stay there. I'll be home soon. Just sit tight. I love you," Matt said as he hung up the phone.

Jessica sat back on the couch, all her fears relieved, all her worst nightmares gone, tears of joy now streaming down her face. Eli stared at her, pleading with his eyes for information, but remaining quiet while Jessica processed the information that she just learned. Finally, Jessica turned to Eli and said "He's alive and on his way here. He didn't give me any more information than that. He'll be here in a few minutes. Please stay with me until he gets here."

"Of course, I will! I have many questions to ask him," Eli said.

"I guess you can call Doron, or his replacement, and tell them they can call off the search, too," Jessica replied.

"No, I can't… and neither can you."

CHAPTER 22

M att was always warmed by the genuine goodness of people, and especially so living here in Israel. The Israeli people are special. Watching the news or social media leaves the impression that people, for the most part, move from one extreme to the next. Hate filled comments in social media posts, hate filled news segments, hate filled screams of a 'cancel culture' were things that the media wanted to focus on, but Matt knew that was only a small segment of society. More often than not, people wanted to do the right thing, wanted to be kind, wanted to help others in need. That was exactly what Matt was experiencing this evening.

Matt was on a bus, having been escorted there by Rabbi Kaduri and his associates. He wasn't allowed to pay the fare, one of the men in the group did it for him. They offered to escort him home, but Matt wouldn't have it. As people boarded the bus at the frequent stops made throughout the city, several of them paused to ask Matt if he was injured, or in pain, or if there was anything they could do to help him, anyone they could call for him. The genuine compassion of the unacquainted masses was truly amazing to him. But something was different about Matt, now. He was seeing things through different eyes. He was looking at each person through the eyes of God's love and it gave him a completely different perspective on everyone. It gave him an unexpected energy as he made his way home.

Matt disembarked at the bus stop closest to his apartment, walked the couple of blocks and with heavy legs, finally made his way upstairs.

Matt tried the handle, but the door was locked so he reached into his pocket and pulled out his keys. Jessica must have heard him and flung the door open. Matt could see the startled look on her face, a look questioning his appearance, but it only lasted a moment as she practically jumped into his arms, burying her head in his chest and kissing him repeatedly.

"Are you hurt? Are you ok? Come in and tell me what happened! Don't you *ever* do that to me again!!" Jessica exclaimed as she took Matt's hand and led him into the apartment.

Walking inside, Matt was a little shocked to see Eli, but extended his free hand to his old friend and said, "I probably shouldn't be surprised that you're here. You're such a good friend. It's good to see you, Eli." As the two men shook hands, Matt pulled Eli towards him and hugged him, a first in their relationship. Matt sat down on the couch, took off his battered shoes and stretched his legs onto the coffee table.

A little surprised by the hug, Eli said, "Ummm… It's even better to see you, Matthew. Tell us what happened. Don't leave out any details."

"Wait a second. I haven't had anything to eat or drink all day. I am *so* thirsty and *so* hungry. Give me a minute," Matt said, starting to get up.

"I'll get it, babe," Jessica said as she nimbly hopped up and headed to the kitchen. Over her shoulder she said, "Don't start until I get back."

Matt nodded and asked Eli, "When did you get here?"

"I got back in the country today and met Jessica at the site this evening. We came back to your apartment a couple of hours ago. She did not want to leave the rescue operation, but there was not anything we could add. The workers know how to get in touch with us, so we came back here. By the way, they found your hat. I doubt it looks much better than you do right now," Eli said with a smile.

"Did you come back to the country just to be with Jessica or is there something else going on?" Matt asked.

But before Eli could answer, Jessica came back with a glass full of sparkling water, a plate with a peanut butter and jelly sandwich on it with some chips on the side, handed it to Matt and sat down next to him. "Now, tell me everything, every single detail since you disappeared. Start at 'I went into the cave that I wasn't supposed to go in' and finish with 'My wonderful wife handed me a sandwich.'"

Matt took a huge bite of the sandwich and fighting through the peanut butter stickiness said, "Well, yes, I went into the cave that I wasn't supposed to go in, but I was only going to step barely inside, just to get a quick look at it. There really wasn't much to it. Just a narrow man-made path that zigzagged around a couple times. I only walked a few paces so that I could see how dark it was. I was using my phone's flashlight app and turned it off and looked back at where I had entered the cave. That's when I noticed the little flashing lights on the cross beams supporting the roof of the cave. Before I knew what was happening, the cave was collapsing around me. I was running for my life in the dark. Then, the next thing I remember I was lying on the ground, waking up."

Eli and Jessica sat there looking at each other, seemingly speechless about what they had just heard. "Tell me about the blinking lights, Matthew," Eli said.

Matt took a huge gulp of water. "Well, there's not much to tell. I just saw these little red and green lights on each of the support beams. I remember thinking that they must have been some sort of stabilizers or something. I only saw them for just a few seconds before I was running for my life. I'm sorry I can't be more helpful."

Matt continued eating his sandwich as Jessica asked, "What happened next and how did you get out?"

"Well, when I woke up, I was lying on my back. Judging by the bloody forehead, I had obviously run into a wall and knocked myself unconscious. I was trapped in a little cavity where the tunnel hadn't collapsed. I don't know how long I was unconscious, but when I woke up, I screamed and screamed hoping one of you or your team could hear me."

The food was starting to help Matt feel like his old self again. He was starting to regain some of his energy and his mood was turning more playful.

Jessica interjected, "Well, we didn't know you had gone in the cave and didn't realize you were missing for close to thirty minutes. Once we noticed you weren't around, the team started frantically digging, trying to rescue you, especially Wally. You know the guy with the big muscles? It was almost like he had personally let you down, so he worked and worked trying to find you. He can move some dirt! And then, he was so concerned about you, he stayed with me all day until Eli got here. Actually, he and Faysal both stayed with me. They really helped."

"Wait…. You didn't know I was missing??" Matt asked with a grin.

"That's really beside the point. Keep going. What happened next?" Jessica said a little sheepishly.

"Well, I was really scared, but I had this feeling rush over me. The only way I can describe it is that it was like a wave of God's love that covered over me, and I *knew* I would be ok. Finally, I was able to squeak out of the cavity where I was and just as I did, the spot where I had been, imploded on itself. It was like an angel was holding it up just until I got free."

"Oh my gosh," Jessica said. "That must have been the secondary cave-in that Doron called you about Eli. That didn't happen until late afternoon. You must have been unconscious for a while."

"Well, when the dust finally settled, I pulled out my flashlight and looked at my surroundings. I was in an incredible tunnel, chiseled out of the limestone. It was obviously carved by the same group or at least in the same manner as the earthen cave, but this was carved completely out of the bedrock," Matt said.

"Incredible," Eli said.

"No, that's not the incredible thing. The incredible thing is that this system of tunnels is a maze, a labyrinth, built, I'm sure, for the express purpose of keeping any unwanted visitors completely confused and lost. The tunnels crisscross underneath the Old City for miles and miles. Each tunnel hallway had openings with rooms and hallways and those hallways had more rooms and more hallways."

"How did you find your way around?" Jessica asked.

"Well, you know that I always carry my *Wild Berry Skittles* in my bag, right? So, I used them to mark a trail and that did absolutely *nothing* for me. I walked and walked and left the candy trail so I would know where I had been. I walked for what seemed like hours, until the battery in my flashlight went out. That reminds me, I need to start carrying some fresh batteries in my bag." Matt opened up his bag to pull his flashlight out and that's when he saw the zip-top bag with the ancient jug handle in it. He pulled it out and handed it to Jessica. "That is officially the first find from inside the cave. Don't worry, I marked where I found it with a pile of green *Skittles*."

"It's not the most scientific way of marking a discovery or practicing archaeology, but I do appreciate the effort. Was there anything else of note in the cave?" Jessica asked while inspecting the pottery shard.

"*Yes!* But I haven't gotten to that part yet," Matt answered.

Eli interrupted, "It wasn't a missing Indian nuclear scientist, was it?"

"Uhhh, no," Matt answered.

"It was worth a try. Everything else in your life is amazing. I thought there might be a chance you found him! Sorry I interrupted, please continue," Eli said with a chuckle.

"Ok. This is the most amazing part of the whole ordeal. See, I walked and walked and walked, lost in the maze. Finally, with my flashlight on its last legs, I found this room that had stacked rocks blocking something. So, I turned the light off and started pulling the rocks away, hoping it was an exit door. When I felt like I had pulled the rocks down far enough, I turned the light back on and saw that it *was* a doorway, but it had been blocked from the other side as well. There were stacks of rocks that had been laid up on that side of the doorway, too. I was certain that this was an exit. I mean, who blocks both sides of a doorway? So, I knocked the rocks out of the way and that's when my flashlight died."

Jessica audibly gasped and Eli asked "Where did the door lead? To a way out?"

Matt answered, "No, not at all. It was a sealed room.... with a dude in it!"

"What?!" Jessica exclaimed.

"Yeah, he was really old... and dead. Maybe I should have led with that. He was definitely dead." Matt laughed. "He was almost mummified. He was wearing a tunic and sandals and had obviously sealed himself inside the room. Strange, right?" Matt asked.

"Absolutely. What else was in the room? Was he protecting something? Wait... if your flashlight died, how did you even see him?" Jessica asked.

"I told you this was the coolest part of the story. Right then, I had a scripture verse come back to my memory, something Jesus said. It's from John 8:12 *"Then spake Jesus again unto them, saying, I am the light of the world: **he that followeth me shall not walk in darkness, but shall have the light of life.**"*[103] All of a sudden, the flashlight came back to life, totally bright, like someone had put fresh batteries in. It lasted for hours and hours, until I was able to get out of the cave system. I can't explain it, but I felt like I was surrounded by God's love the whole time."

"There has to be some explanation for this," Eli said, to himself, but loud enough for all to hear.

Matt nodded and smiling said, "There is. God was with me, Eli. That was just one of the *miracles* during my evening."

"There's more?" Jessica asked.

Matt was really starting to feel like himself again, energized from the food and from being safe and secure in his apartment. He said, "Ooooh yes. So, the flashlight turned on and as I started looking around the room, I saw this black stuff on the ceiling and the walls and on this big stone box. Now, the black stuff wasn't the star of the show, I probably wouldn't have even noticed it except that within the black stuff was something that interacted with the light of my flashlight. It reflected, somehow, the light that was being given off." Matt reached in his bag

---

[103] John 8:12 (King James Version)

and pulled out the zip-top baggie with the black substance in it. "I used my knife to scrape some of it and put it in this baggie and sealed it, like you told me."

Even through the baggie, the black substance glowed and reflected the light of the apartment. It almost looked alive.

"What... in... the... world?" Jessica muttered.

"I've never seen anything like this," Eli whispered.

"Exactly. Those were my thoughts exactly. Which is why I used my knife to collect a sample. Whatever this is, it's very old and I swear I didn't touch it. Only the blade of my knife did." Matt reached down and pulled his Swiss Army knife out of his bag. Looking at the knife, studying it intently, Matt was suddenly very quiet. It caused Jessica and Eli to look at the knife and wait until whatever was on Matt's mind, whatever the continuation of the story was, to be revealed. After a few moments of pondering, Matt finally said, "The Swiss Army must've been pretty confident in their chances to secure victory if they included a corkscrew on their knife!"

"Oh, come on!" Jessica exclaimed while rolling her eyes.

Eli threw his hands up and dropped his head in lighthearted frustration.

"Well, it's true!" Matt said with a huge grin on his face. "Now, where was I? Oh, so I collected a sample. Maybe we can get that tested somehow? Do either of you know a lab we can send it to?"

"I believe we both do," Eli said.

"I'll take care of it," Jessica said, taking the baggie and looking at it intently. "What happened next?"

"It was the strangest thing. I remembered another scripture. It just popped in my head. *"It is his voice that echoes in the thunder of the storm clouds. He causes mist to rise upon the earth; he sends the lightning and brings the rain, and **from his treasuries he brings the wind.**"*[104] It was the last part of the verse that really stood out to me — 'from his treasuries

---

[104] Jeremiah 10:13 (The Living Bible)

he brings the wind.' The wildest part of the evening happened next. I stepped out of the room with the black stuff — it was just a small, little room filled with stacked rocks and that box... and the mummy... but it was a closed room, right? A breeze started blowing out of the room! I couldn't believe it! I put my hand up to the doorway and could feel the breeze blowing out, but it was a closed room!! Four stone walls, ceiling and floor! It shouldn't be possible unless God actually brought the wind from His treasuries!"

Matt looked at Eli and Jessica and they were both a little shocked, trying to process the information he was giving them. He continued, "I was below the surface in a cave, and out of a completely closed room, a breeze was blowing. I recognized God's hand in this, that this was another miracle. So, I followed the breeze, for what seemed like hours, but the breeze led me to an exit! And my flashlight stayed on the whole time until I got there, then it went dead. I stepped out of another hidden cave entrance, just outside of the City of David, south of the Temple Mount. I was able to find someone to let me use their phone to call you, took a bus and made my way here. My story ends with 'My wonderful wife handed me a sandwich.'"

Jessica laughed, but Eli's manner had changed. He was focused, intense, sitting on the edge of his seat.

"You know, now that I know there is another way out, I really want to get back into that room where the dead dude was. I think there are some things buried in there and he gave his life protecting them."

"You are sure that the cave entrance was hidden?" Eli asked, almost on edge, suddenly very alert.

"Yes sir. I'm almost positive that no one has been in that cave for centuries. As I moved closer to the exit, the different rooms and hall-ways had more and more things in them. It was like, when the cave system was first built, the opening I used for my escape was their main entrance. The rooms closest to that exit were the most filled. And, when I say filled, I mean there were odds and ends like jars and clay jugs, not really filled to the rafters with archaeological finds. Anyway, the further inside the cave, away from the doorway, the less stuff there was. Where I first found myself, deep in the heart of the tunnel system, the cave was completely empty except for that jug handle," Matt said pointing to the artifact still in Jessica's hand.

Standing, Eli said, "I have some work that needs to be done this evening. Please do not alert anyone to Matt's safe return until you hear from me in the morning. Get some rest you two. You deserve it." Turning towards Jessica, Eli asked with a sly smile, "Are you still interested in being in charge of an archaeological site?"

ARCHAEOLOGY STAGE THREE: ASSESSMENT

Full-scale excavation and data recovery of site.[105]

"Then the angel brought me back by the way of the outer
gate of the sanctuary (the Golden Gate), which looketh
toward the east; and it was shut. Then said the Lord unto
me; 'This gate shall be shut, it shall not be opened, and no
man shall enter in by it; It is for the prince;
… he shall enter by the way of that gate, and shall go out by
the way of the same. When the prince provides a freewill
offering to the Lord, the gate facing east shall be opened
for him…" — Ezekiel 44:1-3, 46:12

"Humans have 23 pairs of chromosomes, resulting in 46 total chromosomes.
In humans, one copy of each chromosome is inherited from the female
parent and the other from the male parent. This explains why children
inherit some of their traits from their mother and some from their father."
— Dr. Jennifer Marks

---

[105] "Phases of Archaeology," Job Monkey, 2022, https://www.jobmonkey.com/
archaeology/phases/

CHAPTER 23

"Nava? Faysal? Thank you both for coming and agreeing to be part of this *new* team. Would you mind gathering everyone around and being my translators for the meeting?"

Assembling the former excavation crew at the new site and having a morning meeting for the first time was definitely giving Jessica some deja vu feelings. Nervously laughing, Jessica added, "And Matt. You stay right here beside me for this meeting. Don't. Go. Anywhere." Matt clicked his heels together and gave Jessica a salute, all with a wide smile on his still slightly bruised face. Matt had already decided he wasn't going to leave her alone. Matt was determined to stay close to Jessica. So, he resolved that he was going to be a part of the dig team.

After a few moments, the crowd of workers were gathered in the parking lot where the headquarters tent was set up and were awaiting Jessica's remarks. Nava and Faysal interpreted for their respective groups, Nava to the Hebrew speakers and Faysal to the Arabic speakers. Jessica addressed the group in English.

"Thank you all for being here today and agreeing to continue Dr. Kenyon's work, even if it is at a different location. Let me catch you up on what has happened since my husband, Matt, was trapped in the cave-in last week." Jessica pointed to Matt and gave Nava and Faysal a moment to interpret. "Late in the evening on Monday, Matt was rescued by the emergency team. He had some minor injuries, and was very hungry, but otherwise he was safe. We are so thrilled he was found. Not only that, his hat and phone were also found in a small, isolated pocket in the tunnel." Jessica carefully worded her explanation. She knew Matt was found and she knew that his hat and broken phone were found, but in two completely separate places. Eli had *insisted* that no one was to know that the cave where the accident had happened and the cave where Matt exited were connected.

"Where the items were found seemed to be a dead end to the cave. Faysal, Wally and I, sifted dirt and the emergency team worked hard through the day, night, and into the next few days and none of us found anything. Nothing." Jessica paused again for the interpreters.

"With my boss, the man who arranged for me to take over after Dr. Kenyon's accident, we decided to permanently abandon the old site. It looks like it was just a cave. Nothing to discover, no artifacts, no anything. Perhaps it was just an ancient storage shelter. And it obviously wasn't the safest of sites." At this and after the interpretations, there was a smattering of chuckles from the group. "But my boss also knew about *this* site. He knew it was a *very* recent discovery and that it had not been examined yet. It only made sense that since there was a fully formed team with no site to work on and a site that needed a team, that we should be offered the job. I accepted immediately and accepted for all of you as well."

As the interpreters gave their explanations, there was a cheering and round of applause from the group. Jessica continued, "You might be wondering, where is the site? Why are we gathered in a parking lot? Well, please turn to your right." As the group turned, they saw the *City of David* sign. A low murmur ensued. Turning back to Jessica, the group obviously had questions, but she continued, "Matt, would you do the honors of showing the group what they will be working on?"

Matt laughed, gave Jessica another salute and made his way to the hidden entrance to the cave, stepped inside and disappeared from the group's line of sight. There were audible gasps from the assembled group. From where they were standing, it looked like a magic trick, an illusion, like someone making the Statue of Liberty disappear. Jessica watched as the group's collective jaws dropped. Matt gave it a few seconds and then stepped back out from the entrance. Again, there were audible gasps. The cave entrance was *perfectly* camouflaged. *Perfectly* hidden.

"Excavations in the City of David have only been going on for about the last ten years." Jessica continued. "It is our theory that the cave entrance was underground, buried until only recently. Where we are standing, this parking lot is brand new, less than two weeks old. With the way the entrance is so well hidden, it only makes sense that this cave has not been found or explored... until now. Are you excited?" Jessica shouted. The group responded with screams, shouts, claps and even some dancing. "Ok. Ok. Settle down. Back to serious stuff. You see all of these boxes, all of these crates, all of this stuff?" Jessica asked as she was pointing at the various things sitting around the parking lot. "This is all of our equipment from the other site. It will all need to be unpacked and assembled so that we can begin our work tomorrow morning. Feel free to check out the cave, but make sure all of this is set to go so we can start first thing in the morning. One rule: nobody goes in the cave without wearing one of these vests," Jessica held up an orange reflective work vest and pointed out a small electronic device. "Attached to each one is a little transponder that will relay your position, just in case we have any more accidents. Faysal, you're in charge. Make it happen!" Jessica said, finishing her speech.

Littered across the parking lot were large, heavy, wooden crates containing all sorts of equipment. Everything had been packed neatly and in order. Eli and Doron's team had made quick work of packing up the former site and he had even included a few extra pieces of equipment as well. Eli and Doron had thought of everything. There were even brand-new vests with trackers and hardhats with LED lights for longer battery life. Eli's note was even funny. "Put this equipment to good use and let me know if you come across any missing Indian nuclear scientists! I could use the reward money!" The missing nuclear scientist story had been ongoing since at least the night of Dr. Kenyon's death, and it seemed the whole world was aware that Israel was one of the places the authorities believed the missing scientist may be being held. The authorities had even started offering a reward for any information that might lead to his rescue.

Everyone was excited to get back to work and it didn't take the group long to start exploring the cave entrance. After a few minutes, Faysal and Wally found Matt. Wally grabbed Matt, like he had the first day, with a huge bearhug, pinning his arms to his side, and picked him up off of his feet. Faysal said "Wally is glad you are safe, and he has a request. He wants to work with you on this site. Like your personal worker. He wants to stay close, so you are safe. I told him it was dumb idea, but he insisted I ask."

Matt's face lit up and he said, "It's fine with me as long as Jessica is ok with it. Let me ask and I will let you guys know something in a little while." Faysal relayed the message to Wally who, with a big smile, seemed to be fine with waiting on an answer.

"Have you had a chance to look inside the cave?" Matt asked. "There are so many rooms and so much stuff to catalog. This is going to be an exciting place to be for the next few months!"

"How do you know that?" Faysal asked.

"Oh, I got a sneak peek at the cave. How else would I know how to find the entrance? I wasn't allowed to touch anything, but I think there are a lot of things to catalog here. I am really looking forward to exploring the cave! I'll feel much safer having Wally with me, too."

At hearing his name, Wally looked to Faysal for an explanation. Faysal interpreted for Wally and a grin widened across his face. He gave Matt a high five and a thumbs up.

About that time, a commotion, a wave of excitement began rippling out from the group standing around the entrance to the cave. It caught the attention of the three men, and they turned to see what was happening. That's when they heard it:

"A body! We've found a body inside the cave!"

CHAPTER 24

T he young man admired the freshly painted door. He had been very specific in his choice of colors, a royal blue for the base color, white for the background on which the name was written and crimson for the letters. In Judaism, the colors have meaning: red, white, and blue, represent fire, water, and air, respectively.[106] Fire, water, air, and everything in between, he tested it all. The young man unlocked the door, flipped the lights on, shut the door behind him, and put his keys in his pocket. Hanging on the hook on the back of the door was his lab coat. He pulled the white jacket down, adjusted his name tag that was still attached to it and put it on. Still sitting on his desk was the large envelope that the messenger had given him right at the end of business the day before. The envelope was opened but unexplored.

Chad Hudson was a young man, and proud of the fact that he had started his own business, a testing facility, and had managed to keep it afloat during the slow season of the archaeology profession. He was glad he had made friendships in the field before opening his own, independent lab, as those contacts had been the source of his income over the past few months. Now that spring was here, and the archaeological sites were beginning to excavate again, things should pick back up and his income should follow. For the limited size and capabilities it had, his lab was gaining a reputation as a first-class testing site, quick and with dependable results. That was one of the beautiful aspects to his plan. Set up shop close to the different excavation sites, so when they needed a rush job, they

---

[106] "Ask The Rabbi," Ohr Somayach International, accessed March 9, 2022, https://ohr.edu/ask_db/ask_main.php/264/Q3/

wouldn't have to send the items to be tested all the way to Switzerland, Italy, or the United States. They could use a bicycle messenger and send them across town to him. Which is exactly what happened late yesterday.

Hudson reached in the large envelope and opened the note from his former colleague, Jessica Davenport. He knew from his time at Laboratory Nedaviah, that while the science was real and the testing was true, many times the background was illusion. In other words, not all of the testing was done for the reasons he was given. But Hudson had the reputation as someone who knew how to keep his mouth shut and he is sure that was part of the reason why Jessica had continued to send him work. The other part was the fact that while they had both worked together at Laboratory Nedaviah, before the explosion, Chad had extended himself towards Jessica and had invited her to do things with his wife and young son. He knew it could be difficult being alone in a new city without the benefit of friends and family. So, they became friends as well as colleagues. Jessica's handwritten note said:

Hey 'Glad Chad the Rad Dad,'

Hope this note finds you and your family doing well! Please tell Layne I said hello!

Here's an interesting thing for you to test. This black substance was found inside a cave, here in Jerusalem. We'll know more in the coming months, but it looks like the cave has been untouched for 1,000 years or more. One of the team members found this stuff on one of the walls. It is 'unusual.' Shine a light on it and you'll see what I mean. Can you give me any insight into what it is? Is it dangerous? Is it valuable? Call me when you know any-thing. Oh, and keep this between us, ok?

Thanks!
Jess

Hudson pulled the sample out of the envelope and immediately understood Jessica's meaning. The sample reacted to the light of his laboratory in the most unusual and curious manner. This was obviously different from the other testing he was asked to handle on a regular basis. This was unique. Under his breath and to himself, Hudson said "Finally, a new challenge, a new thing to discover, a new answer to find. *This* is why I started the lab!"

CHAPTER 25

"You know, when I agreed to come to work for you, I thought being an archaeologist would be much more…"

"You're not an archaeologist!" Jessica teased from where she was, in the kitchen, to where Matt was, in the bedroom, of their small apartment.

"I know but I'm working at an archaeological site, and I thought being an archaeologist would be much more…"

"Working at a dig site still doesn't make you an archaeologist!" Jessica teased, preventing Matt from finishing his sentence again.

Matt, with wet hair and still only half-dressed, stuck his head into the kitchen and said, "I know I'm not an archaeologist, but what I'm trying to say is that I always thought archaeology *work* would be much more *Indiana Jones* or *National Treasure* than, than, than…" Matt was a little bit surprised that Jessica hadn't interrupted him again and wasn't sure what movie example he wanted to use to finish his thought. "Than, ummm, I don't know, some prison chain-gang movie. Like… Paul Newman in *Cool Hand Luke.*"

Jessica looked at him quizzically and raised an unimpressed eyebrow. Movies weren't her thing.

Matt continued, "Yeah, I feel like all I do all day is lift heavy stuff and carry it from point A to point B. When I'm not lifting something, then I'm pushing or pulling something. When I'm not pushing or pulling something, I'm wheeling something. When I'm not wheeling something, I'm setting something up or tearing something down. I just didn't know archaeology was such hard… *work*. It's not like the movies at all, but I really like it. It's been a while since I had a chance to really get callouses on my hands, to get hot and sweaty, to work those muscles out that have sat dormant for a while. If you don't watch out, I'm going to have a beach body before the summer ever even gets here." Matt stepped fully into the kitchen and Jessica saw that Matt had just stepped out of the shower, threw on some pants and he didn't have a shirt on, yet. They had only been working at the site for a few weeks and Matt's body hadn't changed one bit that she could tell, but that didn't stop Matt from flexing his muscles for her.

"Oh, babe!" Jessica teased. "Those six-pack abs are going to look *so* good once you get that ten or fifteen pounds off of them!" Jessica and Matt both laughed.

"You might not be able to tell it, but I can tell my body is changing. Give me a few months and I'm going to be ripped, with bulging muscles, like Wally. Well, maybe not as big as Wally, but bigger than I am now. Just wait."

"How are things going with him, with Wally?" Jessica asked. "I mean, it's been a little while. Are you guys able to communicate alright even though you don't speak the same language?"

Matt stepped back into the bedroom to finish getting dressed and answered, "Yeah. It's pretty simple. We kind of mime what we need, you know? If we want to eat or something, we just act like we're putting a burger in our mouth or if we need help picking something up, we just act like we're lifting something. It's been really easy. You don't even want to know the sign we give each other if we need to use the restroom!" Matt laughed.

"You're such a boy!" Jessica shouted from the other room.

Matt continued to laugh and then said "For anything else, if either of us come up with something that's a little more complicated or needs further explanation, we just find someone to interpret for us, Faysal, or someone who might be close by. For two people who don't speak the same language, I'd say we're getting to be pretty good friends. There's something about him that seems so familiar. I don't know why, though."

Matt walked back into the kitchen wearing an Alabama t-shirt and in his sock feet, carrying his shoes. "So, did you ever hear back from the lab about that black stuff that I found in that room in the cave?" Matt asked as he sat down and started to put his shoes on.

"No, but I've got it on my list to call Chad about it tomorrow if he doesn't call me about it first," Jessica replied.

"Cool. I know we are taking our time mapping the cave, but I'm ready to find that room again and see what's actually going on in there."

"We'll get there," Jessica said. "We just need to make sure we do it the right way. I've got people mapping the place, workers that do this for a living and that I trust."

"Fair enough. Hey... what's the word on the body that they found in the cave last week? Got any details on that?" Before Jessica answered, Matt added "It wasn't that missing scientist, was it? You're not trying to keep the reward money for yourself, are you?" Matt asked with a smile.

"Very funny," Jessica answered dryly. "No, it wasn't the scientist, but what it is makes me sad."

"Why does it make you sad?"

"Well, it was the body of a young boy. He was killed, murdered, when he was probably only 12 or 13 years old. That's sad. Given some of the clues and putting the pieces together, we think that he was killed roughly 2600 years ago. It's just sad to me that someone so young could have had their life snuffed out at such a tender age." Jessica said.

"Wow. That's a pretty specific timeframe. How did you figure that out?" Matt asked.

"Do you mean how did we figure out his age or how did we figure out the time period?"

"Yes, to both," Matt replied.

"Well, first, from the size and development of his skeletal structure, we can get his gender and age and we could tell by his dress that he was Jewish and lived around 600 BC, give or take, around the time of the destruction of Jerusalem. But the biggest clue was the arrowhead that we found in his back. It was Babylonian from the time of Nebuchadnezzar... King Nebbie. Those arrowheads have a specific shape and are very specific to this historical timeframe and to King Nebbie's people. We think that this adolescent was trying to escape from the invading Babylonians when he was hit by an arrow. He must have crawled into the tunnel, either following people — like the ones who built the room you found — or maybe he stumbled upon it by blind luck. He probably holed up in one of the rooms, waiting for his family or just for the Babylonians and the danger to leave, and unfortunately, he died before he could get out of the caves. And that's where we found him. The remains, as you saw, were in very good condition and had been left untouched for millennia."

"I wonder what it must have been like being a kid in Jerusalem with the enemy army outside the city." Matt had lost his father a few years earlier to a heart attack, and his mind was drawn to him now. "Do you think his dad told him about the danger on the other side of the walls? Do you think the kid knew what was going on? I wonder what their last days must have been like. What was it like going to their last Yom Kippur? Do you think they even knew it was going to be their last?" Matt asked more to himself than to Jess.

Jessica had heard the term Yom Kippur before but didn't quite know the details about the feast day. Matt was better with Jewish holy days and how they related to their shared Christian faith. "Remind me what Yom Kippur is..." Jessica said.

"In English and in the Bible, we call Yom Kippur the Day of Atonement. It is *still* the *most* holy day in Israel."

"Is Yom Kippur the same thing as Passover?" Jessica asked?

Matt answered, "No, they're not. Yom Kippur is celebrated in the fall. Passover isn't too far off from now — it's usually around Easter time — and it celebrates the Israelites freedom from slavery from the pharaoh in Egypt... what is known as the Exodus. There were ten terrible plagues that the Egyptians endured, but the last plague was the death of the firstborn of anyone who didn't follow the Lord's instructions. The Israelites followed God's instructions and were *passed-over* from that death. That was the final straw the led to their release from slavery and every year they celebrate it. In fact, that's what Jesus was celebrating at, what we call, *The Last Supper*. And it's part of what we are thinking about when we take communion at church."

"That makes sense," Jessica said.

"Yom Kippur is much different. In Biblical times, it had to do with sin sacrifices, scapegoats, and, and, well, there is a lot to unpack. Hey! What if I do some research on it and how it relates to us, and we'll go have a picnic and do a Bible study together in a few days. How does that sound?"

Matt and Jessica's relationship had been built on Bible studies, and even though individually they did their own daily Bible devotions, it had been a while since the two of them had made time to do a study together.

"I'd *love* that," Jessica said.

"Me too." Matt smiled, kissed Jessica lightly on the lips and left the room to start his study.

Chapter 26

———— ◆❖◆ ————

THURSDAY. 4 PM.

C had Hudson checked the results for what felt like the millionth time. He had checked and re-checked and re-checked his re-check, but all of the results came back the same. But the same was wrong. There was just no way around it. The results were wrong. Hudson couldn't figure out what he had done to come away with these unusual results. It obviously wasn't human contamination. He was too careful, and the divergent results didn't look like human contamination. It obviously wasn't animal contamination. He wasn't sure there was any cross-contamination, but these results were off… somehow.

Hudson picked up his cell phone, opened the phone app, scrolled the short way down to *Adams* and found Jessica's entry. "I need to change her name to *Davenport* now that she's married," he said to himself. He pressed the call button and waited for Jessica to answer.

It was late afternoon at the new excavation site and Jessica felt like she had a thousand things going at once. Her cell phone rang the now familiar klaxon ringtone she had set to be able to hear over the workers at the site. Looking down and seeing the screen showing *Chad Hudson*, with *LaBro Unlimited* in smaller letters underneath, Jessica couldn't answer it fast enough. She was happy that Chad had called her as she hadn't made much progress on her list and didn't think she would have been able to call him during today's working hours. She also *loved* the name of his lab, a play on the words *Laboratory* and *Bro* and the seemingly *Unlimited* scope of work he did there.

"Hey my friend!" Jessica said, excited to talk to a familiar voice. "How are you and how's the family?"

Hudson, preoccupied by what was happening with the testing, answered, "I've got a problem."

"Oh no! Is everybody ok?" Jessica asked, genuinely concerned. Looking up, she saw Matt walking across the site. Cupping her hand over the phone, she shouted, "Matt, come here!" and pointed to the phone in her hand. Matt changed direction and started making his way to Jessica. Wally, following a few yards behind, changed course as well.

"Oh yes, everybody is great. I'm sorry. Everybody is wonderful. What I meant is, I've got a problem with the results of the testing of that black substance, and I sent some of it to a larger lab in New York City for further testing. I meant to tell you that a few days ago, but I've been working on this thing, this puzzle, trying to find some answers and let time get away from me. I hope it's ok that I sent it," Hudson answered.

Jessica knew that Hudson took pride in his work and that it must be eating him alive not getting passable results himself. She also knew that if he had to send it away there was something definitely unusual or problematic. She said, "Oh, yes. That's fine. What did *you* find? Oh, hey, my husband just walked up. He's the one that found the black stuff. I'm going to put you on speakerphone so he can hear as well. Give me a second. Ok. There. What did you find?"

Matt and Wally had walked up just in time to hear Jessica explain that he had been the one that found the black substance and as she put the phone on speaker, Matt could see the name *Chad Hudson* and *LaBro Unlimited* and pieced together that Jess was talking to the person at the lab doing the testing on the black substance.

"I won't get into the weeds on how the testing process works, but the results are just... out there. First, I can tell you that it is old, really, really old. And it is human, almost... or... more than, depending on how you look at the characteristics and the unusual chromosomes. It also has some radioactive properties…"

"Radioactive properties?!?" Jessica asked incredulously, interrupting Hudson's train of thought.

"Yes, radioactive properties. It's crazy and it makes no sense if it truly has been untouched for a thousand years or more." Hudson replied. Jessica's face flashed a moment of recognition, like a puzzle piece had fallen into place.

"Are we in any danger? I mean, I handled that sample extensively, I mean, I never touched it. There's no contamination. I did it all with my knife, but I held it close to my body in the zip-top bag. Am I in danger?" Matt asked.

"That's another thing that doesn't make sense. It has some radioactive properties, but they are low… or high depending on what test. But definitely not harmful. In fact, it's just the opposite. Everything that the substance has come into contact with has changed the other elements for the better. I am really good at my job, and this has me stumped. What I can tell you is that none of this makes sense."

"What do you mean it 'changed the other elements for the better?'" Jessica asked.

"You know in testing, we apply different elements to the test subject to see how the particles react with our testing element. We can use deductive reasoning to establish the core qualities of the subject matter. In this instance, with *this* subject matter, instead of reacting to the different elements, it changes those elements. Let me make it more plain. It's done on a micro, subatomic level, very small particles, but for example's sake, let's say we take a molecule that is in the shape of a triangle. We knock one of the points off and now we have an unfinished triangle. Then, we add a test particle to it, your black substance. If the test particle joins the triangle, we know it means one thing and if it doesn't join the triangle, it means another thing. Right?"

Matt and Jessica nodded and realizing that Hudson couldn't see them, Jessica answered, "Yes. We're with you."

Hudson continued "Well, when I add your black substance to the two-pointed broken triangle, instead of either joining or not joining, it changes that incomplete triangle in unique ways."

"How so?" Jessica asked.

"Depending on the testing element, your black substance may induce the two-points of the triangle to regrow, from scratch, its third point. With another testing element, your black substance may induce the two points to connect and form a new, different and better shape, like a square. It shouldn't happen. But it does. I am… stumped."

Matt and Jessica were silent, staring at each other with confused looks on their faces. There was a moment of silence among all of the participants on the call when Hudson spoke up. "Tell me again, you said you found this in a cave? Under the Old City?"

Matt answered the question, "Yes. It was me. I found it." Matt glanced around to make sure no one could hear what he was about to say. The only person close enough to hear anything was Wally, and because he couldn't understand English, it wouldn't matter. The three of them were standing around the phone in Jessica's outstretched hand, but Wally was completely uninterested in what was being said and was intently watching the cave entrance. Matt continued, "I was trapped in a cave under the Old City and found this room that had been sealed. Trust me, the room was sealed for a long time. I mean, there was even a mummy inside of it. This black stuff was on the ceiling and the wall and on top of a big broken box that was also in the room."

Hudson replied more to himself than to anyone on the call, "What… in… the… world?"

At the same time, a commotion started rippling from the mouth of the hidden cave. Matt and Jessica turned to see what Wally had been watching for the past few moments. People had begun pouring out of the cave but instead of being excited, it was clear to see that people were scared and they looked like they were running for their lives. People were screaming and running everywhere. They looked like ants from

169

a disturbed anthill. Wally grabbed Matt's arm and pulled him along as he went to find out what was happening.

Jessica said, "I've got a situation going on here. I guess that lab will call me? Did you give them my number?"

Hudson said, "Yes and your email address."

"Fantastic. Thank you. I'll let you know when I hear anything. There's some kind of emergency happening here. I've got to run. Hug Layne for me. Bye!" Jessica said, hitting *End Call* and running from the headquarters tent to the mouth of the cave to try and understand what was going on and why grown men were pouring from the entrance, screaming hysterically.

Chapter 27

———•———❖———•———

Thursday. 4 pm.

The Sun was just beginning to set as Rabbi Eliyahu Kaduri dismissed his students from their lesson outside the Old City walls. The Rabbi had concluded their lesson in the Kidron Valley, which lies between the Old City and the Mount of Olives. He found himself outside the only gate on the eastern side of the temple complex, the Golden Gate, the sealed entrance to the Temple Mount. The Golden Gate was sealed by Suleiman the Magnificent around 1542 in the hopes it would prevent the Jewish Messiah from entering the Temple Mount area as was foretold by the Prophet Ezekiel.[107] It had been a beautiful spring day and the Rabbi had decided to enjoy the wonders of God's creation from outside the confines of a classroom. He and his students had walked as he taught them, and the class had, without intent, concluded on the east side of the city walls, outside of the Muslim Quarter and the Temple Mount.

After speaking with several of the students, Rabbi Kaduri turned to the East and watched as the setting Sun bathed the Mount of Olives in golden sunlight. A soft voice, almost a whisper behind him, caught Kaduri's attention. It said, "Put off thy shoes from off thy feet." Kaduri had a hint of recognition, so he turned around but didn't see anything or anyone close enough to have spoken to him. He looked up towards the Golden Gate, but didn't see anyone in that direction, either. Rabbi Kaduri slowly turned a full 360 degrees but saw no one. Again, he heard the voice,

---

[107] Reference Ezekiel 44:1-3, 46:12

almost in a whisper, say "Put off thy shoes from off thy feet," but this time it added, "for the place whereon thou standest is holy ground."[108]

Rabbi Kaduri immediately recognized the reference. It was the first instruction that God gave to Moses as he visited him through the burning bush. God told Moses to remove his shoes because he was standing on holy ground.

Rabbi Kaduri took off his black shoes and looked for an orderly spot to place them beside where he was standing. When he looked up, he saw something miraculous — a man on fire, but not being burned, radiating light, radiating love, not quite touching the ground, but not quite levitating either. The man, in the most peace-filled voice that Kaduri had ever experienced said, "Fear not..."

Rabbi Kaduri immediately fell to his knees and hid his face. Tearfully, repentantly, and full of regret he said, "Depart from me for I am a sinful man."

"Eliyahu," the man said, "look on me."

With tears in his eyes, Rabbi Kaduri cautiously looked up at the man and felt the love radiating from the essence of him. To Kaduri, it felt as if love was what coursed through the man's veins, the thing that connected the fibers of his being. It felt as if this man was the embodiment of love itself.

The man continued, "Fear not: for I have redeemed thee, I have called thee by thy name; thou art mine."[109] Rabbi Kaduri's spirit seemed to come *alive* within him as he recognized the words of the Prophet Isaiah. Lovingly, the man continued, "Eliyahu, you know *of* me, but you do not actually know *me*. That changes today. I know you and have called you by name. Now, I want *you* to know *me*."

"Wh, wh, who are you?" Rabbi Kaduri babbled.

The man turned and focused his attention on the Golden Gate. Rabbi Kaduri followed his gaze and the man spoke. "Just as there is

---

[108] Exodus 3:5 (King James Version)

[109] Isaiah 43:1 (King James Version)

only one way into the Temple Mount, that Golden Gate," the man said, pointing to the sealed entrance, "So too is there only *one way* to the Father." [110] Kaduri was just as focused on the man's hand, with its gruesome scar, as he was with what the man was saying and where he was pointing. "Eliyahu, it is impossible to have a relationship with the *Law*. It is impossible to have a relationship with a *book*. You must have a relationship with a *person*, not with a *concept* of right and wrong. Do you understand? He that hath ears, let him hear." [111]

Again, Rabbi Kaduri babbled, "Wh, wh, who are you?"

The man, radiating light, smiled, and answered, "Then Nebuchadnezzar the king was astonished, and rose up in haste, and spake, and said unto his counselors, 'Did not we cast three men bound into the midst of the fire?' They answered and said unto the king, 'True, O king.' He answered and said, 'Lo, I see four men loose, walking in the midst of the fire, and they have no hurt; and *the form of the fourth is like the Son of God.*'" [112]

Rabbi Kaduri's heart swelled in his chest and in his throat. He recognized the words of the Prophet Daniel, recording what King Nebuchadnezzar said as he experienced something supernatural. After King Nebuchadnezzar had thrown the three Israelites, Shadrach, Meshach, and Abednego, into the fiery furnace, his eyes were opened to the spirit realm, to God's realm and he saw something unlike anything he had seen before... a man in the image of the Son of God. In an instant, Kaduri understood that just like Nebuchadnezzar, like Adam and Eve, just like Balaam, and just like Elisha's servant, *his* eyes were *now* opened to something different, something unique, something supernatural. He recognized that this man, who had opened his eyes to the spirit realm, who radiated love, somehow, was now claiming to be...

The Son of God.

---

[110] Reference John 14:6

[111] Mark 4:9 (King James Version)

[112] Daniel 3:24-25 (King James Version)

CHAPTER 28

I t should have been a peaceful evening. The Sun was setting on the
Thursday afternoon, casting beautiful colors of orange, pink, and
purple across the sky. Instead, it was a chaotic scene. People were
spilling out of the hidden entrance to the cave as quickly as humanly
possible through the narrow opening. Matt had never seen so many
grown men hysterically screaming. As they exited the cave, each one
of them looked as though they were running for their lives. They were
taking off their hard hats and vests and leaving them where they fell,
screaming at anyone who would listen, in Arabic, and leaving the site.

Matt and Wally had run toward the scene to try and assess the situation and understand what was going on. As one worker came running
by them, Wally grabbed the man by the arm, almost clotheslining him
in the process. The man tried to pull away, but it was useless against the
stronger man's grip. Both speaking Arabic, Wally said something to the
man and the man answered. Matt watched as a shocked look crossed
Wally's face and in that moment his grip lessened, and the man pulled
away, moving to leave the site. Matt turned to Wally and started to ask
what was going on, but just then, Wally grabbed a second man that was
leaving the tunnel, spoke to him, and got a response. Something had
changed. Wally seemed scared.

Finally, Matt saw Faysal and realized he was about to leave as well.
Matt slapped Wally on the shoulder and pointed to Faysal. Wally let
the second man go and he and Matt began jogging toward the foreman.
Matt shouted at him, "Faysal! Hey, Faysal! Don't leave! What's going on?"

Faysal slowed at the sound of his name but did not stop walking. Matt and Wally made their way to him through the crowd of people, and Wally spoke to him in Arabic. Faysal, visibly shaking, responded in English, "Matt, I do not think anyone will come back to work here. The workers have seen djinn inside the cave. I am done. Goodbye." He sounded scared and he sounded angry.

Jessica came running up and asked, "What's going on?"

"Faysal, wait!" Matt said. And, toward Jessica, he answered, "I don't know what's happening. Someone found djinn in the cave? And now everyone is leaving."

"Oh no," Jessica said.

Wally grabbed Faysal by the arm to stop him from leaving, spoke something to him in Arabic and Faysal turned to Jessica and said "You should be very careful, and you should definitely not go in the cave. You should cover your head and face and leave before the djinn finds you." He violently pulled his arm free from Wally's grip and continued walking towards his truck, a 1976 Land Rover.

Jessica chased after him, walking with him to his truck. She said, "Faysal, I understand. I do. Before you leave, wait, look. It's Thursday and it's almost time to quit for the day, anyway. Will you tell everyone to take tomorrow off and just come back on Monday? We can investigate what is going on, make a decision, and tell everyone then."

Reluctantly, Faysal slowed his pace. "Yes, boss. I will do this for you, but you, more than anyone, should be extremely careful around that cave. Djinn bad news."

"I know. I will be. I promise. Thank you for thinking about my safety. And, thank you for doing this for me. Would you mind finding out exactly who saw what and what happened?" Jessica asked.

Faysal reluctantly nodded, made his way to a central location, and started gathering as many of the workers as he could. Wally went with Faysal to help him control the situation. No one would dare say 'no' to the massive Wally. The two men began talking to the group of workers, prodding them, asking questions, and trying to calm fears. It left Matt and Jessica alone together.

"What is djinn?" Matt asked her. "And why is everyone freaking out?"

"Oh, Matt. This is bad." Jessica said.

"Why? What's going on? What is djinn?" Matt asked again.

Jessica began to answer, "A djinn is something mentioned in Islam and something that Muslims *absolutely* believe in. Djinn are mentioned in the Koran. Muhammad spoke about djinn. And because of that, to a Muslim, rejecting the existence of djinn is completely forbidden. In other words, anyone that denies the existence of djinn is basically also denying the Koranic verses that confirm their existence.[113] Almost all of our laborers are Muslim, and it is *required* that they believe in djinn. Even if someone *wanted* to protest, they couldn't. Even if someone *wanted* to say, 'there's no such thing as a djinn,' they couldn't. I mean, it would be like them saying Islam is false, and if they did that, in extreme cases, it could result in them being put to death. If someone says they saw a djinn, it's a really big deal. If it was an evil djinn, which it looks like they think it was, this site is in trouble. I don't know what we're going to do."

"But what *is* a djinn?" Matt asked again.

At that moment, Faysal walked back to where Matt and Jessica were talking and said to Matt, "My friend. You must make your wife leave here. And Nava, too. This is serious. They are in danger. This is why Muslim women cover their bodies, why they wear a burqa!"

"A what? I thought Muslim ladies covered their bodies with a veil." Matt said.

Annoyed, Faysal answered, "They cover their bodies with a Burqa. That is what the veil that they wear to maintain their modesty is called. But the reason they do it is *because of djinn*. According to Abu Ibrahim, a Muslim Islamic religious teacher, women who do not cover themselves

---

[113] Youssef El Kaidi, "Djinn in Muslim Culture: Truth or Superstition?" Inside Arabia, November 24, 2018, https://insidearabia.com/djinn-muslim-culture-truth-superstition/

properly put themselves at risk of djinn falling in love with them and possessing them. He says, 'Djinn possesses people for three main reasons. Number one: out of love. Djinn falls in love with people.'[114][115] Your wife should cover herself quickly. Or leave. Like I am doing now." Faysal began walking towards his truck. "I will see you both on Monday. Or not. I do not know."

Matt started to say something, but Jessica stopped him. Jessica walked and talked with Faysal for a few moments and then made her way back to Matt. The rest of the workers were all leaving as Nava came over to where Matt and Jessica were standing.

"I'm not exactly sure what's going on, but I've had several of the men tell me that we can leave now, we have tomorrow off, and that I should cover myself. None of them would tell me why. I mean, I know in Islam that's what women do, but we have always seemed to have an understanding out here. Do you guys know what's going on? And do we have the day off?" Nava asked.

Matt was already shaking his head when Jessica began to answer. "Yes. You have tomorrow off, and you can go on home if you want. Come back on Monday. The reason is a little bit complicated… one of the workers said they saw a djinn."

"Oh. I see," Nava said.

"Well, I still don't. Could someone explain it to me? *What, in the world, is a djinn?!?*" Matt asked.

---

[114] Abu Ibrahim, "Sign & Symptoms of Magic | Jinn Possession | Eye Evil," Published November 14, 2015, https://www.youtube.com/watch?v=OAPaNOwOBy4

[115] Leyal Khalife, "Women Without 'Proper Hijab' Attract Jinn, Says Islamic Teacher," Step Feed, August 24, 2017, https://stepfeed.com/women-without-proper-hijab-attract-jinn-says-islamic-teacher-0092

CHAPTER 29

Thursday at 11 am was right in the middle of her lunch break, but Jennifer Marks wasn't thinking about the hunger right now. She was waiting for the television crew to finish setting up and she was trying to calm herself down before the interview she was about to give. She was nervously chatting to the young man as he put some extra powder on her face to reduce the shine from the fluorescent television lights.

"Oh, I'm sorry. I'm talking your ear off! I don't know why I always get nervous doing these interviews. I mean, I know it's not live TV and we can just reshoot something if I mess up, but I just hate the thought of the bloopers, you know?" she asked.

The young man smiled and said, "Dr. Marks, you're going to do great. People are always nervous, but once you get into it, once you're explaining this stuff, the stuff you do all day every day, the nervousness will go away. Pretend you're just talking to your husband or one of your friends about what you're doing today at work. Forget the cameras. Just talk to your friend. Or, even better, pretend you're talking to me and explaining all of this deep scientific stuff to someone who does make-up for a living! Make it *really* simple. Dumb it down for me," the young man said with a smile. His words helped the middle-aged geneticist and the tension in her neck and shoulders seemed to relax.

About that time, someone in the lab said "Quiet please! We're rolling."

The room went instantly silent, and everyone's attention was focused on the beautiful television personality wearing a navy dress with a bright yellow jacket and matching shoes. She said, "Hello! I'm Ann

Lauren. Today on *The Science of Stuff* we are in a laboratory in downtown New York City and will be joined by geneticist, Dr. Jennifer Marks. If you are new to our show, our program deals with the science behind the everyday stuff we take for granted. Today, we will be exploring the testing behind the DNA and blood results we see in court cases. Have you ever wondered about the science *behind* the test results? How can the authorities tell if the perp was in the room or not? How do the scientists know if the substance found on the floor was blood and how can they tell if it came from a human? These questions and more get answered today on *The Science of Stuff*." There was a long pause as Ms. Lauren continued to smile and then turning toward the camera man, a tall, lean guy with a dark, patchy beard, she asked, "Do we need to do it again or did I nail it?"

"Nailed it," the camera guy said as he was starting to move his tripod. "Let's set up the next shot."

The young man putting the powder on the much older Dr. Marks, finished, and said, "I think that's your cue. You're going to do great."

Ann Lauren and her tall camera man centered the next shot around Dr. Marks' desk, moved their lights to the perfect angle and went over the questions they intended to ask the doctor.

"Dr. Marks, it is so nice to finally meet you in person. I hope Derek didn't flirt too much with you while he was adjusting your beautiful makeup," Lauren said.

"I tried to get her to leave her husband and run away with me, but she said she has way too much life insurance on him to leave him now!" the young makeup artist said with a smile as he was putting his brushes away. The group huddled around Dr. Marks' desk all laughed at the joke.

Dr. Marks added, "I was pretty tempted, though. Some people want coffee in the mornings. I'd just love for someone to do my makeup every day!" Nobody was expecting the doctor's quick reply, and everyone laughed at the response. It was a great way to ease the nerves and get the interview started on a light note.

"Dr. Marks, I've got your bio and I'll do some voiceover work as we get some stock footage of you and the lab here. I also want to get some information about your lab and then we'll need to get into specifics of how you test materials. Can you and I go over some of that stuff before we start rolling the camera so that I'll have a better understanding of it when we do start filming?"

"Oh, sure! Let me start with the lab," Dr. Marks said. "This laboratory is the largest and most reputable in New York City. We have more state-of-the-art testing technology here than any lab has, outside of *maybe* NASA. In short, we are the lab of final resort. I mean, if the other labs across the country, or really the globe, can't get verifiable results, we are the one they call. Our work has been used to convict or exonerate over 50,000 individuals. In other words, if you want results, we are the place the scientific community comes to get them."

"Does that happen often? I mean, do other labs send you material to test?" Ms. Lauren asked.

"Everyday. Here, this is the next one on the pile," Dr. Marks said as she pulled a piece of paper from a folder sitting on her desk. "This subject is from a laboratory in Israel, which is unusual. Israel is a world leader in the scientific community, so we don't see a lot of things they have trouble with. Meaning, this could be very interesting."

Ann Lauren's eyes lit up. She said, "Could we follow the journey of this particular substance? Make identifying whatever it is the backdrop of our story?"

"That sounds like a fantastic idea! Let me look over the details. It says here that this particular substance was found at an archaeological excavation site, in an underground room that had been undisturbed for at least 1,000 years. The test that the original lab performed showed inconclusive and often opposing results. Hmmm. This *is* interesting. The original tester states that the material is almost certainly human blood but has some unique characteristics such as chromosome abnormality and slightly elevated radiation levels and a unique reaction to light. The material also reacts in an unusual manner when paired with damaged or broken testing samples. Hmmm. This particular case won't be used in a court case. Do you still want to follow this particular materials test?"

"Are you kidding? That looks like a perfect test subject," Ann replied. "What tests do you run to see if it is blood? How do you test blood to see if it is human? What is the background that I need to know?"

Dr. Marks was so focused on her work and explaining things to Ms. Lauren, she didn't notice that the tall cameraman had set up the perfect shot and the cameras were actually rolling. Lauren and the cameraman had perfected the move on a prior show; get the interviewer talking *before* the camera was ready so they were relaxed and then turn the camera on once the interviewer was into it.

Dr. Marks said, "Here are the basics you need to know about forensic blood testing. In 1967 a court case — *Miller v Pate* — showed that the current forms of blood testing were inadequate, so scientists began developing new tests to confirm that substances found at a crime scene are actually blood and not just red colored stains — paint, ketchup, or anything like that. The first thing we try is a luminol test — you've probably seen this on crime scene investigation television shows. Basically, the test consists of spraying a test sample with a solution of luminol and hydrogen peroxide. If the sample is blood, it will glow with a bluish color in the dark. Luminol is a fantastic test as it can detect bloodstains that have been diluted up to 300,000 times.[116] But luminol has its limitations, too. Other things glow besides blood."

"Like what?" Lauren asked.

"I've seen all sorts of things glow... like copper ions and bleach. Shoot, I've even seen horseradish sauce glow," Marks answered with a chuckle. "So, another test we use is called the Kastle-Meyer test. You might have seen this on a crime investigation show as well. The test sample is collected on a cotton swab and then they spray it with a clear liquid. Like magic, if the sample contains blood, the cotton swab turns

---

[116] Brian Rohrig, "The Forensics of Blood," ChemMatters, February 2008, https://lindblomeagles.org/ourpages/auto/2013/11/16/48289636/The%20Forensics%20of%20Blood%20Article.pdf

bright pink. The clear liquid is actually phenolphthalein and hydrogen peroxide. This test isn't perfect either as not only blood, but other substances can cause a positive test."

Marks demonstrated the series of tests for the camera on small samples and they both showed a positive result. It looked like the sample material was actually blood like the original tester has stated. One couldn't ask for better visuals for a forensic television broadcast.

"Now that we 'know' this is blood, we need to see if it is human blood or if this is from some other animal." By this point, Marks had realized she was being filmed and confided in Ms. Lauren, "All of the testing I am doing for you is very unscientific and wouldn't hold up in a court of law. We have several different tests that we would continue to run to prove, without a doubt, that this was *actually* blood. I'm just moving forward now for you and your audience. My technicians will thoroughly re-test this, which will probably use the remainder of our sample material, but they will test it under sterilized conditions. I hope that is ok."

"This is *perfect!*" Lauren exclaimed.

"Great," Marks said. "To differentiate between animal and human blood one of the tests that we use is called the precipitin test. Without going into too much detail the test is based on the fact that human blood will clot if it is exposed to the right antibodies, animal blood won't. When we subject the test material to these antibodies, if it is human blood it will clot. But this takes some time, and we will not know the results for one to two days. But let's just pretend that this *is* human blood. The next thing we want to determine is if this is from a human male or a human female."

By this time, with all of the models and tests performed, the interview had lasted over an hour and Ann Lauren was beginning to lose interest. Except that it provided her a paycheck, she really didn't care for science. She was quite sure she had enough footage for her weekly program. Lauren said, "Tell me about the test to determine gender and then I think we will need to get to our next appointment."

"Oh, sure. So, the next test is a blood chromosome test. Chromosome analysis or what we call 'karyotyping' is a test that evaluates the number and structure of a person's chromosomes.[117] Chromosomes are thread-like structures within each cell nucleus and contain the body's genetic blueprint. Chromosomes help ensure that DNA is replicated and distributed appropriately during cell division and each person's DNA is unique, like their fingerprint.[118] Now, humans have 23 *pairs* of chromosomes, resulting in 46 *total* chromosomes. In the first 22 chromosomes, called autosomes, one side of each chromosome is inherited from the female parent and the other from the male parent. This explains why children inherit some of their traits from their mother and some from their father. But it is the twenty-third chromosome, the sex chromosome, that determines gender. Females have two copies of the X chromosome — one inherited from the mother and one from the father. Males have one copy of the X chromosome — inherited from the mother — and one copy of the Y chromosome — inherited from the father."

It was at that point that Dr. Marks paused thoughtfully and said, "Perhaps that was too technical. Can I restate it? Do you have the time?"

"You read my mind," Ms. Lauren replied.

"Okay. Let me give it another shot." Marks cleared her throat and began again. "To find out the gender of the person whose blood we have, we use a procedure called the karyotype test. The important things to remember from our high school science is that humans have 23 pairs of chromosomes, inherited from the parents. Twenty-two chromosomes are autosomes but for our purposes, the important chromosome is the twenty-third chromosome, the gender chromosome. It is the twenty-third that determines gender. This test reveals whether the sample in question has XX as the twenty-third chromosome, which

---

[117] "Chromosome Analysis (Karyotyping)," Testing.com, January 27, 2021 https://labtestsonline.org/tests/chromosome-analysis-karyotyping

[118] "Learn Genomics," Healio.com, accessed March 9, 2022, https://www.healio.com/hematology-oncology/learn-genomics/genomics-primer/what-are-chromosomes

would be female, or if it has XY as the twenty-third chromosome, which would be male."

"Much better," Ms. Lauren said. "You said it would take some time to determine if this is, in fact, human blood and I guess this karyotype test will take some time as well. When you have the results, would you mind sharing them with me?"

"Absolutely. The karyotype test will take around a week to get results. I will need to remove any specifics as to who submitted it and where the sample came from, but yes, I can send you those results," Marks answered with a smile. "Anything else you want to ask me about before you close up shop?"

CHAPTER 30

R ight there in the middle of the Kidron Valley outside the walls of the Old City of Jerusalem, Rabbi Eliyahu Kaduri felt like he was floating. He knew things were different. His life, as he had known it, was over. He was *new*, somehow. It was as simple, and as complicated, as that. He didn't have a worrying thought. He knew the truth now and he was floating. He floated away from the sealed Golden Gate, as the Man had instructed, and moved north. Normally, a walk like this would take him around forty minutes. He didn't care. It would definitely have been faster if he cut through the Old City, but he was following the instructions he had been given. Kaduri continued north outside the city walls, past the Lions' Gate. He turned left and came to the third gate along his journey, Herod's Gate. Finally, about eight minutes after passing Herod's Gate, the Jewish Rabbi reached his entry point into the city, the impressive and Muslim-filled Damascus Gate on the north side of the city.

Turning south, Rabbi Kaduri made his way into the Muslim Quarter by way of the massive Damascus Gate and through the opening. Surrounded by Muslims, this was not a place he usually frequented, certainly never alone and especially after dark. *There is safety in numbers,* he thought to himself. He was obviously Jewish and anyone who looked at him could tell it. *Tradition,* Rabbi Kaduri thought and nodded to himself. He was wearing his black suit, a white shirt, he had a long beard and a small hat on the crown of his head. *Tradition.*

His emotions and his flight response, both screamed at him to run away, but he was different now and his heart was telling him to follow the directions that he had been given. It didn't matter that he was receiving looks that were full of hate. It didn't matter that people were intentionally bumping into him, making his progress difficult. *Somehow*, he knew this was important and *somehow*, he knew he would be safe.

Almost directly across the city, a Muslim man had walked up the hill and was entering the Jewish Quarter through the Dung Gate on the south side of the city. [119] "Dung Gate," the man said with a laugh. "What a stupid name for a stupid gate. Stupid, but fitting for these stupid, *stinking* Jews." The man, who could have been in his mid-thirties, knew the name was Bab al-Maghariba, or the Mughrabi Gate in Arabic, but he would much rather call it the *Dung Gate*, in English, because of his intense hatred for the Jews. The man was on a mission and walked north towards his intended destination.

The two men couldn't have been more opposite if they actually tried. One was old while the other was young. One was overweight and wearing an ill-fitting black suit while the other was athletic and wearing casual athletic clothing. One was a Rabbi, the other a Muslim zealot. One was filled with love while the other was brimming with hate.

Unbeknownst to either of the men, they were on a collision course.

The younger man pulled out his cell phone, opened the encryption and distortion apps, and dialed a now familiar number to a cheap burner phone. For the first time ever, no one answered the call. *There must be some mistake*, the man thought as he dialed the number again. This time the call was taken before the first tone had stopped. "Alhimaya," he said, "We have another job for you. We need you to kill the woman and her husband, the leaders of the dig. Tonight."

---

[119] This gate's unusual name derives from the refuse dumped here in antiquity, where the prevailing winds would carry odors away. Nehemiah 2:13 mentions a Dung Gate that was probably near this one. See https://israel.travel/the-gates-of-jerusalem/

CHAPTER 31

Matt and Jessica were standing at the mouth of the camouflaged cave entrance, dressed in their vests and hardhats. The vests had lights on them, their hardhats had lights on them, and Matt and Jessica each carried flashlights. They were just about to enter the cave to investigate the reason why all the workers had run away when Jessica put her hand on Matt's arm. "You remember when this all got started? That first night when I came home from work, after my breakfast with Dr. Kenyon?"

"Yeah, how could I forget? That was a rough evening. What specifically are you referring to?" Matt asked in reply. He stopped walking outside the cave entrance and looked Jess in the eye.

"Before we found out about Dr. Kenyon's death, I was so excited about the mystery of why Suleiman had sealed off the caves. It was the thing that initially made you want to help me in this project. Remember? Something freaked Suleiman out so much that one day he came along and sealed every cave in and around Jerusalem. Why did he do that?" Jessica asked.

"That's still a great question," Matt said. "Have you figured it out?"

"Well... what if it was something supernatural that scared him so bad that he sealed all the caves? What if Suleiman or his trusted cave-hunters had a run-in with a djinn and, in an effort to trap it, Suleiman ordered the caves to be closed?" Jessica asked.

"For the final time, *what is a djinn?!?!*" Matt asked, his voice raised almost to a shout.

"It depends on who you ask and what time period and what the context is and..."

"Quit talking in riddles and tell me what a djinn is!" Matt demanded.

"Maybe the best way to describe a djinn is… it's what we, you and me, Christians, would call a demon,"

"A demon?!?" Matt interrupted.

"Yes, but there's more to it than that. In Arabic and Muslim theology, they are a class of spirits, lower than angels, capable of appearing in human and animal forms, possessing people, and influencing people to do evil.[120] There's a deeper context to it, too. Multiple djinn or djinni is actually where we get our word 'genie' from," Jessica said.

"You mean like from the Genie from Aladdin?" Matt asked.

"Yes and no," Jessica said. "Djinn don't grant wishes, but in Arabic and Muslim tradition they *do* have supernatural powers and can use them to hurt or kill humans. They can take on a fiery form, wield power, grow into giants, play tricks on humans. Think about your worst idea of a demon and that's what a djinn is to our Muslim friends. That's why all of our workers took off. They also think that djinn can fall in love with women and will possess them for sexual purposes. That's why everyone kept trying to get me and Nava to cover up, so the djinn wouldn't realize we are women. What if it was a djinn that freaked Suleiman out? What if we are about to encounter a demon, a djinn, face-to-face in this cave?" Jessica asked.

"So, what if we do? I'm not scared of any demons!" Matt said.

Matt was different now.

Matt saw the look on Jessica's face and said, "Look, we are both Christians and the Bible says that *the Spirit of Him who raised Christ from the dead lives in us*.[121] God lives in us! There's no demon that's more powerful than God and He lives **in us**! Jesus himself said that *these signs shall follow them that believe; In my name shall they cast out devils;*[122] the book of James also says that when we *resist the devil he **has** to flee*.[123]

---

[120] "Jinn," Dictionary.com, accessed March 9, 2022, https://www.dictionary.com/browse/jinn

[121] Romans 8:11 (King James Version)

[122] Mark 16:17 (King James Version)

[123] James 4:7 (King James Version)

It isn't an option. We are told to cast demons out and that they have to flee at the Name of Jesus.

"Suleiman might have freaked out, but Suleiman didn't have the Living God residing in him like we do. Let's go see what all the fuss is about!" Matt concluded with a smile on his face.

Jessica just stared at her husband. The change in him over the last year was remarkable. Matt was learning that just because you call yourself a Christian, it didn't mean you were a wimp. She loved that Matt had turned into a man's man, that he had faced his fears and risen above them — and all it took was one life-or-death encounter with a terrorist. She smiled at him, took his hand and they entered the cave together.

"Where do we start?" Matt asked.

"Well, we have several candidates," Jessica said as she held up the electronic device in her free hand. "That's what I was checking on while you were cleaning up the mess that the workers left. Along with a light, in each of the vests there is also a tracking device. So, I know where people were at the approximate time of the sighting, but since I don't know who was wearing which vest, I can't pinpoint which place we need to go. We're just going to have to search them all. This machine will help us do it. It's like a GPS for caves, let's call it a CPS — cave positioning system — and for us, it will give a map of the places that have been explored up to this point. It will be better than just wandering around aimlessly, but with the extreme differences in locations, navigating to each will take some time. Potentially several hours. The other good thing about our CPS, we don't need to have any type of cellular or satellite connectivity. We don't need to be online; the maps are housed in the unit itself."

"Cool!" Matt said. "And, since my boss gave everybody the day off tomorrow, it's not like I have to get up early. We'll just check them all, go home and sleep in tomorrow morning. Nothing quite like date night in a cave, right?"

"We'll certainly see!" Jessica said with a smile.

CHAPTER 32

R abbi Kaduri was following the instructions he had been given. The hardest part of his task had been conquering his own fears of being alone and a Rabbi in the Muslim Quarter of the Old City. He had entered through the Damascus Gate, first-making the sharp left turn and then the quick right-hand turn, turns which had been built hundreds of years before, to slow an advancing army, before airplanes, tanks, and bombs had rendered walls and gates unnecessary. Once he cleared the gate, he followed the Damascus Gate Road for a few hundred yards. He came upon a fork in the road, but he had already been instructed to stay on the left-hand side where it split at Hidmi Falafel. The right-hand road turned into Khaz-Zait Street. That was the wrong street to take. He had been instructed to stay to the left on Al-Wad Street. The road narrowed, but just as he had been told, there was a tourist group being led through the narrow street that was littered with shops and he was able to join the pack without anyone really noticing him. Rabbi Kaduri smiled as he walked along. He stayed with the group and heard the tour guide giving a pretty good explanation of the Via Dolorosa. The misconception about the Via Dolorosa is that it is just one street. The better way to think of the *Sorrowful Way,* is that it is a path consisting of many streets and stations throughout the Old City. It is the path that many Christians believe Jesus walked, forced by the Romans, carrying His cross to His own crucifixion. There were larger numbers of people, mostly tourists, in this area and it gave Rabbi Kaduri a small sense of relief to be in a crowd of non-Muslims.

Rabbi Kaduri came to a building on the left side of the street that had a small plaque on the exterior that said, 'Austrian Hospice,' just like he had been told. He turned left there and walked along the street that had a high wall on the left side and tall buildings on the right. He followed the road for several hundred yards until he came to a cross street, Bab Al-Ghawanima Street that was at the top of a slight rise. As he crested the hill, Kaduri began to look for his intended destination and noticed he was on Lions' Gate Street. "Curious," he thought. "Why was I directed to enter the city through the Damascus Gate only to be directed back towards the Lions' Gate?" He was told to look for a tall tower on his left, the tower from the Church of the Condemnation, and then he would come to a pass-through of an older section of the wall. Kaduri could see the tower almost from the moment he began walking on Lions' Gate Road. He continued walking and then he saw it. At some point, the wall around the city had been expanded or enlarged and rendered the interior wall obsolete. Kaduri was approaching that interior, smaller wall. However, through this interior wall, there was a half-almond shaped opening that had been cut, allowing the road to continue.

Kaduri had been given instructions on what to do. Go to a *certain place*, wait and watch, and then find Matthew at the last place Kaduri had seen him, those several weeks ago. Kaduri was now approaching that *certain place*. He had been told that once he saw the wall's pass-through, he should look for a sign that read 'Herod's Gate Ascent.' It was almost dark now and Rabbi Kaduri had a hard time finding the sign. When he saw it, he understood why — the sign was on a wall but was hidden behind a traffic sign. The sign Kaduri had been told to look for was partially hidden, exactly as the Rabbi would be standing there in the dark. He pulled his black suit jacket closed, closing it tight around his neck against the cool breeze and prepared for the evening. Inadvertently, he made himself virtually invisible, dressed completely in black. He was not sure what he would see or how long he should stay, but after today, things were different in him, and he would do whatever was asked of him.

From his vantage point under the 'Herod's Gate Ascent' sign, and inside the small opening that seemed like it was almost perfectly formed for him, Rabbi Kaduri's eyes were adjusting to the darkness. He could see people inside the wall's pass-through. There were several structural arches along the inside of the pass-through which created small alcoves, small pockets where people had set up shop. Many had shirts, and many had rugs hanging along the walls inside these recesses and the Rabbi presumed that people were selling them, protected from the elements in the pass-through.

"I wonder how long I will need to wait and what I am supposed to be looking for," he thought to himself. It didn't take long for him to find out. As he was looking towards the pass-through, he saw an athletic man walking with a boy of twelve or thirteen coming toward him in the darkness of the pass-through. He saw the faces of the boy and a tall, bearded man. As they were just about to exit the pass-through, the man said something to the boy, and they stopped just inside the opening. The man scanned the area and Rabbi Kaduri eased back into his hiding spot. Once the man was confident no one was watching him, he lifted one of the rugs hanging on the wall. The boy stepped to the wall and disappeared. The man followed, and the rug flapped back down hiding the entrance to a secret passageway in the city. One moment they were there, the next, they were gone.

CHAPTER 33

Six pm wasn't exactly the middle of the night, but it might as well have been to Faysal. The cheap phone ringing in his pocket began pulling him out of the fitful sleep of his pre-supper nap. It was unusual for him to be home this early on a Thursday, but since Dr. Davenport had sent everyone home, he was looking forward to spending some time with his family before the evening meal. Unfortunately, his boys were visiting a friend, Amit, where they were undoubtedly playing his new video gaming system… again. After he realized he had a quiet house, it didn't take but about thirty seconds before he was asleep on the couch as Laila prepared their meal. As he quickly dozed off to sleep, he had visions of the djinn terrorizing him and his family, chasing them, possessing them. The screaming phone just added to the terror of the nap-mare. By the time Faysal realized what the noise actually was and was awake enough to pull the phone from his pocket, it had quit ringing. This was not good. He had instructions to answer that phone whenever it rang. Whoever was on the other end would not be pleased.

The phone, still in his hand, sprang to life again. Faysal answered it before the first tone had stopped and said "I'm sorry! I had fallen asleep. It won't happen again."

"Alhimaya, we have another job for you. Perhaps, after tonight, there won't be a *need* to answer my call *ever* again. Tonight will be difficult for the both of us, but it may be the last thing we ever have to do," the heavily distorted voice said. "It has come to our attention that the cave system where you are now working is connected to the place we have sworn to keep hidden. Precautions are being taken on our end, but we need you to kill the woman and her husband, the leaders of the dig. It must be done tonight. They are still at the site exploring the cave. You will find a gun underneath the seat in your Land Rover. Kill them. Tonight. In the cave. Now."

The door to Faysal's modest home swung open and his sons came running in, surprising him with their playing and laughter. Faysal stepped into another room for privacy and said to the unknown man on the phone, "I cannot. There was a djinn spotted in the cave. I will not enter. The djinn will not let me enter. I cannot enter. I will kill Matt and Jessica at some point before work resumes, but I will *not* do it in the cave."

"Alhimaya, you *will* do it in the cave, and you *will* do it tonight."

"No. I cannot. The djinn..."

"Were those your children I heard in the background? How much do you love them? What would you do to keep them safe?"

"You leave my children out of this," Faysal screamed. "My children will not be used to threaten me." The boys turned quiet in the adjoining room at the sound of their father's shouting.

"You love them all, do you not? Which one do you love the most? Your oldest, Yusef? Is he your favorite? Or..." there was a very long, very uncomfortable pause. "Or... did I grab the wrong one?"

Faysal ran into the other room where his children were. There were only three boys instead of the normal number of four. "*Yusef?* Where is your brother? Where is Yusef? *Where is Yusef?!?*" Faysal shouted. The three boys looked around, confused then sat still, quiet, scared.

Faysal opened the front door and screamed for his son, "Yusef!! *Yusef!!!* Son, where are you?!?" Back into the house he shouted, "Boys, where were you when you saw him last?"

One of the crying, scared boys said, "I don't know. We thought he had already come home. We don't know where he went."

Faysal put the phone back to his ear and screamed, "*Where is my son?!?* If you hurt him in any way..."

The cold, distorted voice on the other end of the call replied, "He is here. With me. You have your instructions. Kill the couple in the cave. Tonight. Once that is done, your son will be returned to you, unharmed. This is just another step in his training and there are some things I will teach him. Tonight, he and I will light a fire."

Resolved, Faysal said "I will do what must be done."

The line clicked and the voice on the other end of the call was gone.

CHAPTER 34

Th realization washed over Matt like the cold water of an *ice bucket challenge*. He realized being this deep inside the cave felt completely different to him than the first time he was here. The differences were glaring. This time he was with Jessica, had plenty of light, had some sense of direction on where they were going and where they had been, knew fairly well how to find an exit, and he didn't care that he didn't have any cell phone reception. He was actually enjoying his time in the cave, especially because he was with his wife. The other big difference between this trip deep in the cave and the time when he was trapped inside was that they were now looking for something supernatural, something potentially evil, something that they may need to confront. In his original time inside the cave, under the Old City, he was hoping to run into *anything* that might point him to a way out.

"Well, we're here," Jessica said as she slowed to a stop in the middle of a hallway. She did a quick 360-degree spin and said, "I guess this isn't it, either. There's nothing here, nothing to see, just more cave. You were right though; this place is a labyrinth. It's a wonder that you found your way out of here."

"Well, I had help," Matt admitted. "As weird as it sounds, the more I have thought about my original time in here, the more I feel like the Lord had a plan. Don't get me wrong, I'm not saying God was trying to trap me or bury me under yards of dirt, but I feel like even if I hadn't discovered this cave through getting trapped, that God would have used me or us to locate this place. Like it's important or something. I think maybe Professor Kenyon had picked up on it, too and that's why he wanted you to take over the dig. I'm still trying to process *why*, but I just feel like there's a reason for it all. Probably sounds silly, doesn't it?"

"No. Not really. Not to me. To someone who doesn't understand that we can have a relationship with God, that He wants to be a part of our lives, that He is here to help us, it might sound a little trippy," Jessica said with a smile. "Keep praying about it. I'm sure God will reveal His plan to us when it's the right time." Jessica pressed a few buttons on her electronic CPS device, and she waited for a new location to be illuminated on the screen. "Has any of this looked familiar to you?" she asked.

Matt replied, "Not so far. Every part of this cave looks just the same as everything else. That's why I was using *Skittles* to help mark the places I had been. I'm guessing that the only thing that will look different are the two unique rooms — the room where the cut rocks were stacked and the room with the black stuff. Oh, and if we come across it, my little pile of green *Skittles*, where I marked the first discovery in this cave will look different, if the pile is even still there."

Matt and Jessica had spent several hours inside the cave and had not been able to locate anything unusual inside. There were only three locations left to check and as they waited for the CPS to pinpoint their next place to investigate, Matt had a simple nudge, something on the inside giving him... something...

Matt said, "I'm not sure why, but I think what we are looking for will be at our next location." Jessica's face flashed an instant of concern, but Matt continued, "But I think whatever is going to be at our next location will be a good thing, not a bad thing. I don't know why, but I do."

Right then, the machine in Jessica's hand chimed. Their next stop had been pinpointed on the device and a rough route had been plotted. "I hope you're right. I'm getting sleepy and it's very late," Jessica said.

At the same time Matt and Jessica were making their way to their next destination, Faysal, armed with a Sig Sauer P320 pistol, was timidly walking through the cave. Even carrying the weapon with its 17 rounds, he was scared. Not scared of killing Matt and Jessica. That would be the easy part. Faysal knew they were still here, their car was in the lot, their belongings were still accessible at the site. He knew how to kill. He had killed in a number of different ways. A gun was just another tool in his arsenal and this particular tool was a fine instrument. No, killing two unsuspecting people, deep in a cave in the middle of the night, would be simple. Too simple, really, for his skilled hands and educated mind. Killing was easy and would never again make him afraid. However, the possibility of an encounter with a djinn scared Faysal to his core. His hands were shaking. His stomach was turning over inside of him. He did not like anything about this and hated anything supernatural, whether it be movies, stories, even talking about it. So, the only thing that could have made him enter this cave was the hope that completing this task, killing these two people, would save his precious son's life.

"I will do what must be done. I will do what must be done. I will do what must be done," Faysal repeated to himself. He was trying to calm his fears by repeating the last words he said to his puppet master, the one giving the orders, the one who had his son. He knew he didn't have any other choice but to put one foot in front of the other. He knew in basic terms where the worker had been when he saw the djinn and he was making his way to the area. Repeating the words kept him from being paralyzed by the fear of the unknown in front of him.

All I need to do now is find them and not the djinn.

Faysal flipped on his flashlight and the light on the hard hat he was wearing. The light cast an ominous beam down the long hallway. Everything was quiet. Everything was dark. He was alone. "I will do what must be done," he again whispered to himself.

It was after midnight and the longer they stayed in the cave, the more tired Matt and Jessica were becoming and the less they were talking. Breaking the silence that had been ruling the past few minutes, Jessica said, "Ok. *Finally*, we are coming up on our next location. After this, we'll have two more to go. But neither of them are very far from here."

That's when Matt saw it. "Jessica," he whispered. "Quiet. Stop walking. Turn your flashlight off. Turn your vest light off. Turn your headlight off." Matt did the same. Matt had seen it first, but now that their lights were off, and the light was gone completely, it was easy for Jessica to understand Matt's concern.

They were still deep in the cave. For hours they had been alone. No sounds but the ones they were making. No lights but the ones they carried. No people except each other. With their lights off it should have been pitch black. They should have been surrounded by a darkness so thick that they couldn't see their hands in front of their faces.

That wasn't the case.

From somewhere, ahead of them, in the direction they were going, but coming from a place they couldn't yet see, there was light.

And the light... *was moving.*

CHAPTER 35

"Yes?" the man said as he answered the cell phone.

"Encryption protocol, 247 — Delta — Alpha — Papa," was the reply from the other end.

"Hold please... Encryption engaged. This is Eli Kaplan. Go ahead."

"Eli, this is Doron. I have news. We are still digging through the rubble and investigating but we have found multiple explosive devices. The explosions that killed the archaeologist, Kenyon, and trapped your friend, Davenport, were both intentional. I will get details to you as soon as they are available, but…."

"What is it?" Eli asked.

"There is something else," Doron said with dread in his voice.

"Yes?"

"The chatter has increased. Whatever is going on, whatever they have been planning, it, or something, it looks like it is happening tonight. You asked me to tell you if it ever looked like it was unsafe for your friends. This is me telling you. It is now. Get them out. Get them somewhere safe. We never had reason to believe that their tunnel system was anywhere near or around the terror tunnels. Now we know. We have heard chatter about 'removing the archaeologist and her husband.' We know it is referring to your friends.

"We have been working around the clock. We have a location and are moving on it soon, tonight, before the break of dawn, once we have assembled the teams and are ready."

"Understood. Thank you."

Eli Kaplan pressed the *End Call* button on his cell phone and immediately dialed Jessica's telephone number. The phone chimed four times and then went to voicemail. Eli said "Jessica, I know it is late, but please call me back. This is important," and pressed the *End Call* button. Kaplan then dialed a second telephone number. It chimed four times and then he said, "Matthew, please call me back, you or Jessica. It is important. I'm on my way to your apartment. We need to talk," and pressed the *End Call* button again. Finally, Kaplan sent a text to each of them: "Kids, please call me when you get this. We need to talk. It is very important. Life or death."

CHAPTER 36

"Your father talks about you often. He's all mouth and no trousers, but you are his pride and joy," the man said to Faysal's son, Yusef. "And I'm chuffed you understand English. I much prefer to speak English than Arabic or Hebrew. It makes more sense to me than any other language. First languages are like that sometimes."

Yusef nodded but said nothing. His father did not like it when he spoke English, especially when he was in the Old City. And even though they had left the city walls a few moments ago, he didn't know if this was a test. So, he stayed quiet. He was so very sleepy, and his tired eyes burned from fatigue. His father never let him stay up as late as this, but he did not want to disappoint the man he was with, and he did not wish to disappoint his father, so he fought to stay awake and kept his mouth closed.

"We are the chosen protectors of the hidden place," the man continued. "I know that you have only just begun your training, but I'm happy that you have started and that you have your father to teach you. It was different for me. I was the last gift my father gave my mother before he died. I was not yet born when my father was killed, so my training came from the mouths of others, people like my brother. He is the chap that you saw earlier, the one in the suit. He just returned from his exile abroad. We have big plans. Big, big plans.

"My brother, your father and even I have different roles, but a common goal: to protect Islam. Sometimes we must do things we do not like, like your father is doing tonight, and sometimes we must do things in horrible ways, but we do whatever it takes in the service of Allah. But don't worry, because tonight, for me and you? Tonight is easy. Carrying all the boxes and equipment was the hard part, but it is over now. The rest will be easy. I know you are tired. Once we do this last thing, we'll go back where we were, and you can rest until it is time for you to go back with your father. He will meet us once he finishes his work."

Relief washed over Yusef. The thought of sleep was almost over-powering, but he knew he was being entrusted to do a task for Allah and he did not want to mess it up. He wanted to make his father proud.

After a few more minutes of walking, the man announced to Yusef, "We are almost there. The man who runs the business found some infor-mation that he was not supposed to find. I want you to remember this, Yusef, we are not cruel or indiscriminate killers. Because he is unaware of how dangerous the information is and what it means, we will let him live. But because the information is here, this place must be destroyed. That is why we are here tonight, when no one else is around, so no one gets hurt. We are going to burn this place down."

Yusef followed the man across the street and through a parking lot until the two of them came to a business that had a royal blue door, with a white background for the red English letters that were written on it. Yusef could speak English, but he could not read it, so he did not know what the name of the place was. It didn't matter to him. He just wanted to finish this night and go to sleep. To Yusef's surprise, the man reared back and smashed the door with his powerful foot. He kicked the door right below the handle and it splintered and opened. Yusef was not expecting the blow and the sound startled the young boy. The man looked around and after he was sure that no one heard the sound, stepped inside the building. Yusef followed the man inside. It took Yusef's eyes a moment to adjust to the dark interior of the building, but when they did, he realized he was in some sort of science room. There were papers and glass beakers and pencils and calculators and different machines on each of the tables. Yusef's eyes eventually trained on the man as he moved through the room. Yusef saw him stop, pull a lighter from his pocket, pick up some loose papers from a desk, light them and drop the slow burning pile into a metal trash receptacle. Then the man did something curious. He walked to each table in the room and turned the little silver knobs that were attached. Then he turned more knobs on the small silver instruments sitting on each table. There were several of them. Yusef began to hear them hissing but was not sure what was happening.

The man said, "That will do it. Let's go. Pull the door behind you please, Yusef."

Yusef was confused but did what he was told, followed the man back out into the parking lot, across the street and back the way they had come. He followed the man back towards beautiful, blissful, sweet sleep. After a few minutes of walking, Yusef summoned the courage to ask, "I thought you said we were going to destroy that building. Why did you change your mind? Did you find the papers you were looking for and just burned them instead?"

The man smiled and said, "We did destroy that building. It just hasn't happened yet." Yusef was confused and the man could tell it by the look on Yusef's face. The man continued explaining. "We set a fire, but more importantly, we added fuel to that fire. Each of those knobs I turned were control valves that released invisible, but highly flammable gas into the room. Some of those knobs were connected to little devices called Bunsen burners, so I turned them on as well. Once enough gas is trapped in the room, it will reach and feed the fire in the trash bin, and everything will go up in flames. And it will happen quickly."

The man barely had the words out of his mouth when there was a loud explosion a few blocks away. The man turned to Yusef, smiled, and said, "Cheers, you corker! You set your first bomb and destroyed your first building. You kept our hidden place hidden. Your father will be proud."

Yusef wanted to smile. He wanted to be proud of his work. He wanted to be excited about making his father happy. But he wasn't. Maybe it was because he was so sleepy or maybe there was something more.

Inside the young boy, conflict was raging. He wanted to make his father proud, wanted to be just like him and follow in his footsteps, but there was something in Yusef that did not like to destroy. This went against *everything* his father had taught him until now. Islam and his parents had taught him to value others' belongings, to share with his brothers, to help those in need, to love those around him, to be gentle to people, especially his mother. Islam is a religion of peace. He had been told. Why did Allah change his mind? Why did Allah now want to destroy? Why wouldn't Allah tell him these things himself?

Yusef decided to think about these things tomorrow. Maybe it would all be clearer then. All he really wanted now was to go to sleep.

CHAPTER 37

E arlier in the day, Faysal had spoken with the worker, Akhmed, who had encountered the djinn. The man was scared, and it was obvious to Faysal that the man had actually been face to face with *something*. Faysal believed it, believed him. The man had given eerily specific details about a glowing, vibrating, undulating... being. He couldn't put a description into words, but it was clear that the man wasn't just using this as a way to get out of work. And there had been other signs as well. He had urinated on himself. So, Faysal had some details about where the djinn had been and where the man had encountered it and even some of the results of that encounter. But that was more than eight or nine hours ago. Would the djinn still be in the same place? He wondered if he would be able to find Dr. Davenport and her goofy husband before the djinn saw him. It was a gamble, but one that he *must* make. His son's life depended on it.

With each step, Faysal's light bounced on the walls, ceiling and floor of the massive cave. All he wanted to do was find the two leaders, exterminate them, and get out of the cave as quickly as possible. He had the flashlight in one hand, the gun in the other.

"I will do what must be done," he whispered again.

Faysal tried to focus on the task at hand. He wanted to kill the couple somewhere deep in the cave where they wouldn't be found for days or weeks, but he was beginning to question whether this was the smartest move. Had the couple left the cave already? Had he missed them? He decided he would continue for one more hour and then he would head back to the entrance to see if their vehicle was still there. "Oh, great. Another room inside a room," Faysal thought and went in to check it out.

The light continued to shimmer from some unknown spot ahead of Jessica and Matt. Until this very moment, Matt had been confident. He was ready to face anything that came at him. Matt was large and in charge. Right up until this very moment. Now, internally, he was questioning everything, every life choice he had ever made, right until this point, every decision flashed through his mind. For a moment, he was glad that it was too dark in the cave for his wife to see him. All of their lights were turned off, which meant she couldn't see the fear that was trying to grip him — it had to have been written all over his face. He had talked a big game, wanting to enter the cave, wanting to confront the djinn, but now that the moment was here, he was questioning why he had been so cavalier about it. His emotions, his intellect was screaming at him to run away. They were screaming loud. So loud. But there was something else, something way down on the inside that was whispering to him *"Keep going. You've got this. 'In the way of righteousness is life: and in the pathway thereof there is no death.'"*[124]

The light ahead of them reminded Matt of something and in that moment, he flashed back to being a child in the suburbs. He was drawn back to his childhood home, looking from his window towards his neighbor's house. More specifically, he thought of his neighbor's swimming pool. Sometimes, in the evening, the neighbor would turn on the light in the pool for an evening swim. From Matt's house, as a little boy, he couldn't see over the privacy fence, but he could see the way the light danced in the darkness, bouncing off of the trees, reflecting off of the house, undulating with each wave and ripple, casting light towards his

---

[124] Proverbs 12:28 (King James Version)

house. Matt had looked at that light dancing in the night and been in awe of the beauty of God's creation. Tonight, the light reflecting off of the walls of the cave looked the same. In an instant, something washed over Matt. A peace. A calm. An awe of God's creation.

Matt reached into the void where Jessica had been standing and touched her arm with his left hand. He slid his hand down to her hand and pulled her towards him. Holding her hand in his, he reached his right hand and found her face, gently cupped it and brought his lips to hers. He whispered, "I love you. Stay here, I'll be right back," and started to move away from her.

Jessica didn't release her grip on his hand and said in whispered tones, "I love you, too, but you're not going anywhere without me. With God, one can put a thousand to flight and two can put ten thousand to flight. We're doing this together." Jessica was referencing a scripture in the Bible found in Deuteronomy that demonstrated God's exponential power when his followers work in concert together with Him. [125]

Even though she couldn't see it, Jessica knew Matt was smiling. He squeezed her hand and whispered, "That's right! There is no weapon formed against us that can prosper against us!"[126] The two of them turned, hand-in-hand, and walked toward the light and whatever it was.

Matt and Jessica cautiously walked down a long corridor with openings on each side. They came toward the end of the hallway and saw the light coming from an opening to the right. Cautiously, they made their way into the opening. Inside the opening was a bare room. Peering into the opening of the room, Jessica could see that along one side, cut in the wall, was another opening, a doorway. There were also neatly cut rocks, stacked in piles. Jessica figured that at one point, the rocks had been stacked on both sides of the doorway. Now the rocks were cleared away and stacked neatly in the larger, outer room. The undulating light was coming from inside the smaller room, its source, still unseen. Matt

---

[125] Reference Deuteronomy 32:30

[126] Isaiah 54:17 (King James Version)

immediately recognized where they were standing. He turned to Jessica and excitedly whispered, "This is the place! This is the room where I found the black stuff! The dead guy, the mummy dude, is in that room, where the light is coming from!"

Faysal thought he heard something, so he stopped and listened. It had been like this all night. He wanted to find Dr. Davenport and her husband, but he did not want to be caught with the djinn. Every time he kicked a pebble, every time there was an unusual sound, every time there was a different sensation of any kind, Faysal was forced to stop, look, listen, see what had made the noise. Over and over, he had repeated this process. It had happened so many times over the hours he had been in the cave that he stopped turning his flashlight off. At one point during his search, he had the realization; perhaps, if the two archaeologists saw his light, they would come to him. That would make things easier. If they heard the noise he was making, they might make their way to him. It was a calculated risk. Would it be the woman and her husband who came around the corner or would it be the djinn? Faysal was ready to shoot if it was the first and run if it was the other. He waited. Quiet. Stillness.

Would this night ever end? The stress was almost unbearable. Not because of the task set before him, not really because of the djinn. The stress came from the unknown surrounding his son. Even if he could complete his task, there were no real guarantees that Yusef would be returned to him.

Another dead end. Endless rooms. Faysal was glad that for weeks he had been working extensively inside the cave and tunnel system and had a fairly good idea or at least a general idea of where he was, where he had been, where he was going, and how to get to an exit if he needed to. There were just so many dead ends and each one needed to be checked. He turned around, flashing his light across the walls of the room.

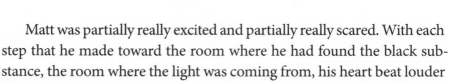

Matt was partially really excited and partially really scared. With each step that he made toward the room where he had found the black substance, the room where the light was coming from, his heart beat louder in his chest, pounded in his ears, stirred in his stomach. It was so loud, he wondered if Jessica could hear it from where she was standing a few feet away, waiting for him. Matt stepped as quietly towards the room as he could, easing to the opening so he could see what was generating the light. What, exactly, did a djinn look like? Matt found himself with his back pressed against the wall just outside the opening of the lit room.

As Jessica watched from across the outer room, she saw Matt lean forward, and crane his neck as he tried to look inside. Then he pivoted, moving his whole body into the light of the doorway which cast a large shadow in the outer room where Jessica stood. He dropped his flashlight and raised both hands, a move that almost looked like he was surrendering and then he stepped fully inside the room and completely out of Jessica's view. The light swallowed him. He was completely out of sight. Seconds felt like hours. How long had he been gone? Jessica didn't know what to do. She stood there unable to move.

From inside the room, Jessica heard a whisper, "Come here."

Jessica stayed still. Something seemed off. A second time, louder, Jessica heard the whispered words, "Come here."

She didn't know what to do. Maybe her mind was playing tricks on her, maybe she was too sleep deprived, but she didn't recognize the voice and so she stayed still. Under her breath she said, "In the Name of Jesus, I command any evil spirits in that room to leave and never come back!"

Matt popped his head out of the room and whispered "Couldn't you hear me? Come here! You have got to see this! You're not going to believe it. You're about to be famous all over again."

Jessica took a step towards the room and the machine in her hand began vibrating and beeping in a low tone. At first, she thought the battery must be running low, but a quick glance showed that the battery was actually three quarters full. It was a radiation warning.

The vests that Eli had provided the team came equipped with a place to clip a light, a tracking chip so they could monitor where the workers were while they were in the cave and the vests also contained a small Geiger counter. The Geiger counter is an instrument used for detecting and measuring radiation and wasn't a normal tool to have at an archaeological site. That instrument was now reporting back to the machine in Jessica's hand and indicating there was radiation present in the room she was standing in.

"How did Eli know?" Jessica whispered to herself. She looked down at the machine and the warning turned off, reading normal levels again. "That's weird," she said. "Matt, something weird is going on."

"Just wait until you get in *here*," was his reply.

Faysal was tired of all of this. Even though he knew he hadn't been, he felt like he was walking in circles. He hadn't seen anything unusual. He hadn't seen the dig leaders. He hadn't seen anything but rocks and limestone walls. Frustrated, he decided to go back to the cave entrance and see if their car was still there. Maybe he would run across them on the way. Maybe he should wait for them out there. He started feeling like a coward and wondered if the man holding his son would honor their agreement if he killed the two leaders outside the cave. Regardless, he needed to check if they were still on site, and he began to formulate a plan in case they had gone home. He could wait for them until morning. If they didn't show up, he could call them and spin a story to them, requiring them to come back to the site. If they were already gone, it might not be a bad thing after all. He began walking with a little pep in his step. Maybe this would be easier than he initially thought.

Jessica stepped into the smaller room and immediately knew why Matt had dropped his flashlight. She dropped hers as well. There was a weight to the room, a presence that was so heavy she couldn't keep the light in her hand. And, just as Matt had done, Jessica lifted her hands into a surrender position and subconsciously whispered, "Therefore, I encourage you to pray on every occasion with *hands lifted to God in worship* with clean hearts, free from frustration or strife."[127] The Bible verse just bubbled up from deep within her; it was a fulfillment of the scripture that said, *'for out of the abundance of the heart the mouth speaks.'*[128] Something inside of her was reacting to her surroundings, to the weightiness of the room, to the presence that was filling it and she was compelled to worship God. She fell to her knees in reverence.

After several moments, Jessica was finally able to understand why Matt hadn't just called her into the room. She could barely speak. All she could do was muster a whisper. She asked, "What is this?"

Matt, who had been in the room for a while longer, and was becoming more comfortable in the unusual atmosphere, said, "This is God's doing, God's handiwork. God's tangible presence. This is God revealing Himself to us. But not only that, look around. This is God returning the things to His people that have been lost for so long. These items will provide undeniable proof that this land belongs to the nation of Israel and was given to them by God."

"I, I, I don't really know what any of this is or what it means," Jessica admitted. She continued to look around the room in complete

---

[127] I Timothy 2:8 (The Passion Translation)

[128] Luke 6:45 (King James Version)

amazement. It dawned on her. The room was completely illuminated, but there was no light source. She said, "I don't understand any of this."

Matt said, "First John 1:5 reminds us that *God is light and in Him there is no darkness.*[129] This room is filled with the presence of God. He is the one illuminating everything in here. Look," Matt said, pointing to the ceiling. "That's where the black substance was, it coated the ceiling and the wall. It's gone now, replaced by the brilliant light." Jessica shielded her eyes as she tried to look where Matt was pointing. The light reflected off of the brilliant white limestone the room was made of. The effect was dazzling, brilliant, blinding light in the room, but it was enhanced by the gold items that Jessica was just noticing for the first time.

Jessica stood to her feet and asked, "Is that what I think it is?"

"Yeah," Matt said reverently. "I think it is."

In front of Matt and Jessica was a box. The box was roughly four and a half feet long, two and a half feet wide by two and a half feet tall and it was sitting on a shelf in the room, elevated higher than the other artifacts. But it wasn't the size or the position of the box that was striking. The box was covered entirely in highly polished gold, and it was radiating and reflecting the light in the room. Adorning the top of the box were two angels with their wings spread, covering the lid and there were four hooks on the corners of the box itself.

Jessica asked again, "Is that what I think it is?"

Matt simply, reverently replied, "It's the Ark of the Covenant."

As he said it, the machine in Jessica's hand started vibrating and chirping. The radiation meter was warning her of unsafe levels, but just as quickly as it started, it stopped again. "What was that?" Matt asked about the machine.

"The CPS machine is telling me that there were or maybe there still are very high radiation levels in here. I guess it's the power of God or something, right?"

---

[129] I John 1:5 (King James Version)

"You better believe it!" Matt excitedly said. "We think of nuclear power as being the greatest energy source on Earth, but the Earth hasn't experienced the kind of power as it did the day Jesus rose from the dead. There was a shock blast so powerful that it pulled His Spirit from the depths of Hell and slammed Him back into His Body. The power from that event then blasted his body out of his grave clothes, leaving them like an empty cocoon where they laid, separate from the handkerchief they used to cover his face.[130] That same power flipped away the huge stone that blocked the tomb and Jesus walked out a new Man! But that was just the beginning! There was so much power in that event that other people who had recently died were brought back to life and showed up in the city, purely from the significant power in operation. I think your machine is picking up on some of the residue of that power!" [131]

The two of them stood just inside the entrance, completely in awe, for what seemed like hours but was more likely just a handful of minutes. Finally, they started to look around the room. Matt said, "When I was here that first night, the room was packed with stones and the dead guy. There was barely enough room to stand. The room seemed so small and so cramped. Now that all of the stones are out of here and the mummy is gone, there's so much more room and we can see what the stones were blocking. But look, even the walls, ceiling and floor of the room have been polished! It is so clean and so bright. Like brand new."

Reverently, Jessica said, "That's exactly what happens to us as well when we invite Jesus into our lives. He cleans us up, from the inside, making us clean and bright and like brand new. He gets rid of the mummified remains and junk in our lives and gives us a brand-new start."

Looking around, Matt and Jessica noticed there were three other pieces of furniture in the space along with the Ark in its place of reverence above them all on the shelf at the back of the room. Looking at the

---

[130] Reference John 20:7

[131] Reference Matthew 27:52-53

objects, Matt realized these were the pieces of furniture that had been kept in the Temple and that these pieces of furniture had been missing since Nebuchadnezzar destroyed the Temple in 586 BC.

"Do you understand what we're looking at? Yes, that's the Ark, but look at the other pieces in here, too! That's *the* menorah," Matt said as he pointed. To their left, Jessica saw a large candle stand with seven individual candle holders that looked to be crafted completely out of gold.

The lampstand had a central branch from which three branches extended from each side, forming a total of seven branches. Each branch looked like a branch of an almond tree, containing buds, blossoms and flowers. Matt continued, "Back during Old Testament times, these seven lamps would be holding olive oil fed by the main central branch and each had wicks at the top. The priests were instructed to keep the lamps burning continuously. Jesus is represented by the main branch of the lampstand, the Holy Spirit is represented by the oil and we, as believers, are represented by the six branches that extend from the original branch. Just like Jesus said, 'I am the vine, you are the branches.'[132] We are connected to Jesus and his Holy Spirit flows to us!"

To Jessica's right, she saw another piece of furniture set directly across from the menorah. It was a small table, from the looks of it, made of wood, but overlaid with gold. Matt saw where her attention had been drawn and said, "This is called the Table of Showbread. It held twelve loaves of bread, representing the twelve tribes of Israel, God's chosen people. The priests baked the bread with fine flour, and it remained on the table before the Lord for a week. Then on the Sabbath day, the priests would remove it and eat it in the Holy Place. Then they would put fresh bread on the table. Only the priests could eat the bread, and it could only be eaten in the Holy Place, because it was considered so holy. The table and the bread were a picture of God's willingness to fellowship and share something in common with mankind. It was like an invitation to share a meal, to fellowship, something friends do together.

---

[132] John 15:5 (King James Version)

God was willing for man to enter into His presence to fellowship with Him, and this invitation was always open. Jesus exemplified this when He ate with tax collectors, prostitutes, and the sinners of Jewish society. But this was more than just a gesture of friendship on Earth. Jesus came to call everyone to Him, make them right with God, so that they could enjoy everlasting fellowship with God. This is what Jesus was talking about when he said, 'I am the bread of life: he that cometh to me shall never hunger; and he that believeth on me shall never thirst.'[133] When people partake of what Jesus offers them, they shall never hunger or thirst for friendship, for completeness, for a relationship with God ever again."

Jessica's mouth was agape, opened in total amazement at what she was seeing and hearing. Her attention was pulled to the last piece of furniture in the room. It was a funny looking table type piece, made of wood and overlaid with gold, but at each corner of the perfectly square table, there were horns. Inside the horns, where the tabletop *should* be, there was a grate. She turned to Matt and asked, "Is this an old-timey charcoal grill? What's it doing in here?"

Matt said, "That is the Altar of Incense. This sat in front of the curtain that separated the Holy Place from the Holy of Holies in the Temple. God commanded the priests to burn incense on the golden altar every morning and evening, and it was to be left burning continually throughout the day and night as a pleasing aroma to the Lord. The incense was a symbol of the prayers and intercession of the people going up to God as a sweet fragrance. The incense is also a symbol to us, of Jesus, our Savior, the one who makes intercession for us just like it says in the book of Romans, 'It is Christ who is risen, and who is at the right hand of God, who makes intercession for us.'[134] Jesus, interceding for us is a sweet aroma to the Lord."

---

[133] John 6:35 (King James Version)

[134] Romans 8:34 (King James Version)

Tears welled up and streamed down Jessica's face. Before he knew what was happening, tears welled up and streamed down Matt's face as well. Jessica said, "I'm so honored that God thought so much of us that He let us be able to find these items. That we're the ones He trusted to keep them safe."

Through tears, Matt answered, "I know." Then he got a curious look on his face. Matt dropped to his knees, closed his eyes, lifted his hands, and said with a loud voice, "Lord, thank You for honoring us with this. You alone are worthy to be praised. You are the Beginning and the End, the Alpha and Omega, the First and the Last, the One who was, and is and is to come! We give You honor and praise for all of your mighty works! Worthy is the Lamb of God! Thank You for sending your Son Jesus, for saving us and thank You for letting us be a part of Your fantastic plan! *We love you! We love you so much!!*"

Once Matt had given thanks, he opened his eyes and the brilliance of the room, the light in the room, the glory in the room was magnified. Jessica, who had dropped to her knees beside Matt, began to sense angelic beings surrounding them, filling the room. They couldn't see them, but somehow, they knew that they were there. Matt and Jessica could hear them speaking, not in English, but they understood what they were saying just the same, "Holy, holy, holy, Lord God Almighty— the One who was, and is, and is to come."[135] After a moment, in the blink of an eye, the room went dark.

It was over.

It was time for Jessica and Matt to leave.

---

[135] Revelation 4:8 (King James Version)

217

CHAPTER 38

Rabbi Kaduri sat huddled in his hiding spot along the Lions' Gate Street, fighting the chill of the evening air. Throughout the night, he had seen many people, twenty or more men, come and go from the secret hidden passageway just inside the first arch of the pass-through of the Old City wall. Kaduri had noticed the pattern. Into the secret door empty handed. Out of the secret door with hands full, walking the short distance to the Lions' Gate and out of sight. Over and over. The men carried bulky items in the opposite direction of where Kaduri was hidden. It looked like the storage facility to some business, and they were liquidating their inventory. The men had carts with wheels, loaded with cardboard boxes, plastic bins, and even shiny metallic boxes. They moved their portable falafel carts from their admittedly strange storage place. They even put the young boy to work, carrying smaller items from the hidden entrance to somewhere out of the Rabbi's view. Whatever the reason, it looked like the group was moving things, possibly moving their base of operation out of their hidden storage place; to what end, Kaduri had no way of knowing.

Two men seemed to be leading the events of the evening. They were completely different, but exactly the same somehow. One was the bearded man who had arrived earlier in the evening with the boy. At first glance, Kaduri thought the boy might have been his son, but through his years of studying human relationships, Kaduri realized the boy did not act like he was entirely comfortable with the bearded man.

But it was the other man, the second man, who commanded Kaduri's attention. He was dynamic. There was something magnetic about him. There was an uncommon energy to him. Even to an aging, straight Jewish man, Rabbi Kaduri recognized that the man was extremely handsome, but there was more to it than that. He radiated leadership. He moved like a man of experience but with the charisma that made men want to follow him. He was clean shaven, and his perfect cinnamon-colored skin glistened in the moonlit night. He was tall, with dark hair and high cheekbones, an athletic build, and was wearing an expensive looking tailored suit. He wasn't doing any manual labor, carrying or lifting anything. He seemed to be the man in charge of the evening. But the other man, the bearded man, who was dressed in more athletic clothing, was somehow in charge as well. He seemed to be the muscle of the operation. He also had cinnamon-colored skin and looked as strong as an ox. The two men were different, but they acted in concert together. Even their movements looked the same.

The Rabbi had seen the man with the beard arrive early in the evening with the young boy. He watched for hours as the group cleared and moved all sorts of things out of hiding. Then the activity died. Sometime after midnight, Rabbi Kaduri saw the boy and the man leave again, hands empty and in deep conversation.

After the bearded man and boy had been gone for a while, the charismatic leader, the man in charge, roughly pulled another man out of the hidden doorway. That man wore a crimson turban and a well-trimmed beard, but Kaduri noticed something as he looked at him through the darkness. He had his hands bound in front of him. It seemed that the man with the turban was a prisoner of some type. Peering through the darkness, Kaduri watched the leader drop his suit coat over the other man's hands, almost as an afterthought, to hide the handcuffs. The prisoner was defeated. He offered no resistance, no sound, no fight, no attempt to escape.

A short while later, the bearded man and the boy, fingers rubbing his sleepy eyes, reappeared and entered the hidden doorway. All of the men who had been carrying heavy objects, the bearded man and the boy, everyone that Rabbi Kaduri had seen through the evening, were back in the hidden place, with the only exceptions being the charismatic leader and his prisoner in the crimson turban.

After a few hours, all activity seemed to stop at the secret hiding place. No one had entered or left the hidden doorway and Rabbi Kaduri was fighting the urge to sleep. Then, to his surprise, Rabbi Kaduri had a sudden impulse that was shocking to him. It was a feeling of completeness. Somehow, he knew he was finished with what he was supposed to do. The next part of his instruction was to find Matthew at the last place they had seen each other, over by the *City of David* sign, those many weeks ago. Rabbi Kaduri eased out of his hiding place and made his way south across the Old City through the cover of darkness.

Chapter 39

"No Matt, *you're* wrong! We have to keep this place hidden. That's why it was revealed to *us*. This has to be a hidden place. We have to protect it," Jessica argued.

Matt and Jessica had stepped from the room with the Ark and the other items and almost immediately had begun arguing about what this meant and what they needed to do with the discovery. They both recognized the importance of the find. They both recognized the value that the artifacts had. But they absolutely differed on what they felt they were supposed to do with them. As they were making their way through the tunnel system toward the exit, the argument intensified.

"I'm *not* wrong," Matt answered.

"Yes, you are. We *must* keep this place hidden. That Ark is much too dangerous," Jessica said.

"What are you even talking about? Dangerous? What? That's crazy! You've seen too many movies! God's not in the face melting business!" Matt was getting more and more upset with each phrase. He was tired and his emotions were getting the best of him.

Their voices were growing louder with each exchange. It didn't matter to them. They were alone, deep in the cave's tunnel system, and no one could hear them. Jessica was reminded of a scripture from the book of Proverbs in the Bible, 'A soft answer turns away wrath, but a harsh word stirs up anger.'[136] Jessica answered Matt in a much softer

---

[136] Proverbs 15:1 (King James Version)

tone. "Husband, I love you, but I think we need to keep this place a secret. Don't you remember what happened to the people who held the Ark when it didn't belong to them? You remember when the Philistines stole the Ark from the Israelites?[137] We can't let this get out into the hands of the public. We just can't."

Matt replied in a softer tone as well, "Yes, I remember what happened. But those were enemies of Israel who didn't respect God and His Ark. The Lord toppled the statues of their gods and caused His enemies to come down with a horrible case of hemorrhoids![138] But none of that stuff happened to God's people, only the people who didn't respect God's property. When God's people came into contact with the Ark, when they respected it as God's dwelling place, they were immensely blessed!"

"What? I've never heard that before. What are you talking about?" Jessica asked.

"Obed-Edom. That's what I'm talking about!" Matt replied. Jessica looked at him with one of those looks that every husband instantly recognizes. Matt immediately knew he needed to explain more. He said, "Remember, God is holy, and His Ark is holy. Think of God's presence like the Sun. The Sun is pure power and it's good! It gives us warmth in the summer, lights our days, gives vitamin D to our bodies, and provides nutrients to plants. However, if anything gets too close to the Sun, it would be destroyed. The Sun can be good and it can also be dangerous. The Bible uses several terms to convey God's pure and powerful presence, terms like "holy," like being "clean" or being "righteous." God's presence, His holiness, is both good *and* dangerous. So, when something unclean, something unholy, something unrighteous comes into contact with pure holiness, pure cleanness, pure righteousness, bad things can happen — like what happened to the Philistines…

[137] Reference I Samuel 5 & 6

[138] I Samuel 5:12 (some translations say emerods, some say tumors)

and to Uzzah for that matter. But when that pure holiness, pure cleanness, pure righteousness is respected, wonderful things can happen."

"Matt," Jessica said, "Just tell me about Obed-Edom! And I guess tell me about Uzzah, too."

"Right. The Ark had been kept by some men from the tribe of Levi, the people God chose to care for the Ark, for like twenty years after its return from the Philistines. The Philistines only returned it to make the hemorrhoids go away. Anyway, David was the king and he wanted to bring the Ark to Jerusalem. So, he went with his men to get the Ark and transport it to be housed in his capital city. God had given instructions on how His holy dwelling place should be transported, on the shoulders of men from the tribe of Levi.[139] They were to use two poles, placed through the hooks we saw on the corners of the Ark. David and his men didn't transport the Ark the correct way, instead they put it on a cart and had an ox pull it."

"Oh no. That sounds like a really bad life choice," Jessica said.

Matt chuckled and said, "It definitely was for Uzzah. Along the trek back to Jerusalem, the ox stumbled and Uzzah, purely by reflex, placed his hand on the Ark to steady it and keep it from falling off the cart. But Uzzah was unclean and uncleanness, unholiness, unrighteousness can't survive in the presence of *pure* holiness. Uzzah died immediately."

"Oh no! Oh my gosh! See! *That's* the kind of thing I'm talking about! I'm glad *we* didn't touch the Ark!" Jessica said.

Dismissively Matt said, "Oh, it wouldn't have affected us the same way. We can touch it. No problem. But... Hang on. Wait. Wait. Wait. I'll get to that. So, it had to have been tough on David and all of those around to watch their friend, Uzzah, instantly die from coming into contact with the Ark. They didn't understand why that happened to Uzzah and they thought God was mad at them, but Uzzah just came into too close contact with God's presence. In other words, he got too close to the Sun. But the people who were around him didn't know why

---

[139] Reference Numbers 7:9

223

it happened. They didn't have the insight that we do now. David was so distraught at the loss of his friend and even more so at the thought of angering God, that he dropped the Ark off at the next house he saw, a farm owned by a man named Obed-Edom. He basically parked the Ark in Obed-Edom's garage and told him to hang on to it and, 'if you're smart, you won't touch it!' David was leaving it there thinking God was angry and going to curse him. So, Obed-Edom kept the Ark at his house and honored it for three months.[140] The Lord blessed him and his entire household. When King David saw that God had blessed, rather than cursed Obed-Edom, his fear of transporting the Ark disappeared and he went back to retrieve it.[141] This time he did it according to God's instructions and brought Levites to carry the Ark on their shoulders. *The thing to understand is that God blessed the man who had honor and respect towards Him, and His Ark.* Obed-Edom was so blessed that the King, in a different city in a different part of the country, heard about how blessed he was! That's what made King David want to go get the Ark, the blessing that accompanied it!"

Jessica said, "Ok, but that still doesn't explain how *we* could touch the Ark and not get zapped like Uzzah."

"Yeah, so, anything unclean, anything unholy, anything unrighteous can't survive in the presence of the Ark. But you're a Christian, right?" Matt asked a little sarcastically, knowing full-well Jessica was a Christ follower.

"Funny," was all she replied.

"Well, the book of Romans says this, 'Since we have been made *right* in God's sight by faith, we have peace with God because of what Jesus Christ our Lord has done for us.'[142] Basically, because of what Jesus did, *we as his followers have been made righteous and clean.* And then in 2 Corinthians, we learn that, 'For God made Jesus who knew no sin to be

---

[140] 1 Chronicles 13:14 (King James Version)

[141] 1 Chronicles 15:25 (King James Version)

[142] Romans 5:1 (King James Version)

sin for us, that we would become the righteousness of God in Him.'[143] See? Jesus made *us* righteous! Jesus took the uncleanness that we had off us and took it on Himself. He became unclean in our place! By doing that, He made *us* clean. He made *us* righteous. He made *us* holy and because we are, we don't have to fear touching the Ark."

"How in the world do you know all of this stuff?" Jessica asked.

"I told you that I would put together a Bible study about Yom Kippur. All of this stuff plays a part in how Yom Kippur, the Day of Atonement, works and how it relates to us, so I just happen to be studying all of this. Isn't God good? He orchestrated it so that we would understand this stuff *before* we knew we needed it," Matt replied.

"Well, when are we going to do that Bible study?"

"Once I get it finished. We'll go have a picnic, like we used to and do the study together, then." Matt said with a smile.

Faysal had been searching the system of tunnels for hours and hours. He had not seen Dr. Davenport or her goofy, wannabe-Indiana-Jones husband since he originally left the dig site over 12 hours ago. The tunnel system was vast and would take days to explore, days Faysal knew his son didn't have. He walked on and on, stopping only to listen for anything that might indicate where the two might be. Listening, willing the couple to be somewhere close. He didn't *want* to kill them, but he knew he *had* to kill them.

Hours ago, Faysal had decided to exit the cave and see if the dig leaders' vehicle and their belongings were still at the site. It was the only thing he could think of that would indicate if the two had left the site or if they were still potentially in the cave system. To his great relief, the car and their belongings were still in the same place.

---

[143] 2 Corinthians 5:21 (King James Version)

"What can I do?" Faysal whispered to himself. He cursed the fact that he was doing this in the service of Allah, but Allah was nowhere to be found. Allah wasn't helping him. Allah wasn't an active participant in the events of the night. Allah wouldn't even talk to him and give him directions on what to do, where to go, how to accomplish the task at hand. There were things about this religion that Faysal just didn't understand, that no Imam had ever been able to explain. He was resigned to the fact he would never understand, and he should just do what he was told. His place in paradise depended on it. It was a deflating thought, a deflating realization, a deflating life. "A religion of peace, but I guess we must *force* that peace on people through violence," he whispered.

Faysal stood there contemplating what to do. "I was instructed to kill them in the cave. That is what I will do," he said to himself and went back into the cave. Before long, he was again deep in the belly of the Earth looking for the two scientists.

Matt and Jessica were sleepy, but they were happy and together they had come to a better understanding about the Ark. They were just able to see the dim light from the soon rising Sun streaming into the tunnel from the exit. They each turned their lights off, one by one. Jessica said, "I can't believe it's morning already. It only feels like we've been in the cave for an hour. We've been basking in the glow of that Heavenly experience, but we really need to figure out what to do. So, let's say, hypothetically speaking, that I agreed that it was okay to reveal this find to the outside world. How would you go about it? Who do you think we should inform?"

Matt had already made up his mind on this topic and replied, "I think we should give it to the religious Jews. It belongs to them anyway. It would substantiate their claim to the land and to the historical accuracy of the Old Testament. We could start by talking with Rabbi Kaduri. He'll know who to give it to. What do you think?"

"Really? That's what you want to do with it? I don't think that's the best idea you've ever had. In fact, that might be the *last* thing I would do with the Ark."

"Why??" Matt asked incredulously.

"Two reasons I can think of just off the top of my head. First, when you say you want to give it to the religious Jews, I think of people like the Biblical Pharisees. The Pharisees weren't the 'good guys' in the Jesus story. They used their knowledge of the law as a weapon against the common people to make them do what the Pharisees wanted. Today's religious Jews would just take the opportunity the Ark provided them and use the perceived power it gave them to rule over the rest of the country's population. Or, the second reason, those same religious people would treat the Ark as a Holy relic and begin worshiping it instead of the God who once dwelled there. It's a lose-lose proposition giving it to the religious Jews!"

"Whatever," Matt replied. "You got a better idea?"

Jessica had also made up her mind and replied, "I think we should give it to Eli. Because he is a scientist *and* a member of every shadow organization in the Israeli government, he will know who to talk with and can find the person that will know what to do with it."

Matt melodramatically rolled his eyes and said, "*That's* the worst idea in the history of bad decisions!"

"What?! What did you just say?!" Jessica asked.

Matt dug his heels in. "Yes. It is! You want to give a religious artifact to scientists? Do you want it to disappear and be written off? Do you want it to be dismissed and scientifically 'proven' to be a fake? Did you learn anything from our experience with the Genesis Machine? Science and religion are still at odds with each other! And you want to give the greatest religious discovery in history *to scientists*? Yeah. Brilliant."

Matt had decided to give the Ark to Rabbi Kaduri and had his mind made up. Jessica was determined to give the Ark to Eli Kaplan, and she wasn't relenting on it. Matt began to dread the next round of arguments he felt was coming. He stopped walking, paused and then said, "You know what? I'm letting my emotions get the better of me. I apologize. I'm so sorry. Sincerely. I know better than that. I shouldn't be talking to you in that tone. Do you forgive me?"

Jessica smiled and even though her feelings were a little hurt, she knew it takes a big person to stop right in the middle of an argument, right in the heat of the moment and apologize. She leaned over and kissed Matt on his cheek. "I do," she said. "Let's go home and get some food and some rest. We can figure out where the Ark goes once we've had some sleep. What do you think?"

"That sounds like the best idea you've had in a while!" Matt said with a smile and a wink. The two of them exited the hidden cave entrance together, hand in hand.

CHAPTER 40

The Sun had not yet appeared over the Mount of Olives on the eastern side of the Old City of Jerusalem, but the early light was making the dig site more visible with each passing moment. Matt and Jessica had experienced a wonderful night in the cave, finding the Ark of the Covenant and some of the Temple treasures and experiencing an intimate moment with God. Now, they were sleepy, but excited and ready to head home as they exited the cave, hand in hand.

As Matt and Jessica stepped out of the cave and into the now familiar work site, neither were paying much attention to their surroundings. That's because both of their phones started chiming from missed calls, texts, alerts, and voicemails. If they had been more alert about their surroundings, more ready, more in-tune or even just a little less sleepy, they would have noticed the man, dressed completely in black, headed their way at a full sprint. But with the Sun still below the horizon and the dark shadows stretching across the site area, neither of them noticed the man until he was right on top of them.

Matt didn't know what was happening as the man approached at top speed. Which, in fairness, wasn't very fast. He arrived breathlessly and hugged Matt with all his remaining might. He picked Matt up and spun him around and around.

"Rabbi Kaduri…. what are you doing here?" Matt asked. "What's going on?" Seeing the Rabbi gave Matt a boost of energy, an adrenaline hit and snapped him out of his tired state. Seeing Matt had given Rabbi Kaduri the exact same experience. The Rabbi had been fighting fatigue on a bench at the site, waiting on the appearance of Matthew so he could continue doing what he was instructed to do.

"You are not going to believe it! You are not going to believe it!!" Rabbi Kaduri was almost shouting. Matt had never seen him this excited. "I have had the most wonderful experience. You will never believe what I have witnessed!" The elderly man took Matt's hands in his and jumped with joy. Matt jumped with joy as well.

Before the Rabbi could continue, Matt interrupted and said, "Oh, you're not going to believe what *I've* seen either! I, I mean, *we* have had the most wonderful experience!!" Turning towards his wife, Matt said, "Jessica, this is my friend, Rabbi Kaduri. Rabbi Kaduri, this is my wife, Jessica."

Jessica said, "It is very nice to meet you. I've heard so much about you and your talks with my husband." Turning to Matt she added, "I thought we had agreed we weren't going to tell anyone about what we had seen until we had a chance to get some rest and make a better decision, *Dear.*"

Matt knew he had spoken out of turn, but Rabbi Kaduri saved him. "It really does not matter to me *what* you have seen. There is no way it will compare to what I have experienced. Let me tell you about it."

Not waiting for their permission, Rabbi Kaduri continued. "I was finishing with my lesson, teaching students outside of the Temple Mount. After the students left, I heard a voice that told me to remove my shoes because I was standing on holy ground. When I looked up, a Man, *the* Man, was in front of me! He was glowing, radiating love. He spoke to me! To **me!** *Then the man took me through the writings of Moses and all the prophets, explaining from all the Scriptures the things concerning himself.*[144] I met… Him. I met… the Messiah. I met Yeshua… the man you call Jesus. He called *me* friend. He spent about two hours teaching me and explaining that I am to be an ambassador of His love! He gave me all sorts of instructions and one of them was to come here and tell you everything that I have seen tonight."

[144] Luke 24:27 (King James Version)

Matt's jaw dropped and just about hit the ground. He turned wide-eyed towards Jessica, but she stood there with body language that Matt recognized. It was a look she gave him when he said something stupid or did something dumb. In other words, it was a look he was quite familiar with. Her arms were crossed, and her weight was on one leg. Matt realized she had never met Rabbi Kaduri before tonight and had absolutely no reason to believe anything he was saying. But Matt knew the Rabbi to be an honest man and was astounded by what he had just heard.

Not even noticing Jessica or her body language, Rabbi Kaduri continued, "The first thing I am to say to you is so you will know that I am speaking the truth. Tell me, does this make sense to you? Yeshua said he protected the room from those that would find and destroy his vessels. Then, He prepared the room for your arrival. He said…. Let me make sure I get this right… He removed the stones and made sure that the dead body, the one you saw so many weeks ago, was gone before you arrived. Then He said He enjoyed His time with you and heard your worship while you were on your knees. He said He loves you, too! Does that make sense to you?"

When Matt glanced at Jessica for a second time, her countenance had changed. She was a different person. Her glare had softened, and she had tears in her eyes and even more streaming down her cheeks. She held her hands clasped in front of her, subconsciously, in a manner that looked like she was praying. "Yes," she answered. "It does. We had an encounter with Him tonight, too! This is the coolest life ever. We need to tell you all about it!"

Before she could start explaining to Rabbi Kaduri about their encounter, Matt and Jessica's car, still parked a few hundred yards away in the parking lot, started honking its horn and blinking its lights. Everyone turned their attention in that direction. "I'm sorry. I must have hit the panic button on my key fob," Matt said as he pulled the keys from his pocket and turned the alarm off. Jessica started to continue, but again the alarm on the car engaged and started honking the horn and blinking the lights. Matt pulled the fob out and beat it against the palm of his hand. He said, "What's going on? I wonder if the battery in the key fob is going dead or something. I'm going to run and check on it. Don't start our story without me!" He pressed the panic button again as he started making his way to the car and the alarm disengaged a second time.

As Matt approached the car, which was still encased in darkness, a man stepped out of the black shadows and grabbed Matt from behind, placing one hand over his mouth to keep him quiet. He said, "Shhh. Quiet. I'm not going to hurt you; I just need to make sure that the man with you is a friend and not an enemy. I have been watching him for over an hour as he lurked in the darkness. I am going to let you go, please don't scream." The man released his hold on Matt, and he spun to face the man.

"Dr. Kaplan! Why are you grabbing me and what are you doing here? Especially at this hour!"

"Matthew, is the man down there with Jessica a friend or a foe? He is dressed in black, was waiting in the darkness through part of the night and looked like he attacked you when you emerged from the cave." Eli Kaplan said with a very serious tone.

"Huh? That's my friend, Rabbi Kaduri. Yes, he's a friend! He was hugging me! Why are *you* here? What's going on?" Matt asked again.

"You haven't received my messages. Let's go see Jessica and your friend and I'll explain it all to you."

"Sure," Matt said as they turned to head back towards the entrance to the cave. After a couple minutes' worth of walking Matt and Eli neared the entrance of the cave where Jessica and Rabbi Kaduri were standing. Matt announced, "Look who I found!"

Jessica practically tackled Eli as she hugged the older, slight, man. She was still overwhelmed by emotion and said, "I am so happy to see you!" Turning to Matt she said, "I think we have our solution." Pointing at Eli and Rabbi Kaduri she continued, "We tell them *both* what we found. There's a reason why we are all right here, right now."

"No. Let's *show* them what we found," Matt said. Jessica's eyes lit up and she nodded her head in agreement.

Rabbi Kaduri said, "No. I need to tell you something important. I've been given some instructions..."

Eli interrupted. "No. *I* need to tell you something important! I've been given instructions by Doron. And then you all need to leave here, right now!"

With authority, Matt said, "We are going back in the cave and the two of you are coming with us. This is not a debate. It is happening. It will take us a little while to walk to our location and along the way, everyone will have plenty of time to talk. Trust us on this. You want to see what we have found. Trust us."

Rabbi Kaduri shrugged and nodded. All eyes then turned toward the aging scientist. Eli looked like he was going to protest and then simply said, "Quickly kids. Quickly."

Matt and Jessica turned and walked toward the camouflaged entrance to the cave, followed closely by the two older men.

CHAPTER 41

M att, Jessica, Rabbi Kaduri, and Eli Kaplan had walked inside the entrance to the tunnel at the site where the Davenports had been working for the past several weeks. After brief introductions, Matt was the first to speak. He told the two older men about the events of their day and evening. Suspected djinn. Searching the tunnels. Seeing the light and going to investigate. He stopped there, telling the men as they reached their destination, he would finish reciting the rest of their evening's events.

Rabbi Kaduri spoke next. He had barely been able to contain his excitement through Matt's unfolding of their night's events. "If it is ok with everyone, I would like to go next, but I will be quick," the elderly Rabbi said. Matt and Jessica nodded, and Eli sighed. It was agreed. Rabbi Kaduri would explain the events surrounding his encounter next.

"I was finishing my afternoon lessons, dismissed my students and said my farewells. I was watching the setting Sun and I heard a voice. The voice told me to remove my shoes because I was standing on holy ground. Before I knew what was happening, the Messiah was in front of me. He told me everything about Himself starting at the beginning, with the Law and then with the Prophets. What you call your Old Testament. He showed me the places where God had told us about Him, the Messiah, and we missed it. We interpreted it incorrectly. We were wrong and didn't recognize Him when He arrived."

The group was still walking, led by Matt and Jessica, through the tunnel network. By this point, Matt and Jessica were pretty familiar with where they had been and where they were going. They came to a place in the cave that Matt recognized and interrupted Rabbi Kaduri. He said, "Excuse me, Rabbi. I just wanted to point this out to you all. The very first day I was here, I was trapped, right? This is the center point of my cave experience, right here. To my left if you follow this path, it will take you to the cave that collapsed on me. It was a second exit to the cave area we are now standing in. If we walk back the way we came, it will take you to the first, main exit. If you walk forward, which we are about to do, you will see the most amazing thing in your life. The funny thing is, to my right, I have never walked that way. I have such an uneasiness about it. Even that first night, I was prevented, by the Spirit of God, from moving in that direction. Four different directions, four different outcomes, four different possibilities. I just wanted to point it out to you because it was such a revelatory moment when I crossed this spot again that first night and it is so easy to get mixed up. Every wall, every turn looks just alike. If you're unfamiliar with the tunnel, it would be easy to miss the turn to your exit. It would be easy to get turned around. Ok, let's head up this way." Matt led the small group across the intersection of hallways and took them towards his destination. He looked at Rabbi Kaduri and nodded.

Rabbi Kaduri took Matt's nod as permission to continue talking about his evening. He said, "After Yeshua, Jesus, showed me all the signs pointing to Him, He gave me some instructions. Some of those are very private things. Some of them are very public things. Some of the instructions I do not understand and some of them I am doing right now. The first thing I was to do was to go into the Old City, to a certain place down the street from the Lions' Gate. I was to hide and watch and then come back and tell you what I had seen."

"Well, what did you see?" Jessica asked with a smile.

"It was very curious," Rabbi Kaduri answered. "I was in a hiding place where I couldn't be easily seen. I saw a man, a large man walking with a boy, down the road in front of me." Rabbi Kaduri slowed and turned towards Eli, who had largely been stressed and silent for most of the time in the cave. The Rabbi said, "Are you familiar with that road? It passes through two places that were once walls."

"Yes," Eli responded. "I am very familiar. What did you see?"

"Well, the large man and the boy walked towards me. I was hiding just outside of the second wall opening. As they were just about to exit the path through the wall, they stopped. The man pulled back a rug that was hanging on the wall and there was a hidden passageway."

Eli stopped walking. Rabbi Kaduri stopped walking. The two men were staring at each other. Kaduri realized that the reason he was there now, was to tell Eli what he had seen. He continued, "After they went in, I stayed and watched. For hours, men exited the hidden passageway carrying things. It looked like they were cleaning out a business. The moved boxes, crates, metallic objects, carts, everything out, for what seemed like hours. They even had the little boy carrying things. One of the last things I saw was a man wearing a turban being led out of the passageway, in handcuffs, by one of the two men who were leading the night's events."

Eli interrupted with a flurry of questions, "Did you get a good look at them, the two men? Did you see their faces? Would you be able to recognize them again? Could you pick them out of a lineup? Could you identify them by their pictures? What about the man in the turban? Did he look like an Indian? Was he hurt?"

"Yes, I could pick them out. Easily. I watched them for hours. The man in the turban looked Indian, I guess. I only saw him in passing, but he did not look hurt. But he looked defeated, resolved to being a prisoner," Rabbi Kaduri answered.

The group had stopped walking. Eli seemed distressed. Rabbi Kaduri seemed more relaxed than he had ever been in his long life. He was completing his task. Matt and Jessica were getting more and more excited. They knew they were close to the room they wanted to show their two mentors. Matt turned and looked towards where he knew the room was and noticed it again, there was a shimmering light. He touched Jessica's arm and once he had her attention, pointed in the direction of the room and the light being emitted. They smiled at each other as they realized what was about to happen and the experience their friends were about to enjoy. They began the process of turning off the lights on their hats, vests and the flashlights in their hands. Matt alone left his flashlight on.

Eli was the next to talk. He did so in rushed tones. He had tried making a call, but his cellphone had no service. "Kids. We must leave *right now*. I must get in touch with Doron."

Jessica asked, "Doron? The guy that led Matt's rescue attempt at the original site? Whatever for? What's going on? And you can't leave yet. We're almost there. Look!" In the darkness, the group turned towards the shimmering light. It was like the small group had not realized Matt and Jessica had turned out most of their lights, they were so focused on the conversation.

Eli continued, unphased. "Yes, Doron. He is the head of an anti-terrorist division. He has been tracking terrorist activity in the country and into the tunnels. Terror tunnels. That's why he was brought in to investigate the cave-in and why you couldn't tell anyone the two tunnels were connected."

Eli paused, pensively, like he was having an inner argument. Finally, resolved, he continued, "Two men have been leading this cell. Brothers. We know about one, but thought he was out of the region." Eli shot Jessica a look that made her unsteady. Then he looked Matt in the eye. He said, "The leader of this cell is a man named Omar Khalid. The other man, his brother, we have never seen before. He is a brand-new player on the scene. We do not even know his name or have his description. That's where you come in, Rabbi." He paused and let the new information hang in the air like the stench of a dead carcass.

Matt and Jessica had not said that name since the events unfolded over a year ago. Omar Khalid was the man who had kidnapped, tricked, and tried to kill Matt, in an effort to use him against Israel and Mossad. Now, it looked like Khalid was up to his old tricks, holding another prisoner, an Indian man, against his will, surely plotting something against the peaceful people of Israel.

Eli continued, "We have used the Genesis Machine, *your* Genesis Machine, Jessica, to find and eliminate the tunnels that they use to bring weapons and fighters into the country, but they have been hiding things, men, weapons, we're not sure what, inside tunnels under the Old City. Since the tunnels are covered by houses, churches, monuments, and people, we can't use your machine to locate them. You know the machine doesn't work like that. But we do know that the terrorists are in possession of highly enriched uranium, and we suspect they are the ones behind the kidnapping of that Indian nuclear scientist that you have been hearing so much about."

Rabbi Kaduri asked, "Highly enriched uranium?"

Jessica had a moment of recognition. "That's why you gave us the Geiger counters! Why didn't you tell us what was going on? Why didn't you tell us what we were in the middle of?"

"I did not know you were in the middle of it. I was just being proactive."

Matt asked, "What is highly enriched uranium?"

Exasperated, Eli said, "To say that terrorists potentially running around the country with uranium might cause a panic is an understatement. That is why I was sworn to secrecy. We are talking about nuclear bombs, kids. Nuclear bombs. You need one of two elements to create a nuclear weapon, either highly enriched uranium or plutonium. While plutonium is radioactive and hazardous to handle, enriched uranium is much easier to handle, and it is more difficult to detect. What this means is enriched uranium is much easier to steal, smuggle, and then hide. A crude nuclear explosive made of enriched uranium can be built much easier than one made using plutonium. Especially if you have a nuclear scientist in your possession. For these reasons, enriched uranium is the material most wanted by terrorists. A few tens of kilograms are sufficient for one explosive.[145] It sounds like your Rabbi friend has found the place where they were keeping the materials and the scientist. I have to let Doron know. Maybe there will be some clues to where they went. We have to go, *right now!*"

Rabbi Kaduri said, "But they are still there. All of the men, but the handsome brother and the man in the turban. I believe it is the place where they are living. The supplies are gone, and the men may be leaving at some point, but I think they are there now, asleep."

Matt turned off his flashlight and said, "Look Eli. See that light?" In the distance was the same glimmering, shimmering light Matt and Jessica had seen earlier. Matt was so excited; he could barely contain himself. He was so excited to show the old scientist and the old Rabbi what they had found. He was so excited, that he didn't notice that scratchy feeling down on the inside. He said, "Give us a couple more minutes to show you this and then we will leave. You need to see it. Both of you do."

Eli looked at Matt. He looked at Jessica who was inwardly willing the old scientist to agree. Eli didn't bother looking at the old Rabbi. He collected himself and said, "Two minutes. That's it."

---

[145] Annette Schaper, "Highly Enriched Uranium, a Dangerous Substance that Should Be Eliminated," Peace Research Institute Frankfurt, 2013, https://www. hsfk.de/fileadmin/HSFK/hsfk_downloads/prif124.pdf

CHAPTER 42

D awn was a good time for a mission. Doron and his men, all dressed in black, had staged quietly outside the Lions' Gate. The Sun was just beginning to rise behind them, which would be to their advantage as they moved west into the kill zone. The Sun would be blinding to anyone stepping out of the darkness of a terror tunnel. They knew this was a dangerous mission for multiple reasons. Any organized Israeli mission, any Jewish related mission into the Muslim Quarter was fraught with dangers. All eyes were potentially enemy eyes. All ears were potentially enemy ears. Every civilian might actually be an enemy combatant, or at the very least an enemy lookout. Dawn was a good time for a mission. Most of those who would intentionally cause harm, those who would raise arms, would finally find the need for sleep by this hour. For those who were only enemy ears and eyes, potentially would not have awoken, yet. Dawn was a good time for a mission.

But this mission was dangerous for other reasons than just the location of the operation. This mission was to confront an enemy. A terror cell that was lurking just out of sight, just below the surface, just out of reach. Plotting. Planning. Preparing. For months, Doron and his team had been tracking the group and their anonymous leaders. They had quietly tracked them, first digitally. They had quietly tracked their electronic footprint, intercepting communications, most recently through a not-so-encrypted cellular telephone. Next, the team had tracked them physically, from point to point across the country. Then their fears had been confirmed. Explosions at a dig site, blocks from the Old

City. They had intercepted the phone calls, but notice was short and deciphering the transmission took time. Fortunately, Doron's team had been brought in to sift through the damage under the guise of looking for missing persons, one Matt Davenport.

The explosions had the markings of the man that terrorists spoke of in whispered tones, reverently referring to him as *Alhimaya*. Doron's team knew the word had many different Arabic meanings revolving around the concept of a protector. Meanings like 'firewall'. Meanings like 'sunscreen'. Meanings like 'nurse'. For their part, Doron and his team called the man they wanted, the man who was the author of numerous bombings in their country, a degrading name, a degrading meaning of the word. They called him the 'Babysitter.' Just like a teenage girl, he took his orders from someone else, unable to think for himself.

Tonight, the team had the opportunity to capture the 'Babysitter' and with him the men who were handling him. The handlers, from the information Doron and his team had collected, sorted, translated, and studied, were brothers. One, an old player on the world scene, was known. The other, his younger brother, was looking to make his initial mark on the world, new to the terror scene. Doron knew the older brother, knew his face. The younger, was a mystery. A successful mission tonight meant the end of the brothers and the 'Babysitter.' Tonight might mean justice for the events surrounding the Sarona Azrieli Tower.

Tonight, if the intel Doron and his team had intercepted was correct, the brothers' plans would be in flux and the perfect opportunity to catch them by surprise. So, his team was staged and ready for combat. They quietly moved in stealthy steps in concert with one another, each man watching the back of his brother or sister-in-arms. Each carried a suppressed IWI Tavor TAR-21, an Israeli bullpup assault rifle, with a full magazine of chambered 5.56×45mm NATO caliber rounds. Each magazine could hold thirty rounds and each member of the team carried five magazines in different pockets of their protective, bulletproof vests. Night vision goggles were fixed to assault style helmets. Each team member had an earpiece in their left ear that allowed for quiet communication. The rubber soles of their black combat boots stepped silently across the stone street. The team was all but invisible as they passed the Lions' Gate entrance to the Old City. They knew there wasn't much cover between them and their destination, so they decided to split the team. Part of the team moved quickly along the street's high wall. There was no pausing. There was no sound. Just infiltration to their second staging point, inside an arch where they believed there was a hidden entrance to a secret lair. An entrance they would need to find before anyone saw them or raised an alarm. The remainder of the team awaited instruction from their position outside of the gate.

Doron, the capable leader of the group, was in the first position and made his way to the rallying point inside the covered pathway, the interior of a wall that once stood impenetrable, but now had an entrance cut in the shape of a half almond. The team formed around him as they reached the entrance. Each knew their assignment. Doron, in the most dangerous position, was first to enter. He checked the wall on the right-hand side for a hidden entrance. The second team member matched his movement on the opposite side of the path, looking for an entrance on that side. The third and fourth team members, with guns raised to their eyes, covered their allies in case of surprise attack. Team members five and six peeled around Doron and team member two, moving ahead to the next section of the pathway. They checked the next portion of the interior's walls. By that time, Doron and the second team member were satisfied there were no hidden entrances in their portion of the pathway. They turned their attention and their guns to cover team members five and six. As they reached their portion of the interior of the archway, team members three and four leapfrogged them and began their search of the next portion of the wall. Each section of wall was checked methodically. This was a life-or-death situation. Real world circumstances. The entrance to the hidden hide-away wasn't going to be concealed by a trap door, by pressing the right combination of piano keys to reveal the Batcave or any nonsense like that. The hidden entrance was big enough for grown men to quickly disappear from view. That meant the entrance was large and only minimally concealed. The terrorists were dependent on the neighborhood people for their true concealment.

Doron and his team worked steadily. They worked quickly. They worked methodically. And then it happened. Team members five and six located the entrance. A large Persian rug, like the ten others hanging on the walls of the interior space, was hung over the hole. It was a rough-cut hole in the stone of the archway, but it was larger than what they were expecting. There was no lip at the bottom of the hole, giving access to most small items with wheels, like carts or wheelbarrows. It was large enough for two or three smaller men standing three abreast to walk through, but easily concealed behind the carpet.

Team member five gave a rapid triple click on her radio announcing to the other team members she had located the entrance. With the barrel of her gun, she pulled the carpet back, away at an angle, and team member six stepped into the secret entrance.

It was a curious feeling to Doron how quickly and in what direction his thinking went. Doron was an educated man. It was at that exact moment that he remembered a line from a poem by Robert Burns, "The best laid plans of mice and men do oft times go awry." [146] He knew that was more of an English transliteration of the original Scottish verse that said something like, "The best laid schemes o' mice an' men gang aft agley."[147] In the flash of an instant, his brain flipped to a more modern retelling of the verse by a more modern-day poet, Mike Tyson. 'Iron' Mike said, "Everybody has a plan until they get punched in the mouth."[148]

Doron's team had just been punched in the mouth.

---

[146] *To A Mouse,* Robert Burns, 1785

[147] "The Best-Laid Plans Of Mice And Men Often Go Awry," Dictionary.com, accessed March 9, 2022, https://www.dictionary.com/browse/the-best-laid-plans-of-mice-and-men-often-go-awry

[148] Anwesha Nag ,"'Everybody has a plan until they get punched in the mouth.'– How did the famous Mike Tyson quote originate?," Sportskeeda, January 5, 2021, https://www.sportskeeda.com/mma/news-everybody-plan-get-punched-mouth-how-famous-mike-tyson-quote-originate.

The hidden entrance was lined with a tripwire that team member six stepped on causing a focused but debilitating explosion. Team member six was killed instantly and team member five was mortally wounded. If the terror group had been unaware of Doron's team, they were aware now. At the sound of the explosion the remaining team members still waiting outside of Lions' Gate, still waiting to be called in once the target had been identified, rushed to the aid of their comrade-in-arms. Before they arrived, Doron began to hear the sound of small arms being fired at his team from somewhere deep inside the hidden entrance.

CHAPTER 43

M att turned off his flashlight. Light radiated from somewhere unseen, down the hallway and towards where the group was standing. He said, "Look! At the end of this hallway, there is a room to the right. Inside the room is the entrance to a second room. Eli, that room is where I found the black substance the night I was trapped. We found something else in there tonight. That's where we are going. That's what we want to show you. This way. You're not going to believe your eyes."

Matt hurried the group down the long hallway towards the light and was first to the room. He stopped short and announced to the group, "We're here! Come on, you've got to experience this for yourselves!" The group made their way the last few yards to where he was, and he led them into the outer chamber room. To their amazement, a blinding light was shining directly in their eyes. But it was different. Matt didn't notice that it was not as brilliant, not as bright. Neither did Jessica. They didn't notice the scratchy feeling, the negative nudge on the inside. They were being led by their emotions, by their excitement. Not the still, small voice on the inside trying to warn them. The light was a spotlight that moved from person to person. First from Matt, temporarily blinding him with the brief but bright light. Then to Jessica. Then to Eli. Then to Rabbi Kaduri. As it moved away from Matt and his eyes had time to adjust to the relative darkness, he saw a man standing in the room with a flashlight. He looked at the man and recognized the silhouette created by the reflected light in the room.

"Faysal? Is that you? What are you doing here?" Matt asked.

In a matter of just a few moments, Faysal had gone from despair to joy. He had come to this room, a dead end, the ten-thousandth empty room he had entered this evening. He had sat down and cried. For the first time since he received the phone call instructing him to kill the dig leader and her husband, he had lost hope. He dropped the flashlight. He dropped the gun. He crumpled to the floor crying in desperation. He sat there for untold minutes. Then he heard it. Faint voices. Distant voices. He scrambled for his flashlight and turned it off. It was dark throughout the cave, but still he heard the voices. He decided to flash his light in the room and out of the entrance of it. The people, the dig leader and her husband, might see the flashing light and come to investigate. They might think it was the djinn. That was why they had entered the cave in the first place. He waved the light in the room. He willed the leaders to come to him.

And they did.

But they weren't alone. Faysal shone his light in the faces of the people who had just walked into the room. The two archaeologists and two old men. This wouldn't be a problem. Not for *Alhimaya*.

"Hellooooo? Faysal? What are you doing here?" Matt excitedly asked again. "Did you see in the room? Did you see what we found?" In his excitement, Matt pushed past Faysal and into the outer room. He didn't notice the gun in his right hand. Faysal stepped aside and the group followed Matt into the room.

It couldn't have been more perfect if Faysal had planned it himself. The tiny group was trapped in the room. Four walls, one exit. And Faysal was standing in it.

Matt walked to the entrance to the smaller room and turned back to the group and to Faysal. He asked again, "Did you see it, Faysal? Did you see what we found?"

Faysal watched as the goofy husband walked over to a blank wall and listened as Matt asked for a second time if he had seen what they found. Something was not registering correctly. It was just a wall. There was nothing there to see.

Matt turned and looked at Faysal. He had a blank look on his face. "Faysal? Are you ok? Do you want to go in here with us?" Matt said pointing at the entrance to the smaller room containing the Ark and other treasures.

Faysal looked at Matt who was still pointing to a blank wall. The goofy husband was acting like there was an opening there, but it was just a solid wall. It was actually the exact place Faysal had been leaning against as he sat and cried just moments ago. Faysal had enough of the games. He raised his right arm. In his hand was the Sig Sauer. He pointed it at Matt.

Matt was still confused at Faysal's silence. Matt turned around to face his foreman, raised his flashlight towards Faysal and that's when he saw it. A gun. Pointed at his face. Faysal was no more than five feet away. There was no way he could miss. Matt had been in a situation like this before, but this felt different.

But then something happened. A series of things. First, there was a loud rumble from somewhere distant, but certainly inside the cave tunnel system. Matt felt it before he actually heard it, a tremor below his feet that vibrated against the soles of his shoes. Then he heard it. A cacophony of sound that washed over the whole of the cave tunnels. That was followed by what sounded like gunshots, lots and lots of them. But not from Faysal. At least, not yet. It sounded like there was a gun battle happening somewhere close, but far away at the same time. The echoing sounds inside the tunnel had that effect, the hard walls keeping the sound waves semi-contained and pushing them throughout the complex. The next thing that happened was Faysal slowly squeezed the trigger to the Sig Sauer, still pointed at Matt's face.

There is a curious phenomenon present in the world of guns and shooters. Many shooters practice hours and hours to rid themselves of the phenomenon. It is called *trigger freeze*. But the name is misleading because there is no real freezing that happens. Neither by the trigger nor by the shooter. For some shooters it only happens rarely, for others it increases over time. It can even cause some shooters to give up shooting altogether.[149] *Trigger freeze* is in actuality, a slight flinch as the trigger is pulled. There are many causes: an inexperienced shooter, a stiff trigger pull, or long trigger pull requiring unexpected pounds of force to be used when shooting. None of those were the reason in Faysal's case. His case of *trigger freeze* was the result of only having three fingers on his right hand.

Eli Kaplan. Scientist. Business owner. Mentor. Secret informant and confidant of Mossad. Small. Frail. All of the time, afraid. Eli saw the gun pointed at Matthew's head and froze in place. He was the last in line, next to him was the overweight Rabbi, then Jessica and Matthew was up front, leading the line of friends. The series of events unfolded in slow motion in front of the slight man. First the rumble from an explosion, obviously Doron's team had reached the tunnel entrance and met resistance. Then the chatter of small arms fire, obviously from the terrorists still in the tunnel system. Then, Eli's attention, in an instant, turned back to the man with the gun pointed at his friend. There was a momentary pause of uncertainty in the gunman's eyes and Eli took action. Eli pushed the fat Rabbi with all of his might towards Jessica. The bigger man's weight crashed into her and the two of them crashed into Matt just as the man squeezed the trigger.

The shot boomed in the small rock walled room. It deafened everyone in the space. It missed Matt by a mile. Matt regained his footing and looked back at Faysal. Faysal was desperately looking for the gun that had recoiled out of his grasp. It was unlike Faysal to use his right hand, but being tired of carrying the heavy gun in his good hand, his left hand, he had swapped it with the flashlight several times during the night. Now he was cursing himself for the stupid decision. With only three fingers on his hand to hold the gun steady, it had missed

[149] Phil Coley, "Trigger Freeze – Or The 'Flinch Effect'. Here's How To Cure It," ShootingUK, March 5, 2021, https://www.shootinguk.co.uk/answers/shooting-answers/trigger-freeze-or-the-flinch-effect-1845

SIXTY SECONDS OF SILENCE

its intended target and gone flying out of his grasp. He searched the floor for the missing gun. Matt took the opportunity to land a massive left hook to the shooter's jaw, sending him sprawling to the floor. Unfortunately, the blow sent him sprawling to the floor and directly into the gun that was laying there, still cocked and ready for the next shot.

Eli grabbed the Rabbi by the arm, pulling him along as he shoved Jessica into the small room, the place they were trying to get to before they were interrupted by Faysal. Matt followed closely behind. Until that moment, Eli was unaware that the room was a dead end. Until that exact moment, Eli was unaware that he had chosen the wrong exit. They were trapped. The sound of gunfire from somewhere deep in the tunnels was getting louder.

Faysal grabbed the gun and pointed it where the small group of people had once been, but they were no longer standing there. It was as if they had vanished. "I will find you!" He shouted. "I will kill you! And then I will get my son back!"

Inside the room, the group was facing in the direction of the entranceway, hiding on either side of the entrance with their backs to the treasures. They could see Faysal and hear him shouting but didn't understand what he meant. "Can he not see in here?" Eli asked. "What is going on, Matthew?"

"Matthew," a weak voice said.

Then it happened. Rabbi Kaduri fell over. Blood pouring from the gunshot wound. Just below his right collarbone, out of the meaty part of his chest, blood was spouting with every beat of his heart. His breathing was labored, his lung having been punctured. Matt rushed over to his side, ripped open Kaduri's shirt and started to apply pressure to the wound. The Rabbi pushed his hands away. Quietly he said, "Now I understand. The next instruction. Ark. Mercy Seat. Rub in wound." And then he lost consciousness.

CHAPTER 44

Just moments ago, Yusef had been sound asleep. He was finally back in the dark cave tunnel system from where they had been moving equipment most of the evening. He had been led into a large room that contained dozens of metal bunk beds. The place was illuminated by two small lanterns on either end of the room, they blinked adding a ghoulish aura to the large space. There were several men already asleep and several others in beds scattered in no discernable order. There were clothes, waste buckets, trash spread all over the room. The place was a dump. Yusef's mother would never let him have such a mess in his bedroom.

The bearded man who had been his caretaker for the evening, showed the boy where he could finally go to sleep, the bunk nearest the door, and then said with a loud voice, meant to rouse even those who were asleep, "This is my special guest. He is not to be touched. If he is, you will first deal with me and then you will deal with Alhimaya. Does everyone understand?"

Some of the men nodded, others looked confused. There was a spattering of responses, affirmative responses.

The muscular man rolled his eyes, and said to Yusef, "See what I mean? Only a handful of them speak English." Then he repeated the warning in Arabic.

The rest of the men nodded their agreement, and several said "Naeam sayidi," Arabic for 'Yes, sir.'

Yusef laid his head down on the hard pillow, which wreaked of sweat. He didn't care. He fell quickly to sleep. It could have been minutes. It could have been hours. Yusef was unsure how long he had slept before it happened.

Suddenly, the room shook, and he was instantly awake. And deaf. He couldn't hear the men scrambling around in the room, scrambling past his bunk. He couldn't hear their shouts. He couldn't hear anything. But he could see them. He could see the panic in their eyes. It made him scared. He tried to stand but was too dizzy. He fell back onto the metal bunk. He saw men stumbling and running from the room. From somewhere, they were pulling guns. He smelled smoke. It wafted into the room he was in. Yusef sat on his bed, panicked. He was crying. Then he started hearing a high-pitched ringing in his ears. He hated it, but he was grateful he was actually hearing anything. He tried standing again. This time there was no dizziness.

The room he was in was suddenly empty. He moved towards the doorway. His hearing was returning. He could hear gunshots blasting away. It sounded like one of those *Call of Duty* games he played with Amit. He was scared but a little excited, too, all at the same time.

Suddenly a massively strong arm grabbed Yusef by the collar of his shirt. The man who had been his caretaker all night, grunted as he said, "Come with me, boy. Come with me or you'll die in this place. They will kill everyone." Then the man picked Yusef up and threw him over his shoulder, carried by his muscular arm. Yusef in one hand, a large automatic weapon in the other. "We have to leave through another exit, if we can find it."

The man exited the room where Yusef had been sleeping and stepped into a hallway. The gunfire was very close now. Yusef could see the men he had been working with through the night were all facing the same direction, firing guns towards an unseen enemy. "It was a surprise attack. Just like those cowards! To attack us in the middle of the night!" The man shouted as he made his way in the opposite direction of his enemy. All of his men began to fall back, moving in the same direction as their leader, deeper and deeper into the cave.

CHAPTER 45

Matt stared at his dying friend; the man was shot in the chest at close range by the bullet that had been intended for Matt's head. The Rabbi had just given him some directions, but Matt wasn't sure what they meant. Kaduri had said, "Now I understand. The next instruction. Ark. Mercy Seat. Rub in wound." And then he lost consciousness.

Jessica said, "Matt! Do it!!"

Matt looked at Jessica and shouted, "Do what?!?"

Jessica said, "The Rabbi got instructions from Jesus tonight. He told us some of them were private and some of them were public. He just told you 'The next instruction!' It's on the Ark!"

Matt jumped up and ran across the small room to the Ark. Without thinking, he climbed up on the ledge, saw a small remnant of the black substance, the last of it, sitting there in between the angels' outstretched wings.

Eli shouted, "*No!* Matthew! Don't touch it! You'll die!"

But it was too late. Matt used both hands and carefully gathered the remainder of the black substance into the palm of his left hand and ran back to the elderly, dying Rabbi. He placed the palm of his hand on the Rabbi's chest and held it there. He said, "Jesus, we're calling on You! Help us! You are our very present help in times of trouble!"[150]

Outside of the room, Faysal screamed, "The prophet Jesus is no match for Allah. You will all die tonight!"

---

[150] Psalm 46:1 (King James Version)

Suddenly, the Rabbi's eyes burst open. He shouted, "Glory to God in the Highest![151] You are worthy of all our praise! Hosanna to the son of David! Hosanna in the highest!"[152] The sudden movement and loud words startled Matt. Kaduri sat up and said, "Thank you, Matthew. I knew I could count on you!" Matt's eyes widened and his mouth moved open and closed, but he wasn't making a sound. Looking at the Rabbi's chest, Matt could see there was no longer a wound of any kind.

Outside of the small room, Faysal was still shouting, "I will kill you. Face me you coward! I know you are here somewhere. I can hear you!"

Eli stood there stunned. Jessica took his hand and asked, "Are you ok, Eli? Are you hurt?"

Eli answered "Not hurt. What is this place? What just happened?"

Jessica turned to Matt and smiling, asked him, "Now what? How do we get out of here?"

The Rabbi sitting up on his elbows, looked at Matt and said, "You got us into this mess. I know you will get us out."

Matt was succumbing to the pressure. He could feel his insides wanting to be on his outsides. He looked at Jessica. Eli was talking. Rabbi Kaduri was talking. Jessica was talking. Matt's world was shrinking in the small room. The walls seemed like they were pressing down on him. Like the atmosphere of the whole world was being compressed onto his shoulders. With a loud voice he said, "Silence!" The group immediately got quiet. With a softer voice he said, "Jess, come here." Jessica walked over and Matt took both of her hands in his. He said, "Lord, we come to You, calling on our covenant. We need Your guidance. We need Your wisdom. Lord Jesus, You said in the book of Matthew that 'where two or three are gathered together in your Name, You are in the midst of them.'[153] We know You are here with us and so we are asking for Your help. Because of what You accomplished on the cross, we can come

---

[151] Luke 2:14 (King James Version)

[152] Matthew 21:9 (King James Version)

[153] Matthew 18:20 (King James Version)

boldly to Your throne room. We know You hear us when we pray, and we thank You for answering our prayers! In the Name of Jesus, Amen." [154]

Jessica echoed, "Amen."

Then the men started talking again. The room filled with confusion. Matt said, "I need *sixty seconds of silence!*" And the room went immediately quiet.

Matt closed his eyes and stood there in the silence, still holding Jessica's hands, listening for that still, small voice.[155] Listening for the Greater One that lives on the inside. [156] After a quick minute of silence, Matt's eyes burst open. His head shot around to where Rabbi Kaduri was sitting and said, "The Spirit of the Lord is upon me, because he hath anointed me to preach the gospel to the poor; he hath sent me to heal the brokenhearted, to preach deliverance to the captives, and recovering of sight to the blind, to set at liberty them that are bruised, to preach the acceptable year of the Lord." [157]

"The prophet Isaiah," Rabbi Kaduri said. [158]

Matt shook his head and continued reciting the scripture, "And he closed the book, and he gave it again to the minister, and sat down. And the eyes of all them that were in the synagogue were fastened on him. And he began to say unto them, **This day** is this scripture fulfilled in your ears."[159]

Rabbi Kaduri shook his head back at Matt. He didn't understand.

Matt answered the old Rabbi, "Not the prophet Isaiah. The Messiah. Jesus. Yeshua. The man you met today said that a couple of thousand years ago. It is found in the book of Luke where Jesus *quoted* the prophet

---

[154] Reference I John 5:14-15

[155] Reference I Kings 19:12

[156] Reference I John 4:4

[157] Luke 4:18-19 (King James Version)

[158] Reference Isaiah 61:1

[159] Luke 4:20-21 (King James Version)

Isaiah. Now, I understand what He meant! *This day! This day! This day* is this scripture fulfilled in *our* ears. I understand!"

"Well, are you going to tell us?" Jessica asked, still holding onto Matt's hands.

Matt was so excited he couldn't stand still. He let go of Jessica's hands and stepped across the empty room where he could address the small group directly. He said, "Rabbi, remember the last time we talked? I asked you about Adam and Eve? *And the eyes of them both were* **opened**, *and they knew that they were naked.*[160] You told me about their eyes being opened to the natural world for the first time, that their eyes were shut off from the spiritual world, from God's world. Remember?"

"Yes, Matthew. I remember. I still don't understand what that has to do with anything..." Rabbi Kaduri's words trailed off.

Matt continued, "Jesus said that He came to do a handful of things. Number one: He came to preach the Gospel, the good news to the poor, to people that don't know Him. He did that with you, right, Rabbi? He came and told *you* the good news!" Kaduri smiled and nodded.

Matt continued, "He brought you the good news that He is real, and He is the Messiah." Matt's eyes subconsciously came to rest on Eli. "Number 2: Jesus said that He was sent to heal the brokenhearted. I'm not sure where that fits in, but we'll come back to it."

"Matt you're not making much sense," Jessica said.

"Stay with me, babe. I'm just getting to the good part! The next thing Jesus said, number three, was that He came to preach deliverance to the captives, right now *we* are captives and need some deliverance. We're going to be delivered, but it's going to happen through the next thing that He said. Here's the part that I've been trying to get to! Number four: Jesus came to preach about *recovering of sight to the blind!* I don't think Jesus was only speaking about people that were *physically* blind. I think He was talking about recovering the spiritual sight that was lost when Adam and Eve ate of the fruit in the Garden of Eden! I think

---

[160] Genesis 3: 7 (King James Version)

Jesus came to give that sight back to the world. I know it! For us, He's going to do it tonight!"

Jessica was not convinced.

Matt said "Rabbi, quickly tell the group about Elisha and his servant."

Rabbi Kaduri looked like he had seen a ghost. His eyes were as big as saucers and his mouth was agape. Everything that Matt said had resonated with him and somehow, deep down, he knew it to be true. Kaduri said, "Elisha's servant rose early in the morning to draw water, feed the animals and get ready for the day. Looking out, he saw the massive Syrian army, their enemies, encircling them. He was scared out of his wits! So, he ran back to his master, screaming that they were doomed. That there was no hope of escape. They were captives in need of deliverance.

"Now the text reads like this, *'And Elisha answered, 'Fear not: for they that be with us are more than they that be with them.' And Elisha prayed, and said, 'Lord, I pray thee, **open his eyes, that he may see.'** And the Lord opened the eyes of the young man; and he saw: and, behold, the mountain was full of horses and chariots of fire round about Elisha.*[161] The servant was able to see into the spirit realm and see the angel hosts of the Lord Almighty. Elisha prayed that the servant could see what was *really* happening. His sight was recovered! His blind eyes were opened!" Rabbi Kaduri was getting excited.

"Jesus said he came to recover sight to the blind. Jesus is going to do that for us tonight! It will be our deliverance!" Matt exclaimed.

Outside of the room, Faysal was still shouting, cursing Matt and his friends. "I will blind you, then I will kill you! I will kill you all! No one escapes tonight!" The gunfire in the cave system was growing increasingly louder.

Matt said, "Everyone close your eyes." Then he began to pray a short prayer, "Lord Jesus. Open their eyes that they may see. Let them see that You are with us and when You are with us, there is nothing that

---

[161] 2 Kings 6:15-17 (King James Version)

can harm us! Keep us free from the terror by night and from the arrow that flies in daylight.[162] Cover us with Your wings and be our shield![163] In Your Name, Jesus, we pray. Amen."

Matt opened his eyes, but he saw nothing out of the ordinary.

Jessica opened her eyes, but she saw nothing out of the ordinary.

Rabbi Kaduri opened his eyes and what he saw was anything but ordinary. The room was glowing bright with white light. Standing in front of him was the same Man he had met only hours ago, smiling, radiating love at the group.

Eli Kaplan, the only secular, non-religious man in the group, the scientist, only trusting in his senses, opened his eyes. Standing there in the bright room was a Man unlike any man he had ever seen. The room was filled with His glory, with His radiance, with His being. It enveloped Eli, wrapping around him in a cocoon of love. The Man spoke. He said, "Hello, Eli. I'm Yeshua. Do not be afraid. I have been waiting for you for a long time. You have been carrying the heartbreak of the loss of Rebecca and Liat, your wife and daughter, for far too long. If you will let Me, I have *come to heal the brokenhearted.*[164] I will take that pain away."

Rabbi Kaduri turned to Eli and whispered, "Just say yes."

Eli, never taking his eyes off of the Man, nodded and whispered, "Yes."

The Man, Jesus, reached his hand into Eli's chest, but instead of causing pain, instead of breaking the flesh, his hand glided right through the skin. It was as if the Man was a spirit, but he was a fleshly Man, too. He reached Eli's heart, touched it and with a twist, a flick of the wrist, He made it whole. The heartbreak was gone. The darkness that once ruled Eli's heart had disappeared. It could not stay in the midst of the overwhelming light in the small room. All Eli felt was overwhelming joy. Peace. Compassion. Love.

---

[162] Reference Psalm 91:5

[163] Reference Psalm 91:4

[164] Luke 4:18 (King James Version)

Jessica and Matt couldn't see what was happening. Their eyes were not opened to the spirit realm like the other two men, but they could tell *something* was going on. They watched in amazement at the physical transformation of Eli Kaplan. When his broken heart was healed, his physical body responded as well. A darkness lifted. His countenance changed and Matt and Jessica could see it.

Then Jesus turned to Matt, placed His hand on Matt's shoulder and announced, like he was speaking to the whole of creation, all of the universe: "Because Matt hath set his love upon me, therefore will I deliver him: I will set him on high, because he hath known my name. He shall call upon me, and I will answer him: I will be with him in trouble; I will deliver him, and honour him. With long life will I satisfy him, and shew him my salvation."[165]

Then the Man, still unseen by Matt and Jessica, leaned over and whispered something in Matt's ear.

Matt stood up bolt straight and said, "Ok everybody. It's time to go. This is going to be cool!"

---

[165] Psalm 91:14-16 (King James Version)

CHAPTER 46

Faysal was getting desperate. The gunfire was obviously getting closer. Louder with each staccato mini-explosion. He had begun hearing men's shouts and then began to be able to understand things being said. Most of the shouting was pure instruction, Arabic. Things like "Ahtami," which means "take cover." As the noise moved closer, he began to be able to distinguish individual voices and then one, in particular.

"Ouch! You're hurting me! Put me down! Please!" the voice said in English.

Faysal recognized it above all the other noises. It was familiar to him. It was dear to him. It was Yusef, begging, pleading to be released from someone's grip. Faysal was drawn to his son's voice. He stepped to the doorway, the entrance to the room he was in. From far down the hallway to his right, he could see shapes, men and the sporadic firing of the AK-47 rifles, the muzzle blast illuminating the barrels of the guns as they were shooting at unknown assailants. They were slowly making their way toward his position. Leading the way and nearing him now was Wally, the muscular meathead from his work site. The man built to move rocks.

"Yusef, speak Arabic!!" Faysal shouted. "Wally doesn't understand English! You have to speak Arabic to him!" And then toward Wally, Faysal shouted in Arabic, "Wally, let him go! What is this? What's going on?"

The muscular man turned towards Faysal, smiled and said, in English, "Have you completed your task, Alhimaya? Did you kill the archaeologist and her husband?" Wally then turned his gun towards Yusef's head.

"I, I, I don't understand!" Faysal stammered.

"It's simple, you twit. You are Alhimaya, *a* protector. I am Walee.[166] *The* protector."

Yusef had heard the term *walee* before, from the Koran. He thought it meant protector. Yes, he was sure of it. He had heard that term used many times in the Koran. It meant guardian or protector. A strong word. Like an Avenger or Guardian of the Galaxy. A superhero. The man even looked like an Arabian *Thor*. But, Yusef had never heard of his father referred to as *Alhimaya*, but he knew what that word meant as well. It was also a protector, but a soft protector like a hat protects from the Sun or a nurse protects a child. That was a pretty good description of his father, especially compared to Walee... a 'soft' protector.

In a flash, all of the dots connected for Faysal. The different pronunciation of Wally/Walee. How could he have missed the clues? Now he understood why he always thought he was being watched. How the person on the other end of the phone always knew the perfect time to call, either when he was alone, or at work, or just as he arrived at home. How easily the gun had been placed in his truck undetected. He even remembered the phone call while he was eating an evening meal with Wally and Jessica. Wally left to use the restroom and suddenly Faysal's phone rang. It all made sense. He understood every word of the English conversations. Walee had been listening the whole time. He even spoke with a British accent.

"Please, Walee. Please, don't hurt my son." Faysal pleaded.

"Have you completed your task, Alhimaya? Did you kill the archaeologist and her husband?" Walee repeated the questions again.

---

[166] "Walee, A Quranic Name For Boys," Quranic Names, accessed March 9, 2022, https://quranicnames.com/walee/

"Not yet. I have them trapped in a room, in here." Faysal stepped back into the room where he had watched the group disappear. He continued, "We were all in here. The husband punched me, and I dropped the gun. When I picked it back up, the group was gone. The entrance to the room must be hidden. But they are close. I can hear them talking. Listen."

From somewhere, Walee could hear conversation. It was faint and hard to hear over the shots being fired, but it was clear. Their prey was close. Walee said, "Good. Good. This is where we make our stand. We will bring our men in here. It will be easy to defend because of only having the one entrance. We can use all of these rocks as cover. We will find the hidden passageway and escape as our men fight off the cowardly Jews."

Walee stepped to the doorway and shouted in Arabic, calling all his men to their location. As quickly and as safely as they could, they made their way into the room. They pushed rocks up in piles to create barricades against the bullets that would soon be shot at them.

Inside the room with the Ark, the small group could hear more and more gunfire, gaining in intensity as it moved closer to them. They also could hear conversations among men, although they could not make out what was specifically being said. Matt was smiling from ear to ear. He knew something the others didn't.

"Rabbi Kaduri, would you continue the story and tell the group what happened, when Elisha's servant's eyes were opened to the spirit realm?" Matt asked.

"I did that already, Matthew," Rabbi Kaduri answered. "The servant was able to see into the spirit realm and see the angel hosts of the Lord Almighty."

Matt chuckled, "The rest of the story, if you please!"

The old Rabbi's eyes opened wide. A moment of recognition. A smile crossed his face.

Doron and his men chased the enemy combatants down the tunnel system, but they had to be supremely cautious. The initial tripwire may have only been the first of many. They were methodical in their pursuit. Advance. Scout. Fire and move. Fire and move. Fire and move. Advance. Scout. Investigate.

"Clear!" Someone would shout giving the rest of the team members the signal to move forward.

Advance. Fire and move. Scout. Investigate.

Then Doron saw it. A muscular man carrying a small boy, running for his life. "Hold your fire! There are children here. We must use caution," Doron shouted in Hebrew.

It became a mission of precision. Surgical shots were fired. Only when the team was positive of a hit and never, ever around the child.

Walee was directing the activities of his men. He was calling them into the small room where he had found Faysal. From their position, just a very small number of men could keep the enemy at bay. The narrow opening minimized the well-trained enemies' numbers, and the child minimized their thoughts of using an explosive to neutralize the men in the room. Walee knew the boy would buy them protection. He knew the Jews were too soft when it came to children. He knew they would never breach the room with Yusef in there with them. Now, it was up to Walee to find the other exit and get out of there alive.

He knew he should have gone with his brother, but perhaps he could still make him proud.

The Rabbi, still smiling knowingly, said, "Oh, Matthew. This is good. This is good. The Lord is good; his mercy is everlasting; and his truth endureth to all generations!"[167]

Matt said again, "Rabbi Kaduri, tell the group what happened when Elisha prayed that his servant's eyes would be opened. What happened?!" Matt was so excited; he could barely contain himself!

Kaduri, giddy with excitement said, "Elisha prayed, and said, 'Lord, I pray thee, open his eyes, that he may see.' And the Lord opened the eyes of the young man; and he saw: and behold, the mountain was full of horses and chariots of fire round about Elisha. And when the enemy army came down to him, Elisha prayed unto the Lord, and said, 'Smite this people, I pray thee, with blindness.' And the Lord smote them with blindness according to the word of Elisha."[168]

Eli, the pragmatic scientist said, "What are you even talking about?"

Jessica was puzzled as well, but Matt and Rabbi Kaduri were smiling. Matt said, "Come with me," and moved towards the exit to the small room.

"Matt, no!" Jessica screamed.

"Trust me," Matt said sweetly to his wife. "Jesus will never leave nor forsake me!"[169]

Matt stepped out of the doorway and into the slightly larger room. He was followed by Rabbi Kaduri, Jessica, and a reluctant Eli. What Matt saw in the space shocked him. There were over a dozen terrorists, holding machine guns, firing them out of the doorway and into the darkness.

Rabbi Kaduri stepped out of the doorway into the small room behind Matthew. What Kaduri saw in the small room shocked him. There were over a dozen men with machine guns, but there were five times as many large, muscular, heavenly creatures, angels, filling the room, filling every

---

[167] Psalm 100:5 (King James Version)

[168] 2 Kings 6:17-18 (King James Version)

[169] Reference Hebrews 13:5

empty space, shielding his group from harm, awaiting their commands. In the corner was Yeshua, the Messiah. Jesus. Smiling.

Jessica stepped from the room and was paralyzed with fear. They were completely trapped by scary men with big, scary guns. They hadn't noticed their group yet, but Matt was standing tall and proud and at any moment, he might be shot.

Eli stepped from the room and stood in amazement. The man who had just healed his broken heart was now in their little room. There were things going on, people, guns, children, angels, death, life, confusion, but all Eli could focus on was the Man standing there smiling at him. Radiating life. Radiating peace. Radiating love. The Man who had healed his broken heart.

As Rabbi Kaduri began to look closer, he could see small impish creatures. They seemed to be giving directions to the sweaty men in the room. Their eyes glowed an evil glow. Their mouths dripped with saliva as they whispered in the terrorists' ears. They were small, very small. Demons. Devils. They were so small, so powerless that Rabbi Kaduri felt he could thump them into oblivion if he tried. They snarled and growled and whispered into the ears of the men in the room.

Matt stepped into the room and boomed, "In the Name of JESUS!" As he did, the group of terrorists turned to look at him. The impish creatures turned to look at him, but there was something different. It was fear. At the sound of Matt's words, the impish creatures reacted in fear. Rabbi Kaduri watched as the Man, Jesus, Yeshua, the Messiah, stepped from the corner and just as he had done when His hand had penetrated Eli's heart, Yeshua stepped fully, *into* Matthew.

Matt continued, "I command you, evil spirits, flee now!"[170]

Now, when Matt spoke, it wasn't his voice alone. It was Yeshua's voice *in* Matt's voice. It **boomed** in the room. There was authority to it. His voice filled the room. Filled the whole of the Earth. It filled the whole

---

[170] Reference James 4:7

of the universe as far as Rabbi Kaduri could tell. He watched as the evil spirits fell off the shoulders of the terrorists. They were shaking in fear.

"Be gone!" Matt and Jesus shouted abruptly, and Rabbi Kaduri watched the evil imps flee, running away in terror. Then, with commanding authority, Matt said, "Lord, smite this people, I pray thee, with blindness!" Rabbi Kaduri then watched as the heavenly beings placed their hands over the eyes of the men holding guns. Other heavenly creatures stepped in front of Matt and his group, protecting them. The men, experiencing emotions beyond common fear, moved in wild panic. Several of them began shooting, wounding, and killing some of their own men. Others tried running, but they crashed into each other and into the walls and rocks. Eventually, they all made their way to the floor, groping around, trying to find anything familiar. Not knowing what else to do.

Matt saw Faysal standing there, the gun, no longer in his hand, replaced by a young boy with tears in his eyes. Faysal said, "Who is the man that stepped into you? What are all of these creatures in this room? Why did they protect us from the bullets?" It seemed, Faysal could see into the spirit realm as well.

Rabbi Kaduri started to explain, but then saw Yeshua step from Matt's body. He stood in front of the man and his son and said "Faysal, Faysal, why do you persecute Me?" Matt and Jessica couldn't see what Faysal was looking at, but they could hear the voice. It filled the room.

Faysal replied, "Who are you, Lord?"

"I am Jesus whom you persecute.[171] I am the risen Savior. I am the Lord. I AM."

As soon as He had said unto him, I AM, Faysal went backward, and fell to the ground.[172] Faysal eventually moved to his knees under the weight of the revelation, under the power with which the words were spoken. He bowed himself in surrender and said, "Forgive me. I have

---

[171] Reference Acts 9:4-5

[172] Reference John 18:6

been deceived. *Please* do not kill me or my son and we will follow you the rest of our lives. I believe. I believe. I believe."

Jesus smiled and Faysal's eyes were once again tuned to the physical world, blinded once again to the spiritual world, but he was different. He sensed the change and turned to look at Matt and Jessica with tears in his eyes and running down his cheeks. Kneeling, he said, "I am so sorry. I did not know. From my youth, I was so deceived. I am a sinful man, but I did it in service of what I thought was right. Please forgive me. I will do whatever I can to make this right."

Doron and his men burst into the room shouting commands and creating a stir. They did not realize that the terrorists had been subdued. They were slapping them, grabbing guns, controlling the situation. Matt, Jessica, Rabbi Kaduri, Eli Kaplan, and young Yusef all raised their hands. Faysal kept his face to the ground. In the instant that Doron and his team had moved in, the room went back to normal. All supernatural activity was again relegated to an unseen world.

Doron said, "Eli? What, what are you doing here?"

Eli responded, "It is a long story and one that you probably will not believe. Let's get these men into custody. Tonight was a success?"

Doron looked intently at each of the terrorists in the room. "No. We have lost them. Unless there are some more men running around in the tunnels, these are the only men who were in the secret hideaway. It's obvious that Omar Khalid is not here. We missed them. Both have escaped. And when they did, they took the uranium and the scientist." Doron said. "Worst of all, we still do not know the younger brother's face."

Rabbi Kaduri stepped up and pointed to the muscular man scrabbling on the floor, blind, lost, confused, and bewildered. He said, "Excuse me. He is the one you are looking for. He was one of the men in charge tonight. He is the one that moved all of the boxes out of the tunnel."

Young Yusef also stood up and walked to Doron. In English, he said, "This is the man they call Walee. He is an evil man. He destroyed a science place tonight. I didn't want to, but he made me go with him. I am sorry."

Matt stepped over to get a better look. "Oh wow! I see it now! Jess, now I know why he looked so familiar. If he didn't have the beard, he would look just like his brother. Their faces look just alike."

"Doron," Eli said. "Get these men out of here and take special precaution when you move them from the tunnels. We do not want any more surprises. Be aware of ambushes. In fact, use the archaeological site exit. Matthew, will you show him the way?" Matt nodded.

"What is wrong with them?" Doron asked.

Eli responded, "They have been blinded, but we do not know how long it will last. And this one," he said, pointing to Faysal, "he is not blind. Do not be fooled."

Doron said, "Yes sir. I have also called in reinforcements. We will have men all through this tunnel in a matter of minutes, if it is not done already."

Eli answered, "Very good. Please leave some men as guards outside of the door and keep a guard on this room for the next several days. People you trust. And leave instructions that no one is to enter this room until I personally give the all-clear. I'll give you more details soon." Doron nodded and started barking orders to his men in Hebrew and to the terrorists in Arabic.

Turning to the remainder of his group, Eli continued with a smile, "Jessica, you, me, and the Rabbi still have some things to discuss about what to do with those special, wonderful items in the next room. Let's go have another look, shall we?"

Jessica turned to Matt asking the unspoken question. Matt said, "Can Jessica and I have a minute?" Eli and Doron both nodded.

Matt said, "Go. I don't need to be in there. The three of you do. Don't you see? Represented in that room is Science, Government, and Religion, but now they are represented by a scientist and a government official who is a believer in Jesus. Eli knows the truth, and even he can't deny it. Represented in that room is the Jewish religion by a Jewish

Rabbi. But now the Jewish religion has a Yeshua follower. A Christian. Rabbi Kaduri will never be the same. And then there is you. The leader of the dig. The one who found the Ark and the one who actually *knows God's heart*. You will need to help them follow God's plan in this. *That's* the reason why Professor Kenyon wanted you for this project. Somehow, the wily old professor knew. With the very last phone call to his wife, he was listening to the direction of the Holy Spirit and giving her instructions about *you*. You guys will have some big decisions to make, and it is important that all three of you make them, together."

Jessica's eyes were misting over. "You're right," she said as she leaned into her husband and kissed him. "I love you, Husband. Thank you."

Matt smiled and said, "I love you, too, Wife. I'll see you in a little bit." Matt turned, found Doron and the men left together.

ARCHAEOLOGY STAGE FOUR: CONCLUSION

Writing of official archaeological report and submission to proper agencies[173]

"Jesus saith unto him, I am the way, the truth, and the life: no man cometh unto the Father, but by me." — John 14:6

"The man surrendered his life to Jesus on the spot. He had been convicted of his sin and saved to eternal life, not because someone had rebuked the darkness that imprisoned him, but because he had seen the shining light of God's glory in worship. Similar phenomena are taking place throughout the Muslim world. In fact, today, nine out of ten Muslim converts to Christ encounter Him in a dream or vision."[174] — Matthew Davenport, to the sentencing judge of Faysal Mohy al-Din abu Yusef

---

[173] "Phases of Archaeology," Job Monkey, 2022, https://www.jobmonkey.com/archaeology/phases/

[174] Terry Law and Jim Gilbert, *The Power of Praise and Worship,* (Destiny Image, 2011), 84.

CHAPTER 47

T he harmonic notes produced by the electric guitar screamed in unison over the driving beats of the bass, drums, and electric rhythm guitar. The thumping of the song pulsed like a hard rock heartbeat through their small apartment. It was easily the third time in a row the song had played, and it showed no signs of changing. Matt was blasting *The Writing's on the Wall* by *Stryper,* again. He knew it wasn't Jessica's favorite song or even her favorite type of music so he hoped it would hurry her up. He was hungry and he was ready to go.

"Really? Again?" Jessica asked in mock frustration. She knew the song was special to Matt, for a lot of reasons and it was to her as well.

"Yep! I'm rocking out to this song until we leave," Matt said jokingly. Even he could only listen to it a couple more times before he would be tired of it, and he knew it.

"Ok. Ok. I'm coming. I just got an email from some doctor in New York. It looks important. Let me print it out, and I'll read it in a little bit. Grab the food, will you? Oh, and put a couple drinks in the backpack, too, please."

"Already done. You about ready?" Matt started making his way towards the front door when their doorbell rang. He opened it just in time to see a messenger heading into the elevator. Matt looked down at his feet and saw a couple of boxes with their address on them. He picked them up and walked back inside. By the time he returned, Jessica had turned the music off.

She said, "Who was that?" as she stuffed the printout into her purse.

"We got a delivery, one box, addressed to you and one box addressed to me. It was the mail carrier that rang the bell."

"Care if I open it before we go?" Jessica asked. The answer didn't matter, Jessica was determined to open the box and see what was inside. She grabbed some scissors and snipped the tape along the edges. She pulled back the flaps to reveal the contents. On top was an unsealed envelope with her name written on it. She recognized Eli's handwriting. Below that, was a small velvet bag with something inside. She pulled the handwritten letter out of the envelope and read it aloud to Matt.

Jessica,

> *I have told you some of the circumstances surrounding the death of my wife and daughter. Everything about that day, even before the Coastal Road Massacre, brought me pain. We had made plans to take our daughter to the beach, but my wife and I had an argument that morning. I received a call from my boss and because I was upset with Rebecca, I decided to go to work instead of going on holiday with my family. I canceled our beach trip. In a form of protest, Rebecca said that she was going to take our daughter, Liat, to the beach without me. Those are the last memories I have with my wife. A selfish act by a selfish man. I have lived with that pain for over forty years.*

> *Liat was sad that I was not going to the beach, but I told her we would have a tea party after she returned home. She loved the tea parties with me and with her special stuffed animals. It has been one of the fondest memories I have of my short time with Liat. I have missed her so much.*

> *As silly as it sounds, the stuffed animals, Fred the Bear and the Monkey Prince, have brought me a measure of comfort over the years. I kept them. And somehow it*

271

almost kept part of her alive for me. But since our time in the cave and the experience I had there, something inside of me has changed. I have found that I do not need the false comfort of the stuffed animals. My broken heart has been healed. Yeshua did that for me.

Jessica, you are the closest thing I have to a daughter. While I do not need the false comfort of the stuffed animals, I also could not bring myself to throw them away. I want you to have them. Do with them what you wish, but please never talk to me about them. I am free from the pain and never want to go back to it.

Forever free.
Eli

Jessica refolded the note and placed it back inside the envelope. She looked at Matt with compassionate eyes and smiled. Inside the velvet bag were two aged and weathered old stuffed toys, a friendly looking, fluffy teddy bear with bent ears and a smile on his face and a cute little monkey, ready for a banana. She placed the animals sweetly on the shelf beside the front door. "Now, they can watch over the place when we're not here," she said.

"That's the perfect place for them," Matt said in agreement.

"What's in your box?" Jessica asked. Matt took the scissors and cut open the box, pulled back the flaps to reveal a brand new, crimson baseball cap with a script 'A' on it.

"You bought me a new Alabama hat! Thank you, sweet wife!"

"Try and hang on to this one, ok?" Jessica teased. She said, "You ready?" and opened the front door. "See you in a little while, Fred and Monkey!"

"We're going to have to come up with a new name for that little guy," Matt said. "I can't refer to him just as *Monkey.* He needs a name."

"Well, make up your mind! Do you want to go to our picnic and do the Bible study or do you want to stand here and think up names for stuffed animals?" Jessica teased.

Matt looked down at his watch and said, "Oh, no. We've got to go. I've got this all timed out and we are behind already!" And out the door they went.

Chapter 48

"Matt, where in the world are you taking me?" Jessica asked. Now she understood why Matt had asked her to wear 'durable shoes' and 'long pants,' even though they were planning an outside picnic and the weather was considerably warm. They were on a hike. After leaving their apartment, Matt and Jess went back to the original dig site. Nava was waiting for them there. She handed a printout to Matt and did something with his phone, then said her goodbyes. "Where are we going?" Jessica asked again.

The hike was not like any she had been on before. There was no path. They were just outside of the city, trekking through the countryside, looking for something. They cobbled through brush and around steep ledges, overlooking the city to the south of them. The whole time, Matt looked at his phone, moved, climbed, then looked at his phone again. Matt answered, "You'll see. We're almost there. Just keep going."

Finally, the couple reached their destination. It was a fairly level spot on the side of a large hill. It was not an easy place to reach, but it was a nice, private spot overlooking the city and a perfect place for a picnic and Bible study. It was the termination point for the path that made its way down from the top of the hill.

"Probably would have been easier to get here if we had started at the top, but I didn't know. Wow! Would you look at this view? You could stand right here and if a group gathered down there, everyone could see you," Matt said as he shrugged off the large backpack. He stared at the view for a moment longer and then started unpacking the contents of the bag. He laid out a blanket in the center of the ledge and noticed that right in the middle, there was a raised shape. He pulled the blanket back and realized there was a perfectly square, flat stone about twelve inches on each side that was raised about an inch or two out of the ground. It was covered with dirt and loose straw which is why Matt hadn't seen it until that point. He wiped it off and cleaned around it. "Perfect," he said. "That's where I'll put our drinks!" He laid the blanket back down and finished unpacking the rest of the gear. Paper plates, sandwiches, chips and cans of soda were laid out. Lastly, he pulled out his notes and their Bibles and took a seat on the blanket.

"Why did we come here, to this exact spot? Couldn't you find somewhere closer or easier to get to or even a spot that actually meant something to us and our relationship?" Jessica asked, still a little bit winded by the physical exertion of the climb. She sat down across from him and waited for his answer.

Matt just laughed. He pulled out the piece of paper that Nava had given him. He said, "I asked Nava to analyze the data from our special night in the cave. She used the cave positioning system, *your* CPS, to find out *exactly* where we had been, *exactly* where the special room is. These are the coordinates." Matt showed her the piece of paper. "Then, I had her drop a pin in my map app on my phone so I could find the place. What better place to do a Bible study about Yom Kippur, the Day of Atonement, than the place where we found the Ark of the Covenant? Except, you know, we can't get to the place where we found the Ark of the Covenant. But we can get to the place, directly above it. If we were to dig straight down, from right here, probably right where this square block is, it would lead us directly to the room where we found the Ark. *This* is as close as I could get us. How is that for a spot that actually means something to us and our relationship?" Matt was grinning from ear to ear.

"I should have known better than to doubt you, Husband," Jessica said. "This is the perfect spot. Let's eat and then you can teach me about Yom Kippur."

Matt and Jessica ate their picnic lunch and enjoyed the warm, early summer day. When they finished, Matt picked up his notes and said, "Yom Kippur, the Day of Atonement. This is a great big subject, and I could talk about it for hours and hours. What I would like to do is tell you about the ceremony that the ancient Israelites performed under the old covenant, the people in the Old Testament, and then tell you about how Jesus fulfilled that and how it affects us, in the new covenant, the people in the New Testament."

Jessica nodded. She had been looking forward to this for several weeks. "Sounds good to me! Let's do it."

Matt paused and said, "I hope this doesn't sound morbid, but I have been thinking about that little boy's body that we found at the dig site. Remember, you said he was probably around twelve or thirteen years old? I think I want to go through this Bible study with him in mind. So, if it's ok with you, let's do it this way. Let's put ourselves in that boy's shoes, er, his sandals," Matt said with a smile.

"What do you mean?" Jessica asked.

"Let's pretend that we are with that little boy as he attends his very first Yom Kippur ceremony at the temple in Jerusalem. He didn't know, but we now know, it was the very last Yom Kippur celebration before Nebuchadnezzar destroyed the city, that's when he was killed. But let's put ourselves in his sandals for that celebration day." Jessica nodded.

"I want to be very clear about this. I have done a lot of study on this subject, but I found a wonderful book titled, *The Miracle of the Scarlet Thread*, by Richard Booker. I have it back at the apartment and if you want to read it, I really encourage you to. Mr. Booker explains this all in a very simple to read way.

"God gave instructions to Moses about the Atonement ceremony and how each part was to be performed. You can read about it in Leviticus 16. It starts with the death of Aaron's sons."

"What?!?" Jessica asked.

"Yep. And they were priests. But Aaron's sons didn't follow God's commands, didn't respect His ways, and when they approached the Ark, they had sin in their lives. That sin made them unclean or impure and as we know, nothing impure or unclean can survive in the presence of God. They died. So, after that, God laid out even more, explicit commands on how his Ark was to be treated and how the sins of the people were to be covered. That's what this ceremony is about, covering the sin of the priest and covering the sin of the people."

"That's a hard way to learn a lesson," Jessica added.

"Yeah. Exactly. So, let's put ourselves in the shoes of that little boy on the last Day of Atonement before King Nebbie destroyed Jerusalem, and watch the ceremony as it unfolds before us.

"One of the first things we see is the priest washing himself. He is cleansing himself so that he can perform the functions on this day and represent the people. He is going to stand in their place. You'll see what I mean in a minute." Jessica nodded.

"So, we're watching the High Priest get clean, but he's not wearing his usual elegant, priestly garments. The clothes he puts on are not beautiful. He's actually wearing very simple, plain clothing. He puts on a pair of white linen pants, a white robe and sash, and a turban. There is nothing special about him. In our eyes, he looks like every other man attending the ceremony.

"So, we see him and he's ready to start the ceremony. First, he needs to sacrifice a bull for his own sin. Because the priest is just a man, I mean, he even looks just like every other man in attendance, he has to take care of his own sin before he can represent the nation and help do something about all of ours. But that's when we realize that he is *just* like us. He's a sinner and has uncleanness in his life too. That's a little scary, right? *This* is the guy that's going to be representing *me* before God? The only really good thing about this is the fact that he knows what we have gone through, the things we have been tempted with, the personal battles we have fought this year. He's had to fight them as well. So, he kills a bull and takes some of the blood into the Temple."

"Wait," Jessica said. "Why is he killing a bull? How does that do anything for his sin?"

"Oh, that's a great question," Matt said. "Romans 6:23 tells us 'For the wages of sin is death...' When Adam and Eve sinned, death showed up on the planet. Romans 5:17 says, 'Wherefore, through one man (Adam) sin entered into the world, and death by sin...' Death has a right to be here, and sin will always lead to death. The paycheck of sin is death.

"So, we go back to our ceremony and a death is required to pay for the sin that is present. God made a way for a bull to pay for the sin of the priest. This is actually great news! That bull's death can stand in for the priest's sin! But it would only last for a year and then the ceremony would need to be repeated.

"So, the High Priest goes into the Temple with the blood of the bull. We can't see him, but we know that he is going into the Holy of Holies, where the Ark is. To make atonement for his sins, he takes the blood of the bull and sprinkles it seven times on the lid of the Ark. That lid is called the Mercy Seat and that was God's throne. With that act, the High Priest has made atonement for *his* sins. Basically, he has taken care of himself so that he can now take care of us, the people watching the ceremony. So, he comes back out to get ready for the next part of the ceremony."

"What happens if the priest didn't do something right?" Jessica asked.

"If the high Priest didn't do something right, in any individual part of the ceremony, it could actually lead to his death. So, there was always a lot of pressure on the priest to get things right. He didn't want to die, *and* he wanted to help remove the sin from his people," Matt said.

"Glad I wasn't the high priest back then!" Jessica said.

"No kidding!" Matt replied and then continued with the Bible study. "So, the High Priest comes back out and now he starts with the part that will cleanse the people of the nation. Two goats are brought to him. One of them is chosen to be the sacrifice for the people. The High Priest leans his hands onto the goat to symbolically transmit the sins of the nation to this animal. The goat is the one that will be dying in our place. This goat becomes *our* sin substitute. The High Priest kills the goat and takes some of the blood back into the Holy of Holies and all of us on the outside of the temple? We wait on pins and needles."

"Why?" Jessica asked.

"Because this is the most important part of the ceremony, and we don't really know what the High Priest is doing inside the Temple. Did he get scared? Is he just hiding out of sight, just inside the door? Is he actually atoning for our sins? We hope he is. But we don't know for sure. We hope that he has gone into the Holy of Holies and continued the ceremony. Has he done everything right or did he die in the middle of the process? If the High Priest did everything correctly, God sees the blood of an innocent sacrifice on His throne that tells Him a life has been given to pay the penalty of sin. *The blood-covered Mercy Seat changes God's throne from one of judgment to one of mercy.*[175]

"If he did everything right, the High Priest comes back out. Our sin has been atoned for, but we didn't see any of it. We weren't in the room. So, the High Priest needs a way to show us that our sins have been separated from us. He takes the second goat and lays his hands on it, like he did the first goat, symbolically transmitting the sins of the nation onto it. Then they take that goat out into the wilderness and set it free. This is where we get the term *scapegoat* from. The second goat, the scapegoat, could only go free after the blood from the first goat had been used to atone for our sins. Now that we can see the second goat being led out of the city gates, we know that our sins have been forgiven and they are separated from us!"

"Cool! So, is that the end of the ceremony? And what does any of that mean for us today?" Jessica asked.

"Almost done. The ceremony finishes up with the High Priest changing into his priestly, elegant, expensive garments inside the Temple. Once he comes out, he concludes the ceremony by offering a burnt sacrifice to God. God accepts the sacrifice as a sweet-smelling

---

[175] Richard Booker, *The Miracle of the Scarlet Thread,* (Destiny Image Publishers, 1981), 123.

aroma. That gets us all clean, separated from our sins… until we have to do this again next year." Matt said.

"Wow. That's a lot of formality to go through to get our sins away from us," Jessica said. "But at least God made a way for us to have the sins removed."

"Yeah," Matt said. "But as we sit there at the end of the ceremony, we think that there has to be a better way. There has to be a way to remove our sins from us once and for all. We hate having to go through this process *every* year. Couldn't there be a better way? A better sacrifice?

"God actually set this ceremony up so that the Israelites would recognize that better sacrifice, that better way, when it showed up. But when it got there, they didn't understand."

"What do you mean?" Jessica asked.

"Well, the old system, with its sacrifices, could never permanently remove the sin from the people. Maybe a better way to say that is that the old system could never remove the sin *nature* from the people's hearts. The High Priest's job was never finished. He had to keep sacrificing animals year after year after year. But just like God had established this temporary way to cover the sins, he sent a *perfect* High Priest to finish things once and for all, to provide a way to remove the sin *nature* from the people's hearts."

Matt could see the confused look on Jessica's face. He smiled lovingly and continued, "Look. The High Priest changed out of his elegant robes and into regular clothes, right? He looked like a normal guy and went through the same stuff we do and was tempted by the same things we are, right? In the book of Hebrews it says that Jesus *laid aside His own heavenly glory to be a High Priest for us who would feel our infirmities and be tempted as we are.*[176] Jesus changed out of his elegant, heavenly garments and into regular human garments so he could be a guy who would go through the same stuff and be tempted just like we are.

---

[176] Reference Hebrews 4:15

He looked just like one of us. He came to Earth as a baby, and he wore a simple white robe."

"*Wow!*" Jessica exclaimed.

"You ain't seen nothing yet!" Matt replied. "The next thing the High Priest did at the ceremony was to ceremonially wash. Once Jesus was ready to start his ministry, the first thing he did was go get symbolically cleansed. He was baptized in the Jordan River by John the Baptizer. Jesus never sinned, so He didn't *need* to be cleansed. He did that for our benefit!"

Jessica had a look on her face. She said, "Ok. The next part of the ceremony the High Priest killed a bull and splashed it on the Mercy Seat, for his own sin. You just said that Jesus never sinned. So, what comes next?"

Matt nodded and said, "Because Jesus never sinned, He was perfectly righteous, and it wasn't necessary that He make a sacrifice for Himself. He skipped that step. Instead, He went right to making the sacrifice for the people. Instead of placing the sin onto a goat, He took our sin on *Himself.* II Corinthians 5:21 says that 'He who knew no sin became sin for us.' And, Hebrews 10:10 says that 'we are sanctified through the offering of the body of Jesus Christ, once for all.' *He* became that "once and for all" sacrifice. He hung on the altar, the cross, of his own free will *for* us. He sacrificed Himself for us."

Matt looked down at his notes and said, "I loved this quote so much, I wrote it down. Mr. Booker says this, 'Jesus appeared to His disciples and said, 'Behold My hands and My feet, that it is I Myself. Handle Me and see, for a spirit does not have flesh and bones as you see I have.' Jesus said flesh and bone rather than flesh and blood. That's because all of His blood was poured out at the foot of the cross. But now that His work was over, they could touch Him. On resurrection morning, He entered a more perfect Temple in heaven. He went right into the heavenly Holy of Holies. *It was the real High Priest, entering the real throne room of God, with the real sacrifice. The real sacrifice was His own blood that He sprinkled over the heavenly Mercy Seat.* With His blood, He purchased our eternal salvation."[177] Isn't that awesome? Because it was a *perfectly sinless* sacrifice, it paid for our sin forever. It actually removes the sin nature from us and makes us a new creation![178]

"Not only that, but unlike the Old Covenant High Priest, Jesus lives forever. Because Jesus lives forever, He is always there with God to remind Him that He paid the price required by sin *for* us! And Jesus paid for it with His own perfectly sinless blood! We never have to worry about Jesus atoning for our sins. He's not hiding in the corner. He's not doing something incorrectly. It's already been done! All He ever has to do is remind God of it!

"So, in the old ceremony, the next part deals with the scapegoat. The scapegoat was the evidence that the people's sin had been removed from them, remember?" Matt asked.

Jessica was a little beside herself with all of this new information. She nodded and said, "Yes. And the second goat couldn't go free until the blood from the first goat had been used to atone for the sin of the people."

Matt continued, "Right! Well, Jesus' sacrifice was the atoning blood for the sin of the people. When we accept Jesus as our sin substitute, He removes our sin from *us*. We are like the scapegoat because *we have been set free!* We have been set free from our sins! The Bible tells us that our sin has been removed from us as far as the East is from the West.[179] Have you ever tried to measure how far east is from west?"

"I don't follow what you mean," Jessica said.

"Let me put it to you this way. If you were to travel north on an airplane, at some point you would hit the North Pole and as you followed the curve of the Earth, you would start traveling south again, right?"

---

[177] Richard Booker, *The Miracle of the Scarlet Thread*, (Destiny Image Publishers, 1981), 127

[178] Reference II Corinthians 5:17–Therefore, if anyone is in Christ, he is a new creation; old things have passed away; behold, all things have become new. (King James Version)

[179] Reference Psalm 103:12

Jessica nodded and Matt continued, "Or if you were to travel south on an airplane, at some point you would get to the South Pole and as you followed the curve of the Earth, you would start traveling north, right?" Matt asked.

"Sure," Jessica said.

"Well, if you were to get into an airplane and start flying east, when would it hit the point that you were flying west? You wouldn't. It would always just be *more* east. Or, if you turned around and started flying west, you would never hit a point and all of a sudden be flying east, right? East and west are different from north and south. North eventually turns south and south eventually turns north, but east and west are *always* separated. *That's* how far our sins have been removed from us! They are *always* separated!"

The revelation of Yom Kippur was not lost on Jessica. She was beginning to understand the magnitude of what the day and the ceremony meant. "Is that the end of the ceremony?" she asked.

"Almost," Matt answered. "In the ancient ceremony, the priest would change back into his priestly garments and offer a burnt sacrifice to God. That concluded the ceremony."

"How does Jesus fulfill that or how does it relate to us?" Jessica asked.

"This is so beautiful. The Bible says in Ephesians 5:2 that Jesus gave 'Himself for us, an offering and a sacrifice to God for a sweet-smelling aroma.' His broken body that hung on the cross and then his Spirit which endured the fires of hell were the burnt offering for us that God accepted as that same sweet smell as the Old Testament High Priest made.

"The final piece of our Bible study today is Jesus putting back on his elegant garments, His priestly garments, the pieces of clothing He removed so that He could perform this task. The Bible says that after His resurrection, Jesus had a glorious body.[180] He put back on his heavenly attributes, having accomplished everything during the ceremony

---

[180] Reference Philippians 3:21

that needed to be done. But here's the really cool part. You ready for this?" Matt asked with a huge smile on his face.

Jessica nodded and Matt continued, "In I Corinthians, the Apostle Paul describes what the body of the believer will be like in heaven. He tells us that our heavenly bodies will differ from the ones we have now in-splendor, in power, and in longevity. He also states that the believer's body will be an image of Christ's body.[181] That same body that Jesus has, with its priestly, elegant garments? We'll have glorified bodies like that, too!

"One last thing: we've put ourselves in that little boy's sandals and we've been walking through the ceremony with him. When he finished that ceremony 2600 years ago, his sin was removed. He's clean. The little boy might not understand the ceremony and what it was pointing to, but by trusting God in this ceremony, the little boy was placing his trust in the Messiah and the redemptive work He will eventually do. That's how I choose to remember the boy. Not as the boy who was killed by King Nebbie. I choose to remember him as clean from his sin and believing in and looking forward to the coming Messiah. I choose to believe that I'll meet him in Heaven one day."

Matt finished up the Bible study and Jessica sat there for a long time in thought without speaking. Finally, she said, "I can understand why the ancient Jews didn't understand the significance of the sacrifice Jesus made. I mean, here I am two thousand years later. I grew up in church, heard about Jesus all my life and I never knew *any* of that stuff. If they didn't have someone to explain it, I can see how it was so easily missed."

"I guess that can be said about the goodness of God toward man, too," Matt said. "Unless there are people who are willing to teach of God's goodness, of His Grace, of the sacrifice He was willing to make for all of humanity by giving His Son to die in our place, it would be easy to be missed. That's why one of Jesus' last commands before He ascended

---

[181] Reference I Corinthians 15:35-49

to heaven was 'Go into all the lands and make disciples of all people and teach them what you know.'"[182]

Jessica smiled. "What a wonderful God we serve and what an honor to be able to share His goodness with others! People like Eli and Rabbi Kaduri will never be the same."

Matt smiled and leaned back on his hands, pointed his face to the sky and enjoyed the warmth of the summer day on his face.

---

[182] Reference Matthew 28:19-20

CHAPTER 49

T he quiet of the afternoon was interrupted as Jessica's phone rang. It startled Matt as he was relaxing after finishing the Bible study with Jessica. She dug around in her purse until she found it. "Hi Eli!" she said. "Yes, he's with me… Yes, I'd say we're in a *very private* spot… Sure. Hang on." Jessica pulled the phone from her ear and turned the speakerphone on. "Are you still there, Eli?"

Eli said, "Yes. Can the both of you hear me?"

Matt said, "Yes sir!"

Eli said, "Good Matthew. I wanted to update you, both, on the things we have learned from the captured terrorists."

"Did they lead you to Omar?" Matt interrupted.

"Unfortunately, not. But we do have his brother. The one you know as Wally. He has not told us anything yet, but it is only a matter of time. *Then,* we will use him as bait for his brother. The rest of the men in the cave that night were poor, uneducated refugees, just trying to get out of the hellhole they live in. They are not 'true believers' or even radicals. They were just foot soldiers and they do not know anything of any value," Eli said.

"Well, what *do* you know?" Jessica asked.

"I guess we should start with Faysal Mohy al-Din abu Yusef. As you know, he had an encounter, similar to mine, that night in the cave and he has had an amazing conversion. He has held nothing back. His son, Yusef, has been very informative, as well.

"Faysal is a bomb maker, the son of a bomb maker who was the son of a bomb maker. As far back as his family can remember, they have been bomb makers in the service of Allah. Suleiman the Lawgiver conscripted his family to protect the cave where the Ark was hidden. It seems in about 1540, Suleiman's workers found the Ark and either to protect Islam or because of something that made them afraid, Suleiman sealed all the caves in the area. Our best guess is he sealed them all so that there were no ways to find the room with the Ark. No connecting passages to get there. But for months or years, people had been in and out of the caves, quarrying them, and when Suleiman abruptly sealed them, the people knew there was something special, perhaps something valuable inside. So, Suleiman commissioned a small group of men to guard and protect the hidden cave. That 'honor' was passed from generation to generation. Faysal was part of that lineage. He did not know what he was protecting and had no idea who was giving the orders. Somewhere along the line, the terrorist we know as Wally, took over the duties as Faysal's handler.

The brothers, Wally and Omar Khalid, were raised in England. Wally never knew their father, as he died during the Coastal Road Massacre before Wally was born. These men are the 'true believers,' truly radical. At some point, the brothers stole the highly enriched uranium and kidnapped the Indian Nuclear Scientist. Then, they used Faysal to keep their base of operations hidden. That's the reason why he detonated bombs when Professor Kenyon was in the cave and then again while Matthew was in the cave. He thought he was trying to keep the 'cave of wonders' hidden — but in reality, the brothers were using him to keep their base of operation hidden. We do not know their specific plans, but with the amount of nuclear material they have and having a scientist with knowledge of how to assemble a device, it has horrible implications. Doron is still working to find Omar and he will continue as long as it takes. For now, it seems that you guys have saved the nation of Israel, again. We owe you a debt of gratitude. You will probably get to meet the Prime Minister again."

287

Matt said, "I'll see if I can squeeze him into our busy schedules." The group collectively laughed at the silly joke.

Once the laughter subsided, Eli continued, "There is one other thing, kids, and it's not great news that I need to tell you. We found out from Yusef that he and Wally torched a building the night of our encounter. It turns out, the building contained a laboratory and was owned by one of our friends, Jessica."

"Oh, no!" Jessica said. "It's Chad, isn't it? They blew up his lab? But why?"

"Yes. Wally has not told us why they did it. So, we are trying to piece it together. Yusef only knew that Chad had found out some information he was not supposed to know and so they destroyed the evidence to keep it from coming to the surface. Do you have any idea what that could have been?"

Jessica's head slumped. "I think so. I sent the black substance from the room with the Ark to Chad. He tested it for me. One day at the site, he called me, and I put him on speakerphone so that Matt and I could both hear the conversation. I think Wally was standing there. I didn't realize he could speak English and didn't think anything of it. Chad told us that the black substance was radioactive. Since Wally was hiding nuclear material in his part of the cave, he must have thought we were going to find out about his hidden base or that we were getting close to it or something."

Eli said, "Yes. That makes sense."

"Wait a minute!" Jessica exclaimed. She started digging through her purse. "Chad told me he couldn't figure out the test results and he sent them to a larger testing facility in New York City. I got an email from a doctor in NYC today. I haven't read it because Matt was in such a hurry to leave the apartment. I printed it out. Let's see. Yes, here it is. There's a note and some test results." Jessica read for a few seconds and finally said, "Inconclusive. They don't know what the material is. And there is nothing in these results that would give any other explanation than the one we already have — that there were some slightly elevated radiation levels in the room and Wally thought we were getting close to his cave."

"That makes sense," Eli said. "Well, I will let the two of you get back to your day. I am going to be out of touch for the next little while but will check in with you in the coming weeks."

"Hey! Wait a minute!" Matt said. "You don't get off that easily! Jessica won't tell me anything about what has been done with the Ark and the temple treasures. Will you fill me in?"

There was a long, long pause. Matt was just about to ask if Eli was still on the call when the old scientist spoke up. "Matthew, I really want to. For right now, I cannot tell you anything, especially on an unencrypted phone. Let's revisit this the next time I see you. How does that sound?"

"Horrible," Matt was fake pouting. "But I'll take it. Whenever you get back, let me know. I've got some questions for you."

"Agreed. You kids have a wonderful day. Shalom!" And with that, Eli was gone. Jessica put the phone in her back pocket.

Matt started gathering up the remains of the picnic, used paper plates, plastic bags and all the trash. He stopped what he was doing and turned to Jessica with a quizzical look on his face. When Jessica saw it, she stopped, too. Matt asked, "What *were* the results from that lab in New York City? What did they say?"

Jessica pulled the printout back out of her purse, scanned over them and said, "They basically say what we already know, what Chad told us. The black substance had some radioactive properties to it. They said it looked like human blood but there were some abnormalities to it. It didn't act or react like purely human blood should. They have not been able to isolate the other substances involved. Actually, they have asked if we could send them another sample as they have used all of what they had. Too bad it's all gone. None left on the Ark. None left at Chad's lab."

Matt nodded and resumed cleaning up the picnic materials. The last thing he picked up was the blanket the two of them had been sitting on. He grabbed it by the corners and began shaking it to knock the loose grass and twigs from the bottom. As he did, he stepped forward and tripped over the raised square rock, the one they had used as a table for their drinks during their picnic. He tumbled parallel to the edge of the cliff, so there was no real danger of falling off. But he did fall down. When he came to rest on his stomach, his face was about four inches from another perfectly square stone, about twelve inches on a side. Matt stood up and dusted himself off. Jessica, after realizing he wasn't going to fall off the hill and wasn't hurt, couldn't control her laughter. Matt didn't even notice. He was looking at the square stone. Slowly, he turned and looked back to the original stone that he and Jessica had used and following the same trajectory, his eyes continued forward. He stood there quietly for a moment and then Matt walked back to the center stone and stood there, frozen in thought, frozen in revelation, frozen in time.

Jessica was still laughing. She said, "What? What is it? Are you alright?"

Matt, never taking his eyes off the stone, said, "I'm fine. I need to know about the abnormalities with those test results. Break it down for me so I can understand *exactly* what they are."

Jessica didn't understand. "Why Matt?"

Matt looked her directly in the eye and whispered, "Please."

Jessica sensing that something serious was going on, fumbled through her purse again, until she found the test results. She said, "Aside from having slightly radioactive properties, the biggest anomaly is the number of chromosomes the sample has. Different living things have a different number of chromosomes. Humans have 23 *pairs* of chromosomes, for a *total* of 46 chromosomes. All humans have 46 chromosomes. In fact, each species of plants and animals has a set number of chromosomes. A fruit fly, for example, has four pairs of chromosomes, while a rice plant has 12, and a dog, 39.[183] They are set numbers. Every *normal* dog has 39 pairs of chromosomes for a total of 78 and every *normal* human has 23 pairs for a total of 46. This sample looks like

---

[183] "Chromosome Fact Sheet," National Human Genome Research Institute, accessed March 19, 2022, https://www.genome.gov/about-genomics/fact-sheets/Chromosomes-Fact-Sheet

human blood. It responds to other tests like human blood. *But* this sample doesn't have 46 chromosomes. It has 23 *single* chromosomes. Not pairs! So, how is this even possible? How can it only have 23 and still be *human* blood? That's the anomaly in a nutshell. That's why they want more of the sample. They think there has been some cross-contamination somewhere."

Matt's eyes welled up with tears. He sat down and cleared the grass, dirt and rocks off of the square stone they had used during their picnic. Matt scraped away the dirt along the edges. He pushed the stone and it moved. He pulled the stone and it moved more. He rocked it back and forth. With very little effort, Matt was able to remove the rock from the ground. It was the cap, a stopper, a plug to a deep hole. Matt looked at Jessica and said, "I know what the black substance is."

"What? How?" Jessica asked. She was rightfully confused.

Matt said, "Yes. And you're not going to believe it."

"Did you bump your head when you fell? Are you dizzy?" Jessica teased an unwavering Matt. He never flinched.

Matt said, "We just finished a Bible study where I told you about the sacrifices that the High Priest made. He took the blood of the bull and goat into the Holy of Holies and sprinkled it on the covering of the Ark, on the Mercy Seat. Jesus fulfilled that. He died as a sacrifice for us and shed His blood in our place. He went into the heavenly Holy of Holies and sprinkled His own blood onto the heavenly throne, the heavenly Mercy Seat. We didn't talk about His crucifixion. He was nailed to a cross, and He was killed in between two criminals.[184] There were three men killed that day. Three men were crucified, three men hung on crosses." Matt looked down at the stone and the hole that was exposed. He pointed to the square rock to the right, where he had fallen, and another square rock on the left-hand side of where he was standing. His eyes came back to the center stone where he was standing. "There are three stones, plugging three holes where three crosses once stood. Look here at this center hole.

---

[184] Reference Matthew 27:38

This has to be the place where Jesus was crucified. This is the hole where His cross was placed. *Directly* below us is where we found the Ark. Jesus not only sprinkled his blood on the Mercy Seat on the Ark in the heavenly Holy of Holies… His actual, physical blood was placed physically on the physical Mercy Seat on the Ark of the Covenant directly below us. That black substance was the remnant of Jesus' physical blood that ran down the cross, into the hole, through the Earth and sprinkled on the Ark. It only has 23 chromosomes because He only had *one* Earthly parent, Mary. The other set of chromosomes were spiritual, ones that can't be recorded on any measuring instrument. The sample was Jesus' blood, and it *did* have **cross**-contamination! *That's* why they couldn't identify what the additional components were, why it defied the laws of physics, why it responded uniquely to light, why it had radioactive power to it, why it responded abnormally when it came into contact with broken things — it healed them!! Just like…" Matt's words trailed off. There was a long pause and then Matt finished the sentence, "It healed those broken molecules that they used to test it… just like it healed Rabbi Kaduri that night in the cave."

Matt sat down and Jessica sat next to him. A peace settled on them, a knowing. The two of them sat there in the quiet of the summer afternoon and held hands for a long time, basking in God's presence. Finally, Jessica said, barely above a whisper, "Thank You, Lord, for Your goodness to us. We will praise You and worship You the length of our days. We love You. Amen."

"Amen."

"For the Lord is good and His mercy endures forever."— I Chronicles 16:34, II Chronicles 5:13, II Chronicles 7:3, Ezra 3:11, Psalm 100:5, Psalm 106:1, Psalm 107:1, Psalm 109:21, Psalm 118:1, Psalm 118:29, Psam 136:1, Jeremiah 33:11.

The end, for now.
Matt and Jessica will return…

Note from the Author:

Dear Reader,

Thank you for finishing *Sixty Seconds of Silence*! I hope you enjoyed the thrill and adventure of it, but more importantly, I hope you understood something that I genuinely believe. God loves YOU, and He genuinely wants the best for you. He's not mad, upset, or disappointed with you. It doesn't matter what you may have done in your past. Just as with Matt and Jessica, God *wants* a relationship with YOU and in order to have that relationship with YOU, He was willing to sacrifice everything, even His Son, Jesus. You don't have to do anything to earn that relationship or even prove you're worthy of it. All you have to do is accept it.

A relationship takes two, and God is ready and willing, if you are. Starting that relationship is as easy as saying something like this: "God, I want a relationship with You. And I believe we can have that relationship. I believe Jesus made a way, even if I don't understand it. Through His death, burial, and resurrection, He made a way for us to communicate! I want to be saved from a life without You in it." It really is that simple.

You might not feel any different, physically, after saying that prayer, but if you truly believe that you have a relationship with God, I promise, God is moving to make Himself known to you, just like He did with ME and with our book's hero, Matt Davenport. It doesn't matter what you feel like; God is making a new life with you and in you. Now you are connected with God, and in His eyes, you are completely new.

One translation of the Bible says it this way: *"This means that anyone who belongs to Christ (Jesus) has become a new person. The old life is gone; a new life has begun!"* You are starting a brand-new journey as a brand-new person, connected to God and brand-new in His eyes! *That's* the good news of the Gospel.

Finally, if you prayed that, especially if you prayed it for the first time, let someone know or let me know. I have a 'Contact Me' page on my website, DavidPorterBooks.com, and I would love to hear from you!

David

Supporting scriptures:

> God is Love. (I John 4:8) For God so loved the world (that's YOU) that He gave His only Son (Jesus) that whosoever believes in Him would not perish, but have everlasting life. For God sent His Son (Jesus) into the world not to judge the world, but to save the world through Him. (John 3:16-17) This means that anyone who belongs to Christ has become a new person. The old life is gone; a new life has begun! (2 Corinthians 5:17) For whosoever shall call upon the name of the Lord shall be saved. (Romans 10:13)

Acknowledgments:

My wife, **Lauren Porter** and my parents, **Dave & Virginia Porter:** Thank you for all of your help, support, work, encouragement, and love during this process. Thank you for not giving up on this project even when I wanted to. I hope seeing it completed blesses you as much as it does me!

Mark Machen, Pastor of Life of Faith Church in Birmingham, Alabama: Thank you for being a sounding board for this project from well before I ever started writing it. I *appreciate* and *thank* you for all the time you spent reading different early drafts and for all of the amazing ideas and feedback along the way. And most of all, thank you for helping me hear God's voice during *my* sixty seconds of silence. A short paragraph at the end of a book doesn't do justice to the friendship you given and the love you've shown. I appreciate you more than you know. Thank you! https://www.lifeoffaith.church/

David Seymour, Pastor of Victory Church in Chattanooga, Tennessee: Before he founded Victory Church, he was the children's pastor that I referenced in the introduction to this book. Thank you for making the Bible interesting and fun for a little kid. Your storytelling ability always sparked my imagination and became my inspiration to tell stories that keeps people's attention and points them to Jesus. https://www.VictoryTN.org

John Grunewald and **Chad Gonzales** are two ministers who have encouraged me to write, supported the books once completed and helped spread the word that God can use fiction to bring people to Jesus: I thank you both for always encouraging me, supporting me and my writing, and giving your honest thoughts about the book and the message contained within. I also sincerely thank you for being my friends. We *will* take that trip to Israel together!
https://grunewald.org/ and https://www.chadgonzales.com/

Dr. Shahar Shilo, former Director of Marketing for The Biblical City of David and Tourism Director of the Friendly Negev Desert Tourism Association and Lecturer for the Israel Ministry of Tourism: He is one of the biggest influences in the substance of this book. I watched hours of YouTube videos of Dr. Shilo giving interviews and lectures while doing the research for *Sixty Seconds of Silence*. When I contacted him, he was incredibly helpful offering his services, support, and knowledge to help me get things right. Shahar, I cannot thank you enough and look forward to the time when we can meet face-to-face.
http://www.allaboutjerusalem.com

Archaeologist **James R. Strange, Ph.D.,** the Charles Jackson Granade and Elizabeth Donald Granade Professor in New Testament in the Department of Biblical and Religious Studies at Samford University and Director of the Shikhin Excavation Project located near the Beit Netofa Valley in Lower Galilee, Israel: Thank you for your help, information, and details that added to the realism of life on a dig site.
https://shikhinexcavationproject.com/

Ron Peled served in the Education Corps of the Israel Defense Forces teaching about the history and geography of Israel, with an emphasis on the Old City of Jerusalem and he continued as a guide in Jerusalem and the surrounding area after the army, working with all the important institutions in the city: Thank you, Ron, for answering all of my detailed questions and for sending me the videos you shot in the caves in and around Jerusalem. Because of the pandemic, the videos, and the information they contained were vital to the writing of this book. http://www.allaboutjerusalem.com

Jason Shingleton, my friend, and original contact at Xulon Press: Thank you for the encouragement (every time I called) and always patiently answering each of my questions. I appreciate you helping me land at Xulon and everything you have done for me along the way.

My friends who read early copies of this book – THANK YOU. Thank you for having faith in me and for the feedback, both positive and negative. Even if I didn't end up making your suggested change, I considered each one thoughtfully and prayerfully.

Finally, I need to acknowledge **Ron Wyatt**. He was the Christian adventurer that I mentioned in the introduction to this book. I have no idea if the things he claimed to have found were actual archaeological treasures or completely fabricated, but the thoughts of his treasure hunting around the world for the Gospels' sake had a profound effect on me in my younger years. Finding the Ark was an idea that I got from Ron Wyatt, not Indiana Jones. I look forward to meeting Mr. Wyatt in Heaven one day (many, many years from now) and asking him all about his life and adventures.

For Further Reading and Research:

Booker, Richard. *The Miracle of the Scarlet Thread*. Pennsylvania: Destiny Image Publishers, 1981.

Cargill, Robert, R. *The Cities that Built the Bible*. New York: Harper One, 2016.

Damkani, Jacob. *Why Me?* Pennsylvania: Whitaker House, 1997.

Free, Joseph, P. *Archaeology and the Bible History*. Michigan: Zondervan Publishing House, 1992.

Kennedy, Titus. *Unearthing the Bible: 101 Archaeological Discoveries that Bring the Bible to Life*. Oregon: Harvest House Publishers, 2020.

Telchin, Stan. *Betrayed!* Michigan: Chosen Publishing, 1997.

ABOUT THE AUTHOR:

 David Porter jokes that his religious education began in church nine months before he was born. In addition to an undergraduate degree, David also has three Bible school degrees, including a Master of Theology that his wife, Lauren, is elated he has finally put to good use. He is a successful entrepreneur and keynote speaker with a passion for writing suspense novels in the light of current events. With his attention to detail and ability to make even the most complex concepts simple, David's other books, novel *Five Minutes to Live* and non-fiction investment book *Juror Number One and the Alternate Retirement Plan,* are consistently featured on bestseller lists. David and Lauren currently reside in Birmingham, Alabama.

Connect with David at his website, DavidPorterBooks.com.

CPSIA information can be obtained
at www.ICGtesting.com
Printed in the USA
LVHW102050311022
732015LV00016B/299/J